BLACK
SHIELD
MAIDEN

BLACK SHIELD MAIDEN

WILLOW SMITH
& JESS HENDEL

13 5 7 9 10 8 6 4 2

Del Rey
20 Vauxhall Bridge Road
London SW1V 2SA

Del Rey is part of the Penguin Random House group of companies
whose addresses can be found at global.penguinrandomhouse.com.

Penguin
Random House
UK

First published in the US by Del Rey in 2024
First published in the UK by Del Rey in 2024

www.penguin.co.uk

A CIP catalogue record for this book is available from the British Library.

Hardback ISBN 9781529101980
Trade Paperback ISBN 9781529101997

Printed and bound in Great Britain by Clays Ltd, Elcograf S.p.A.

The authorised representative in the EEA is Penguin Random House Ireland,
Morrison Chambers, 32 Nassau Street, Dublin D02 YH68

www.greenpenguin.co.uk

MIX
Paper | Supporting
responsible forestry
FSC® C018179

Penguin Random House is committed to a
sustainable future for our business, our readers
and our planet. This book is made from Forest
Stewardship Council® certified paper.

Dedicated to those whose stories
have yet to be told

FROM THE AUTHOR

Dear Reader,

I want to let you know just how important this novel is to me. I have always been deeply interested in the evolution of humanity and society into what we see today.

About five years ago I became intrigued with Viking culture through various books, YouTube videos, and the very well made TV show *Vikings*. I was struck by the deeply rooted polytheism and how they allowed women to become warriors and wield greater amounts of social autonomy than I've observed in other ancient societies.

As my rabbit hole got deeper and deeper, I started to wonder: Did the Vikings ever encounter Black or brown people? Could there have been such a thing as a Black Viking?

My research then became rigorous. I discovered the story of Thorhall the Hunter, a character from the Old Norse saga of Erik the Red, who served as Erik's right-hand man on his escapades in Vinland. Thorhall is described as being dark-skinned, and some speculate that the "real" Thorhall—the historical figure whom the character may have been based on—could have been a Black man. I also discovered that Vikings from Norway made it as far down as Morocco in their quest to plunder new shores, meaning they likely had at least some interaction with Arabs and Africans. Maybe even more important, though, I discovered just how difficult it is to find substantial information on early medieval African history. It struck me that I'd been taught so much more about Western history than about the history of my own ancestors. And that Black and brown people's enormous contributions to civilization—and the ways in which people of all different races learned from one another throughout the Middle Ages—have been erased from our understanding of the past. (I want to explicitly thank my parents for having so many informative books on the subject when I literally couldn't find them anywhere else.)

Thus the character of Yafeu started to take shape in my mind. As a young Black woman with a platform, I am part of the fight to give marginalized characters a voice. Yafeu struggles not just because she's a woman in a patriarchal society, but also because she's a Black person in a white culture. And those two aspects of her identity birth new struggles that are faced by neither Black men nor white women. I'm glad to live in a time when feminism is finally starting to become both intersectional and mainstream; when feminists are starting to care about more than just the struggles of white women, and people across all kinds of divides are eager to inhabit the subjectivities of "others." Nowadays, a story can have a young Black female protagonist without being categorized as a show, movie, or book that is "for" Black people alone.

But even as I was developing Yafeu's character, I knew that her journey wasn't the full story. There was something more that I wanted to say. Yafeu is clearly a badass. She's strong and powerful in ways that are universally recognizable. But there are many other kinds of strength and power, and many different paths to finding one's own expression of those two things. What is to be said of the women who find strength in spirituality, or the "soft power" of interpersonal skills? Women come in all different sizes, shapes, colors, religions, personalities. Our definitions of strength and power should reflect this diversity.

That's how I came up with Freydis. Yafeu and Freydis are opposites in many ways. They have a different set of strengths and weaknesses, different wants and needs, different self-expressions—but they are equal in strength and beauty. And they need each other to create a world that they both can thrive in.

We all find it difficult to connect with those who have beliefs that actively oppose our own. When we assume that someone is "other," we dehumanize and ostracize them, making it impossible to communicate in the ways that are necessary to create any semblance of human decency.

We have a tendency to compare our pain and suffering—or ignore each other's altogether. It doesn't help that male-dominated media tend to portray women as competitive with one another, as pitted against each other (in fights that are usually over men—or over male conceptions of power). But I believe that radical equality can't happen until we stop keeping one another at a distance. We must be willing to search for some kind of common ground, while at the same time celebrating what makes us unique. We can build something beautiful together if we have the willingness and the compassion to do this.

With Yafreby—the Norse-African city that Yafeu and Freydis found together, complete with its own pidgin language—I imagine the new form of community that would be born from enacting that philosophy. Yafreby is what cultural blending would look like if one culture wasn't dominant over the other. Ultimately, that's what *Black Shield Maiden* is really about, that's the theme that lies at its heart: connection and community. I hope that reimagining the past through this ancient lens will open up new possibilities for more connection and community in our own future.

Something else happened in the writing of this story, and especially in the process of developing the secondary characters. I realized that, in my quest to portray a variety of manifestations of strength and power, I ended up creating characters that were "gender fluid"—men who had so-called feminine qualities, and women who had so-called masculine qualities. My generation is evolving past the outdated binaries of gender, sexuality, and gender expression.

Women my age can wear traditionally masculine clothing without being called "boyish" or "gay." Men my age can paint their nails and wear eyeliner without being called "girlish" or "gay." Your self-expression is just that—personal to you. I wanted my characters to reflect this societal shift, to resonate with the young people of my generation. Ultimately, though all the characters in *Black Shield Maiden* make sense for the circumstances of their time, they remain modern characters at heart. And their journeys are timeless.

Willow Smith

To rule well is to find balance on the tip of a
blade. True leaders must see beyond their own
desires: They are chosen by the gods, but bound
to the people. They must wield power, but never
hunger for it. Such power is rooted in tradition,
but only those who question tradition—
and *create* it—live on in myth and song.

—NYERU, HIGH PRIEST OF THE CITY OF YAFREBY, 861 CE

BLACK
SHIELD
MAIDEN

1

YAFEU

The antelope calf strays too far from his mother.

I crouch behind a boulder, tracking his movements as he combs the parched riverbank for sparse clumps of hippo grass. My ankles are strained, my thighs tight as bowstrings. From the moment I spotted the small herd trotting toward the White River, I haven't moved a muscle. After years of practice, I can ignore the discomfort, keeping my breath steady, even stopping my joints from creaking as I slow my *nyama*—the energy that flows through all things—until I'm as motionless as the boulder.

You must be as still as death itself.

Papa's rich, deep voice booms in my mind, as though he had just spoken aloud. As though he were here beside me.

Focus, he says.

I ride the breath as it leaves my body. Soon I can feel the *nyama* of the herd as clearly as my own. It flows between the calf and his mother, her presence always mindful of his, and his of hers. He's old enough to have weaned, but young enough that his sense for danger is dull. A new blade in need of grinding.

The White River is shallow and murky, its bank naked without the grasses that once speckled the red-brown mud like spots on a giraffe. All around me, the land is dry and brittle and nearly empty of life; it will be a full moon cycle or more before Sogbo blesses us with rains and we can sow the loam with seed. But pink light softens the barrenness of the earth as Lisa peeks above the horizon. He blankets my dark skin in a welcome warmth, lights up the scattered acacia trees, and rouses the firefinches to their morning song. Even the birds were asleep when I rose, stirred in the middle of Mawu's reign by the restlessness that seizes me when the hour is ripe for a hunt.

The calf ambles closer still, his shadow creeping up the boulder in the dawn's half-light. I can already picture his tiny horns joining the teeth and claws on my hunter's tunic. Tokens of the animals I've given to the long night.

Trust your instinct. Yet another of Papa's lessons. *It is instinct that acts through* you *to make the kill.*

My patience is poised on the tip of my throwing knife as I slide it out of its sheath. I raise my arm so slowly it aches and bring the blade behind my ear.

Now.

Just as I'm about to strike—a flash of brown and black darts from behind an acacia trunk. A painted wolf lunges at my prey.

The herd scatters. The calf flees with his mother. The wolf snaps her teeth and gives a moment's chase before slowing to watch the antelope disappear into the horizon. There's no chance of outrunning the herd; we both know that.

Legba's cunning! My heart sinks into my empty stomach. All that patience—wasted!

I stand, relieving the ache in my thighs, and level a glare at the painted wolf. She stares after the herd, apparently unaware of me.

Maybe I should add *her* teeth to my collection. She's probably too heavy to carry all the way home, but I could skin her and give the pelt to Mama. The morning doesn't have to be a total waste.

I raise my dagger again, but something makes me hesitate. She's little more than a cub, and the bones jutting out from her haunches betray the meagerness of the dry season. Perhaps she was separated from her mother during the last rains. Only an inexperienced huntress would spring too soon like that, ruining an easy kill.

Hunger makes us all too bold.

As if sensing my thoughts, she swivels her head back, meeting my gaze.

Her umber eyes bore into mine, and suddenly the Sahel fades to a blur.

Time slows to a crawl. The air thrums with a nameless foreboding. It coils around my heart, like the great snake Bida tightening around a fresh kill.

But then the wolf turns and trots away, and the feeling passes as quickly as it came.

I shrug myself back to my senses. My tongue is swollen, and my mouth tastes like dirt. How long has it been since I had any water?

I grunt my frustration and sheathe the dagger. Dangling bones thwack against my chest as I walk toward the river. I swallow a few gulps of water, then splash some on my face, enjoying the shock of cold against my skin.

But I can't wash the little wolf from my mind.

It reminds me of something that happened years ago, on the banks of this same White River, though many days' ride from where I am now.

It was back when we lived on the roads between cities and home was only each other. I was at that age when my body didn't know itself yet, when I always had scrapes on my arms and my knees knocked together when I ran.

We had set up our tent outside the city of Jenne. Papa knew

some nobles there who would pay handsomely for the new weapons he had forged, and Mama was planning to coax their wives into buying a few of her necklaces.

Papa and I woke early in the morning to fish, before the air grew too thick and hot to bear. Kamo and Goleh were too young and unruly to come along, so we left them sleeping in the tent with Mama. I remember the thrill I felt at that; there was no greater treasure to me than the time Papa and I spent together, just the two of us.

It was right after the first floods of the rainy season, and the river was teeming with life. I struggled to haul a full net of butter fish onto our little canoe and tipped us over, sending both of us, along with our catch, splashing into the water. Mama would have been furious, but Papa howled with laughter and dunked my head beneath the surface. He tugged the boat to shore while I swam behind.

Papa saw the crocodile before I did. I only saw his eyes go wide, heard him shout at me to swim faster. I pumped my arms and legs as hard as I could, knowing it didn't matter, that the crocodile would easily catch me here in the water and my short life would be over soon. But some stubborn instinct drove me to keep swimming. My whole body pulsed with my heart when I finally scrambled onto the bank.

Papa lifted me up and set me down behind him like a sack of millet. I turned back to see him facing the crocodile, who was waiting half submerged in the shallow waters, his eyes fixed on Papa. He drew his dagger and passed it from hand to hand. I still remember how it shimmered in the sunlight, as if Gu had ordered Lisa to send his power into the blade.

It seemed like an eternity passed while Papa and the crocodile stared each other down. Then the crocodile spun around and swam off, disappearing into the depths of the river.

"The gods have saved us!" I cried out, triumphant.

"No." Papa sheathed his dagger. He knelt and took my hands in his own. "People want to believe that the gods or the spirits are responsible for everything that happens in their lives. The truth is that belief *itself* is what controls their fate." His mahogany eyes shone with conviction. "Belief is power, daughter of mine. But it's also a choice. When you *choose* to believe in something, you give it power. I chose to believe that I was stronger than the crocodile. And so I was. That is why he left. Not because the gods saved me. Or, perhaps, the gods *did* save me. Perhaps they saved me because I was willing to save myself."

I felt my brow scrunching. "Mama says we must honor the gods, and the ancestors too. She says I have much to learn from them."

He smiled one of his mysterious half smiles, where only one of his dimples appears. "Your mother is very wise."

Bewildered, I could only gape at him. But one thing was clear: My Papa was no ordinary blacksmith. From that moment on, he was like a hero from one of the old stories in my eyes: Yafeu, the man who cowed a crocodile!

When we returned to our tent, I told Mama what had happened. I thought she would be as amazed as I was, but instead she became wary and told us to pack our things. The crocodile was a warning from the gods, she said. It was a sign that the city wasn't safe for us. I shared a knowing smile with Papa, but we did as she asked and left Jenne that same day.

The day after, Jenne was attacked by unknown warriors from the North. Word spread that they swarmed the city, burned the sacred groves, destroyed the statues of our gods, and killed anyone who stood in their way.

A chill dances up my spine despite the swelling heat.

If the crocodile truly was a warning from the gods . . . What does the painted wolf bode for me?

2

YAFEU

With a heavy sigh, I turn and follow the bend of the river until I reach the array of small canoes resting under the mangroves, marking the junction to our village.

The thatched clay hut nearest to the river is also the largest. It belongs to my uncle and his family—one of the many luxuries of his chiefdom.

When Papa was young, his skill as a blacksmith grew so great that he surpassed all his brothers and gained renown across the land. Merchants and nobles as far north as Fes and as far south as Igodomigodo commissioned his weapons, and Papa was happy to oblige. But Papa's older brother—who was not gifted with Papa's talent—chose the life of a millet farmer instead, eventually becoming chief of the village in which they were born.

My heart sinks as I draw closer: My cousins are already outside. I was hoping to get back to my own hut before they woke. They don't approve of a girl going out to hunt by herself. Not that I have a choice, given that they won't share their kills with us. Almost no one in the village shares anything with my family. I *have* to hunt to feed Mama, Kamo, and Goleh, and to get the bones and skins we need for our work.

Still, my uncle and his family despise me for it. They used to ridicule me for using a throwing knife instead of a bow and arrows. But Papa never taught me how to use a bow; he left before I was tall enough to even carry one. Instead, he taught me how to wield a blade—and how to make one.

Yet another thing my so-called kin disapprove of.

My uncle's family would never recognize a girl as a true blacksmith. But even if I had been born a boy, my mother does not come from a long line of blacksmiths, like Papa and his brother did. My blood is impure in the eyes of Papa's family.

Mama isn't even Soninke, making it even worse for us to live with Papa's tribe. They met when Papa was traveling to the South on a commission for a prince of Igodomigodo, the jungle kingdom. He was just passing through Mama's village, but from the moment he first laid eyes on her, he knew she was destined to be his wife. When he left, she joined him—despite both their families' disapproval.

A disapproval I have inherited.

As usual, my cousins make the gesture to ward off malevolent spirits when I pass. They believe I am haunted by the spirit of a vengeful ancestor—from Mama's line, of course—and that's why I act so much like a boy and not a proper girl. That's why Papa abandoned us here, they say. To escape it.

To escape *me*.

I roll my eyes and rest my hand on the dagger at my hip. Hardly an act of defiance, but it's all I can get away with.

The trick, Papa always said, with a wink and a grin, *is to learn how to make trouble without getting into it.*

Only once did I get into it: with my cousin Masireh. As he glowers at me now, I feel a tiny trickle of rage spill over the dam I've built around my heart. Normally I would tamp it back down and ignore him. But I'm already sour from losing the calf, so I allow the rage to seep into my thoughts, daydreaming about the time his blood painted my knuckles red.

It was right after Papa left us here, entrusting us to the "care" of my "beloved" uncle. I was coming back from the river, balancing a basket of clay for our hut on my not-yet-widened hips, when I noticed Masireh huddled with the other village boys. They whispered to one another and shot suspicious glances my way like little arrows.

I held my chin high, ignoring them. Until Masireh spat at my feet and whispered loud enough for me to hear:

"*Jugu.*"

Jugu. Evil.

The word had barely left his mouth when I dropped the basket, whirled around, and swung at his nose with my fist, throwing my weight into the punch like Papa taught me.

I heard a loud crack. Then Masireh was on the ground, his hands muffling his screams as blood gushed between his fingers. Another boy leapt at me, but I used his own force against him, grabbing his arm and tossing him to the ground with ease.

I whipped around and stared down the rest of the boys.

"Try it!" I shouted, though my breath was coming in ragged gasps. In truth, I had no idea how many more of them I could take. But I never had to find out. They shrank from me, their eyes wide with fear.

No one ever called me *jugu* again. Well, not to my face, at least.

Mama gave me the scolding of a lifetime that day. "Whatever they believe about us," she said, "you've only made it worse."

I knew she was right, and the shame of it hurt worse than my bruised fist. As the old saying goes: People are always in the hands of speech, not the other way around. Fear spread across the village like a fire across dry brush, leaving hatred in its wake. Soon the whole tribe saw me as a scourge.

Jugu. Evil.

For a long time, their hatred nipped at my heels like a hyena, bringing me to tears night after night. Mama would wrap me in her arms and be very tender with me then. "Your tide flows *with* our ancestors' wishes, not against them," she'd say, stroking the long dark coils of my hair.

Eventually I stopped crying. I resigned myself to turning a deaf ear to all the whispers, all the taunting. But no matter how high I build the dam around my heart, their contempt oozes through the cracks.

My one refuge is the little forge I've built in the back of our hut. I love the rhythmic clang of my hammer striking the white-hot iron, the smell of coal that clings to my skin and never quite goes away. I love how it keeps my arms strong and my mind clear. So what if my uncle's family sneers at me? No one who has seen my handiwork can deny that Papa trained me in the secret wisdom of Gu. He trained me as his own father trained him, and his father before him—all the way back to the first people on earth, who were blacksmiths, just like us.

My uncle trained his sons too, but their daggers are crude carving knives compared with mine. Despite my gender, despite my mother's "impure blood," I still have more *nyama* in my little pinkie than they have in their whole bodies. They can spread their hatred and lies all they want: I have my craft, and that's something no one can ever take away from me.

I'm so consumed by these dark thoughts that I almost miss what Masireh is holding in his arms: a bundle, tied up with thick leather straps. It's then that I notice the donkeys weighed down with packs, lashed to the wooden post outside their hut.

I freeze, remembering.

Today is market day!

How could I have forgotten?

Market day is my one escape from this tiny village and its suffocating superstitions. Many different kinds of people converge on the markets of Koumbi Saleh, people from different lands, with different goods and different gods. It's exhilarating to see all of them, to become just one of many among them. It almost reminds me of my old life with Papa, of the awe and delight of visiting new cities—except the strangers come to our lands now, instead of us going to theirs.

I sprint the rest of the way home, weaving a shortcut through the dozens of identical mud-brown huts and hoping against hope to get there before Mama wakes up. But when I arrive at our own hut on the far edge of the village, she's already outside, along with my twin brothers.

She kneels by a thick woolen blanket, carefully wrapping her new necklaces as Kamo and Goleh wolf down bowls of millet porridge. I hesitate, preparing myself for a scolding.

"You're late" is all she says.

"Sorry, Mama," I reply.

I add a silent prayer of gratitude to Agé—he must have sent the wolf to chase away the herd. We wouldn't have had time to prepare the meat before the long walk to Koumbi Saleh, and it would have spoiled. Agé hates wastefulness even more than I do.

Mama rises to her feet and looks me up and down, taking in the dirt covering my arms and legs. I should have thought to bathe before I came home; I don't have time to go back to the river now. She puts her hand on her hip and meets my eyes, her gaze piercing.

"You're in trouble," Kamo says through a mouthful of porridge. Goleh, always the more reserved of the two, fixes me with a look not unlike Mama's.

I stick my tongue out at them and follow Mama into the hut.

Inside, I grab a spare bit of cloth and rub as much dirt off my body as I can. Mama rakes a comb through my hair, loosening the knots before tying the strands into braids. Then she hands me her old kaftan. It's a bright sumac yellow, with an elaborate silk brocade adorning the neckline. One of the few luxuries we've held on to from our former life.

I grit my teeth, but I take off my hunter's tunic and put the kaftan on without complaint. Admittedly, the smooth cotton feels pleasantly light and breezy against my skin. Sometimes I forget what it's like to wear clothes that aren't weighed down by animal bones. A reminder of how much more comfortable I'd be every day if it weren't for my pride.

Besides, Mama is right to make me wear it. We'll sell more of our wares at Koumbi Saleh if I play my part as a wealthy blacksmith's daughter.

If I look more like the girl I used to be.

Satisfied with my appearance, Mama hands me a bowl of cold millet porridge.

Porridge is all we've had to eat for almost half a moon now. That's how it goes in the long stretch between market days after we've eaten the chickens, especially in the dry season when game is scarce. I'm sick of it—we all are—but I force the thick globs down my throat with haste. It takes several hours at a brisk pace to walk to Koumbi Saleh from here, and we're already running behind. Thanks to me.

I set down my bowl and reach for my dagger, steeling myself against another disapproving look from Mama as I strap the sheath like a belt over the yellow kaftan.

She arches an eyebrow at me as she takes my empty bowl. "Don't forget the rest of them, child."

Mama goes back outside, and soon Kamo and Goleh's giggles turn to yelps. No doubt she pinched them for goofing around instead of packing up Fàré, our donkey. "Stop wrestling and help me pack, you lazybones!" I hear Mama scold. My smile widens.

I grab my empty satchel off the wall and fill it with jugs of water. I do every task I can until finally I have no choice but to turn to the one I dread.

With a sigh, I push aside the dark-purple curtain that leads to our workshop. I pass our heddle loom with the forgotten strip of cloth half woven across its beams, pass the explosion of Mama's beads, strings, and stones on the rough-hewn wooden table, pass the ashy little forge and the anvil covered in bits of slag, and come to a stop in front of the wall of daggers. Sunlight slithers through the holes in the thatched roof and paints circles on the blades. Some are Kamo and Goleh's practice knives, too crude or mis-shapen to be worth much; some are my own unfinished creations. Three are ready to be sold, each with precise, if simple, designs carved into the hilts of bone.

My favorite, of course, is the throwing knife, with several blades branching out at different angles from a main shaft. I steal a moment to handle it one last time, enjoying the feel of the smooth iron as I inspect my handiwork. The fruit of many moons of labor. I'm getting better, though I'm nowhere near as skilled as Papa.

Still, he would be proud.

Pride and anguish weld together inside me. I swallow my feelings and wrap each dagger in the goatskin sheaths I made for them and place them carefully inside the satchel, along with one of the practice blades, which we might be able to trade for a chicken or two.

I head back outside and secure the satchel onto Fàré. The old beast whinnies his complaint. I stroke his neck, commiserating. We all bear more than our fair share in this family.

It was all so different when Papa was with us. Or rather, when *we* were with *him*. We were always in motion in those days, always traveling from village to village, market to market, never resting in one place for longer than a few weeks. But we traveled in great luxury, with many camels to carry extra stores of food, water, and co-conuts, and tents with thick carpets for us to rest in at night. Not to mention a handful of mercenaries to protect us and our goods. As the family of a renowned blacksmith from the great empire of Wagadu, we expected no less.

Now we only have Fàré.

I lift my gaze to the trail behind Fàré's haunches, following it with my eyes as it winds a dusty auburn through the withered yellow grasses. It's been six years since I watched Papa's back disappear down that same trail over the horizon. Six years since the first log of the dam around my heart fell into place.

Papa often left us with our uncle's family for many moons, when a commission took him to some dangerous place we could not follow. I always counted the days until he came back—and he always did, with precious gems for Mama to make her necklaces and solid ivory for the hilts of my daggers. He would scoop us up in his arms and hug us close. "I missed you so much!" he'd say. "I thought you might disappear before I returned."

Mama would laugh and shove him in response, but tears would well in my eyes as I clung to him, gripping his fine tunic in my small fists. I worried we would disappear without him too.

Then, one morning, a traveling Wangara merchant came to deliver a message to Papa. A foreign explorer had heard of Papa's great skill in the forge and was willing to pay handsomely for Papa to make swords for him and his men. The explorer traveled across the seas in a marvelous ship, discovering new lands. It was the greatest ship the merchant himself had ever laid eyes on.

I still remember how Papa's eyes lit up at the idea of the ship, of the explorer from across the sea. When I saw that look on his face, I felt like I'd swallowed a pebble of raw ore.

Papa was born a blacksmith, and he loved his craft. But more than anything, it was adventure that he craved. It's why we lived our lives on the road with him; he could never rest in one place for long. By then, he'd already crossed the desert many times over, including twice with us. But the seas—the seas would be a new challenge.

He promised us that when he came back, we'd be richer than the Ghāna himself.

But he never did.

Somehow, we didn't disappear. We lingered on, hope thinning with our bodies after each moon he didn't return. Eventually we realized that we would have to survive on our own.

I was ten years old then, but Kamo and Goleh were eight—only two years younger, but not old enough to grasp the sands of memory and keep it from sifting through their fingers.

I turn from Fàré to watch them scuffle in the dirt, folding my arms across my chest.

"Goleh—knee him in the stomach!" I shout as Kamo pins him to the ground. Goleh throws a good kick and Kamo doubles over, giving Goleh the chance to roll out from under him.

"No fair!" Kamo gasps. "It's cheating if Sister helps you!"

Perhaps it's better this way. At least they don't bear the burden of remembering a better life than the one we live now.

Sometimes even I struggle to recall the details of Papa's face. I remember only his wide smile with the lines cutting down his cheeks, the dimples that deepened when he laughed.

But I remember his lessons as clearly as Lisa shines down on us now. He was playful and carefree in all things, except when he was teaching me something—then he grew very serious, and I knew I must be serious too. Those lessons held the secret wisdom of the gods, and I committed them to my heart.

Kamo, Goleh, and I follow Mama as she leads the now heavily burdened Fàré to the road. Most of the other families in our village have already left; they'll be the ones to nab the best spots at the market. My eyes anxiously scan the road for Ampah. Did she leave already?

Someone shoves me and I stumble forward. I wheel around, raising my fist to Kamo or Goleh to return the blow. But instead of their cocoa eyes, I meet Ampah's dark and dancing coal ones.

"Think I would leave without you, night owl?" She winks.

"Ampah! I almost punched you!" I say, though I can't help but grin. "I thought you were one of my idiot brothers."

"Oh, please! When those lugs try to sneak up on me, their footsteps are as loud as Sogbo's thunder."

Kamo and Goleh rush past us that very moment, blushing furiously. Only Ampah can make their brown cheeks turn so red. I smirk at her, and she giggles and grabs my hand. Our mothers trail behind as we begin the walk, palm-to-palm, to Koumbi Saleh.

Ampah is my best—well, only—friend on this earth. Before Papa left, we didn't stay in one place long enough for me to get to know anyone else; Ampah is the only good thing that has come from his absence. She and her mother are the only people in the village who are kind to us, probably because they are despised in their own way.

Ampah's mother is the youngest, and therefore lowest-status, wife of Tummu, the griot. But despite their status, Ampah attracts the attention of all the village boys—including my cousins, the chief's sons. Unfortunately, this means that she also attracts the jealousy of the other village girls. She's always had a striking face, with smooth, dark skin, prominent cheekbones, and large eyes so earnest and expressive anyone can tell what she's thinking. But now her slender figure is blossoming into the fullness of woman-hood. Where I'm all brawn and hardness, Ampah is all lissome curves. When she walks by, the boys start roughhousing with one another, flexing their muscles and strutting for her attention. She always elbows me and rolls her eyes, as if their foolish displays are for me as well.

As if the boys ever look at me with anything but fear.

I shake my head and return my thoughts to the road, to the warm feeling of Ampah's hand in mine. Today will be a much-needed rest from the village and its small-mindedness. Today is market day, and in Koumbi Saleh, I'm just one of many *nyamakalaw* who jour-ney to the city to trade their family's wares. I'm no one to fear, no one to hate.

I'm no one at all.

Lisa climbs in the sky and beats a blistering heat down upon us. Ampah and I while away the hours gossiping and teasing each other. We catch up to a group of older women from our village, who frown at me as we glide by. But Ampah, still wearing her playful smile, switches to my other side to walk between me and them. That's her way: pretending nothing is happening, even as she's shielding me from their disapproving glares.

My skin prickles with anticipation as we come to the training ground outside the city. I crane my neck as we pass, staring through the gaps in the thorny acacia fence at the warriors within. They spar with one another, a handful of older soldiers barking instructions and correcting their form. I ache to join them, to test my strength and skill against theirs. But only the Ghāna's soldiers are allowed on the grounds.

Of course, I could never become a soldier myself.

Because I'm a girl.

The thought is so bitter I can almost taste it.

Finally, with the frenzied shouts of bargainers and the scratch of cart-wheels on the ground as a greeting, we enter the brick walls of Koumbi Saleh. Kamo and Goleh race ahead, kicking up dust in their wake.

Koumbi Saleh never ceases to inspire me. I've been to many cities around Wagadu, and even a few outside the empire's borders, but I've never seen one so splendid as Koumbi Saleh. Little wonder, given that the Ghāna himself lives here.

Papa once told me that our Ghāna is the richest king of all the kings in the world. Looking around, it's easy to believe. There's gold everywhere: carved into the wooden doors of the massive stone palace, forged into sword-mounts for the Ghāna's many sons, plaited in the hair of his daughters, embroidered in robes of his diviners. Not to mention the protection that gold can buy: Royal soldiers with gleaming swords and spears stand guard at every turn.

We pass the Ghāna's cavernous stables on the way to the market square. Even the horses are treated like royalty, with reins of silk and soft furs for them to sleep on.

It sets my blood on fire to know that horses live in such luxury when there are people in Wagadu who are struggling just to survive. I've gone to bed without food myself more nights than I can count—and we're some of the luckier ones. At least my uncle lets us stay in the village. Those without tribes don't last very long; they either starve or get picked up by slavers.

The square is already teeming with peddlers and packmen and other *nyamakalaw,* so I lash my focus to finding an empty plot among the horde of stalls and carts to set up our things. Ampah waves goodbye and saunters off with her mother to search for their own space.

After a while, a luckless potter decides to leave early and we slide into her plot. Kamo and Goleh are given the task of finding Fàré some water as I arrange our goods on the selling cloth. Mama sets another cloth over our heads to shield us from the violence of Lisa, now at his highest peak. I lay out Mama's creations: her beautiful beaded necklaces and a handful of stone pendants of different shapes and pigments, intricately carved in the likenesses of the gods. Beside them my daggers look rugged and uninviting.

"If anyone asks—" Mama begins, turning to me.

"I *know,*" I say fiercely, rolling my eyes. "Papa made these weapons. Not me."

After we finish setting everything up, we wait for someone to perceive our creations as worthy of being coveted. Soon, three men start toward us.

I study their unfamiliar tunics, trying to place their origin. The man on the right looks about my age, small and slenderly built compared with his older, broader companions. Like many here today, their skin is the color of the lightest shea nuts. A heavy *nyama* radiates around them, seemingly pushing others from their path. My stomach twists; they move like they expect others to move out of their way.

I look to Mama. Her face is calm, but as they approach, she takes a shaky breath.

"I greet you, gentlemen," she says, smiling politely.

They say nothing, scanning our creations with furrowed brows.

The burly man in the center runs a calloused finger down my throwing knife. He has a round face with close-set eyes and a lumpy nose that curves at an unnatural angle, like it's been broken too many times to set straight.

"This one isn't as bad as the others. Which of your boys made it?" He speaks our language with an accent I can't place, holding the dagger up to examine it in the sun.

I clench my jaw but say nothing. He's only insulting us to get a better price.

Mama shoots me a wary glance. Kamo and Goleh are roughhousing in the dirt a few paces away, paying no mind to the men at our table.

"They are too young for such fine handicraft," she replies smoothly. "My husband made it."

The man smirks at Mama, then at me. "No wonder he sends you to the market alone. He hopes your pretty faces will make up for his lack of skill."

Heat rushes to my face.

He's haggling. He's just haggling.

But I hear my uncle in his scathing words. I see Masireh in the cruel twist of his lips. And something inside me refuses to be hidden any longer.

"What if I told you it was me?" I blurt out before I can stop myself, looking straight into the man's beady eyes.

He shares a look with the man on his left, and the two of them burst into laughter. The smaller man nudges him on the arm and mutters a few words in a language I don't recognize, seemingly rebuking him. But their laughter only grows louder. A molten ball of anger forms in my chest.

"Don't be silly, little girl," he replies, his tone mocking.

I hear a flinty ringing between my ears, like a hammer striking a blade. The ball of fire in my chest breaks apart and flows down my limbs, flooding them with energy.

I spot a goshawk soaring in the air behind his head. Quick as a flash, I snatch the dagger out of his hand and hurl it into the sky. The blade skims his hair as it whizzes past.

Wide-eyed, all three men turn to watch the bird drop out of the sky.

Dead.

I have only a moment to relish their shock before those callused fingers wrap around my neck.

The burly man lifts me off the ground like a doll.

"How dare you!" he snarls. Mama screams and lunges for me, but the man on the left steps between us and swats her to the ground. Hard. I cry out to her, but only a choked gurgle comes out.

I struggle to get air back into my lungs as I watch him turn to the cloth, grabbing fistfuls of Mama's necklaces along with my daggers and shoving them into a pouch on his belt. The smaller man seizes the thick arm holding me up, hissing some urgent words in their strange tongue, but the burly man simply laughs and tightens his grip.

My eyeballs feel like they're bulging out of my head as I scan the square for help. Everyone—from the *nyamakalaw,* to the merchants, to the beggars on the street—averts their eyes. Even the Ghāna's soldiers do not intervene. After all, I'm no one worth protecting.

I'm no one at all.

The smaller man is shouting now, turning back and forth between his two companions. They both ignore him. They don't even seem to hear him.

Blue spots creep into the edges of my vision.

Just when I think I'll never breathe again, the burly man lets go of my neck. I drop to the ground, gasping and sputtering.

"Let this be a lesson to you," he says.

My vision returns to normal as I suck the dusty air into my lungs. Kamo and Goleh cling to Mama, crying softly. She wraps her arms around them, keeping her eyes down as the men finish stuffing their pouches. When they finally leave, all three of my daggers and most of Mama's necklaces and pendants are gone.

I glare at their backs with half a mind to go after them, to show them what else my father taught me. But then a group of diviners walks between us, their flowing white robes obscuring the trio of thieves.

When the crowd clears, they're gone.

3

YAFEU

The four of us walk home in silence, our moods darkening with the sky as Mawu takes over Lisa's reign. Every glance at the dirt marring my yellow kaftan sends rage and guilt ripping through me like twin sandstorms through the desert. The only happy one is Fàré, who carries a much lighter load than he did this morning.

Thanks to my stupid pride.

I shove open the wooden door to our hut and look to Mama as she sets down the empty blanket and lights the hearth. I study her face in the flickering firelight. She looks as calm as ever.

Isn't she as angry with me as I am with myself?

After my brothers fall asleep, I tiptoe to the back of the hut and push aside the purple curtain to find her working on a new pendant. Her shadow looms on the wall, cast upward by the candles on her worktable. I approach hesitantly and peer over her shoulder; she's carving a vibrant parrot-green stone into the shape of a painted wolf.

My breath hitches in my throat. Could Mama have known about this morning? I open my mouth to tell her, then close it, my heart heavy as I remember all that's happened since then.

"Mama," I whisper.

"Yes, child?"

"I'm sorry." Tears sting my eyelids and I blink ferociously, willing them back down. I am far too old for tears.

Mama sighs. Her heartwood stool groans as she turns and opens her arms to me. I snuggle into her lap and inhale the warm, spicy scent of ginger and berbere that always clings to her skin. The familiar scent bears down on my self-control, and suddenly the tears spill out into a sob.

"You always tell me not to say anything," I say, gasping between sniffles, "and the *one* time I do, something terrible happens!"

She turns back to the table and picks up a long cord of tanned sinew, threading it through two tiny holes at the wolf's head and tail.

"I've been making this for you," she says, placing the necklace in my palm.

I study it with awe, running my fingertips over the etched canals. I don't recognize the type of stone she's used, but it's undeniably beautiful; it would fetch a high price at the market. And she's giving it to me instead. Even after we lost so much today.

She takes the necklace, tilts my head, and ties the cord around my neck. "They have strange beliefs in this village of your father's kin," she continues. "They believe the creator, Nana Buluku, gave birth to many twins, one male and one female. They think this is the proper order of things."

I nod. "Like Mawu and Lisa, the moon and the sun."

"Where I grew up, they are called Mawu-Lisa. They are not twins, but rather one being with two faces, neither male nor female but *both* at once."

One being, both male *and* female? I can hardly wrap my mind around the thought. I try to picture what such a being would look like, but no image will come.

"Why are you telling me this now?" I ask.

She takes my hands into her own. "You are your father's child, my daughter. You have his boldness, his tenacity, his talent."

I return her smile with my own, feeling the soothing swell of pride in my chest at her words.

"And you have his dimples too," she teases, poking the grooves under my cheekbones. "But I am within you, as well." She touches my chest tenderly. "Grace, compassion, wisdom . . . Father *and* Mother. When you were a child, it was my duty to teach you balance. To teach you restraint. But you are a woman now, and it is up to you to decide who you wish to be."

Fresh tears well behind my eyes, but I nod my understanding.

Her own eyes glaze over, taking on a faraway look. "You have a great destiny, child. Great and harrowing, for the world will always fear your strength. But the spirit of the painted wolf remains by your side. Always has it been so—ever since the night you were born, when I heard a wolf howl at the end of my labor. Remember to honor her, and she will guide you on your path."

Again, my mind flashes to the little wolf this morning. Unease sinks its claws into my chest. If Papa were here, he'd laugh at Mama's strange words. *Don't fill her head with your superstitions,* he'd say, swooping her into his arms. *Our daughter will make her own destiny.*

But Papa isn't here.

The full force of my exhaustion hits me all at once. I slide down on the floor and rest my head on Mama's lap.

"Tell me the story again," I plead, softly.

"You're getting too old for this," she chastises, but I can hear the smile in her voice. She clears her throat and begins stroking my hair.

Yafeu, a great hunter who could invoke the spirits of nature and find his way in the most remote places, had been sailing with the Majūs *for days on end, discovering new lands and col-*

lecting riches. The Majūs had a great knowledge of the sea and thought themselves its masters—but they had grown arrogant. They'd been out at sea for so long that they ran out of food, and the fish were failing. So they decided to dock on a stretch of coastline where the mountains met the sea to search for animals. Right away, Yafeu vanished for three days and nights, and no one knew where he had gone.

On the fourth day, the Majūs found him on the peak of a jagged mountain with his face turned up to the sky. He was calling on the gods with ancestral movements—a spell passed down from his grandfather, and his grandfather before him. The warriors watched him in horror, shocked by his dance, for they had no such wisdom of their own. They begged and pleaded for him to stop, to come back down the mountain with them. Only when he had finished the spell did he comply.

They returned to the beach to find a giant beast of the sea lying motionless on the shore. Right away, the warriors sprinted over to the carcass, cheering at their sudden good fortune. But Yafeu stayed back. The crew ate well that night, until a sickness arose from the meat. Yafeu then said to the sickened Majūs, "Has it not been that Agbe and Naete, gods of the seas, are better protectors than your giant gods? My dance was an offering to Agbe and Naete; they have never failed me." So the men spit out the fish and burned the rest of it, sacrificing the meat to Agbe and Naete and their giant gods together. After this, there was an abundance of food for the rest of their journey...

My eyelids lower as the sound of my mother's voice becomes a soothing hum, her words melting together like the images dancing behind my eyelids.

"Mama?" I ask, my tongue heavy with the threat of sleep.

"Yes?"

"Is Papa ever coming back?"

I feel her stiffen. I know the answer already—I've asked her many times before—but tonight I need her to say it again.

"Before he left to follow his destiny with the *Majūs,* your father promised us that he would return. And there are two things that no one—not even the gods—can deny about Yafeu: He always gets what he wants, and he *always* keeps his promises."

That night I dream of the muted *thwack* of Papa's bow, of his focused gaze through stalks of thistle, of his hands caressing Mama's face. I drift into this world of memory, real and imagined, still clasping the stone wolf in my hand.

4

FREYDIS

O ne last stroke and the final rune is complete.

The knife slips out of my aching grasp. I let it disappear into the depths of the bracken, grateful to be rid of it. I lean over and plunge my stiff fingers into the narrow stream trickling down to the Agdersfjord, sighing with relief. I doubt my hands will ever grow accustomed to such strain. Beads of sweat fall from my forehead and merge with the water. Me— *sweating in the fields*! I almost laugh at the absurdity. But the whalebone at my side tugs soberly at my attention.

I shake the water from my hands and throw yet another glance behind my shoulder. The late-evening sun sends a soft and sloping light across the grassy knoll. I am alone, save for perhaps the hidden folk, who are known to make their burrow-homes in hills such as this.

It would be almost peaceful, were it not for the reason I'm here.

Once my hands have regained some movement, I pick up the newly inscribed whalebone, clutching it to my breast. It's nearly the length of my torso, and a third as thick, but surprisingly light. It cost me an entire ingot of silver at the market, traded with a merchant who no doubt wrested it from some Sami hunter in the North. I realized from the weaselly grin on his face as he turned away that I'd likely paid double its worth.

Next time I'll take off these garnet beads and wear an old, worn cloak over my dress. He may not have known who I am, but a merchant knows wealth when he sees it.

No—there won't *be* a next time. Not if this works.

And it *must* work.

The little stream is paltry compared with the mighty fjord it feeds, and I briefly wonder if it will anger Freya to call on her in such an ordinary place. Perhaps I should go to the sacred Lake Vítrir instead.

But the risk is too great. I might be spotted by one of the cityfolk, who sometimes go there to seek Odin's wisdom, or a farmer leaving an early offering to Frey in the hope of a rich harvest. Then the flame of gossip would leap from one log to another, and the rumor would spread to everyone in Skíringssal that the king's daughter practices magic, like some lowborn witch. A shudder runs through me at the thought.

Father would kill me if he knew what I was doing.

I glance around one more time, twice as anxious as I already was. No; this was the safest place I could have chosen. Besides, I must remain close to the bath chamber, in case Mother decides she needs me after all.

I bow my head to the stream and hold the whalebone out in front of it, just as Fritjof, Father's skald and the most powerful seer in all of Agder, instructed me to do. I clear my throat then, slowly, begin to sing the impromptu rune-charm I've carved into its sides:

Hail, Freya, ruler of Folkvang! Hear me and ease the labor of the queen. Save her from sorrow and pain as she births an heir to the throne. Bless her with a hearty son and prince.

Nerves lace my voice with tremors, like an unsteady hand weaving a thread-picker through finespun yarn. I can't boast of a worthy singing voice, not like Fritjof can. Though he eventually gave in to my pleading and taught me the art of rune-casting, Fritjof remained firm that my voice could not be trained. As with the Sight, a song-voice is a gift from the gods. You are either blessed with one or not.

Still, I hope with all my heart that my clumsy charm will win my namesake's favor. Or if the goddess would spurn me, I pray at least that Mother's midwife can help her. No doubt she's already cast a more powerful spell than I could ever invent.

Renowned for bringing many a strong and hearty babe into the world, the midwife was sent for all the way from Hordaland in the west, at my tight-fisted father's great expense. Of course, there are plenty of midwives closer by, each capable of aiding women through the ordeal of childbirth. There used to be one right here in Skíringssal, but Father had her executed when Mother's last babe was stillborn. Though her belly swelled again shortly thereafter, not one midwife in all of Agder dared come forward after that.

As usual, after the birthing began this morning, the midwife wouldn't let me in the bath chamber. Not that Mother wanted me to stay; she only wanted Helge by her side. "You will understand someday, Princess Freydis," Helge said before slamming the door.

Helge may be right, but I had to do *something* to help Mother— something I'd never attempted before.

There is great risk in rune-casting, but I had to try. It was the only thing left *to* try. All my heartfelt prayers over the years, all the offerings of silver and gold I've laid at Freya's altar, all the ewes and heifers and sows Father has sacrificed . . . it's never been enough to change the tide.

As if cued by my black thoughts, a bloodcurdling scream resounds from the bath chamber.

Mother!

My stomach spasms again as my feet rush me to the source of

the scream. Just as I reach the door, a thrall emerges, carrying out a sheepskin dripping with red ocher dye.

Not dye.

Blood.

The metallic scent fills my nose as the thrall scurries past. A wave of dizziness washes over me. I put a hand on the peat wall to stay myself.

"Mother!" I call from the doorway, but my voice is feeble.

Another scream sounds from inside, then stops short. I wait. For a few long moments, silence. Then—wailing.

Unthinking, I toss the whalebone aside and burst into the dark chamber. The air inside is close. In the dim light from the soapstone candles, I can just make out Mother on her knees.

My heart lurches at the sight. Her beautiful face is caked in dirt and sweat and tears and twisted in an expression of pure agony. She squeezes Helge's hand; the midwife kneels behind. Blood stains the bottom of her tunic and pools beneath the three women.

I gasp at the sharp scent of metal.

That smell.

It roots me in place. I couldn't move my legs if I tried.

"Get out!" the midwife shrieks.

I barely hear her; the dizziness has taken hold of me again. My vision blurs. I'm sure I'm about to faint.

I feel myself being shoved toward the door. I catch a flash of Helge's gray hair whipping out of her unkempt braid, then I'm outside once again.

I stumble back, blinking in the soft light, disoriented. I make my way to the outer wall and feel around for the discarded whalebone. My fingers clasp the bone as my vision starts to clear, and I let myself slump against the peat.

I turn over the whalebone and examine the runes one more time, just to be sure. The bone seems to vibrate, until I realize it's my hands that are trembling.

Mother.

I've never seen her like that before. So much pain, so much blood . . .

I try to force the image from my mind. With nowhere better to go, I decide to wait. If I can't be of any other use, at least I can sit and pray.

A rough kick to my shin jolts me awake. I yelp and shrink back against the wall, squinting up at my assailant. In the dim light of dusk, I can just make out the dark eyes and gaunt frame of the midwife.

"Foolish girl!" she hisses, snatching the whalebone from my grasp. "Did not your teacher warn you that just *one* wrong mark will incur Freya's wrath?"

The runes.

"It—they are perfect," I say, though fear wavers my voice again. "I'm sure of it. I-I've spent years learning—"

"Be silent!"

She turns the whalebone over in her hands. I watch with my breath in my throat as she scrutinizes the sacred marks for errors. Finding none, she purses her lips and thrusts it at me.

But before I can take it back, she drops it and falls to her knees, bowing her head in sudden deference.

As if snapping awake from a dream, I suddenly remember my place. Father's favorite reprimand comes to mind, the one he's repeated over and over for as long as I can remember: *Never forget who you are, and never let anyone else forget either.*

I rise to my feet and brush off my dress.

"The king," I hear a nearby thrall whisper.

My body goes rigid.

Of course. That's why the midwife is kneeling. Not for me.

The painful smack of wood against wood fills my ear as the door to the bath chamber ricochets off the wall. And again, moments later. From the corner of my eye, I see Father rushing out. Neither the midwife nor I dare look at him.

"King Balli, the Norns did not weave it—" the midwife begins, but he storms past the both of us without so much as a glance.

A shaky exhale passes her lips. She stays on her knees, even after we hear the door to the Great Hall slam shut in the distance.

She's terrified of him. That can mean only one thing.

My rune-charm failed.

The babe is dead.

My heart plummets. Sixteen winters have passed since my own birth, and Mother has borne many since, boys and girls alike—yet I have neither brother nor sister who still draws breath. Babe after babe, snatched away from the womb before their time, or born lifeless.

I look down at the midwife with newfound pity; she must have known the fate of her predecessor after all, and she answered the call nonetheless. A brave woman—or a foolish one.

"If you wish to keep your head on your shoulders, you'll leave before sunrise," I say, doing my best to sound commanding. I unhook the string of garnet beads slung across my dress and offer them to her. "Use this to bribe a fisherman to take you to Eikundarsund. From there, you can make your way back to Hordaland."

She blinks up at me, confused.

"Go now, before he returns!" I snap.

At that, she snatches the beads, scrambles to her feet, and rushes off.

I watch her disappear down the hill, then turn back to the bath chamber. I take a deep, steadying breath of clean air before stepping inside.

More soapstone lamps have been lit, but they do little to fight the gloom within. It's as though the darkness is thick with grief. I can just see Mother's form shuddering in Helge's embrace. Her cries bounce off the cramped walls—which seem to be closing in around us, threatening to swallow us whole. Helge murmurs in soothing tones and rocks her back and forth, like a mother with her child.

I know Helge rocked me like that when I was young, though I can scarcely remember those days. It seems more like a dream than a memory now. Since then, I've earned nothing but her scorn. And Mother's, too. I try my best to please them, but I can't seem to do anything right in their eyes.

I know they wish I'd been a boy. Everyone in Skíringssal does, though none more than I.

A pang of despair rises from my stomach, only to lodge itself in my throat. I glance around for the newborn's body, but I don't see it. Of course, a thrall must have taken it away by now.

"My son," Mother moans into Helge's shoulder between sobs. "My son!"

It was a boy.

Another boy, lost. How could the gods be so cruel?

"Mother," I choke out, crouching down beside her. "I'm so sorry." I reach my hand out and place it gently on her back.

She recoils at my touch as if from a bee sting. "Leave, Freydis!" she shrieks. Helge glares at me, and even in the dark her eyes are colder than the winter frost.

Sorrow knots itself in my throat as I take my leave from the bath chamber. Helge quickly resumes her murmuring. At least she can comfort Mama, even if I can't.

Though the evening air sends goosebumps across my skin, at least it's unmarred by the smell of death. I glance at the sky. Dusk has given way to twilight; it never truly grows dark this time of year. The stars struggle to shine through the blue haze that swathes the sky.

I know how they feel.

My eyes glaze. I take a deep breath, letting a familiar current of imagination sweep me away.

In my mind, I'm no longer in Skíringssal, no longer in the kingdom of Agder at all. Instead, I'm in Vestfold with my husband, King Harald. Our children are fast asleep, and we're taking a nighttime stroll through our gardens. His copper keys dangle from a knit chain at my chest. The breeze is warm and gentle and the air smells sweetly of gardenias. And now we stop to gaze at the stars. My husband stands behind me and wraps his arms around me. And now he murmurs in my ear that he loves me even more than Thor loves Sif.

In this future—*my* future—my heart is whole and full. And nights like tonight are only a distant memory.

Feeling slightly lighter, I come back to the present. I start walking toward my family's longhouse, to the extra room I have all to myself—the room Father had built for the many sisters and brothers I was supposed to have. I don't really want to go back; I want to go down to the docks, cut loose one of the boats tethered there, and sail out of Skíringssal and into the future that awaits me. But that won't happen until Harald comes to claim me.

How much longer will I have to wait?

I pause when I spot the whalebone in the grass where the midwife dropped it. I pick it up. As I stare listlessly at the runes carved into its side, I'm struck by the overwhelming desire to hurl it into the stream.

I was right: The runes are perfect. Freya simply ignored my plea.

"Princess Freydis."

"Yes?" I hold the whalebone behind my back as I turn to face Orm, Father's youngest guard. Even in the wan twilight, I can see his round cheeks flush. Orm is only two winters my elder, and he's always been ill at ease in my presence. "What is it?"

He shuffles awkwardly. "The king wishes to speak with you. He awaits you in the Great Hall."

5

FREYDIS

The Great Hall looms at the crest of the hill, a stark edifice cutting into the blue-black sky. I force my feet to carry me to it, fighting the dread rising in my chest as the towering oakwood walls draw nearer and nearer.

A moment ago, I was avoiding returning to my room. Now I desperately wish I could head straight there, burrow into my bed, and disappear under the furs.

As I reach the apex of the hill, the city of Skíringssal comes into view below. The fires of a hundred hearths wink at me through the roofs of the densely clustered homesteads. It always seemed to me that the Great Hall was watching over them, like an eagle scanning the wrinkled fjord from a bluff.

Tonight it feels like the hall is watching me.

After losing yet another heir, Father is surely in the throes of one of his rages. If he's had any henbane tonight, that rage will only be magnified. I'm a skiff sailing into a storm.

I pause in front of the runestone, resting my hand on its cool, smooth face. After he finished building the Great Hall, Father erected the runestone to declare his kingship over Agder. I linger for a long moment, hoping the marks will infuse me with some of their power, before pushing open the heavy wooden doors.

Instantly I'm greeted by a deafening clash. A drinking horn smashes against the wall, barely an arm's length from my head. I flinch reflexively. A splotch of liquid mars the oak, dribbling down toward a cowering mass of scraggly white hair and homespun wool.

Fritjof!

"You swore to me that I would have sons!" Father thunders. I look up to see him pacing in front of the massive hearth, his blood-red cloak swishing violently behind his slight frame.

"Please, no more!" Fritjof cries out. "I see only what they choose to reveal!"

I feel an urge to throw myself on top of the old skald, to shield him from Father's rage. But fear roots me where I stand. I expected Father to take his anger out on a thrall, but he must be out of his wits to brutalize the gods' messenger to Agder. Of all the people in our kingdom, I thought Fritjof would always be safe from Father's wrath.

Fritjof is not simply a skald. He is also a seer, with one eye in Midgard, and one eye that sees into the other eight worlds. Sometimes he even sees into the Well of Fate, the hall beneath Yggdrasil where the Norns reside. I've seen firsthand the toll it takes on the poor man; it has cost him a great deal of his soundness of mind. But he is irreplaceable to Father because of it. Everything he has foreseen has come to pass.

Everything except this.

"You're a fraud!" Father bellows. "You know nothing of the will of the gods!"

Fritjof winces and peers up at Father with wide, mismatched eyes, his craggy face half in shadow in the dim torchlight. A trickle of blood drips down from his hairline, where Father's last blow must have hit its mark. His confusion is evident. It makes my heart ache. Fritjof taught me everything I know about magic, from rune-casting to herblore. Above all, he's the closest thing I have to a friend.

"Please," he begs again. "Please."

I know Fritjof; he can't speak plainly enough to defend himself. Not that there's any reasoning with Father when he's like this.

My heart is thumping, but I do my best to keep my face expressionless. The worst thing to do around Father is show fear. Or show any feeling at all.

"You sent for me, Father?" I ask blithely.

He stops pacing and shoots me an irritated glance, as though I've interrupted a game of *tafl*.

"Leave, Skald." He flicks his fingers in annoyance. "I'll deal with you later."

Fritjof climbs shakily to his feet. I hold out my hand to steady him, giving him a slight smile. I hope he can feel the reassurance I'm sending his way.

The moment his arm touches mine, his face jerks upward into the light, as if drawn by some invisible string.

My breath hitches in my throat. Father goes very still, knowing as well as I do the look of a man in the grips of the Sight.

The world seems poised on the edge of a knife.

Fritjof looks straight into my eyes as he speaks. The words tumble out in a high-pitched whine—not *his* voice, but someone else's speaking through him:

They'll come in a pair, one light and one dark, the sons of Balli of Skíringssal.

Relief blooms in my chest. It feels like the first snowdrop flower after a long winter frost.

Freya hasn't forsaken me. She has simply been waiting for the right time to give Mother not one, but *two* sons.

Twin boys! At her age, it's almost inconceivable. But the Norns have made it known, and age is but a taper in the gale of their will.

Fritjof's head lolls forward. He staggers on his feet. I catch him just before he crumples onto the ground. He shoots me a dazed smile, the blood trickling down his forehead and matting his bushy white eyebrows. The wound needs tending; I'll go to his longhouse and fix him a salve after this.

Poor Fritjof. Father keeps him fed and housed, but he has no one to keep him company, nor look after his well-being—no one but me, and I can't visit as often as I'd like. It would provoke too much suspicion.

As I help Fritjof to his feet, I send a silent prayer of thanks to each of the Aesir for giving him this vision. This hope.

I glance at Father. Sure enough, a look of cold satisfaction rests on his face. "Go, Fritjof. I release you," he says, his tone notably gentler.

Disoriented, Fritjof jerks his body forward into something resembling a bow before skittering out of the hall. He may not be fully present in our world, but he's sane enough to know to leave my father's sight when he's not wanted.

Father releases a heavy sigh and turns toward the hearth, folding his arms across his chest.

It's my turn to face him now.

My footsteps echo across the lofty hall, filling the silence between us. With just the two of us in here, the hall seems even larger than usual. I pass rows and rows of longtables, each flanked by wooden benches softened with sheepskins. The roof is bolstered by thick, tree-like columns delicately carved into reliefs of warriors locked in battle, who seem to dance in the firelight.

I spare a quick glance over at my own contribution on the eastern wall: a tapestry depicting Father with his sword raised high in the air, the ravens Hugin and Munin perched on his byrnie-clad shoulders to signify the Allfather's blessing as he leads the *hird-*

men to victory at the Battle of Geirstad. It's a story every child of Agder knows by heart, even before they learn to walk: how Father used the strength and cunning of Odin, patron god of all rightful rulers, to lead our men to victory against impossible odds, snatching the kingdom of Agder from the iron grip of King Godfred of the Danes. Even now, the sight brings me comfort. It reminds me that Father is a hero, a man chosen to rule by no less than the Allfather himself.

Father built the Great Hall just before I was born, after the old mead hall burned to the ground in the battle. We won our freedom, but at great cost: Half of Geirstad was lost in a devastating fire, becoming what we now call the Dead City. So Father renamed what was left Skíringssal and set about building it anew. He cleared the path to the farmland and expanded the harbor and the market, drawing the best craftsmen in the land and merchants from far and wide to our shores. Skíringssal grew into a great center for trade, and Father grew powerful along with it. So powerful that Godfred himself was forced to acknowledge Agder's sovereignty.

But for all Father's many achievements, he still has no heir. No true heir—no *male* heir.

As I approach, I study his profile, at once familiar and strange to me. His is a severe face, with an aquiline nose and thin lips that are often twitching, even when he doesn't speak. Lichen-green eyes—so very like my own in color, or so I'm told—stare moodily into the flames from behind drooping eyelids.

He's getting old.

The realization hits me like a bolt of Thor's lightning. The rings of gold and silver look heavy on his bony arms, the sallow skin sagging beneath their weight. Even his cloak looks like it's bearing down on his hunched shoulders. His beard is already more gray than tawny, and droplets of ale cling to its fringes.

But as his gaze flickers to mine, I notice that the whites of his eyes are clear instead of bloodshot, the pupils focused on my own; at least his ale wasn't laced with henbane tonight.

I come to a halt several paces before him and bow my head in deference.

"I assume you know why you're here, though the seer's portent may change things somewhat."

I shake my head, keeping my gaze planted firmly on the ground in front of me.

It is best for the unwise to sit in silence. Father himself taught me that, though he would never know he did. I overheard him say it to Alvtir as a child, in one of many nights spent with my ear pressed to the northern door of the hall, praying Helge wouldn't catch me out of bed and box me for eavesdropping.

He grunts in annoyance. "Have you bled?"

I look up, startled. I was not prepared for *that*. "... Father?"

"Your woman's bleeding," he snaps. "Have you had it yet?"

"Y-yes, Father."

"For how long?"

"Two winters."

"Good." He scratches his beard. Fittingly, he appears to be standing under his sigil—Hugin and Munin, emblazoned on the shield that hangs on the wall behind the dais—as he falls deeper and deeper into deliberation. *Allfather,* I pray silently, staring at his favorite pets. *Give me the strength to face whatever trial Father has in store for me. Bless me with your guidance, as you have blessed him.*

"Harald has invoked the pledge," Father says finally. "One way or another, you'll be married within the year."

Harald.

A flutter rises in my chest. Nervousness and excitement swirl together inside me, like Frey gathering the clouds around him before a summer storm.

Harald has finally invoked the pledge.

I've waited for this moment for years and years—ever since the day Harald and I met, though we were only children then. It must have been just before his father died. The ailing King Hálfdan of Vestfold brought his son with him on a rare visit to our neighboring kingdom. No doubt looking to secure his son's marriage prospects before he passed into Niflheim.

I was summoned to meet them. I had been amusing myself in the garden, and Mother chastened me for my face being dirty. I stood awkwardly in front of the throne facing the doors, Mother's hands heavy on my shoulders, as Hálfdan called for his son to come inside.

Even at eight or nine, Harald was a sight to behold. As he entered the hall, I remember Mother whispering to Helge that his honey-colored hair, which fell freely to his shoulders, was even comelier than mine. He had bright, keen eyes, and not one feature on his face stood out as unlovely.

It was the first time I ever felt embarrassed about my appearance. I reached up to my face and desperately tried to rub off the dirt before he came near. If he noticed, he said nothing, a prince to his core. Instead, he smiled and bowed low before me.

"*Heill,* Freydis. My name is Harald," he said. When he straightened, his chin was raised with a confidence I had never seen in someone my own age. "You are most beautiful," he continued. "If it pleases my father, I hope you will be my wife someday."

I gasped, but Mother laughed and clapped her hands in delight. "What a charming young man," she said. "You've raised him well, Hálfdan."

"He gets it from his mother," King Hálfdan replied, grinning through his thick, gold-flecked beard. "Though she died in his birthing. Odin knows, I have no such charm of my own."

I spared a glance at Father out of the corner of my eye. He was leaning on the arm of the throne, staring listlessly into the distance. The exchange of courtesies must have bored him near to tears.

"Be polite, Freydis," Mother urged, giving my shoulders a hard squeeze.

"*Heill.*" The word came out in a squeak. But Harald only smiled wider. Our parents' idle chatter became a hum in the background, and his eyes never left mine.

I was overjoyed when Father announced that very night that we were betrothed. I haven't seen him since, but rumor has it that Harald has grown into a noteworthy man, both handsome and brave. Harald the Fine-Haired—that's what the traders from Vestfold call him.

"Do you understand me, Freydis?" Father bangs his fists on the column beside him, jolting me back into the present. "Or are you even more dim-witted than you appear?"

I shrink back, despite myself. My chin trembles, but I hide it by nodding. "Y-yes, Father. Thank you."

Never let a man see your tears. That's what Mother always says. Besides, it's better that he takes this frustration out on me than on some unfortunate thrall later on. Or on Mother herself.

Not that he won't do that as well.

The thought makes me shiver, even through the stuffy heat emanating from the hearth. "I await my wedding with great joy," I add, "as I await the birth of my brothers, despite the sorrow of this night."

With an approving nod, Father reaches for his belt and unloops a small pouch of coins, holding it out for me to take. "In the morning, you will go to the market and buy the finest silks from Bulghar to fashion a new dress."

I take a few steps forward, hesitant, then take the pouch from his hand. "Thank you," I say again. Feeling utterly drained, I give him a short bow before turning to the door. I'm eager to head back to my room, where I can sort through all the tumult of this day.

My beloved will claim me. Mother will have sons. All will be well. Just not tonight.

"Freydis," Father calls after me, his eldritch voice etching itself into my bones. "Tell the guards to fetch me a thrall. The gods will receive a special gift tonight."

6

YAFEU

Falling, falling in blackness.

Soon I find the ground. I feel the side of my torso hit the dirt and suck in a breath. Immediately I retch, coughing and sputtering as though I've swallowed a swarm of gnats. My eyelids feel sewn together, but I pry them open. Through two slits, I see the purple cloth flutter to the side as Mama's blurry silhouette runs through.

Smoke and screams. Our hut is filled with both, filtering in from outside.

Fear settles over me, as heavy as the gray haze in the air. I rub my eyes and struggle to my feet. Kamo puts his arm around a whimpering Goleh as Mama shoves the last of our millet stores into her satchel.

"What's happening?" I croak.

She puts her finger over her mouth and kneels to the ground, pointing to the crack between the door and the wall. What I see through it makes my knees buckle.

The village is on fire.

The thatched roof of a hut only a stone's throw away from ours blazes brightly against the night sky. As I watch in horror, the flame spreads to the huts on either side. It won't be long until it reaches us.

But that's far from the worst of it.

The fire lights up the sight of strange soldiers with glistening blades—blades poised on the necks of Ampah's family.

Ampah!

I watch helplessly as Ampah is yanked from her mother's side by her hair. She screams and claws at her attacker, but he overpowers her easily and lashes her to a camel with a piece of rope.

It's then that I see the long line of camels, and the throng of weeping, shaking people—half the village at least—bound together between them.

A slave caravan. They're not soldiers; they're slavers.

Fury explodes in my core. The clink of metal on metal grabs my attention, and I turn to see Mama brandishing two of my unfinished daggers. We nod at each other in silent understanding. I strap on my own sheath and slip on my shoes, the leather soles worn thin from too many years of use. I grasp Kamo's and Goleh's hands with my own, squeezing tight.

Mama kisses us each on the forehead. Then, with a strength I didn't know she possessed, she kicks open the door and makes a run for the White River. The three of us follow close behind.

Villagers dart everywhere, desperate to escape. An icy panic floods my veins despite the scorching heat in the air. I grip my brothers' hands and force myself to run faster than I ever thought I could. Thank the gods I fell asleep in the yellow kaftan, which flows noiselessly around me as I pump my legs to their limit.

"Jump!" I shout to my brothers. We leap over a girl named Newma as she's tackled to the ground by one of the slavers. Mama sprints ahead and I pull my brothers forward, desperate to regain the lost momentum.

But we can't outrun the flames traveling from hut to hut, ravaging everything in their path. The skin on my face and arms grows blisteringly hot. Smoke fills my eyes, my nose, my throat. Each new breath brings a searing pain to my chest.

Just as we reach my uncle's hut on the far edge of the village, the roof suddenly falls inside the dome with a deafening crack, sending a cloud of fiery flecks into the night sky. Did my kin make it out? Either way, there's nothing I can do for them now. I sprint by without so much as a second glance.

As soon as we break free of the smoke, I start to see the river and the outline of the mangroves. My heart swells with hope as my mind fixates on the little canoes waiting for us in the thicket. They're squat, hollowed logs that barely seat two people, used only for light fishing in the rainy season. But they're the only chance we have to escape.

"Stop!" I hear someone shout behind me. I glance over my shoulder to see one of the slavers running after us.

My feet grind harder into the dirt.

We'll make it. We have to make it.

Something strikes me between my shoulder blades and shatters. A blinding pain ricochets through my whole body, stifling the scream in my throat. I let go of my brothers' hands just in time to break my fall.

"Mama!" I hear Goleh shout.

Then I hit the ground. Another spasm of pain rocks through me.

"Get up!" the slaver growls at me, jerking me up by my arm.

Without thinking, I throw a kick to his groin. He grunts in agony and folds into himself. Before he can recover, I slam my fist into his temple, reveling in the sight of him keeling over, unconscious.

But my victory is short-lived. Two more slavers are already on me.

I turn toward the river just before they grab my arms and twist them behind my back. Dread dulls the twinge that shoots through my shoulders. I thrash and kick out wildly, uselessly. I can no longer see my family up ahead. I can only hope they've reached the mangroves by now.

Take the canoes, I pray silently. *Let me go.*

But a moment later, Mama comes racing back. A couple more slavers jump between us, facing her. She screams and rips my daggers through the air in front of her.

I had no idea she knew how to wield them with such ferocity.

I watch in awe as she spins like a tornado and leaves a gash across one of their stomachs. The other steps back, missing the blade by a hair, then lunges.

"Mama—no!" I scream, but I'm already being dragged toward the caravan. I struggle against the vise-like grip on my arms. I can just see the slaver's shoe come down hard on Mama's hand, eliciting a painful shriek as she drops the dagger.

And then he's on top of her.

Terror seizes me. My voice, numb with the violent vibration of my screams, grows weaker and weaker.

Someone removes the sheath from my hip, then fastens a thick rope around my wrists and ankles, lashing me to the long stretch of camels and bodies.

Dizziness hits me first—then nausea.

I watch in a daze as the last of the huts collapse one by one into smoldering heaps. The wind picks up, blowing ash and dust in the air. The slavers continue to tie villagers to the caravan, snatching weapons and jewelry as they do. Others comb the rubble for valuables, and still others carry jugs of water from the well at the center of the village, tying them to the camels' saddles. It's all so orderly, so matter-of-fact. I dimly wonder how many times they've done this before.

A low, close moan tugs me back to the present. A girl hunches over in front of me, whimpering to herself. It takes a moment for her high cheekbones and large, frenzied eyes to register.

"Ampah!" I reach out and seize her arm, straining against the rope. "Are you okay?"

She stares like she doesn't recognize me, then shifts out of my grasp, revealing a gash peeking through her torn kaftan at the rib cage.

"Ampah," I whisper, dread rising in me once again. But the wound doesn't look like it's still bleeding; it can't be that deep. She's just terrified.

"Sit down if you can," I say gently. "Put your head between your legs." I move closer to give her more slack in the rope, but she doesn't comply. I doubt it would help if I forced her.

Ampah and I are flanked by two camels, each carrying hefty loads, making it difficult to see who else has been captured. I lean to the side and squint up and down the line for my uncle's family, but in the faint glow of the embers, I can only make out Masireh standing toward the front. Maybe I just can't see them.

Or maybe they *were* in the hut when it . . .

The thought twists my stomach, sending another wave of nausea up my throat.

Thankfully, I don't see Mama. I don't feel her *nyama* here either. She must have escaped with Kamo and Goleh after all.

I let out a shaky breath of relief and shut my eyes, sending a silent prayer to Agbe and Naete, who rule over river, lake, and sea.

Please, watch over them. Let the White River carry them to safety.

When I open my eyes, one of the slavers is walking down the caravan, inspecting the interlocking stretch of camels and villagers. He pauses several people ahead of me, next to Newma. She's shaking violently, her kaftan hanging off her in rags. The man motions to one of the other slavers, who undoes her bindings and takes her out of the line. The first man spins her so her back is to him.

Then he takes out a dagger and plunges it into the base of her skull.

Ampah lets out a sharp cry as Newma crumples to the ground. At the sound, the man swivels toward us.

I know that face.

It's the man from Koumbi Saleh.

My gaze fixes on the dagger in his hand.

My dagger. One of the many he stole from me. And now he's using it to kill my people.

My blood boils. The thought of lunging forward and strangling him with the rope around my wrists consumes me for a moment— until he continues down the line, and I realize what he's doing.

He's searching for anyone who, like Newma, is too badly injured to survive.

My eyes flicker to poor Newma's corpse, lying facedown in the dirt. Blood stains her kaftan, which billows around her bare legs in the breeze. Stomach churning, I straighten and distribute my weight evenly, fighting a wave of dizziness.

"Stand tall and be quiet," I hiss at Ampah through gritted teeth.

Gratefully, she listens this time, and the man walks past us without a glance. I hear him pull a few others out of the line and slaughter them like animals, but I don't look back. I can't.

I provoked these same men at Koumbi Saleh yesterday.

Did they follow me here?

Is all of this my fault?

I shut my eyes again, wishing I could shut my ears as well, so I wouldn't have to hear the villagers weeping and pleading in vain. I force myself to picture Mama and Kamo and Goleh disappearing down the river, all huddled in our tiny canoe.

Let it be so, Agbe and Naete, Mawu and Lisa. Let them be safe.

In the distance sounds a piercing scream. No . . . a howl. Despite the heat emanating from the smoldering huts, a chill rips through me. Somehow, I know it's the painted wolf.

Someone shouts an order from the front of the line, and the camels begin to move, dragging nearly an entire village with them.

The slavers each have their own camel to ride, and it makes me hate them even more. We veer north, crossing over the road to Koumbi Saleh. It doesn't take me long to realize where we're headed.

The desert.

Another wave of fear crashes over me, dousing the last of the fire in my blood. I take a deep breath and look up at the fumy sky, the painted wolf's death cry still ringing in my ears.

7

YAFEU

The sand has long turned cold beneath my feet when the caravan finally slows to a stop at the outskirts of the Sahara.

At the order shouted down the line, the camels flanking Ampah and me fold their legs and lie down, letting out a low bleat as they do. My own legs tremble from walking through Lisa's rise and set and I collapse willingly onto the sand, finding a peculiar comfort in its grainy caress. I'm aware of a sensation between my shoulder blades, and I know it to be pain, but it feels far away. Ampah thumps down in front of me and curls into a ball. The slavers hop off their camels and start to make their own camp, setting up tents and lighting fires that carve yellow orbs of light into the night.

Warmth radiates from the camel behind me. I lean on him, releasing my own heavy sigh. Camels can be snappy, but this one is too tired to protest my closeness.

It won't be long until Lisa rises again. I remember how we slept in shifts when we crossed the desert with Papa: resting only a few hours at night, then resting again during the hottest part of the day. We traveled at dawn and dusk, when we had enough light to see danger coming from far away but Lisa wasn't hot enough to slow our movement. Maybe that's also how the slavers do it. If so, we won't get much sleep tonight.

I look over at Ampah. Silhouetted by the light of the campfires, the outline of her torso shivers and convulses, racked with quiet sobs.

A stiff, cold feeling settles in my chest, and soon my cheeks are damp with tears too. I lick them off my face as they fall, hoping they will slake my aching thirst. Or at least wash the taste of ash off my tongue.

The sounds of celebration from the slavers' camp mingle in the air with the soft cries of their captives. It strikes me that these ropes have connected me to the villagers for the first time, in more ways than one. They've never thought of me as one of their own, but to the slavers, we are all the same.

The stiffness in my chest pulses, but I force myself to stop crying. The tingle in my throat has built to a painful dry cough, and I know I need to conserve the water in my body.

While I've crossed the Sahara twice before with my family, we would never dream of making the journey on foot. We traveled with all the comforts that a famous blacksmith of Wagadu could buy. But even then, water was precious, and we drank sparingly. I remember sucking on a pebble to keep my mouth wet.

I sift through those memories for any clues to where the slavers could be taking us. Most likely, they will take us to Sijilmasa, the northern trade city that rivals Koumbi Saleh. We went there once with Papa, and once to Anfa. But they could also take us to Fes or Nekor, or Tahert. Any of those cities would have a profitable slave market.

My blood turns to ice as I remember another possibility: Idjil. They could be taking us there, to work in the dreaded salt mines.

Based on the hair-raising stories I've heard, Ampah wouldn't last a day in the mines. Maybe I wouldn't either.

I push the thought away. No matter where we're headed, we must first survive the desert. Even the shortest route to the closest city will take over a month by foot.

I'll have to track our position relative to Lisa's rise and set to get my bearings. After a week or two, I should be able to figure out which route we're traveling.

And then . . . what? What will I do then? Come up with a plan to escape with Ampah? Or better yet, kill all the slavers and free my people? Both thoughts are so absurd, I might laugh if my throat weren't so raw.

Instead I heave myself onto all fours and crawl over to Ampah, laying a hesitant palm on her shoulder. She flinches at my touch.

"It's just me, Ampah." I hold my hands out to show that I have no weapons. Her eyes are wild and unrecognizing, her beautiful face slick with sweat despite the chilly night air.

Fever from the wound, I realize. Another pang of dread rocks through me.

"Let me see," I say softly, pointing to the gash running across her rib cage. I try to lift her kaftan to get a better look, but she bolts upright and grabs my wrist—the cloth has dried onto the wound, her blood blending into the red dye. "It's okay." I take my hands away. It's better that the cloth is covering it anyway, to protect it from the sand. I certainly don't have anything better to dress it with.

"It's very warm when you lie here," I add, patting the camel's belly. After a few moments, she scoots closer and curls up against the camel, facing away from me. I decide to take it as a good sign.

I lie on my back and gaze up at the sky. It's cloudless, flecked with stars and the sliver of Mawu ruling over them, beautiful despite all the anguish beneath it.

Night owl. That's Ampah's nickname for me, because I wake so often before the end of Mawu's reign. I can't help it; I've always felt so much freer at night than during the day. Like the coolness of Mawu is balancing me, focusing me. Mama would say it's because I'm all fire, like my father.

Mama.

The thought of her slices through the numbness and clogs my throat, blurs my vision. My hand flies to the green wolf at my neck as Mawu's face begins to shimmer.

Does Mawu see us here now? Does she—he, they—see our suffering?

Do they care?

With both Ampah and the camel radiating heat, exhaustion quickly overtakes me. Still clutching the wolf, I drift into darkness.

8

YAFEU

Right foot, left foot. Right foot, left foot. I force myself to think of nothing but the motion, repeated over and over again. It doesn't take long for me to fall into a trance: me staring at the back of Ampah's head, our feet mindlessly, unwillingly, moving through space and time.

At first, I tried to count the days. One, then two weeks went by before a heavy fog settled over my mind and I couldn't keep track anymore. Now the days—or rather, nights—swirl together like grains of sand in the wind. By the time the caravan stops midmorning, we are ready to collapse into a fitful sleep; when we wake in the evening, we are given a meager amount of bread and water, no more than what we need to survive. In between we are marching, always marching.

I never knew the wrath of Lisa like I do now, but time is truly the cruelest god. When you start to feel every flake of skin, feel your saliva thickening and the air scraping through your chest as it dries, feel the sweat-hardened rags of your kaftan chafing against your skin as you walk, rubbing it red and bare—it all happens over time.

Somehow time seems to ravage me less than the other villagers. Every day, more and more of them buckle and fall, unable to keep marching. The dying are untied and left to rot in the sand or be scavenged by the circling buzzards above. My chest clenches at the sight of the bodies disappearing behind us, at the plaintive wailing of their families and friends. I mouth a silent prayer to Mawu-Lisa for every one of them.

Ampah still hasn't shaken the blood-fever. She has yet to speak or show any other sign of recognizing me. Already so slender before we were taken, she's beginning to look frighteningly thin. I note with a creeping sense of trepidation how each successive step seems harder and harder for her to take, her legs wobbling like stems of hippo grass in the wind. Not like my own sinewy, baobab-thick legs. I can stand more of a beating from the desert.

Even the slavers look worse for the wear, and two of their own have already joined the corpses of the villagers in the dunes. We didn't stop to mourn them either.

Slave or slaver: The desert doesn't know the difference.

It's not as comforting a thought as I want it to be.

Finally, we come to the first oasis. We stop for the slavers to refill their water bags and gather dates and coconuts for the next leg of the journey. The cluster of palm trees around the peanut-shaped lake tugs at an ancient thread in the fabric of my memory.

I've been here before.

All of a sudden, I recognize our route. They're not taking us to Sijilmasa. Nor to Fes or Nekor or Tahert. Nor, thank the gods, to the mines of Idjil. No—we're veering west to the ancient city of Anfa. I've made this same journey with Papa once before, though it seems like a lifetime ago.

The thought of Papa stirs another memory—another lesson that cuts like a dagger through the fog of weariness and thirst:

You must link your breathing to your steps, to stop your nyama *from spilling out into the sand.*

As we're dragged out of the oasis, I match my breath to my footsteps. Five in, five out. Sure enough, I notice the haze lifting slightly from my mind. Hopeful, I tap Ampah's shoulder to show her, but she recoils from me again, still in the throes of the fever.

I send a prayer up to Mawu-Lisa. *Please,* I beg silently, *don't take my Ampah from me.*

9

YAFEU

L isa is especially punishing today. Heat shimmers above the sand, rippling the air like waves of water.

All I want is water.

A sickly feeling bubbles up from my stomach and spreads throughout my body. The ringing in my ears won't go away; I start rubbing them with my shoulders, then mashing them, anything for the ringing to stop. My legs are suddenly unsteady, my steps uncertain. My eyes sway from left to right. I don't know how much more I can take of this heat, this thirst, this endless, endless walking.

You must believe you will survive.

In the distance I see a silhouette of a man, a tall man with skin the color of mangrove heartwood and arms that could crush a buffalo. He waves at me from afar, and the *nyama* emanating from him is unmistakable.

My heart leaps in my chest.

Is this really happening? Has he finally come back?

"Papa?" My cracked lips sting from the effort of whispering. He breaks into a run, still a silhouette with Lisa's rising face behind him.

"Papa!" I scream, lunging forward. I strain with all my might against the ropes before I'm jerked back. The camel behind me falls over, causing the next one to stumble and the man riding him to fall off.

I crawl forward on my stomach, squinting at the blinding light. The silhouette stops moving. A huge gust of wind blows the sand in the air, and when it settles, the figure is gone.

The sound of my own breathing fills my ears. Through the corner of my eye, I can just make out the fallen slaver drawing his short sword and starting toward me.

Then—red.

The red of a kaftan, with two toothpick-thin legs poking out from underneath it. Ampah has jumped in front of me with a vigor I didn't know she still possessed.

"She's sick! She's seeing things!" she warns the slaver in our tongue. I hear the man scoff, then a sickening crack as he hits her head with the butt of his sword.

I look up, alarmed. The flash of the blade in the sun is the last thing I see before all goes black.

A sharp sting on my cheek brings me back to life. My eyes open slightly at the pain, and I register two figures hunched over me, the sky blazing red and orange behind them. Maybe Mawu-Lisa set the world on fire. I wouldn't blame them if they did.

I blink away the spots crowding my vision and glare up at the men. They regard me with dispassion, murmuring to each other; I don't need to speak their language to know they're debating cutting me loose.

I also know I'll die if they leave me here, so I fight the crippling pounding in my head and drag myself to my feet. The men exchange a glance but head back to their camels, leaving me be.

"Are you okay, night owl?" Ampah's voice is so weak I almost don't hear it at first. I look up to meet her large round eyes, blood-shot and defeated from the beating she took on my behalf.

Somehow, despite everything, she's smiling at me. I let out a bleat of relief.

Ampah!

She remembers me. The delirium must have broken—she's healing!

For the first time since we were captured, I feel something akin to hope.

"Ampah, did you see him?" I barely recognize the rasping voice that comes out of my own mouth. "Did you see my father?"

Ampah's face falls. She shakes her head no.

So it was just an illusion, a trick of the desert.

I want to cry, but I find that I can't, so I pretend the specks of sand on my cheek are tears.

I have to stay strong. For Ampah. And for Papa, even though he wasn't really here.

I study her beautiful features for a moment. Left for so long to the wind and sand, her raw cheekbones jut out in stark relief. She's barely more than a skeleton, but at least her dark eyes have the shine of awareness again.

She turns around as the caravan starts up again, but she reaches back and grabs my hand while we walk. I relax immediately into the familiar sensation.

If I make it through the desert alive, it will be because of the power of two palms reaching out to touch, cutting like shards of light through the darkness, sharing *nyama* where they meet.

Two palms clasped together can survive anything.

The next morning I wake again to the sensation of being dragged. I hop up abruptly, cringing as I realize I'm getting used to this routine.

It takes me a moment to notice the empty space in front of me. I look down to see Ampah dragging facedown through the sand.

No.

She was better yesterday. She was getting well. We were going to survive this together.

I bend over and flip her body around. Her sunken eyes stare through me, lifeless. I grab her shoulders and shake her anyway, hoping against hope that she's just unconscious. That she's still there.

"Ampah!" I whisper. "Ampah, get up!"

But she doesn't.

A scream rips through the air. I know it's coming from my mouth, but it feels like it's coming from someone else. Like this is *happening* to someone else, and I'm just watching through her eyes.

I don't even notice that I've stopped walking, until I hear the shouts coming from the back of the line. Someone speaks to me in my own tongue, heavily stilted.

"Stop that! Be quiet!"

I turn to see one of the slavers hop off his camel and lumber toward me.

The same man who nearly choked me to death at Koumbi Saleh.

Something inside me snaps. He notices Ampah and stoops down to cut her loose. I lunge forward and coil the rope binding my wrists around his neck, yanking poor Ampah's body through the sand with the effort. I manage to kick away two other men before I feel the shock of heavy leather thwacking across my back.

The pain is paralyzing. I open my mouth but no sound comes out. Instead I fall to my hands and knees, remaining there as the slaver whips me a few more times for good measure.

Dizzy with agony, I can only watch helplessly as they untie the ropes from Ampah's wrists and tie them around mine, binding me twice over.

They waste no time starting the caravan up again. The sandy tatters of my kaftan chafe against my back, sticking to the wet blood. But I can hardly feel it through the pain in my heart. I crane my neck to look back even as my feet stumble forward, watching

Ampah fade to a red-and-brown blur against the endless sea of tan. As if staring at her hard enough will bring her back to life.

Ampah. No, no, no, no.

When the last speck of her disappears, it hits me: My only friend is gone forever.

Despite the dozens of people bound to me with this same rope, I am completely alone.

My hand curls around the stone wolf at my neck. I can feel myself weeping, though the tears won't come. I weep for Ampah. I weep for Mama and Papa, Kamo and Goleh.

I weep to be so achingly, crushingly alone.

10

YAFEU

Through my grief, I'm dimly aware of the sand turning to rock beneath my feet, of the barren limestone peaks replacing the dunes ahead of the caravan. We stop at a large trading post near a river, and the slavers let us drink our fill of water. It lifts the fog from my mind, but that only sharpens the pain of losing Ampah. The image of her limp body dragging through the sand is branded in the supple skin of my memory.

We were almost out of the desert. If she'd only held on for a little while longer.

It takes us over a week to cross the arid plains and canyons of the low mountains, passing only shepherds and the occasional far-flung village. Then, suddenly, we're surrounded on either side by fields of grass and golden grains and the reddest soil I've ever seen, its rich, earthy scent filling my nose. The air is mild, the breeze moist enough to soothe my parched skin, and I almost feel glad that I'm still alive.

It continues like this for two more days, until, at last, we reach the city of Anfa.

I take in the imposing rammed-earth walls, only a few heads taller than me but stretching as far as the eye can see. The rusted metal gates heave a great sigh as they rise, revealing a swarm of people against a backdrop of brightly colored stucco homes. My senses are overwhelmed by sights and sounds and smells, a jarring contrast from the void of the desert and the mountains and the stillness of the farmland. The clinking of metal blends with shouts, laughter, music. The scent of incense wafting through the air gives way to sizzling meats and tantalizing spices trickling out of the gated courtyards, making me even dizzier with hunger than I already was.

But the scents also conjure the vague memory of when I was here with Papa, so many years ago. I remember the arched doorways and mosaic swirls, the crumbling ruins of a distant past forgotten and built around.

Our captors lead us deftly through the maze-like streets. I wonder how they remember where to go. *The city of alleys*—that's what Papa called it.

At last, we arrive at the market district. Each craft has its own section: leather-workers standing knee-deep in honeycomb vats of dye; weavers selling tapestries in breathtaking, intricate designs; herbalists waving pungent concoctions in the noses of our captors, who wave them off like flies. I don't have time to take in all the details as we're hurried to a large, covered space that looks like a resting spot for camels.

New men come to greet our captors. They pass around more stale bread and pour water into the troughs, motioning for us to drink. *Like we're animals,* I can't help but think to myself again, but the thought washes away in the gulps of water sliding down my throat. The camel I've been sleeping on leans down beside me and slurps water up his long neck. It's been days since we cleared the desert, but I don't think I'll ever quench this thirst.

A cool breeze sends a loud *whoosh* through my ears. I raise my head and breathe deeply, smelling salt in the gust. I can't see the sea, but it must be close.

Our captors untie the camels and tether them to posts, leaving two men to guard them while the rest lead me and the villagers down to a large open square with a rickety wooden platform in the center. This is where they will hold the auction.

I look over the caravan with renewed worry. I'm shocked to see how short the line is without the camels; many more than I realized died in the desert with Ampah. Those who survived are little more than walking skeletons draped in skin. Including me.

The slavers jostle us into an orderly line around the platform. More and more people crowd around as they notice our company.

People who want to buy us.

My stomach twists. What kind of life awaits me here? Most likely, someone will buy me to work on their farm or serve in their house. But what if I'm bought by a merchant, just to be taken across the sea and sold again? Al-Andalus—that's what Papa said the kingdom across the sea is called. I don't know what happens to slaves there. Anfa is as far as I've ever traveled; other than the name, I know nothing about al-Andalus. The thought fills me with dread. My entire future is dependent on who buys me, and what they want from me.

I scan the faces in the crowd pushing in toward the rickety stage, searching for a hint of—I don't know what. Kindness? Compassion?

No. Even if I found it—even if I could choose who I left with today—it wouldn't matter. Ampah is dead, but my family is still out there somewhere. So I will find a way to escape. I will make my way back to Wagadu. By all the gods, no matter how long it takes, I will find Mama and Kamo and Goleh, and together we'll start a new life.

One of the slavers climbs onto the platform and points to a gangly boy at the front of the line. Two of his companions untie him from the rest of us and bring him forward onto the platform. When I recognize him, my blood grows cold.

Masireh.

The slaver shouts some sort of advertisement, loud enough for all to hear. He points to Masireh's arms and legs, then grabs his jaw and yanks open his mouth to show off his teeth. Three moons ago, Masireh would have spit in his face for such an insult. Now he just stands there and wilts, like a stem of hood grass.

The other slavers chuckle, revealing their yellowed, rotten smiles. I cringe, feeling a wave of nausea wash over me.

A hand raises a bag of coin above the crowd. The figure holding it pushes his way to the front, revealing himself as an elder with faint, discolored skin. The slaver kneels down at the edge of the platform and takes the man's pouch. He pours six gold coins into his callused palm and hands Masireh to the old man, along with the empty pouch.

Masireh was never anything but cruel to me. Still, I watch with a sinking feeling as he bows his head in defeat and disappears with the old man around a corner.

The slaver points to the second person in line. As the people call out their bids, I spot a tall, lean man at the front of the crowd. His skin is even darker than mine, and he's dressed in a gossamer red-and-gold tunic and a finely embroidered round red hat—the garb of a wealthy man, a noble or more likely a merchant.

The man shouts something out. All at once, the crowd stills and goes quiet.

Then he points to me, holding out a hefty sack of coins.

I hold my breath. Two other slavers start to untie me.

What?

I have no time to rub my aching wrists before they bind them together again with a separate rope. They yank me around the wooden platform and shove me over to the merchant.

He looks me up and down, licking his cracked lips with a hint of lust that makes my blood boil, even as my throat closes in on itself in fear. He circles me like a vulture and utters some words whose meaning I can well guess.

I feel a harsh grip on my backside. Instantly, rage uncoils within me, tensing my limbs. The merchant's hand snakes up my waist and fondles me roughly over my kaftan, eliciting laughs from the other men at the market.

I whip around and strike my head against his. Hard.

He screams, stumbling backward. When he regains his balance, he raises his open palm to slap me. I shut my eyes and steel myself for the blow.

"*Aieeeeeeeaaa!*"

Instead of his palm, a piercing shriek hits my ears.

Where did it come from?

A murmur goes up among the slavers and buyers alike. They glance around nervously.

The merchant digs his fingers into my braids and yanks my head back. Out of the corner of my eye, I watch his own eyes darting around the square, searching for the source of the shriek.

A spear flies over my head, fast as a bolt of lightning. It soars over the crowd and buries itself in the wooden platform behind me.

What in Legba's name is—

I get my answer before my mind finishes forming the question. But when I see her, my first thought is that I must be dreaming.

A woman with skin the color of bone and hair the color of night flips off the balcony of a house on the edge of the square. She lands in a crouch behind the crowd.

She looks like no woman I've ever seen before. Long black hair falls flat as a board next to her deathly pale cheeks, but every other part of her body ripples with muscle. Despite the heat, she wears a fur vest adorned with the face of some animal I don't recognize, its jaw open, pointed teeth bared in a fearsome display.

Her light-blue eyes graze mine. A shiver washes over me, as though I've been doused in a bucket of cold water.

The hilt of her blade seems to wink at me, and I lower my gaze to the sheath in her hand. I can't see the sword itself, but a powerful *nyama* emanates from the inlays on the silver cross guard.

The markings of magic.

She flips the sheath from one hand to the other and the sword flies out in an arc above her. I gasp as it soars through the air, glittering in the sunlight.

"Valhalla!"

The bellow is so deep and rumbling, I can hardly believe it came from her mouth.

She catches the hilt of the sword in her other hand. Not a moment passes before she slices it through the air, cleaving the unlucky man closest to her in two.

My jaw falls open.

"Majūs!" The screams go up in a chorus all around me.

Majūs. *I know that word.*

But I can't think. All is chaos. The slavers shout and draw their swords, starting toward the woman. The auction-goers push past one another, trampling each other in their rush to flee the square. The villagers, still lashed together, try to run in different directions and wind up pulling one another to the ground.

The merchant tightens his grip on my hair as he backs away, dragging me with him.

"Valhalla!"

I yank my head straight just in time to see two more pale-skinned women leap down from the balconies around the square and move to flank the first. The one on the right is short and sturdily built, with pinkish skin and straw-like hair shorn close to her head. She holds an ax in either hand. The one on the left, a lithe woman with a single braid cascading to her waist, brandishes a sword and a yellow wooden shield painted with two black birds on either side. The shield immediately goes up to block the blow from the first slaver to reach them.

And then the battle truly begins.

The first woman carries no shield, but it quickly becomes clear that she doesn't need one. She whirls around, parrying blows with her sword and hewing down the slavers with ease. I watch in awe as she runs the glittering blade through one slaver, kicks his body away, then spins and hacks off the arm of another before he can even raise his weapon. A wide grin lights up her otherworldly face as the bodies fly from her path. It's glee, I realize—a rabid, animal glee. The woman on her right wears a far more focused expression as she sinks an ax into one slaver's neck. Blood spurts from the wound as he goes down. Meanwhile, the one on the left races forward and uses her shield to knock the weapon out of another slaver's hand.

My view is suddenly obscured by the back of the wooden platform as the merchant hauls me out of the fray.

Fury courses through my veins, giving me new life. I dig my heels into the dirt and propel myself backward, slamming back into his chest with full force.

He lets out a snarl and staggers back. My hands are still bound, but I throw an elbow at his nose and draw blood. As his hands fly to his face, I drop down and sweep my leg under his, swiping him clean off his feet.

I turn to run—and crash right into a panicked slaver doing the same.

A split second of confusion, but it's all the time the merchant needs.

I feel his grip locking around my ankle just before I hit the ground.

The fall knocks the wind out of my lungs. As I struggle to suck in air, he grabs my hair again and resumes dragging me out of the square, away from the commotion.

Lisa is blinding, spotting my vision. I feel my back scraping against dirt and stone. I hit the merchant's hand over and over with the thumbs of my bound palms. A sharp pain blossoms in my shoulder. I howl.

All the fire leaves me at once. My body goes slack. The merchant looms over me, a blade in his hand and a murderous look in his eyes.

Suddenly I'm no longer the bold heart my father raised me to be. I'm just a girl, weak and helpless.

I fought. I fought with everything I had, but it was no use.

I'm going to die.

Fight harder, my daughter, Papa urges me in my mind. *Believe you are stronger than your enemy.*

I'm sorry, Papa. I can't.

I shut my eyes.

But a gruesome squelching sound pries them back open.

Blood spatters across my face. A blade juts out through the merchant's eye, skewering him from behind. His mouth lolls open as his body sags and crumples to the side, revealing another silhouette behind him.

I blink up at the ivory-skinned woman towering over me. Her left eye is a shard of ice cutting through the tattered curtain of her straight black hair as she holds my gaze.

It's Mawu. Lisa's other half, the darkness to the light, who holds both life and death at her command.

The goddess herself has come to my aid.

A wordless moment passes between us. Time slows to a crawl. The screams and shouts in the distance fade to a dull roar.

She says something to me. The flowing vowels of her strange tongue seem at odds with the grindstone roughness of her voice. I continue to stare at her, still dumbfounded.

She repeats herself, more urgently this time. I shake my head, trying to convey that I don't understand.

A horn blasts out from somewhere inside the city. She looks over in the direction of the sound and grunts in frustration. Before I can blink again, she flicks her sword up between my wrists, slicing the binds.

I force myself to sit up, fighting a wave of dizziness. The woman quickly searches the merchant's corpse, tucking a coin purse into her vest. She starts to jog away, then stops and looks over her shoulder at me.

A silent question hangs in the air between us, the clarity of its meaning bursting through the barrier of our different tongues.

My mind flashes to the image of her sword arcing through the air, to the look of savage exultation on her face as she cleaved that wretched man in two.

I've spent six long years feeling ashamed of my own wildness. Part of me believed that I really am *jugu*. So I built a dam to contain that wildness, to keep it inside, where it couldn't hurt anyone—or get me hurt.

But she is wild, and she is not ashamed. Neither are the other two. They are *warriors*. I don't know how it's possible . . . but somehow it is.

By the time the horn sounds again, I've made my decision.

I scramble to my feet and take off after her. My legs scream in protest, but I force them to match her long, thunderous strides as she runs back into the square. It's almost empty now, the slavers and buyers all dead or fled. The two other women are looting the bodies that litter the ground. I scan for the villagers, but I don't see any of them among the dead. They must have escaped.

The black-haired woman shouts something to the other two as we race past. Instantly they're on their feet, falling into step behind us.

The four of us skid to a halt at the wall that separates the city from the sea. Bloodcurdling screams and the clang of iron on iron emanate from the other side, coming from about a stone's throw to our left. That's why no reinforcements came to the square: The guards are busy with the real battle. The gate to the sea must be over there—but there's no way to get there without leaving the square and finding our way through the maze of alleys, and from the sound of it, there's no way we'll make it out regardless.

What now?

The black-haired woman whips an ax out from her belt and

slams it into the wall with all her might. The first blow ricochets off, but the next catches a groove and holds fast.

My jaw drops open. I've never seen a blade so strong it can cut through rammed earth.

She grabs the handle with both hands, pulls her body up, and swings her legs over the ledge with astonishing nimbleness. I wonder again if she isn't a goddess in human form.

From astride the wall, she pulls the two other women over. Then she holds her hand out to me.

I throw one last look over my shoulder at the auction square.

No, there's nothing but death in that direction. Which means there's only one way to go.

Forward.

I take her hand.

On the other side of the wall, my aching legs sink into the white sand of a vast beach. My eyes widen at the sight of the battle we were just hearing.

To our left, a horde of bone-colored men are locked in a battle with Anfa's guards.

No—not a battle. A slaughter.

Most of the guards lie slain, their blood staining the white sand red. The surviving guards are surrounded on all sides, save for the gate behind them, on which they bang their weapons in desperation. That's what we were hearing on the other side of the wall.

But the gates won't open.

The bone-colored men throw themselves on the helpless survivors with abandon, hacking and mauling like buzzards tearing into a buffalo corpse. My stomach churns, but I can't look away. The pale men fight like they'd welcome death if it came, but they know it won't.

As if summoned by my thoughts, more guards appear from behind the gate.

Archers.

Panic grips me. A handful of the bone-colored men go down. An ax flies from their ranks, spins through the air, and strikes one of the archers between the eyes. Blood pours from his head as he tumbles over the wall into the sand.

With the three of us at her heels, the black-haired woman takes off toward the sea, barking something at the men. The order echoes down their ranks, and soon everyone is falling back from the assault.

Do all these soldiers follow her orders?

A woman—in command of a whole *army*?

How can that be? My heart swells with awe and confusion.

An arrow whizzes by my ear, banishing the questions from my mind. The black-haired woman grunts as it skims her outer thigh but keeps running. The two other women overtake us both as another bone-colored man goes down to our left. I pump my legs with wild abandon, my thighs stinging with the strain of pushing off the sand. It's as if the sand doesn't want to let me go, like it's greedy for the life it couldn't take from me in the desert.

It feels like forever until we're out of the archers' range, and still we run with everything we have. My heart threatens to burst through my rib cage.

Then I finally notice what we're running toward.

Dragons.

Not dragons—dragon *ships*. There are maybe two dozen of them looming over the merchants' skiffs tethered to the docks. They have green-and-white-striped sails and sit impossibly high on the water, almost as though they float just above it, like water-insects resting on pond film. The head of a dragon glares at us from every prow, and on the decks, yet more ivory-skinned men rush about, reeling in anchors and lowering oars into the water.

I don't see any other women.

The men from the beach wade into the sea and are hauled by their comrades onto the ships, which are surprisingly shallow for their size. I splash in after the three women, and we wade almost up to our shoulders before we're pulled aboard the last ship, the only one with red-and-white sails.

The black-haired woman starts shouting commands, and the ship lurches forward. A spasm of pain rocks me as my body slams hard against the deck. I roll onto my side and suck air into my ravaged lungs. I try to stand up, but my head spins and my knees buckle beneath me. Instead I grab onto the bulkhead with both hands and peer over it, watching the bay of Anfa as it slides farther and farther from view.

Darkness creeps in around the edges of my vision. All at once I'm overwhelmed by a bone-deep exhaustion. I notice a tingling in my shoulder and look down.

Blood blooms red against the sand-covered tatters of yellow cloth.

A voice crashes over me like a wave. I turn to face it, but all I can see are curtains of night around two piercing blue eyes.

I feel myself fall, and all is darkness.

11

YAFEU

There are flashes of awareness through the turmoil. A burning pain in my shoulder. Someone forcing me to sit up and pouring hot, salty broth down my throat. Retching the liquid over the side of the ship. Shivering in the dark against the thick, spiny fur of an animal whose feel I don't recognize, my own skin slick with sweat or rain while the creamy blur of stars whirls through the blue-black sky overhead. The wind howling against the rain like the howl of the painted wolf when she was dying that night, the last night I spent in my mother's arms.

I heard her dying from across the White River—yes, I'm sure I heard her, it must have been her. That's the message she had come to deliver to me: that she was dying, and I am dying, my *nyama* linked with hers. Once I think I see land. Once I am on the land, though I am still in the boat. But then it recedes again, and I am being rocked, always rocked, cradled in the undulating arms of Agbe and Naete, the gods of water, herself, himself, themselves...

*   *   *

My mind returns to the world in the wake of the storm. When I sense myself in my body once again, I feel better than I have in a long time. I reach immediately for the green wolf around my neck, relaxing when I find it's still there.

The rains have stopped and Lisa is high in the sky. It must be close to midday—whatever day this is.

As I stiffly sit up, it hits me that I'm chilled to the bone, even under Lisa's bright glare. I pull the strange fur draped over me around my shoulders. The coarse spikes are drenched on the outside, but the inside is somehow still dry.

So it wasn't all a dream: There really was a storm. It's a marvel that the ship is still intact, if Agbe's rage was as violent as I remember.

The wound. I was bleeding.

My hand flies to my shoulder. Someone must have tended to it, since it's healed over neatly. It's tender and will scar, but at least I'm alive.

I'm alive.

I climb to my feet, noting the weakness in my thighs with dismay as they adjust to the gentle sway of the ship. The wind blows my fraying braids in front of my face. I sweep them aside and find myself staring down a long, narrow deck at the back of the dragon head. The woman who saved me leans out over it, holding on with one arm as her own black hair whips around like licks of fire in the unfettered breeze. The other two women stand at either side, both wearing furs like mine, the soft tones of their hushed conversation only barely reaching my ears.

The same breeze puffs out the massive sail as we ride the dragon through the water with astonishing speed. The oars have been pulled onto the ship—except for one, which one of the men seems to be using to steer. The other men are either lounging on the deck or adjusting the ropes of the sail, the well-hewn muscles in their arms taut with strain.

Looking around, I see nothing but placid waves in all directions, save for the fleet of ships trailing behind us. A desert of water.

I stumble toward the women, nearly tripping over the interlocking planks as Agbe and Naete lurch beneath my feet. The men crane their necks as I pass. The stink of their bodies is nearly suffocating.

As I get closer to the prow, I notice the sturdy, straw-haired woman, the one who fought with axes, staring down into the water, as though looking for something to emerge out of the endless, formless blue. She's the one who fed me in the night, I realize. She mutters something to the black-haired woman, who responds in kind.

As if sensing my approach, the black-haired woman lets go of the prow and spins to face me, her long hair brushing the edge of her belt. I'm surprised to see a simple tunic in place of the fearsome vest; perhaps I only imagined that she wore the face of an animal on her breast? Her icy-blue eyes send a jolt through my core like a bolt of Sogbo's lightning.

She says something to me. That voice, like a man's but conveying a uniquely rugged grace. I shake my head, expressing my inability to speak her tongue. The words are as fluid as I remember, wavy and flowing like the water itself.

I take a moment to study her face. Lines on her forehead and eyes, drawn by time, tell me that youth has long faded and wisdom has taken its place. She might have been handsome in her girlhood, but I can only imagine that her face had a wildness about it even then; the wildness is set in her features. For hard men, a harder woman.

Majūs. That's what the slavers called them back in Anfa.

The memories flood back to me all at once. Mama's story . . . Everything makes sense! My heart leaps in my chest.

That's why Papa left—he went to sail with the *Majūs*!

"Yafeu," I croak, wincing as my dry lips crack with the effort.

The black-haired woman hands me a jug of water and I drain it in one gulp. With a quick wave of her hand, she dismisses the women, who join the men at the sails, leaving us alone. She leans back against the bulkhead, her bottom resting precariously on the edge. In one blindingly fast motion, she whips a small dagger out of a sheath strapped to her calf and plunges it into a satchel hanging from her belt. I force myself not to flinch.

She smirks as the dagger emerges, spearing some kind of purple fruit. My mouth waters at the sight of it. She slides it off the blade and begins slicing it into pieces, and I have to tear my eyes away to see that she's waiting for me to continue.

"Yafeu," I say again. "My father, Yafeu. Do you know him?" My voice gains strength as I speak, eased by the smooth honey of my native tongue. I wonder how long it's been since I've spoken at all. I feel a strange sensation in my mouth, like it's starving for more words.

How far are we from another Soninke speaker? How many days by ship, by camel, by foot?

The woman shakes her head and hands me a slice of the fruit, her callused fingers scraping against my palm.

Either I'm that hungry, or it's the best thing I've ever tasted in my life, sweet and juicy and crisp against my tongue. Maybe both.

She pops a slice in her own mouth. "Plum," she says, spewing juice between bites. She holds up the rest of the fruit.

I nod, letting her know I understand. "Plum," I repeat, pointing to it.

She gives me another slice, then pats her chest twice before speaking: "Alvtir."

She's telling me her name. I swallow and try to make the noise: "Ahh-ehl-ve-ter." The watery sounds strain against my tongue.

She nods and gestures to me. "Yafoo," she says.

She thinks that's my name. Which means she's never heard of Papa.

I feel my heart sinking into my gut again, a sensation that's become all too familiar over the last few moons. Are these not the *Majūs*? And doesn't Papa travel with the *Majūs*?

She asks me something else, throwing in another "Yafoo." I shake my head again, feeling embarrassed for some reason.

The corner of her lip curls into another lopsided smirk. She reaches out and claps my good shoulder through the fur before turning her gaze to the sea, murmuring something under her breath.

I take it as a sign that the conversation is over—for now. Until I start to learn her language, there's nothing more we can say.

Lisa sets at our left and rises at our right the next morning, revealing our heading as north. Getting my bearings is a small comfort, but a comfort all the same.

The cold seems to bother me more than it does the ivory-skinned warriors, who seem as at ease on the open sea as I am in the sunburnt lands of Wagadu. It feels right to me that their tongue should be as billowing as the wind that fills their sails, as undulating as the waves that carry their nimble ships.

I wonder what Papa felt when he made this journey. Did the waves echo the vibration of his *nyama,* or did every instinct in his body scream for the safety of land, as mine do now? In Mama's story, he summoned Agbe and Naete at will . . . but that was just a story. She couldn't possibly have known about his adventures with the *Majūs* after he left us.

Still, the thought of Papa surviving, even thriving, on these same waters wraps around my heart like a warm blanket, alleviating some of the agony of the last few moons. Someone, wherever we're going, must know of him. Maybe he'll be there himself.

But a strange discomfort settles over me as the hours wear on. My eyes have combed the blurry faces on the ships that follow behind us in the fleet. I've seen no one else with skin like mine. I feel like a raven among doves. I keep fingering the wolf around my neck, the last token of Mama, of the family that was wrenched away from me. But I won't let myself give in to tears—not in front of Alvtir.

I distract myself by studying the other two women warriors.

They look to be about the same age: definitely younger than Alvtir, but older than me by at least several years. I have a fragment of a memory, a blurry image of the long, leanly muscled arms of the taller woman wrapping this fur around me during the storm. She has willowy limbs and light-brown hair like a desert mouse, most of which flies free from the messy braid that stretches down her back. I watch her as she cajoles the men, moving as easily among them as if she were one herself. She laughs loudly and often, and I can't help but like her. She isn't especially pretty, not like Ampah or Mama, but she carries herself with an effortless poise that makes the men follow her with their eyes. They turn in a half circle toward her when she speaks, and though I don't understand her words, I know she steers the conversation.

The only person she follows with her own eyes is the other woman, the sturdy one with the cropped yellow hair, who is as quiet and stoic as the other is boisterous and jovial. But I remember the way she fought in Anfa, and I know she's eloquent with her axes if not her words. She spends most of the hours sharpening those axes on a whetstone, or watching the water with her arms folded across her chest, conferring with Alvtir here and there—who then barks orders at the steersman, who then makes small adjustments to our course. I can't imagine what she gleans from the water, which looks unchanging to my untrained eyes. Maybe Agbe and Naete send signs only she can interpret.

The sturdy woman looks at the tall woman, and the tall woman looks at her, and the *nyama* that flows back and forth between them tells me they are only for each other. I wonder if the men don't see it, or if they don't pester the women out of respect for Alvtir. Or fear *of* Alvtir. Despite the narrowness of the ship, everyone manages to stay out of Alvtir's way.

At some point we lose the wind, and the oars are hauled out again. One of the men thrusts an oar into my hand and shoves me toward an empty seat. I glance at Alvtir in confusion, but she gives me a stern look in return, so I sit and row without complaint, despite the ache of protest from my shoulder.

Later that very day, a steep green landmass rises in the distance, a chorus of whoops and cheers rising from the ships along with it. We turn to the east and follow the sea with Lisa at our backs as it narrows into a kind of river, the tide carrying us faster and the air growing warmer as the flanking mountains close in.

I can't help but marvel at the hills as we pass. They are greener than any hill I've ever seen, every inch covered in thickets of trees and undergrowth. As they get closer, I squint to make out the strange vegetation. Some of the leaves are spiky and needle-like, similar to the hairs of this fur. I've never seen a tree that grows needles instead of leaves before, and for a moment I lose myself in wonder.

The river snakes through the hills, winding this way and that. Lisa disappears behind the clouds, and finally we arrive at our destination. It's a place called Skíringssal, or so I've gathered from the men's eager shouts. Our ship and most of the others turn in toward the harbor, but some continue on down the river, splitting the fleet in two.

The first thing I notice is the ugliness: gray wooden docks, framed by rows of squat, gray wooden dwellings. Why would anyone build so many houses out of *wood*? With such mighty winds racing around us, I wonder how the rickety structures don't blow over.

A jostling crowd of faces ranging from ivory to faintly pink wait at the harbor for our arrival. As we draw near, it strikes me that even their clothes are ugly, with faded dyes and little patterning at the hemlines. Despite the crisp air filling my nostrils, I can't help but wrinkle my nose in distaste. The women wear a short dress over a long one, with tools and baubles dangling from brooches at their shoulders. The men wear belted tunics over trousers and wrap their legs all the way up to the knee, like the warriors do.

I would think they take no pride in their appearance, were it not for the elaborate styles of their limp hair. I've never seen hair like the kind that spills down the backs of the *Majūs,* long and feathery and ranging from yellow to red to dark brown in hue. Men and women alike wear their hair carefully combed and braided, some with lines and circles shaved into the sides.

As soon as the ship reaches the dock, the warriors drop the gang-plank and rush across. Alvtir waits for the others to disembark first, then motions to me.

I stumble across the dock, my legs struggling to recall their balance yet again. Tentatively, I step down onto the sliver of soggy shingle that separates the water from the land. Instantly I'm enveloped by the eager townspeople—mostly women and children, but quite a few men as well—all searching anxiously for their loved ones aboard the ships. The number of squirming, swarming bodies is overwhelming. I feel my own body seize up as my mind hurtles into memory.

I'm at the slave auction in Anfa. The shouts are bids on my price, and now I'm being sold to the man who will use my body for his plea-sure. I can't move. I can't breathe. A hand locks onto my arm.

But it's Alvtir's hand, not the merchant's. She leads me onto the shore and through the fray. The people move hastily out of her path.

An explosive cheer goes up around us, and I turn to see a hefty chest being carried off one of the ships. Alvtir shouts something to the men carrying it, then pulls me into the city.

I try to absorb all the strangeness around me as Alvtir leads me through some kind of marketplace. This city—if I can even call it that, after the golden grandeur of Koumbi Saleh, the dark magic of Anfa and its maze of alleys—is all wood and hay and mud. Long, narrow houses line both sides of a wooden walkway. Alongside the houses are dozens of patched tents and lean-tos open to the air. I peer inside as we pass. The *Majūs* stare back at me with naked curi-osity, craning their necks. Not one other brown face meets mine.

They're hawking all kinds of wares, spread along trestle

benches—more strange furs, pots of clay, combs made of bone, a variety of glass and amber beads. It's not entirely unlike the markets at Koumbi Saleh and Anfa—though much smaller. And dirtier. And the stink of fish is inescapable.

But the hills surrounding the city almost make up for its lack of charm. Every inch is burgeoning with green, with grasses and shrubs and trees of all sizes seemingly growing on top of one another, clamoring for space. There is so much more growth than I've ever seen at home, even after the rainy season. I wonder if the people here eat well all year long.

We pass a smithy at the edge of the market. The quenching hiss of iron plunged into water sends steam billowing out, and my heart clenches at the sharp smell of coal and slag. It smells like Papa. Like home.

The familiar *nyama* of the forge beckons to my own, and I desperately wish we could go inside. But Alvtir pulls me forward, unrelenting, toward some other fate. At least I can take comfort in the knowledge that Gu's magic is here, too.

There are other familiar sights, sounds, smells: a cowhide stretched across a frame, the clack of beads rolling across a jewelry-maker's table, the flinty sound of some talisman being carved with the point of a delicate knife. I stumble over an odd-looking chicken, who lets out an indignant squawk before roaming over to his companions to peck at the grains scattered across the ground. I try to cling to these sensations, desperate for a way to make this "Skíringssal" feel less overwhelmingly strange.

But something inside me revolts against the effort. I ache for the flat red stretch of the Sahel, the hippo and crab-crab grasses that line the banks of the murky White River, the sacred groves of sturdy-rooted baobabs on the fringes of Koumbi Saleh.

I want Wagadu. I want Mama, Kamo, and Goleh.

I want to go home.

As if responding to my thoughts, Sogbo thickens the blanket of gray over the sky and sends a light rain. We reach the end of the walkway and cross onto a wide, rutted dirt path, trudging through the mud. The clamor of the market fades away. The houses are fewer and farther between now, the land around us less tame. We pass a set of wooden totems standing in a circle. One has a long, swirling beard and a single eye; another has a protruding belly emblazoned with three interlocking triangles. Their faces are egg-shaped, their expressions distant. These must be their gods. They seem to mark the edge of the city, like the groves of Koumbi Saleh. Though this "city" is only half the size of the golden city at most.

I follow Alvtir into a much larger stretch of farmland. Squinting into the distance, I can just make out the wattle fences that separate the land into holdings.

My mind races. Alvtir didn't greet anyone at the harbor, nor in the market. And she hardly strikes me as a farmer. So where is she taking me?

The rain stops and starts again as we walk. Lisa falls under the mountains, and a chirping noise rises up all around us. It reminds me of a locust's song, only it pulses in and out, rhythmic like the beating of a drum. Only a few people are out in the fields at this hour, bent with labor, finishing up their day's work harvesting some kind of grain. Their clothes are an undyed brown, even uglier than the clothes I saw on the *Majūs* at the docks. Not that I'm one to be talking right now. Under this cloak, Mama's kaftan hangs off my body in tatters, soiled beyond recognition.

At the very end of the road, we veer left, heading for a cluster of buildings. It looks to be another farm compound, larger than the others we've passed. At last, we come to a stop at the biggest structure on the compound. It's long and narrow, with an uneven triangular roof. Alvtir pushes the door open and motions for me to go inside.

I step in, blinking at the sudden darkness of the windowless room. The familiar scents of hay, livestock, and burning wood overwhelm my nostrils. As my eyes adjust, I realize there are two women huddled around a firepit in the near end of the room, stoking the low flames. They shrink back from us, fearful. Clearly, we're unexpected guests.

The rustle of animals prompts me to look past them, to a row of stalls with cattle shifting and stamping inside, sensing a stranger in their midst. Various farming tools and cookware line the walls and hang down from the beams. The space seems to be part barn, part living area.

Suddenly the sliver of twilight filtering in from the doorway disappears with a bang as Alvtir shuts the door behind me.

My chest clenches. Panic overwhelms me again. "Wait!" I call in my own language. "Alvtir!"

I fling open the door and start after her, but stop short when I see a large, sour-faced man approaching. He has a round belly and a head of patchy, pale-yellow hair, too pale for his pink skin—sickeningly pale. He gives Alvtir a hard look down his nose, then turns that look on me. Disgust instantly washes over me. He starts arguing with Alvtir about something, waving his meaty hands in the air.

An instinctual awareness of danger prickles the hair on my arm, warning me not to interfere. I creep back into the barn and shut the door behind me.

The panic drains away, banished by exhaustion. I sink down against the wall.

The two women peer over at me from the other side of the fire. I can just make out their features. One of them has curly red hair, and faint little dots cover her face—though that could be a trick of the fire. She looks about my age. The other has a small frame and an ageless, triangular face, with thin eyebrows and hooded eyes framed by dark hair that stops short at her cheekbones. It's a face unlike any I've seen today—or ever before. Maybe she's from somewhere far away, like me?

The first girl gives me a reassuring smile. "Bronaugh," she says. She points to the other girl, who keeps her gaze trained on the fire, her mouth pressed into a line. "Airé."

"Yafeu." I say Papa's name in place of my own. The title I unknowingly gave myself, the title Alvtir knows me by; that's the name I will take. For now.

Bronaugh rises and reaches into a basket on the far wall, emerging with a bundle. Despite a warning glance from Airé, she strides over and hands it to me: a long, plain dress and a shorter one with shoulder ties to change into, pointing to her own dresses for guidance.

I nod my thanks. I briefly wonder why I need to wear one dress over another, but as the night quickly descends, I'm grateful for the layers of cloth. I pull the fur cloak off my shoulders and lay it close to the fire. It's not exactly comfortable, but it's all I have for a bed.

It's funny how a few moons in the open desert—or open sea—can make you grateful for the tiniest comforts.

A small, bony cat emerges from the darkness at the other end of the barn. She perches near Airé and studies me, swishing her tail in a state of calculated observation.

I gaze into the flames, reaching inside for my inner awareness, for that quiet place within where strength and wisdom reside. But all I feel there is emptiness.

Why did Alvtir leave me here? Is she coming back for me? In Anfa, I sensed we were . . . connected, somehow. Like she *knew* I was a warrior too. I thought that's why she saved me.

Doubt seizes me. I ran after Alvtir without knowing the first thing about her. I was injured and weak, maybe even delirious . . . I could have been imagining the strong *nyama* between us.

What am I doing here?

I reach for the wolf at my neck, grasping onto the last remnant of Mama. *Oh, Mama, I'm so sorry. I should have stayed in Anfa. In all the chaos, I could have escaped. I could have found my way back across the desert to you and Kamo and Goleh. Now the whole world stands between us.*

Maybe I really am *jugu*. After all, *none* of this would have happened if I'd just kept my mouth shut that day in Koumbi Saleh.

I've lost everything and everyone I've ever loved—and I have only myself to blame.

At first, the shame is too overwhelming for tears. But the shadows on the wall become menacing to me in their strangeness, and finally I cry, letting the fear and shame settle in deeper than ever before.

When the tears subside, I find a morsel of comfort in listening to the familiar sound of the fire. The fire breathes; I too still breathe. I survived the desert and the sea. I survived hunger and thirst, beatings and lashings and even a knife to the shoulder. If I'm alive, it's because the gods have a plan for me. At least, that's what Mama would say.

But Papa... Papa would say that my will has sustained and saved me. That I can save myself again, so long as I believe in my own strength.

I don't know which is true, if either. But I know one thing for sure: Papa was with the *Majūs,* and now *I'm* with the *Majūs.* That means I'm closer to him than I've been in six long years. It can't be a coincidence.

The thought brings a glimmer of hope to the darkness and I cling to it as I fall into a deep and dreamless sleep.

12

ALVTIR

"Twenty silver ingots for a thrall girl? You're as mad as they say, cousin!" Broskrap laughs and slaps his thick knees, sloshing ale out of the brew-barrel in his grasp. A familiar twinge of annoyance runs up my spine. By Loki, how is it that he can shift his shape from a grown man to a fatuous child in the blink of an eye?

"A paltry sum for a rich man like yourself," I reply, leaning against the beam of his brew shed.

"You'll get no more than five. And I'll throw in a barrel of ale for good measure." He swirls his pinkie in the amber liquid as he speaks, bringing it to his lips and wincing at the sickly sweetness. Broskrap could always *drink* his ale, but he couldn't *brew* a decent batch if his life depended on it. He never did anything all that well— other than swaying the minds of the other Thingmen, who have even less wits than he.

I ignore his generous counteroffer. "She's hardy, Broskrap. She can help with the harvest, grind flour. She'll carry more than her own weight."

"The boys who mind my pigs are hardy. A hardy *woman* doesn't suit my needs."

"Oh, I know all about your *needs*." I take a menacing step forward. "In fact, I know your bed has hardly cooled since Siv died—"

He holds out a hand to silence me, the nostrils on his knobby nose flaring in anger. "Step carefully, cousin, lest you tread on my honor."

How can I tread on what does not exist? Under other circumstances, I might have said it aloud. I've never cared for my lecherous, ill-tempered cousin, and he's certainly never cared for me. But as it is, I need him to take the girl off my hands, among other things.

"It's one thing to rut with a thrall here and there—but Knut's *sister*?" I can't help but revel in the dumbstruck look that flattens his already dumb face. Yes, Broskrap. I know everything that happens in Skíringssal. *Everything.*

"It'd be a shame if my brother found out," I continue, gazing past him to the golden rows of barley that fill the sizable swath of farmland my brother gifted him. A reward for gathering the support of the Thingmen in favor of Skíringssal's sovereignty from the Danes. But that was years ago, and Broskrap's usefulness to my brother has waned as his belly has waxed. Now he must prove useful to *me*. "Or Knut himself. How difficult it would be to find a husband for the poor girl, with such a stain on her reputation!"

Broskrap climbs to his feet and closes the gap between us, doing his best to leer through his ale-soaked haze. I stifle a snort of laughter at the display. He's a good head taller and thrice as large as I, but we both know who would win in a fight, if it came to that. I'd best the lumbering troll on my worst day—even if he weren't as drunk as Loki in Aegir's winter hall.

"You ask too much, Alvtir." He spits out my name, his stinking breath hot on my face. "One day you might regret fleecing your own kin."

"You know my rules," I say coolly. "*No rutting.* Beyond that, you can work her to the bone for all I care."

Broskrap growls, but he runs a hand through the few strands of blond hair he has left, and I know I have him. After all, I don't make idle threats. Everyone in Skíringssal knows that.

"I'll wait while you fetch the silver."

He lets out one final grunt of frustration and kicks over the barrel of ale before stomping off, muttering to himself all the way back to his longhouse.

By the gods, how is it that I share a bloodline with such a dim-witted, dung-bearded man-child?

"To Odin!" I hear my twin brother shout as I enter the Great Hall. A thrall rushes to place a horn of mead in my outstretched palm.

"To Odin!" the men of the *hird* call back in unison, sloshing their own brimming horns as they raise them high to the Allfather.

"To Njord and Frey, for a good harvest, fair weather, and peace."

"To Njord and Frey!"

"To the king!" I shout, raising my horn and locking eyes with the man himself across the hall. He sits at the far table, overseeing the festivities with the air of a fox in a henhouse. "Balli the Fearless, the greatest king in all the land!"

"To the king!" the men shout back.

"Long may he rule!" I drain my horn in one gulp and belch loudly, eliciting whoops and laughter from the men. From *my* men. I shake the droplets of mead off my hair and grin, feeling the sweet liquid warm my bones, softening the edges of the day, soothing the fire burning in my belly from Broskrap's insolence.

My brother stares at me expectantly, unamused.

My boots crunch on the ground as I make my way over, littered as it is with gnawed, discarded bones and the drying blood of sacrificed pigs. Their flesh boils now in a massive cauldron at the hearth, sending the tantalizing scent of meat and thyme and lovage into the air. The tables are already laden with a feast: black pudding with plums, honey-glazed ham, crisp bread with butter, smoked cheese with caraway, stewed lamb's-quarter. And, of course, mead. Always mead.

My brother spared no expense tonight. But Njord knows, the chest of Saracen treasure we've dragged across the sea more than makes up for it.

The benches wobble under the weight of nearly two hundred men; almost the entire *hird* is crammed into the hall. I look for the shield maidens, but they're nowhere in sight. I suppose they left early, if they came at all. Hetha and Wisna are never much for these feasts, and young Ranveig has yet to earn her seat at one of these tables. My brother's simpering girl-child is also notably absent. Smart to hide her away, given her recent blossoming and the state the men are in. I wonder if the bevy of thrall girls warming their laps now will be enough to sate their hunger after a long journey at sea.

Save for the thralls, the only other woman in attendance is my sister-in-law. Yngvild waits on the men like the gracious hostess she was trained to be, smiling politely as she refills the mead in their horns, pretending not to notice when they grab at the tail of the gaudy snow-fox fur adorning her shoulders or mock her high-minded gait when she turns her back. After all, this is a feast befitting a successful raid. The *hird* has enriched her husband, and at least for the night, he must enrich us back. What's his is theirs, including Yngvild's servitude.

Unless she'd finally borne him an heir. Then she'd be allowed to sit out the feast, to suckle and tend the babe instead of playing nursemaid to a hundred drunk men.

So she'd miscarried yet again.

Good. Odin smiles upon me still.

I halt and signal for Yngvild to refill my own horn. The beads dangling across her chest clack together as she stops in front of me, her smile tight. She pours the mead unsteadily from a glazed green water jug with an unusually long neck and large basin—one of the

Saracen treasures we brought back from Iberia. It's a symbolic act on my brother's part, forcing her to use such an unwieldy thing. It calls attention to the fact that the loot is his, not ours, until he apportions our shares later tonight.

Even though we're the ones who risked our necks to claim it.

I can't help but smirk as Yngvild pours, refusing to meet my eyes. I revel in the fury scrunching up her haughty face as she's forced to wait on me, to treat me like a hero.

Tonight, I am a hero. But tomorrow may tell a different story.

Stay with me, my protector, I call silently to the Allfather. *Even this "hall of light" will not shelter us from the coming darkness.*

With my horn full, Yngvild rushes away, careful to keep an arm's distance as she passes. I continue on toward my brother, guzzling mead as I go. The raucous laughter of the men mingles with the lush and merry sound of the lute. The skald's honeyed voice swells over it all in song. For a moment I almost wish I could forget myself like I used to.

For a moment I almost wish I were young again.

"Alvtir." Balli shoots me a crooked smile as he rises, though it doesn't quite reach his eyes. Eyes, I note, that are bloodshot and puffy, the pupils plump and glittering with madness. How much henbane has he already had tonight?

"Brother."

We embrace. "I was expecting you earlier," he says, lowering his voice so that only I can hear.

My eyes flicker to the shield hanging from the wall behind his throne, painted with the same depiction of Hugin and Munin that adorns the shields of every soldier who fights for him. Only their shields are covered in notches, collected over the years from the blows of swords, spears, axes, and arrows.

His shield stays on the wall, collecting nothing but dust.

"I had to check on my pups," I lie. The hounds are more than capable of looking after themselves. I doubt I have a hen left alive by now.

Balli snorts his indifference. I wonder if he's ever given a thought to what I do in my spare time, outside of raiding and plundering for his gain. Or for "the glory of Agder," as he prefers to say.

"There are important matters to discuss," he continues. "After the feast."

"Of course."

"With Snorri," he adds.

I grimace but nod my assent as my brother releases me. I glare past his shoulder at Snorri Broskrapsson, seated at his left. Farmland isn't the only gift my brother gave to Broskrap for keeping the Thingmen in line: He also made his son a captain in the *hird,* complete with his own ship and crew. The *only* captain who didn't earn the privilege with years of sweat and blood.

Snorri shoots me a snide smile, preening; it sharpens his already sharp features even further. He's dressed like a trussed-up grouse tonight, in a fur-lined navy tunic hemmed with golden thread at a low-cut neckline, an amulet of Mjölnir poking out from the pale, wispy fuzz of his chest hair. Like his father, his hair is so pale it's almost white, making him look sickly even in the flattering candlelight.

But unlike his father, the head beneath that mop of hair isn't hollow. Indeed, Snorri might scheme his way to the top of the *hird* if I weren't here to stop him. Must've gotten his wiles from his mother's side. If only he'd put them to use in battle, instead of dreaming up ways to snatch my army out from under me. I must keep an eye on the dung-bearded little wretch. He's growing too ambitious for his own good.

"I hear the Saracens fought well," my brother says loudly as I take my seat at his right-hand side.

"Like grains at the scythe," I retort.

The men bellow and cheer. This is the show we put on for them every time, brother and sister; it never fails.

"They were ripe for harvesting," Snorri adds. No doubt he wants the men to think that he's part of our little performance. It would bolster his image as a leader. Maybe even as an equal of mine.

"Tell me, Snorri," I call out, "were you able to see the brown of their skin all the way from the stern of your ship?"

The men guffaw again. I probably shouldn't have said that, but I can't keep the smirk from my lips as Snorri's narrow pink face turns red. I hide my grin in my horn as I take another gulp of mead.

"Save your petty banter," Balli drawls. "Our entertainment has arrived." I turn to see an elderly thrall being dragged in by the guards. He hangs limply in their grasp, barely conscious, his wrists and ankles bound needlessly. He was probably beaten to within an inch of his life just moments ago. And starved for a lifetime before that—even in tatters, his homespun tunic threatens to swallow his thin frame whole.

I wonder what his crime was. Stealing food from the cookhouse? Collapsing from fatigue before finishing his chores?

Or maybe there was no crime. Maybe my brother no longer bothers with an excuse.

I drag a tray of black pudding over to my plate and steal a glance at Balli, who takes in the new arrival with hungry eyes, like a fisherman eyeing a sizable cod on the hook. His lips twitch in anticipation.

"Lash him to the column," he orders the guards, who hastily comply. The man slumps against his bonds, letting the column hold him up. My brother uses his knife to spear a morsel of pork before rising to his feet. He nibbles it as he circles the old thrall.

"To thank the Allfather for such a fruitful raid—and for blessing the great city of Skíringssal with peace and prosperity," he begins, "we will make another sacrifice."

I have to bite my tongue. This is no gift to Odin. This is for *him*, to slake his hunger. His sickness.

The old man eyes him with more resignation than fear.

"A sacrifice the old way," Balli continues: "the *true* way." He runs the dirty knife down the thrall's chest, causing him to scream out in agony. I can see the gleam in my brother's eyes as he tortures the man, the way he revels in his victim's pain, in draining the life out of him as slowly and excruciatingly as he can. Blood pools at the man's feet, joining the pool of pig's blood. From the corner of my eye, I see Yngvild turn away, unable to watch. She could never even feign to stomach this side of her husband, weakling that she is.

I look past her to the tables. Many of the men raise their horns or clap their hands in delight, but an equal number shift in their seats, betraying their discomfort.

I wonder, for those men, how far their loyalty can be stretched before it snaps.

I wolf down my pork, keeping my own face impassive. If I don't, it will raise suspicion. I must continue on as though everything were the same as it has always been.

As though I really were young again.

A dagger hurtles through the air, aimed at my forehead. I sidestep it with ease, and it plants itself in the wooden plank beside me. Yet another indent in a scarred doorway—the doorway to the king's bedroom. It's the king's favorite game with his sister: dodge the dagger. He knows I will. Every time.

Balli laughs a squealing, fitful laugh, a lingering effect of the henbane. His aim was surprisingly good, given how much he must have taken tonight. I chuckle and give him a playful shove on the shoulder. Behind him, Snorri is leaning against one of the dragon-headed legs on my brother's pine table, a piece commissioned many years ago to celebrate our victory against the Danes. The same dragons mark the prow of my ship, and every ship in Balli's fleet. Including that of Snorri, who glances back and forth between my brother and me now, likely wondering if we've both gone mad. I shoot him a wide grin for good measure, reveling in the way the blood drains from his face as his eyes flicker down to my teeth.

The points are no longer sharp, but just the echo of the fangs I used to bare is enough to remind him of who I am.

"Our kinsman has told me all about the long journey—in your *absence*," my brother says, emphasizing the last word. So, he's still angry that I didn't meet with him immediately upon my return. "But I wanted to hear my *stallari* tell the tale."

Snorri grimaces, visibly irritated by my brother's choice of words. *Stallari,* the leader of the king's *hird* in his stead. A title Snorri the Snake wishes he could slither into.

"It is a tale of triumph," I say, striding purposefully over to the table. The map I acquired from the Frankish merchant last summer has been spread across it, littered with *tafl* pieces. The king's piece marks Skíringssal, and the light pieces represent the *hird,* one for each ship in my brother's fleet. The dark pieces are our enemies. I stop near Snorri, standing just a little too close for his comfort. "Our timing was blessed. My contact among the merchants told of Christian uprisings drawing the emir's eye to the eastern part of his kingdom. With the bulk of his forces occupied, we caught the western shore with their breeches at their ankles. We passed over the walled cities, opting instead for smaller, less defensible settlements." I move one of the light pieces from Norveg down to the Iberian Peninsula. It was my idea to venture south, instead of repeating our old attacks on the newly fortified coastlines of the Christians. "The rumors of their wealth proved true," I add, nodding to the heavy chest of Saracen gold at the foot of my brother's bed. "Even in the early days, the Christ-monks never boasted such a treasure."

Balli glances at the chest, then back at me, impassive. "I'd expect no less, since you were gone for three whole moons." He begins pacing around the table, circling me and Snorri like a buzzard around the battlefield.

I move another white piece down to the uncertain mass at the bottom of the map—what is supposed to be the tip of Africa. "Africa is farther than this map tells, even with Njord's winds at our back," I say calmly. "And more dangerous than we could have known. If there truly is a 'land of gold' there, it must lie far from the shore. The cities we attacked were well guarded, though we found no stockpiles of riches to defend. Word of us likely reached them before we did. We escaped with few gains—and many injuries, which slowed the journey home."

"It's the journey home that concerns me, sister. Snorri informed me that my fleet overnighted in Ireland and the Norðreyjar, instead of taking the North Sea through Neustria and the Danelaw as we had agreed."

"Did he?" I turn to face Snorri in mock surprise.

Yes, I will have to put him in his place. And soon.

Snorri clears his throat and looks away. Clearly he wasn't expecting the king to test his version of events. He underestimates the bond I share with my brother.

Oh, Snorri, don't you know how many souls we've sent to the gods together? How many lives I've taken in his name, for his glory?

"It does well for an unwise man to listen more than he speaks, Snorri." I keep my gaze hard on him as he shifts from foot to foot.

"So says Odin, wisest of all the gods," my brother adds. He stops at the edge of the table and stands across from us, waiting for me to explain myself.

"The Mercian king has rallied the Christians against the Danelaw," I begin, turning back to the table. "And the cross-worshippers' hold on Neustria grows stronger by the day. When we first made camp in Brittany, we heard rumors that Rollo the Bastard had forsaken the old ways in exchange for a title from the Frankish king. It is said that he and his men slaughter other Northmen in the name of their new god. Even his fellow Danes are not safe." Balli's lips thin at the mention of King Godfred's unclaimed son, betraying his unease. I grab a handful of black pieces from beside the map and place them on Neustria, just across the Western Sea from our own shores. "So I ordered the *hird* to make for Dublin, where the northern rule still holds—for now—instead of taking us back into Rollo's territory. We sailed straight through from there. In all, a moon's delay is but a small sacrifice for the safe passage of your men. *And* your treasure."

My brother studies the map grimly. Agder and its king are half surrounded by black pieces. Christians to the west, Christians to the south. And our own people among their ranks.

"Have the Christians truly grown so fearsome, sister?" He lifts his gaze to mine.

Now is my chance. Ideally, I would have waited until Snorri had slithered back into his hole, but the snake has given me little choice.

"There is a shift in the winds, brother," I say slowly, almost pleadingly. "We thought this Christ god was weak, but we were wrong to underestimate him. He wields a great power over the hearts of men."

"I'm more concerned with their sword-arms than their hearts," he replies.

I regard him earnestly. "We've won many wars on the battlefield, that is true. But we cannot fight an idea. It has no weapon to shatter, no shield to knock, no body to kill—yet it is stronger than a thousand armies. It turns honorable men into oath-breakers, and nithings into fearless warriors. It unites kingdoms that have warred for generations and makes bitter foes of neighbors who have known only peace. *That* is the power of this Christ."

"Who cares what god they pray to?" Snorri jumps in. "The *hird* of Balli the Fearless is second to none. Christian or Dane, it matters not; we will send them all to Niflheim!" He slams his fist on the map for emphasis, scattering the *tafl* pieces.

"Not all enemies are alike, foolish boy," Balli snaps, glaring at Snorri. "And this table is worth more than your life."

Snorri pales and stiffens. He gambled that stroking my brother's ego would win him favor. A sound bet, if only his timing hadn't been so poor. Balli is many things, but he is no fool. And only a fool makes light of his enemies. Now the scorn on Snorri's face has been supplanted by something else: fear. Good, Snorri—if you don't fear my wrath, at least you have enough sense to fear my brother's.

Balli turns to me, squeezing my shoulder affectionately. "You were wise, sister, to choose the safer route. We must protect these riches over all else, for the good of the kingdom."

I bow my head in assent, hoping it masks my relief.

"Leave us." He dismisses Snorri with a flick of his wrist.

"Yes, my king." Snorri bows low and scurries out. *Like a kicked dog with his tail between his legs,* I think to myself with satisfaction.

But knowing Snorri Broskrapsson, I've only won the battle, not the war. No doubt the little nithing is already scheming up another way to ingratiate himself to the king.

Once he's gone, all semblance of tenderness vanishes from my brother's visage. His hand falls from my shoulder.

"Snorri the Snake tries hard to manipulate you, brother," I say quickly. "He likes the sound of the word *stallari* on his forked tongue."

He gives me a patronizing smile. "Oh, sister. We're so fortunate, you and I. I'm fortunate that you have the taste for combat I never did. And *you're* fortunate that I allow you your nature. I saved you from a life of dishonor when I let you lead the *hird* in my name, though I knew other kings would mock me for it."

And there it is: the lie that he planted between us all those years ago. In truth, it was no more than a strategic decision on his part: He was too paranoid to trust another man to lead the *hird* he'd amassed—even a kinsman like Broskrap—lest that man turn his own soldiers against him. He knew firsthand how easily the allegiance of men could be swayed. But he was too much of a coward to raise a sword himself. Hence his "gift" to me: Making his twin sister his *stallari* was the only way to ensure that the *hird* would remain under his control. After all, I'm a woman; I would never pose a threat to his rule. That's all there ever was to it.

But I let him believe his lie. I let him believe that I believed it too. And while I was quenching my thirst for vengeance against our enemies, that lie was taking root in the very soil of our bond. It grew as wide and tall as the ancient oaks in Frey's grove. Now it has more branches than Yggdrasil itself—and is just as impossible to fell.

Only Ragnarök will bring it down. And I can't let that come to pass.

"Someday even you will have to hang up your sword," he continues. "It is only natural that the young should replace the old. But that reminds me—we have more important things to discuss than our kinsman's ambition." He turns to study the table once again, folding his arms across his chest. "There are arrangements to be made for the future of Agder."

I couldn't agree more, though I fear my brother and I do not have the same future in mind. "What do you mean?"

"Yngvild has failed to produce an heir. But Fritjof has foreseen that I will have sons yet. Freydis must be married before they are born, while the other kings still believe that a son by her would inherit what is mine."

The skald says what he must to keep his head on his shoulders and food in his belly. Of course, I would never tell my brother that.

"Freydis is pledged to our dear neighbor, Harald of Vestfold," he continues. "But that was an arrangement between me and his father Hálfdan, and Hálfdan is long dead." He picks up one of the scattered black pieces and places it on Vestfold.

For once I am grateful for my brother's lack of honor. A better man might value the weight of his own word. "Then—you won't give Freydis to Harald?"

"I knew Hálfdan never truly respected my sovereignty, and now his arrogant son has all the makings of a conqueror. Merchants from Svealand and the Rus already pass through Vestfold. With Skíringssal, Harald would add the Anglian trade to his sway." He traces the Skagerrak with his finger, following its flow beneath Agder to where it spills out into the Western Sea. "Even with my son on the throne, he wouldn't hesitate to claim Agder as his own. With our ports combined, he'd grow rich enough to amass an army that could conquer all of Norveg."

My ears must be jinxed by Loki himself. "I am surprised—but relieved—to hear you say so—"

"Then you agree. Freydis should marry Hakon of Trøndelag instead. Hakon's *hird* is the best in Norveg after mine and Harald's. Together, Hakon and I can form a stronghold against Harald before his head grows too big for his crown."

I sigh and pluck the white king piece from the map. I place it in my brother's palm and gently curl his fingers over it. "No. Neither."

He frowns. "You're saying there's another?"

Odin, make me the vessel of your wisdom. Open my brother's mind to reason.

"Brother, what I say of the Christians is true. Their faith spreads like a plague. Rollo is the first to fall, but he will not be the last. Sooner or later, the Christians will set their sights on Norveg. The White Christ will cast his spells on Harald, Hakon, and all the weak-minded kings of the North. Bewitched, they will take up arms against any who honor the Aesir—even their own kin. War and chaos will rip through our lands. It won't end until every man, woman, and child is dead or pledged to the cross. Without our worship, the gods will abandon Midgard. Loki's children will break free of their binds. Giants and demons will march on Asgard, and Christ will be the one who leads them." I seize my brother's bony fist and squeeze hard, taking him by surprise. "Don't you see, brother? Don't you see why the winters grow colder and longer with each passing year? It is just as the skalds have sung since the days of our ancestors."

Balli stares at me with an expression I can't discern. "Ragnarök."

Finally, he sees! "We need stronger allies than the likes of Harald and Hakon. Allies with courage and honor to spare. We should look to the Saracens. Marry Freydis to one of their princes. Together, Saracen and Northman can stem the Christian tide."

He turns from me, breaking my grip. The smooth white king piece winks in the torchlight as he weaves it between his knuckles. "Your words have an ill ring to them, sister," he says finally. "Not the ring of prophecy, but the ring of treason."

I scoff, taken aback. "*Treason?* Never! I only want to *save* our people from annihilation!"

He wheels back around, his face suddenly red with rage. "Is it not treason to imply that I am as 'weak-minded' as the other kings of Norveg? You say I must forge an alliance with those strangers from the South, or else prostrate myself before the Christ. You've forgotten that the Allfather himself chose me to rule, for I proved myself to be the strongest and best of men. Unless you think Odin gives his favor lightly."

"No, brother," I say calmly. "I know we are the strongest and best of our people. *That* is what frightens me."

His eyebrows rise in surprise, then he barks out a laugh. I hold my breath as he reaches out and strokes my cheek.

"My *berserker*," he murmurs. "My sister with whom I shared the womb, whom I've loved so well ever since . . ." His eyes swivel down to my teeth as he lifts my top lip with his thumb. "Have you finally lost your *edge*?"

I lift his thumb from my mouth and replace it on my cheek. "I am ever your sword. As you are my king."

"It's funny," he continues, a cruel smile playing at the edge of his own lips. "All the world thinks you little more than a rabid bear. I alone see what hides behind those fangs of yours: a helpless little girl." Fury surges through me, but I keep my face as clear as a cloudless sky, betraying no emotion. He drops his hand abruptly. "Your past has poisoned your mind, Alvtir. In the shadows of our enemies, you see the ghosts of the men who took your life from you, all those years ago. But those men are long dead by now. Let them lie."

I stare at my twin brother dispassionately. I'm not the only one who hides behind a mask. Behind his mocking, I see his fury. And beneath his fury, I see the old fear in his eyes. He remembers just as I do that I was always our father's favorite when we were young, always the stronger and the brighter of the twins, always besting Balli in our training. Besting him even in play. I know he's spent more than a few nights lying awake in his luxurious bed in the dead of night, stirred by a small, ancient voice in his head whispering that his sister would have made a better ruler than he.

And just as I know that Balli has wondered this to himself in his most private moments, I know I must never let him believe it is so. I can see that I've overstepped my role this time, the role I am always playing as his "rabid bear" of a sister, good for nothing but carnage.

I let out a heavy sigh and bow low before him. "Forgive me, brother. You are right, of course. You always see the true path, even as I stumble in the dark."

At that, Balli softens. He leans down and plants a kiss on my forehead. "And you have served me well, dear sister."

I straighten to see him gently setting the king piece back on the map, back in its place atop Agder. And just like that, the future the Norns could have woven for my people unravels, spool by spool.

"You are a warrior—*not* a ruler," he continues. "The Allfather himself has given you his strength, and me his wisdom. I know in my heart that he will protect us, as he always has."

I say nothing. The fate of our world rests heavier than a byrnie on my shoulders.

"You can go now," he says, an edge of decisiveness cutting through his voice.

I give another short bow and head for the door.

I failed to convince my brother today. I failed my people, my city. And now my brother has given me no choice but to take matters into my own hands. He is right about one thing: He has not lived the life I've lived. He has not seen what I have seen.

I will force his eyes open.

Just as I reach the door, Balli calls out: "Alvtir."

I pause but don't look back, keeping my gaze ahead of me, fixed on the future.

"I expect you to follow my orders next time—Christians or no. Defy me again, and it will be the end of you."

13

YAFEU

"There is only one God, but he has ... three sides," Bronaugh says, stumbling through her Norse. She sweeps the barley from the millstone into the wide mouth of the clay pot, her hands completing their task on their own while her mind searches for words in a tongue she hasn't mastered.

"And his son Christ is one side of him—but not *also* a god?" The pestle grinds to a halt and ricochets pain up my arms. I grimace.

Well, I could use a break anyway. I stop milling and fish out the culprit: a lone husk that slipped through the threshing.

"That's how they teach me, in my home," she replies.

"What's the third side?"

"I don't know how to say ..." She thinks for a moment, wiping sweat from her neck with her apron sleeve.

My own neck is cool and dry, though I've been at the pestle for longer than my turn. It's too cold for me to sweat. It was warmer when I first arrived, two moons ago. Even then, though Bronaugh and I spent the long days out in the field, hacking row after row of golden grain, I rarely perspired. A fact that never ceases to impress Bronaugh, whose shift could be cracked in two after it dries.

The only time I sweat is when I'm asleep—and it's not the kind of sweat that comes from toil. It's the cold kind. The kind that reeks of fear.

For the first few weeks, I could hardly sleep. In the dead of night, I would surge awake, shaking with panic, convinced that the village was under attack and some unseen force was bearing down on our hut. I would grasp for daggers that weren't there and whimper in terror when I realized I was defenseless. Some nights I dreamed I was still in the desert and would wake with Ampah's lifeless face burning into the back of my eyelids. Some nights it was Newma's face that I saw. On the worst nights, it was Mama's, or Kamo's, or Goleh's—deaths I never witnessed but that haunted me all the same.

Slowly, I'd remember that my village was already long gone, burned to ashes. That I was not in my hut, nor in the desert, but in a cold, dirty barn far across the sea, surrounded not by my kin but by pale, indifferent strangers. That I was all alone. It was like waking from one nightmare just to find myself in another. Only this time, the nightmare wouldn't end. It was real.

Now the night terrors have subsided, but the feeling of living a nightmare hasn't. There's a weight in my chest that never goes away, an anchor. Grief rolls through me in waves throughout the day. With each wave the anchor sinks a little lower, a little deeper.

The anchor draws mass from the sheer foreignness of this place. The animals, the weather, the men, women, and children with their marble skin and watery tongue. Even Lisa himself is peculiar here, his light unfeeling and cold.

"Ghost!" Bronaugh says finally, her soft brown eyes lighting up with satisfaction. The way she smiles through pursed lips gives her a mischievous look and I can't help but smile back, feeling the anchor lighten a little. "The ghost is the third side," she finishes.

"A *ghost*, Bronaugh?" A chuckle escapes me before I can stop myself. I don't want to insult her, but thankfully she joins me.

"I know, I know. That's why my people—"

"Hey, you two!"

Bronaugh and I flinch in unison, our heads swiveling to face the longhouse. Broskrap scowls at us from his stool.

Bronaugh was dumped here by Alvtir a year ago. She says that occasionally, when Broskrap is traveling, Alvtir will drop by and offer fresh honey cakes and other treats in exchange for information on Broskrap's latest doings—namely descriptions of the men and women Bronaugh and Airé had seen him with. Outside of those brief exchanges, they neither see her nor hear from her.

I try not to think of Alvtir myself. The memory of what happened in Anfa makes my stomach churn with a sharp bitterness. I was a fool to trust her so blindly. She only "saved" me to sell me as a slave—a "thrall," as they call us. I narrowly escaped one master only to trade him for another.

"Back to work!" that master snaps now.

Bronaugh and I share a look. I resume churning the pestle through the barley, despite the spasm of protest from my arms.

The *Majūs* use barley for making ale, a foul-tasting drink that warms the belly and slows the mind. Airé has pilfered a bucket for us more than once, but I don't like it as much as she and Bronaugh do. It lifts the anchor for the night, but the next morning there's a pounding in my skull and a thirst on my lips that sends me right back to the desert.

Broskrap drinks ale morning and night, and most times in between. At the height of the harvest, he would work alongside us in the field during the day. But now that the time has come for grinding and storing, he's happy to watch us do all the labor from his little lean-to outside the longhouse, while he sits on that stool and brews his precious ale. I, for one, prefer him like that—at least a stone's throw away from us—even though it means I have to take on twice the work myself.

I level a hateful glare at him. Heedless, he goes back to brooding over the large pot of barley mash simmering over the firepit.

"Yafeu want switch now?" Bronaugh asks.

"Not yet," I reply. "Grinding makes Yafeu strong again." I flex my arms for show, making Bronaugh giggle. I can tell from her grateful smile that she's relieved to avoid the wrong end of the millstone for a while longer.

The truth is, despite all this strain, my muscles aren't nearly what they used to be. Broskrap keeps his thralls underfed; it leaves us weak and compliant.

Gods, I never thought I'd miss the days of millet porridge. Now I ache for it.

Before the wave of grief can hit me, Broskrap's two toddlers come bounding out of the longhouse in the nude. Airé runs out after them, her short black hair whipping across her furrowed brow as she chases them around the empty fields.

"Back inside for your bath, *stallos*!" she yells. The boys cackle and run faster.

Bronaugh told me that ever since Broskrap's wife died several moons ago, it's fallen to Airé, as the thrall who's been here the longest, to play nursemaid to the children. It's not a chore I envy, though it must be easier on the arms than grinding grain.

Soon she manages to wrangle the boys, who are now screaming with laughter. Bronaugh and I half smile to ourselves as she scolds them mercilessly and shoos them back toward the longhouse.

But the smile dies on my lips as I watch Broskrap stagger up from his stool and cut her off, blocking the door. He tugs at the hem of her apron and leans his head down close to hers, whispering something in her ear. She manages to squeeze past him into the house with the children, but the hungry look in his eyes as they follow her is enough to spark the fire in my veins.

My hand flies subconsciously to the knife strapped to my outer thigh, hidden beneath my shift. The outline of the handle feels good against my fingers. Reassuring.

It was the very first thing I took from Broskrap, my first small act of defiance. Every day, Broskrap circles his stores like a vulture, making sure none of the thralls have taken more than he's allotted for our rations. Half the time, he's probably too drunk to notice even if we did. But the other half . . . I once saw him use the back end of a hoe to bludgeon one of the scrawny boys who look after his sheep, just for slaughtering a sickened old ewe without asking him first. No matter that the sickness would have spread to the other sheep; no matter that the boy acted wisely.

But I felt too vulnerable without my daggers, and when I spotted the knife hanging down from the rafters of the brew shed—a stubby, shoddy woman's tool with a spiraling bone handle, designed to hook onto a key ring or an apron—I knew it wouldn't be missed. It probably once belonged to Broskrap's wife. With its owner gone, its *nyama* called out to mine. Bronaugh kept an eye out while I took it down. I've worn it ever since, like a secret jewel only I know I'm adorned with.

I can feel Bronaugh watching me. "Yafeu speak Norse better than Bronaugh already," she says quickly.

I drop my hand, tearing my eyes from the yellow-haired demon. "That's not true."

But it is true. I've been listening to Broskrap talk with his boys, and with the men and women who visit him from time to time. I've been practicing speaking their tongue as they do, making rippling waves through the vowels, refining the little inflections.

"Oh yes. Yafeu better at grinding too," Bronaugh teases, nodding at her own joke. She winks and opens her palm, revealing a handful of ground barley before slipping it furtively into a small pouch tied to her apron. As long as Broskrap is distracted, he won't notice if we take a little from the millstone before it ever gets to the storage vats. "*Much* better."

I force a grin, but a wave of grief washes over me.

She's distracting me from my anger, just like Ampah used to do.

The thought of Ampah threatens to bring up tears, so I shove it away and focus only on my hatred of Broskrap, pouring all the fire coursing through my body into grinding. Bronaugh falls silent as I pummel the kernels like I wish I could pummel him.

It surprises me how quickly Bronaugh has come to understand me, and I her. I would even call her a friend, which makes her the second friend I've ever had. She was taken from a place called "Ireland," from a village where the cliffs meet the sea and the ale is even stronger than Broskrap's. The *Majūs,* whom Bronaugh calls "Northmen," seized the two largest ports, turning them into strongholds before plundering the nearby farms and villages. She was separated from her family when they came; like me, she doesn't know what happened to them, if they still live.

But Airé remains a mystery to me. She spends most of her time with Broskrap's children, and even when we are together, she barely speaks. Everything I know about her, I learned from Bronaugh. It isn't much: All I know is that she's from a land even more north than here, and that the *Majūs* took her from her family when she was still a child. Even Bronaugh doesn't know how long she's been in Skíringssal.

After grinding the rest of the dried barley, we still have some light left in the day. Broskrap prepares to leave for some celebration the king is holding, something called a *"Freysblót,"* or so I've gathered from his conversations with visitors over the last few days. The sheep are happily at pasture, the barley we haven't ground is still drying in bundles against the barn, and it's too early to pick the hardy greens that will ripen at the start of the cool season, so he sends us off to do what we wish with a mutter and a wave of his hand.

Broskrap doesn't care where I wander in my own time. He doesn't need to—there's nowhere for me to run. Skíringssal is enclosed by densely forested hills to the east and west, stretching farther than the eye can see, and a towering mountain range to the north. I haven't been able to find any kind of trail in my brief forays into the western woods, past Broskrap's grazing lands—the only two paths are the one cutting through the heart of the city, connecting the farms to the harbor, and a branching path from the harbor to a compound atop a shorter hill. Unless the woods on the eastern side of the city are different, the only way in or out of Skíringssal is by boat.

So, today, I do what I've done with every precious scrap of time I've been given since I discovered the western woods were a dead end.

I head to the harbor to plan my escape.

14

YAFEU

I keep up a light trot down the rutted dirt path, ignoring the cries of protest from my swollen feet. They long to be free of these too-large old boots I've been given and rubbed with tallow by the fire, but they have a way to go before they've earned it.

The path is just wide enough for a wagon, so the farmers can cart goods to and from the artisans and traders in the city. Broskrap's holding is the largest, including the pastures bordered by the forest, which I've taken to mean that he is a rich man, as far as the *Majūs* go. The plots I pass get smaller as they get closer to the city, with fewer thralls toiling outside. It's not only thralls—some of the soldiers from the ships work alongside them. After watching them battle Anfa's guards, it feels strange to see them threshing grains and shoveling dung.

Lisa disappears and the sky resumes its usual ashen color. I scowl at the clouds; it might rain, but I can't be sure. Sogbo is still deciding.

Weather is fickle in this land. It's as if the gods are wrestling for control over it. Lisa can only shine down for an hour or two at a time before Sogbo grows jealous and blankets the sky in gray, threatening a storm. Then, despite all his bluster, it rains like a hare dashing over a hill—a light spray one moment, gone the next. In the blink of an eye, the sky clears and Lisa is back again, as if he'd never left. All day long, they go back and forth like this. Maybe that's why Lisa lingers so long in the sky, long after Mawu should have started her reign of night.

It's Agé who reaps the rewards of their battle, with green shooting up from the ground, green hanging down from trees, green spiraling off dense bushes on either side of the path. I scan the leaves and stems as I trot past. So many plants whose names I don't know, whose uses I don't know.

It's a painful realization, adding yet more weight to the anchor in my chest: All the things Papa taught me, all the things I've learned on my own—it all adds up to nothing here. It's like I've lived my whole life sitting on a turtle's back in the middle of the sea: Just when I thought I'd memorized all the planes and angles of the world, the turtle lifted herself from the water, and I saw that she had a much bigger shell than I ever imagined. Not to mention legs, a tail, a head.

The gray sky now seems to match my mood as it settles over the equally gray markets, which I hurry through without meeting anyone's eyes.

The first time I ventured here on my own, I barely made it through the marketplace before nightfall, stopping to ask every merchant and artisan in my broken Norse if they knew Yafeu. Most of them just gawked at me, their expressions both flustered and morbidly curious. A kind few remembered their manners after some moments and responded—but it was always "no." No one had heard of Papa. I barely got home in time to sleep that night, and I had nothing to fill my belly but disappointment. Now I don't bother talking to anyone.

The wind picks up as I get closer to the water, and I'm grateful for the warmth of the blood pulsing through my limbs as I jog. I wish I'd brought my fur; I'll get cold as soon as I stop moving. But the sight of the twisting waterway they call the "fjord" lessens the heaviness in my chest, and I stop caring about the weather even before my boots sink into the shingle.

The gods may squabble over the weather, but when it comes to the heart of the people, there's no question that Agbe and Naete have won. Even out in the farmlands, you can feel the tug of the fjord, hear its whisper bounding up the path from the harbor. Every building in Skíringssal seems to lean toward it.

The sea gods have stolen my heart too—but for a different reason. Somewhere out there, another *Majūs* ship is carrying my papa. Farther away, across the many seas, Mama, Kamo, and Goleh are waiting for us both. The water connects us all.

I gaze out at the handful of boats gliding across the surface. Lisa peeks out from the clouds at that moment, easing the weight in my chest even further. The tips of the waves shimmer his reflection back to him. The breeze blows my tight braid back and I wish I could let my hair free, to feel the wind caressing the thick curls. But I don't want to draw any more attention to myself. I stand out too much as it is.

A trading boat with cream-colored sails pushes away from the wharf, catching my eye. I've seen it here at least once before. It's similar in design to the warship I came in, but much smaller and rounder-bellied, and missing the dragon prow.

I study the two men within it. One unfurls the sail, lifting his finger to the wind to detect the direction. The other untethers the boat from the wooden post and takes out an oar. Then the man at the sail angles it to fill up with wind, straining against the force that would blow it out of his hands. The other man uses the oar to maneuver the boat through the narrow waterway: left to move right, right to move left. Simple enough.

And yet, there are so many more minute movements than that, more than I can keep track of—different ropes they pull and let out and tie down, parts of the boat that swing to and fro, the men ducking and jumping with practiced ease.

Of course, as my luck would have it, sailing is one of the skills Papa never taught me. I'm not sure if he knew how himself; we never needed a real boat in landlocked Wagadu, only rafts and canoes to traverse the White River. That's probably why he left to sail the seas with the *Majūs:* It was a new challenge, a new domain to conquer.

I can imagine how awed Papa must have felt when he first laid eyes on that foreign ship. The *Majūs* live crudely compared with us, making homesteads out of rickety wooden hovels—but the quality of their ships is matchless. They make ships that can glide across a mild chop with staggering speed, that bend against waves that should break them.

Looking around, it's easy to understand why: The water is the pathway to the world for the *Majūs*.

Which means that a boat is my only means of escape.

Again.

The irony is so bitter I can taste it on my tongue.

The trading boat trails farther and farther down the fjord until I can no longer make out the men inside. As it rounds the bend, I walk west along the rocky shingle, trying to keep it in sight. I shield my eyes with my hand, straining to watch the sails until they disappear.

Eventually, if I keep coming to the harbor and watching the *Majūs* sail, I'll figure out how to do it myself. Then I'll tell Bronaugh of my plan, and together we'll convince Airé to join us. On some clear, quiet night, when Broskrap's slumber is heavy with ale, the three of us will sneak out of the barn, make our way down to the harbor, and steal a small boat like this one.

We'll head west along the fjord until it spills into the sea, then we'll turn north, or maybe south, hugging the shoreline until we find the nearest settlement. I'll ask the people there about Yafeu, a traveling blacksmith with skin as brown as mine. We'll search up and down the whole coast if we must. *Someone* will know of him, or the ship he travels with. *Someone* will be able to tell us where he is. The danger will lie in finding him; once we do, he'll be able to protect us. We'll take Bronaugh and Airé to Ireland, or wherever they want to go. Then we'll make our way back to Wagadu together, Papa and I. We won't rest until we find Mama and Kamo and Goleh. We'll be a family again, no matter what it takes.

What if Papa can't be found?

The question hits me out of nowhere. After all, he left with an explorer, a man who wanted to discover new lands. That ship could be anywhere by now. Farther from here than Wagadu, even.

What would we do then? Where would we go? My mind flashes back to the blur of the storm on Alvtir's ship. Even the half memory chills me to the bone. We would never survive the open sea on some stolen fishing boat.

"It's not as complicated as it looks."

I wheel around to meet blue-gray eyes. Not ice, like Alvtir's, but water, like the fjord. The eyes of a man maybe a year or two older than I am, resting on a wooden stake with his arms folded across his chest. His light-brown hair is shaved around three clean lines at the sides, the top bundled neatly at the nape of his neck—except for one blade of hair dangling at his cheekbone. A handful of dots, like the ones Bronaugh bears all over, pepper the skin under his eyes. "Sailing, I mean. But stealing a boat in the first place—that's the real trick."

My gaze sweeps over him: he has a fighter's build but wears only a worn gray tunic, no armor, no weapons at his belt. I cross my own arms, acutely aware of the woman's knife strapped to my thigh. "Oh?"

He lifts his angled jaw to the compound atop the hill, and I notice his close-shorn beard contains a mix of red and brown. "You can't see it from here, but there's a watchtower up there, and a guard with his gaze trained on the Agdersfjord at all times, day and night. He's watching for enemy ships coming in, of course. But a lone boat going out, say, in the middle of the night, that would raise suspicion. Even if you escaped unnoticed, you'd find no safe harbor for a runaway thrall on a stolen boat. Not in King Balli's lands."

His tone is gentle, his expression soft, but the words themselves are like piercing arrows. "And why do I need to know this?" I snap. "I may be a thrall, but I'm no thief."

He cocks an eyebrow. "Not yet."

"I have no plans to become one."

"Then why do you study the boats so intently, whenever you come here?"

My eyes narrow. "Have you been watching me?"

"You're hard to miss."

I let out an exasperated snort. It's one thing to be scorned and ridiculed. I'm used to that. But I don't know what game this stranger is playing with me—and I don't like it. "Perhaps I enjoy watching the boats," I reply. "Perhaps it soothes me. Perhaps it reminds me of my home, of my family. In any case, it's none of your concern."

His brow furrows, red-flecked eyebrows turning inward, and he falters for a moment, as though suddenly unsure of himself. Then, to my great surprise, he stands and bows his head to me—as though I were some noble lady, and he a servant. "I'm sorry. I was once someone who longed for an escape; perhaps I'm too given to seeing myself in others." He straightens, his sea eyes catching mine. "I promise, my intention was not to offend. Only to advise."

His apology catches me even more off guard. I open my mouth to reply, but I'm not sure what to say, so I close it again, holding his steady gaze.

He looks himself about to speak again, when a deep voice booms out: "Shield-Breaker!"

We both look over at the voice's source, an enormous man with a wild mop of black hair emerging from a nearby stall. He holds up a dead fish the size of his bulging forearm, grinning like a dog with a bone. "Got us a bargain for dinner. Let's eat before it rots."

The stranger turns back to me and bows his head once more, then follows the giant man into the streets without another word.

No sooner do I find myself alone again than a wave of despair crashes over me. Hot tears rush to my eyes, blurring the boundary between water and hill, hill and sky. I hurry away from the shore, pushing against the current of day visitors and dusk fishermen flocking back to their ships before Lisa disappears on them. The artisans and craftsmen pack up their stalls for the evening as I weave through the market, keeping my head down, retracing the same steps I took with Alvtir when I first arrived.

Gods, was that only two moons ago? I followed her blindly then, straight to my doom. Now my eyes are open, but it doesn't matter. I walk the same path, even knowing what lies at the end, because I have no other choice.

Because there is no escape.

Because I'll never see my family again.

Another wave of despair breaks over me, threatening to swallow me whole.

The haze of dusk presses in on me as I make my way back to Broskrap's farm, so thick I can barely see the next step ahead. By the time I reach the barn, the anchor in my chest feels heavier than ever.

15

YAFEU

I t used to be that the sky didn't fully blacken at night; it remained in the cobalt blue of twilight, as if Lisa was reluctant to give Mawu her turn. But as the air grew cooler, the nights grew darker, and I sleep much better now because of it. Or maybe because I'm getting used to this new life.

Bronaugh and I usually share what we've managed to pocket during the day to supplement our "supper," as she calls it—a handful of extra grain, or some berries from the bushes at the edge of the forest. Whenever I can get away with it, I'll snatch a fresh-caught fish from one of the stalls at the market. Those are the nights when we eat like free women. But today the market wasn't as crowded as it usually is, and I didn't think I could take anything fresh without losing a hand for my trouble. I like my hands, so I settled for a small piece of salted cod from a smokehouse, which was unattended while the stout cook haggled with someone outside.

I usually have supper with Bronaugh alone—or rather, with Bronaugh and Saint Brigid, as she calls the little barn cat. But Broskrap took his boys to visit his eldest son in the city today, freeing Airé from her cooking duties, so tonight all three of us huddle around the firepit as the old bones of a ram long since slaughtered boil in the clay pot above. Bronaugh tosses in an extra handful of ground barley. Even a bland, chalky soup is better than a *thin,* bland, chalky soup.

Now it's my turn. I shrug apologetically as I take out the small parcel of salted cod, hastily wrapped in a strip of spare cloth. Saint Brigid trots over from her hay-bale perch, as she always does when I have fish. I hold the parcel high, and she flicks her tail in annoyance. "There's not enough for you tonight," I scold her.

I'm about to throw the fish in the pot—it needs to boil for a while before it softens enough to eat—when Airé grabs my arm. "Save it, Yafeu," she says. She shoots me a smile that looks almost coy in the dancing firelight. Then she reaches into her woven basket and emerges with the hindquarters of a freshly slaughtered lamb.

Bronaugh gasps and throws her hands over her mouth. My own belly flips with joy. Even Saint Brigid meows plaintively, weaving herself between Airé's legs.

"Airé!" Bronaugh exclaims. "How?"

"One of the young ones had foot rot, so Broskrap slaughtered it," Airé says. "He gave the rest to me."

I hesitate. Why would Broskrap do such a thing? He's hardly generous with the rest of us, let alone any of the other thralls. But Bronaugh gets up and starts to dance, and my worry fades away. I can't help but laugh as she hums atonally and twirls on her callused toes, her long red hair swishing around her shoulders. Even Airé lets out a giggle.

For once, the three of us are all smiles. "Can I prepare it for us?" I ask, already reaching for my knife.

I can't remember the last time I tasted meat, tasted the fullness of its flavor. Maybe none of us can, as no bite goes untouched.

After the feast, our minds fall into a pleasant lull. A full belly will put your woes to bed—even without any ale. The sounds of cattle shifting in their stalls forms a lullaby with the sizzle and pops of the fire. Feeling indulgent, I feed a small piece of the salted cod to Saint Brigid as Bronaugh entertains us with a story from Ireland. It's a strange tale about a priest who chased all the snakes around the island until they fled into the ocean, and everyone celebrated. I stare into the crackling fire, picturing the licks of flame as snakes. My mind flits back to the sorcerer in Anfa, to the way he bewitched the rattlesnake and made it dance.

"Why did they celebrate?" I ask, confused. "Did the snakes attack people?"

Bronaugh giggles. "Snakes are bad, Yafeu. They are . . . messengers. Of the bad angel. We call him the Devil."

I look to Airé, wondering if she agrees. She says nothing. In the glow of the fire, I can just make out the languid rise and fall of her thin torso. Fast asleep.

"Bronaugh?" I lower my voice to a whisper.

"Mmm?"

"Was it so bad in Ireland that being a thrall here is better?"

She shrugs. "My family is poor, and I have many sisters. My father . . . he make me live in convent."

"Convent?" The word is unfamiliar. It sits heavy on my tongue, unwieldy.

"Where women go to worship God."

A temple just for women? How could that be bad?

"When you are in a convent, you never have love with a man," she continues, answering my unasked question. "Never marry, never have family."

"Why?" I ask, taken aback. "What kind of god wants its worshippers to live without love?"

"Because you are married to God, they say. And loving God is . . . like a big meal." She gestures to the empty pot. "No love left over."

"My mother told me that we show love for the gods by honoring all their creations," I say.

"The—*gods*?" Now it's Bronaugh's turn to be surprised.

It hits me that I haven't told Bronaugh very much about my own people. "In Wagadu, where I'm from, we worship many gods, not just Nana Buluku, the creator."

"That is beauti—"

"There are no gods." The edge in Airé's voice silences us both. "Not the god of Ireland, not the Aesir and Vanir of Skíringssal, not your gods in Wagadu. They are all lies. Lies our parents tell us, just as their parents told them, so everyone believes that the world is full of magic and justice and everything makes sense. But the world has no magic. No justice. Not if you are a *thrall*. Not if you are a *girl*."

She spits out the last word, and it sinks into me like a poison-tipped dagger. I shudder but say nothing, not wanting to upset her any further. Bronaugh stays quiet too.

I roll to face the wall, watching the hills of our shadows mingling with the shadows of buckets and baskets and the tools hanging from the beams. These shadows no longer make me cry, but thinking about Airé almost does.

Airé is gone, but Bronaugh is still snoring when I wake the next morning.

Strange. Airé is always the first to rise, but I never wake up before Bronaugh. Ordinarily, I savor every extra moment of blissful unconsciousness before she gently shakes me awake for the day of chores. But now I find my limbs are restless, full of a bouncy, roiling *nyama* that needs to be unshackled in movement. Perhaps it's the richness of the meal we had last night.

I throw on my apron, strap the knife to my thigh, and put on the large old boots. A few moments later, I push open the barn door.

The cold air slaps my face. I can see my own breath billowing in front of me. Lisa has not yet appeared above the bushy hillside to the east, though the sky has lightened from twilight to dawn, signaling his approach.

If only I could go hunting. A thought that's occurred to me countless times over the last two moons. But I don't even know if this stupid kitchen knife is sharp enough to kill; with its odd shape, I couldn't throw it with any accuracy anyway.

Frustrated, I decide to walk to the forest for a bath. Bronaugh showed me where the stream widens and forms a little pool, just a short hike past the lea. The frigid water will help douse the fire in my blood.

Soon I quicken my pace to a jog. The light exertion and the sound of my feet hitting the dirt in a steady rhythm calms my restlessness. I take in the beauty of the white-capped mountains rising in the north, the ancient massifs huddled as if for warmth under blankets of shadow and light.

It's not just the mountains. Endless greens, blues, and shades of gray form the unique personality of this place. At first, I found it lacking compared with the palette I'm used to, the rich browns and reds and tans of Wagadu. I still ache for those colors. But as the weeks have passed, I've come to accept that Skíringssal is simply its own painting. No more or less; just different.

I enter the woods, breathing in the fresh, resinous smell of the trees. Supple brown spikes litter the ground, cushioning my step. After a short trek uphill and back down again, I hear the familiar sound of running water, and I come upon the pool.

I approach it with my heart feeling lighter than it has in a long time—even more so when I notice Airé, already shoulder-deep in the chilly blue water. She's facing away from me, but her calm movements and small splashes reveal a peacefulness I rarely see in her. It brings a smile to my lips. No wonder she always wakes before the sun.

I am wondering whether I should join her or leave her be when a hulking form emerges from the other side of the dell.

I freeze. From the corner of my eye, I watch Broskrap spy on Airé as she bathes, unaware of the intrusion.

At least he's unaware of me. For once, luck is on my side.

Slowing my *nyama,* I duck silently behind the trunk of a tree.

Broskrap lopes over to the stream. The look on his face makes my stomach twist. Airé spins and stares up at him, eyes widening in alarm. Her hands fly to cover her naked chest.

"Come here, girl," he says, grabbing her thin arm and yanking her out of the water onto the bank. She lets out a strained yelp. I can feel the pain and fear in her *nyama*. My breathing quickens, every muscle tensing with rage.

Broskrap kicks her down and holds her there with his mud-covered foot. She lies there limply, facedown in the grass.

I can't wait any longer. I reach under my shift, my fingers clasping around the spiral handle of the knife. I remove it from the strap as Broskrap undoes the knot that holds his pants closed and lowers himself over Airé.

With my measly weapon in hand, I creep forward. Their backs are to me, his over hers.

The ringing between my ears grows louder and louder. I feel myself trembling. The dam breaks, and this time I don't care. I want it to flood. I want every last drop.

I expect a sea, but what I get instead is fire. It burns away everything between me and Broskrap.

I finally see the truth of it—the truth I spent so many years trying not to see, not to *feel*. I was always pushing it away, but it was always pushing back. It lingered in my blood. It lurked in my bones. Not an evil spirit, not a vengeful ancestor: just *me*. The other part of me, like Mawu and Lisa are two parts of one being.

Rage.

Rage is focus. Rage is power. Rage is the instinct that acts through me to do what must be done.

I raise my arm and spring. A primal yell rips through me as I tackle him to the ground, setting Airé free.

Hoarse gasps ravage my lungs as I tower over Broskrap's lifeless body. Blood spurts from the large vein in his neck and pools around his head, like the unraveling of a lustrous red scarf. His face is beaten raw. I feel my own face and find drops of his blood sprayed there, still warm.

I killed him.

I should be upset. I should be horrified. But I can't feel anything other than exhilaration, sweet and pure and shockingly potent, like the first bloom after the rains. It's the same feeling that was written on Alvtir's face as she butchered the slavers in Anfa.

Broskrap is dead. I killed him.

As my breath slows, I wait for a blanket of guilt—or grief, or even fear—to snuff out the exhilaration, but it doesn't come.

After a long moment, I turn my attention to Airé. She sits with her arms wrapped around her legs, still naked and shivering violently.

It's then that I finally feel something: worry.

I kneel next to her. She doesn't acknowledge my presence, her wide eyes glued to Broskrap's corpse. I reach out to touch her shoulder, but she squeaks and recoils, and I realize that my hands are soiled with Broskrap's blood.

I flash to the moment I touched Ampah's shoulder, that very first night in the desert. Her reaction was the same.

"Are you okay?" I whisper.

Airé flings her gaze like a dagger in my direction. The anger in her eyes hits me harder than Broskrap ever could. "You have no idea what you've done."

I frown, confused. "I s-saved you."

She shakes her head from side to side, as if the force will fling her from this moment.

Now I feel afraid.

"You've killed us!" she shrieks. "You've killed all of us, Yafeu!"

Her words dance around me, just outside my grasp. I hadn't thought—I had only seen her suffering, his monstrosity… "I wanted you to be safe," I say again, like an idiot.

"But *they* don't! Don't you understand? How could you be so foolish?"

I don't know what else to say, so I just kneel there, dumbfounded. Abruptly, Airé stands and throws her shift over her mud-caked body. Broskrap's handprints look like burn marks on her arms; soon they will blossom into purple-blue bruises.

She stalks off toward the barn. My feet follow her, but my mind stays in the pool, drowning in disbelief.

I saved her. I saved all of us.

Didn't I?

16

FREYDIS

"I can't start making exceptions, Tófi."

As my eyes adjust to the gloom of the Great Hall, I find two strangers standing before my father, who sits on his throne on the dais, leaning his head against his fist. Aunt Alvtir stands at his side wearing a similarly bored expression. Her brawny arms are folded across her chest, a pair of leather bracers wrapped tightly around her plain black tunic, as though she's just come from a hunt.

Father continues on, ignoring my entrance: "How would it look to the others if I showed you such leniency? They would storm this hall just to grovel at my feet, each spouting their own most *noble* cause."

As I draw nearer to the older man, I realize that I recognize him: He's one of father's jarls, Jarl Tófi of Hvitbjorg. He's been to Skíringssal before, to deliver our share of the harvest or attend the Althing, the assembly where the jarls and other prominent men gather and discuss the affairs of the kingdom. When Father became king, he made it law that all ancestral lands in Agder belonged to him, and that all the farmers, no matter how humble, must pay him a tax. He was savvy in choosing loyal jarls who will carry out this levy, compensating them with a third of the taxes for keeping the farmers in line.

I remember Jarl Tófi for his auburn hair, now laced with white, and his kindly blue eyes. He's not like the other jarls; there's a gentleness about him that has always stood out. Next to him stands a lanky boy with the same auburn hair and kind eyes. His son.

I pause a few paces back from Tófi and his boy, unsure of my place in this strange unfolding. *Why have I been summoned?*

"King Balli, I would not ask if the need were not dire," Jarl Tófi begins. "The winter frost lingered long past the seed moon this year. The soil was so hardened that it would not yield to the plow. It was lamb-fold before we could sow the fallow. We sacrificed several boars to Frey, and my two finest bulls to Skadi and Hod. Nonetheless, the barley and hay crops were weak, and the harvest was the poorest in all the summers I've drawn breath. If I ask any more of my farmers, they won't have enough to feed their animals this winter. Their families would go hungry. Some would not survive."

I feel my lips part in surprise. Jarl Tófi must have fallen short on the tax this year.

No jarl has *ever* fallen short on the tax before. But Tófi is known to be an honorable man, and his voice has the clear ring of earnestness today. He's telling the truth.

Even so, Father has that look on his face. The look that's both cold and feverish at once. A familiar dread seizes me at the sight of it.

I know that look.

"That's quite a story," Father says, flexing his fingers and examining his nail beds in apparent disinterest. "But if it's true, then why were all the other jarls able to pay their full shares? This was a cruel winter for all of Agder, but summer was not unkind. Why was Hvitbjorg the only province who did not reap her full bounty?"

"Because Hvitbjorg lies at the northernmost edge of Agder, my king. We are farthest from the sea, and the land has always been colder for it. Still, the winters are growing harsher and lasting longer. Not just for us, but across the lands. Every year is worse than the last. Hvitbjorg may be the first to go hungry, but I promise you, sooner or later, the other jarls will come to stand before you as I stand now, with the same plea on their lips."

"You would lecture *me* on what is happening in my own lands?" Father grips the arms of the throne. "What I hear is that *you* allowed the farmers to idle away the spring. So *you* should have compensated for the loss in yield with a percentage of your own share."

"We already have, King Balli," Tófi's son cuts in, stepping forward.

Father's gaze flickers to the boy as Tófi reaches for his arm. "Magnus—"

"There is simply no more to give," the boy continues, shrugging his father off. "Can't you see? We would not have come to you otherwise."

A long moment passes. Father relaxes his grip, a smile spreading across his face. The throne creaks as he stands. His footsteps are the only sound as he steps off the dais and comes face-to-face with the boy, Magnus. My breath is stuck in my throat, along with everyone else in the room save Alvtir, whose expression remains aloof as ever.

"He meant no disrespect," Jarl Tófi says quietly. He's trembling now, his face white as a sheet. A look of confusion passes across Magnus's face, but he holds Father's hard gaze. He's a skinny, pockmarked thing; a boy who hasn't yet broadened into a man. Maybe three years younger than me.

"Tell me." Father begins circling the boy. My stomach tightens. "Why did you bring your son with you?"

"I . . ." Tófi trails off, his voice now quaking as violently as his body.

What can he say? He brought his son with him for no other reason than to stoke the embers of Father's mercy.

But Father isn't known for his mercy.

"A fine young man." Father pauses, draping his arm around the lad's shoulders and giving him a firm, paternal squeeze. Magnus looks to his father, clearly baffled, but he stands tall. Perhaps he's flattered to receive such praise from the king. Perhaps he thinks he earned it with his reckless words. I cast my gaze to the floor, but I can still hear Father's next words with painful clarity. "Old enough to learn an important lesson, don't you think?"

"Please . . ." Tófi begs, his voice weak. "He is my only son."

"You are blessed to have one." I can hear the sneer in Father's voice. "I wish I had been so blessed. But sometimes the gods have other plans."

I feel the familiar pinch of shame in my stomach. I wonder if Father was looking at me when he said that.

I force myself to look back up. I won't let him see my weakness; that will only inflame him further.

A mistake. Tófi's kind eyes meet mine, a silent plea. But I can't do anything for him.

The pinch of shame becomes a crushing grip.

"Sister." Father motions to Aunt Alvtir. She strides over to the jarl, awaiting Father's command. "What do we do to thieves who steal from their king?"

It happens so fast. One minute Jarl Tófi is trembling next to Alvtir, the next his head is rolling across the ground.

My entire body seizes up. The boy cries out, but Father's arm around his shoulder holds him in place.

Alvtir remains in a slight lunge. Her long black hair hangs in front of her face, like the curtains of Hel obscuring a wraith. If just seconds before she moved with uncanny speed, now she's as still as the runestone outside. Then she straightens, lifting her sword above her head. My heart skips a beat as she flings it to the side, whipping the blood from the blade onto the floor.

Father grins as she sheathes the sword. He murmurs in the ear of the ashen-faced boy: "I suppose you're the jarl now, son. Do you think you'll do better than your father, or do you need another lesson?"

"I . . ." The boy gathers himself quickly. "I will deliver the full tax before winter."

"Good lad," Father says, patting his shoulder before releasing him. "Once I receive it, I'll send your father's body for you to bury."

The boy doesn't waste a moment—he turns and walks out of the hall as quickly as he can without running, brushing by me without a glance.

Alvtir lets out a laugh like a tern's screech, and for a moment I almost think I see her *berserker* bloodlust flashing in her eyes.

"Get Werian to clean this up," Father orders the guard at the entrance. As the guard rushes off, Father heaves himself back on his throne. Alvtir takes her place at his side, looking as indifferent as ever. And why wouldn't she be? To her, it's just one murder among hundreds. Maybe thousands.

Mother's anger can be terrible sometimes, and Father's is far worse. But both are nothing compared with Alvtir's feral rage. She deserves every horrible thing people say about her.

I do my best not to look at the corpse, fighting a wave of nausea as I catch sight of Tófi's head at the edge of my vision. I keep my chin down, hoping Father sees it as deference and not weakness.

"Now, on to more important matters. Freydis." Father waves me forward.

I take a few steps closer and give a short bow, keeping my usual distance.

"I've come to terms with Hakon of Trøndelag," he says. "You'll be married in the spring. We will host the wedding here, after the last of the winter frost has melted."

I blink at him, thunderstruck. It takes several long moments for his words to sink in.

Hakon of Trøndelag?

But . . . I was pledged to Harald!

"Father, I thought—Harald . . ." I stammer, feeling my face grow hot.

"Forget the boy-king. Hakon is of more use to us."

My heart shatters. The shards fall into the pit of shame in my stomach. I should never have nourished the dream of Harald, never have allowed such fancies to take root in my heart.

But . . . Hakon of Trøndelag?

All I know about Hakon Grjotgardsson is that he's an old widower. As old as Father at least.

But perhaps age doesn't matter when it comes to love. And Hakon is still a king. So I will still be a queen, and I will still have my own hall—one that's far away from here.

"What's that, girl?" Father snaps.

"Th-thank you, Father," I say hastily. "I will make an offering to Frigg that she may bless this marriage." My mind jumps into motion again. I wonder . . . "If I may have one request?" Father makes a sound of irritation in his throat but gestures for me to continue.

"Now that I'm to wed, perhaps it's time that I have my own handmaiden? Like Helge is for Mother? I'll need help with all the preparations . . ." I trail off.

"Fine. Alvtir will find some girl for you on the next raid." Aunt Alvtir glances down at Father in apparent surprise.

Is Loki playing tricks on my mind, or is she just as unaware of Father's plans as I am? I thought Father told Aunt Alvtir everything.

"There's no need to send the *hird* out for a mere handmaiden," Alvtir scoffs. "I have a girl for her now."

"Oh?" Father questions. "I thought you didn't keep thralls." It's well known that Aunt Alvtir shuns all company, save for her savage shield maidens. She'd rather live like a common milkmaid than accept the help of a thrall in her own home.

"Not mine, one of Broskrap's girls," she continues, picking something out of her teeth and flicking it onto the floor. I cringe and force down another wave of nausea. "She's not worth her weight as a farmhand, and he wishes to be rid of her. But I suspect she's well suited for more . . . *feminine* tasks. Perhaps she and Freydis would get on well." Her tone is mocking, her thin lips pulled up into a smirk.

I wonder how often Aunt Alvtir engages in "feminine" tasks. I can't imagine her sitting in front of a loom. But someone has to make the clothes you wear, dear Aunt. Even if they are the clothes of a man.

"It's settled then. The girl is yours." Father swats the air as though the matter were a fly buzzing around his ear.

"Thank you," I say again. "And thank you, Aunt Alvtir."

She spits on the ground. And with that, I figure I'm free to leave.

As my feet carry me back to my room, my mind attempts to unravel the thoughts and feelings tangled together inside me.

I've always known that I would never have the freedom to marry solely for love. I'm the daughter of a king; it is my duty to marry the suitor who best strengthens the kingdom. I thought I'd accepted that. But perhaps it was easy to accept when I was pledged to Harald, since loving a boy—now man—like him seemed . . . inevitable. It wouldn't be the *reason* we married, of course, but love would grow between us sooner or later. Because he is handsome and brave and kind, and I . . . well, I know I am pleasing to look upon at least, and I would try my hardest to be good in other ways as well. And we would understand each other: I know what it's like to grow up as the only child of a king. I know how lonely it can be. How isolating.

And yet, there must be a reason Father chose Hakon over Harald. Father is nothing if not opportunistic, but he is also shrewd, and he knows the weight of breaking an oath. The drawbacks of marrying Harald must somehow outweigh the risk to his honor. Perhaps it has to do with Vestfold's key positioning along the Volga trade route . . . or perhaps it's something else entirely. I sorely wish Father would share his reasoning with me. I know I'm not good for much, but I have more of a mind than he credits me for.

But that is a fruitless line of thinking. I must try to focus on the good. Before the year is done, my birthright will be fulfilled. Like a swan in molt, I will slough off Skíringssal and all its loneliness and violence. I may not have a great romance, but I will do my best to be loved as a queen by the people of Trøndelag.

No matter what, I'll have a home of my own. A *family* of my own. Perhaps that's enough.

But as soon as I set foot in my room, a ferocious despair sinks its sharp teeth into me. For years, I've been dreaming of Harald, of the beautiful life we would lead together . . . and in the span of a single heartbeat, that dream was snatched away. Stolen. I fall onto my bed, forcing the thoughts of marriage from my mind. At the very least, there is something I can look forward to right away: I will finally have a handmaiden! She could be my friend and confidante, like Helge is to Mother. If I'm being honest . . . I don't know what Mother would *do* without Helge. If things don't go well between me and Hakon, then this girl could be my own source of comfort and companionship.

I hope Alvtir spoke the truth when she said we would get along.

ALVTIR

I make sure my niece has finished sulking her way out of the hall before I turn to my brother. "*Another* raid?"

"You will take the *hird* out on the next full moon."

I frown. "For what purpose?"

"I need you to find a suitable dowry for Freydis."

Rage clouts me like a swing from Mjölnir. Only a moon ago, I brought him a sea-chest brimming with gold and silver. Even before that, he was as rich as Njord himself. But he won't give up even one of those coins to his daughter's dowry? He'll send weary soldiers out into the frigid winds and stark-raving seas of winter, just to keep their recent plunder for himself?

"Summer has ended," I say, struggling to keep the anger from my voice.

He shrugs. "Go back to Iberia, then. You say it's warmer there. And you can avoid your dreaded Christians."

As I stare into his dull green eyes, I realize that every shred of love I once felt for him is gone. Now there's nothing but shame. Shame that his blood also courses through my veins. Shame that I've let him control me for so many years.

I shove my indignance away to think for a moment. The Saracen cities far outclass the stray Northumbrian monasteries we've raided before, and the Saracen soldiers are no helpless monks. If their soldiers have returned from their own war with the Christians, there's no telling what we'd face if we attempted another raid.

"I'm not certain such a quest would be fruitful, given the cost of payment to the *hird*," I begin. "That jarl was right about the winters growing colder: It will feel like Fimbulwinter on Njord's rough chop. And the soldiers have barely had time to warm their beds with their wives—those that even have beds, or wives."

"They are *Víkingar*. They were born with the call to battle in their hearts."

"And if they die—"

"Then the Valkyries will take them to Valhalla," Balli replies casually. "What more could a warrior want?"

"—who will protect Skíringssal?"

"Sell-swords aren't hard to find."

"But good, loyal men are."

"Dear sister," he chuckles. "You worry too much. Odin will grant his favorite warrior the victory she seeks."

Suddenly an opportunity I hadn't seen before crystallizes in my mind's eye. An idea so full of potential, it must have been sent to me on the wings of Hugin himself.

My eyes flicker to the shield hanging behind us. *Thank you, Wise One. I know what I must do.*

I watch my brother as he gulps down his henbane-laced ale from a Saxon goblet, one of many treasures from the earliest raids. His greed is like ice-water around the molten iron of my resolve, hardening it forever.

They say money makes a beast of a good man. But my brother was never a good man.

I'll gladly go on this mission, dear brother—for now I have a mission of my own.

"I am yours to command."

I step outside and blink in the sudden brightness, surprised to find Sól's chariot still so high in the sky. It seemed like I spent an age in that cursed hall today.

I hurry down the path toward the city, only slowing when I enter the marketplace. Trade is always frenzied this time of year, and the port is indeed full of fat-bellied *knarrs,* the stalls crowded and the alleys bustling with activity.

If I needed yet more proof of Odin's guidance, the Frankish mineral trader is here today, haggling with a woolworker over one of his glittering rocks.

The woolworker ducks inside his shed at my approach. "Chlothar," I call out in greeting.

Chlothar's jowls shake as he sighs. "You are bad for business, Alvtir."

"But I always pay for the privilege."

He crosses his chubby arms and turns to face me. The many bejeweled rings on his thick fingers boast of just how much I pay for that privilege. "And what is it you're buying today? It better be this lovely fluorspar crystal, since I have no new information to sell."

"It's not information I've come to buy, nor crystals."

He frowns. "Then what can I offer you?"

I glance about. As usual, everyone from weaver to woodworker keeps their distance from me. I've never been more grateful for that than I am today. "Some of your crystals are from al-Andalus, are they not?"

He frowns. "Why?"

I lean in close. "I need your help arranging a meeting."

17

YAFEU

Lisa's descent stretches our shadows across the barn. I close the door out of instinct, and then I remember—there's no master left to overhear us. Only Broskrap's two boys, who are off playing ball somewhere, probably giggling at the groaning of their empty bellies and wondering why that cheerless thrall hasn't wrangled them for dinner.

Boys who will grow up without a father. Because of me.

"We don't tell anyone he's dead," Bronaugh reasons, her voice shaking. She tosses another log into the fire, then goes back to stirring the broth simmering in the pot above it. Since we returned from the woods, she hasn't stopped moving. "We take care of the farm and the boys. We keep going. Nothing is different."

"And what do you think they'll do when they find his body?" Airé hisses. "We'll be the first people they blame!"

I stand there mutely, staring at Airé's shadow pacing back and forth across the wall.

"They won't find him. Yafeu and I put his body in the stream—"

"It's only a matter of time until he washes up!" Airé tugs at the edges of her short, dark hair. "They will find his body and they will kill us! Or worse!"

Their hushed voices fade to a murmur as my mind drifts back to the bank of the pool.

All I saw was Airé in pain, helpless at the hands of that man. That *jugu* man. I didn't think about the consequences. I just wanted to help my friend.

And to wrap my hands around Broskrap's neck. I wanted that too.

"Airé," I begin. She rips her panicked glare from Bronaugh to me. "I understand that you're afraid. So am I. But the stream will carry his body far away from here. You are safe—"

"No! You *don't* understand. You don't know them like I do. We will *never* be safe!" Tears slide down her cheek, glinting in the dim light of the dying embers. And then she crumples, like a crane flower wilting after bloom. Only Airé never got the chance to bloom in the first place.

Sorrow snakes up my chest and throat. "I'm sorry," I whisper for the hundredth time. "I wish I could take it back."

But even as I say the words, I know they're a lie. I wouldn't take it back. No matter what happens now, Broskrap deserved to die. I only wish I had made him suffer more.

Bronaugh ladles the soup into three wooden bowls. It hadn't occurred to any of us to take more food for dinner, even though there's no one to beat us for doing so. She tries to hand the steaming liquid to Airé, who ignores her and flops down next to the fire.

Bronaugh sighs and shoots me a look, both fearful and frayed. She hands some broth to me and I accept, cradling the warm bowl in my hands more for comfort than anything else. We take our usual seats around the fire.

"Do you know what happens to a man's thralls when he dies?" Airé begins, staring emptily into the flames. "Sometimes, they bury them with him. Alive. So he can take them with him into the next life."

An eerie silence fills the room.

I glance at Bronaugh, who holds her untouched soup close to her chest. "Come, Airé," she says gently. "We don't know if—"

The door bursts open. A familiar voice, rough as raw ore, rides a gust of cold air into the barn.

"Yafeu."

Startled, I drop the bowl and jump to my feet. A rugged silhouette stands backlit in the doorway. I am suddenly reminded of Sasabonsum, a forest demon Mother told us stories about when we were young. It had long, dark hair and teeth as sharp as nails, which it used to feed on human victims.

"Alvtir." I tremble despite myself. What is she doing here?

She strides into the barn, leaving the door ajar behind her. "Come with me," she says, leering at me from behind a curtain of black hair.

She knows. Somehow, she knows what I've done to Broskrap.

Thick silence fills the room again. I search the *nyama* that radiates from Alvtir for a sliver of empathy or compassion. I find nothing.

So be it.

The trembling subsides as I turn to Bronaugh and fold her into a fierce embrace. "May God be with you," she whispers, trembling in my arms. She squeezes me hard one last time before pulling away.

I pick the fur off the ground and turn to the woman who gave it to me. She jerks her neck toward the door, signaling me to follow.

I spare one last look at Airé. Her jaw is clenched, her gaze inscrutable.

Then I follow Alvtir to my death.

We walk in silence for a long time, following the same furrowed path to the city that she led me up two moons ago. Only this time, we're headed down, away from the farmland. The orange-blue sky casts an uncanny glow on the barley fields. They almost look like they're on fire. I flash back to my village burning, the bright-orange flames thrashing against the black night.

Alvtir quickens her pace as the path widens at the mouth of Skíringssal. In the twilight, I can just make out the thatched roofs of the longhouses, crowded together like a bloat of hippos. But then she takes a sharp turn east, bypassing the city entirely. We scale the hill adjacent to the harbor, eventually meeting up with a narrow, steep path to the top.

She's taking me to that compound on the hill? I open my mouth to ask her.

"The king would like to see you," Alvtir says before I can speak, seemingly reading my mind.

"King?" I say, confused by the word.

"Chief. Leader. Ruler."

Fear sinks into my chest like a newly sharpened dagger. At the top of the hill, we come to a large building, by far the grandest of the houses I've seen in Skíringssal. It nearly spans the length of the hilltop itself. Two soldiers stand guard in front of the doors, and in front of them stands a single raised stone with strange markings on its face. I wonder if the markings are some kind of writing. Whatever the markings are, they clearly signal the importance of this place.

The wooden walls of the structure tower above me, at least three times my own height or more. I glance around, measuring the building in my mind. A field of barley could fit inside. Of course, it's barely a stable compared with the home of the Ghāna. But the *Majūs* are a crude people; their king would probably consider himself lucky to live in one of the Ghāna's gilded stables.

Alvtir nods to the two guards, and they step aside to let us pass. We approach the wooden doors, trimmed with sinuous gold braids interwoven around more of the foreign markings. A simple design, laden with an import I can't discern. But as with stone, I can feel the weight of its meaning.

I glance at Alvtir, searching her stoic profile for any hint of what's to come. Will there be a trial? Will I be thrown in the king's prison? Or will he order me to be killed at once?

"You'll be serving Princess Freydis from now on," she says.

Serving a princess? I have a new master? That's . . . my punishment?

Does this mean I'm not going to be killed?

Before I can ask, she leans against the heavy doors, pushing them open.

I let out a shaky breath, feeling the pressures of dread and confusion settle into their familiar knots within me as I follow her in.

The inside of the building is not what I expected. Instead of many chambers, there is one single, vast room, supported by columns. It reminds me of the banquet halls I once glimpsed at Koumbi Saleh, only this one is filled with shadow and torchlight. Rows and rows of tables and benches stretch out in front of us, enough to seat nearly half the city, at least. At the opposite end is a dais bearing a heavy-looking wooden chair. A throne. This must be where the king holds festivals for his people.

Right now the hall is nearly empty—save for three figures seated at the far table, another pair of guards, and a handful of servants standing behind them. The rich colors of the trio's clothing tells me they are the royals we came to see. Even at this distance, I feel the curious stares burning into me.

First among the trio is a severe-looking man. The king.

His features grow sharper as we approach. He's either an elder or a man aging before his time. The gold of his armbands twinkles in the light of the massive, blazing hearth in the center of the room. They look too heavy for his bony arms. He stares at me through lusterless eyes, and I feel every muscle in my body tense in response. There is something wrong with his *nyama,* a sickness I can't name.

To his right sits a lavishly adorned woman with straw-like hair twisted in braids around her head. Beside her is a girl who looks much the same as the woman must have looked at my age, her own wispy golden hair cascading freely down her shoulders. The way the woman sneers at me—along with the glittering baubles strewn across her chest, and the white fur draped around her shoulders—tells me she is the queen. The girl next to her must be the princess. Princess Freydis, Alvtir called her.

She doesn't strike me as much of a princess. Where her mother sits still and tall, with an air of regalness in her raised chin and disdainful expression, the princess hunches and squirms in her chair, her *nyama* wavering and unspooling at the seams. I find myself drifting closer to Alvtir, feeling as acutely aware of my difference, of my otherness, as I was when I first woke on her ship.

Alvtir takes her time leading me toward them. I glance around. Tapestry after tapestry line the walls of the hall, most of them depicting scenes of battle. Even the wooden columns have images of warriors carved into them. On the far wall hangs the same shield the warriors bore in Anfa—yellow with two dark birds on either side.

This entire hall is a tribute to war.

We come to a stop in front of the table. The smell of the meal they're eating washes over me, the scent so rich and varied that it makes me dizzy with equal parts hunger and nausea. Alvtir opens her muscled arms in greeting, and I notice that her wrists are cuffed with smooth, black skins fastened with red sinew. "My beloved family." She smirks.

Family.

She's one of them.

A royal.

I stiffen as a fiery burst of anger sweeps over me.

How could I have been so wrong about Alvtir in Anfa?

"She's as dark as a black elf," the king says, eyeing me up and down. It reminds me of the man who tried to buy me at the auction. "Are you sure you didn't take her from Svartalfheim?"

I ball my fists and shove away the memory before I do something

I'll regret. *Don't lose your head,* I steel myself. *You've made it this far. Now stay alive.*

I take a deep breath and hold my head high. Ignoring the king, I stare directly into the eyes of the princess. Her round, birdlike face twitches under my gaze. She fiddles nervously with her fingers and glances away, to her father. My stomach tightens with anger at the thought of what she must think of me. She in her delicate linen shift and brocaded red dress, and me in my simple thrall's shift and apron. Her skin whiter than the tusk of an elephant, and mine as brown as marula bark.

"This is the girl I mentioned," Alvtir says. "Her name is Yafeu."

"Can it speak?" asks the queen.

"I speak well enough." I spit the words like venom. The queen arches an eyebrow, but Alvtir chuckles.

"She's learned our tongue, but that's about all she's learned. Broskrap tells me she's useless in the fields."

I cut Alvtir a look. There's no way Broskrap would have said that. I know I wasn't useless—certainly not compared with his other thralls.

Why is she lying? What game is she playing?

Her face remains impassive, revealing nothing. "He said she's better suited for women's work," she continues. "He has no need for that, of course, but she'll make a fine maidservant for Freydis."

It's all I can do not to snort. *Women's work?* I'm the *least* suited for that. But a small cinder of hope sparks to life inside me: She must have some reason for moving me to the royal family—to *her* family.

Apparently losing interest, the king grabs a horn from a hole in the table and holds it out. Instantly, one of the thralls standing behind him, a boy several years younger than I, scurries over with a pitcher of amber liquid and refills it.

"Is that all, sister?" he asks, then takes a large gulp from the horn mid-pour.

Sister.

Before Alvtir can reply, the king jumps up, his chair tipping over from the force, and spits out his drink—all over the boy who poured it. I draw back instinctively. Even the princess and the queen flinch.

"What is this, Werian? Broskrap's barley wine?" he screams, his face red and twisted with rage. He sloshes the rest of the drink onto the quaking thrall boy for emphasis.

Unfazed, Alvtir shoots me a wink. It passes faster than Sogbo's lightning.

Did I just imagine that?

What in all the gods' names is happening here?

"Bring me some real ale, you chicken-brained fool!"

"Y-yes, my lord." The poor thrall boy rushes past us, disappearing out the front door.

I stand stiffly, utterly bewildered.

Alvtir clears her throat. "If I may take my leave, brother, I have my own meal waiting for me at home."

The king dismisses her with a wave of his hand. He resumes gorging himself on his meal, his face as dull as before, as if his outburst never happened. Begrudgingly, or so it seems to me, the queen picks up her fork as well.

Alvtir starts toward the door, leaving me standing there. I turn to stare at her receding form.

"Thank you, Aunt Alvtir!" Freydis calls after her. I wince at her tone, so giddy and shallow. Like I'm some trinket Alvtir has gifted her.

Freydis scoots off her chair and approaches me. Her shy smile immediately fills me with an acidic hatred. She has the round, childlike face of a girl who has never gone without a meal. Pale-yellow eyebrows sit atop wide, mossy-green eyes brimming with innocence. An innocence I recognize only because I lost my own long ago.

"Here, I'll show you to your room!" She practically skips with glee. Reluctantly, I follow her out the back door.

The usual chirp of insects greets us outside. Mawu is only a sliver in the sky. I blink, my eyes adjusting to the darkness as she leads me toward another dim set of structures at the back of the hilltop.

"Next time, you should grab a torch from the hall . . . for light. A torch. Fire." Freydis speaks deliberately, as if I'm slow-minded. As if I haven't been forced to speak her slippery tongue for the last two moons.

"Are there any torches left, or did your father's spittle put them all out?"

To my surprise, Freydis lets out a high-pitched giggle. Then she clamps her hand over her mouth, as though the giggle escaped without her permission. "You mustn't disrespect the king."

Silence thickens the air between us. She drops back to walk at my side. "What was your name again?" she ventures. "Yafoo? Is that right?" She butchers it the same way Alvtir did the first time.

"*Yafeu,*" I say through gritted teeth.

"*Ya-fe-u,*" she echoes, emphasizing each syllable. "I'm sorry; I promise I'll remember it from now on."

There's genuine contrition in her tone. For a moment, I almost regret being rude.

But then I remember Mama crying out as the slavers tackled her to the ground. Kamo's and Goleh's screams in the smoky air. Ampah's limp body dragging across the sand. My own desiccated body crumpling helplessly as the merchant's blade pierced my shoulder. The warm spray of his blood as Alvtir's sword sliced through his skull. *Aunt* Alvtir. I remember how *Aunt* Alvtir rescued me—only to throw me into slavery the moment we landed in this cold, gray place. I remember that this princess is my *master,* just like Broskrap was before her. And whatever concern I felt for her *feelings* evaporates into the night air.

"My name is—"

"Freydis." I cut her off. "I know."

Freydis leads me to a squat, shoddily built shed next to a sizable longhouse. No doubt the thralls' shed, from the look of it. At least it doesn't smell like livestock.

"Do you have a task for me tonight, or can I go to sleep now?" I keep my voice flat.

She cocks her head to the side like a bird. "This—this is not how Mother and Helge are," she stammers. Tentatively, she reaches for my hand. It takes every ounce of control I have not to yank it back and slap her. Instead I let it hang limply in her grasp. She brightens, apparently mistaking my restraint for acceptance. "You're my maidservant now, but I also want us to be friends."

A strange feeling bubbles up inside me. I can't help it; I start to laugh. Freydis drops my hand and soon I'm leaning with my palms on my knees, convulsing with laughter. My belly aches and tears fill my eyes, blurring my vision.

"*Friends!*" I choke out through peals of laughter. "*Friends!*" Her expression, pinched with confusion and worry, fills me with a morbid joy, and I laugh even harder.

Eventually, the laughter subsides, and I wipe my eyes, breathing deeply until my lungs are filled again. Suddenly exhausted, I ask again, "Can I go to bed?"

Speechless, Freydis opens the door and gestures into the dark room. I take a hesitant step inside. The fire has almost gone out; in the glow of the embers I can just make out a small, simple room with benches skirting the two longer walls. On the far bench, a form stirs awake.

The haggard face of an older woman peeks out from underneath a fur. The creases on her forehead deepen as she scowls at Freydis. "What is it?" she asks sharply.

"Sorry, Helge," Freydis says quickly. "Just showing Yafeu where she'll sleep."

Sorry? She's apologizing to a thrall?

"You'll be sharing this room with Helge," she says to me. "Mother had her prepare a bed for you."

A bed. How long has it been since I slept in one of those? I nod

slowly, my eyes trailing from the fur-covered bench to a wooden
tub in the corner. I point at it. "To bathe?" I ask, my heart quickening at the appearance of this new luxury.

"Yes. There is a well outside. You can use the fire to heat the
water and then pour it into the bath."

A thrill runs through me. I turn around to face her. "I'd like to
use it in the morning," I say, already picturing how glorious the
warm water will feel on my skin.

Freydis's wide eyes meet mine for a peculiar moment before she
scans my body. "That will be good. You're a member of the king's
household now. You'll need to look presentable." Her tone has
taken on a clipped, haughty edge, the pretense of friendship all but
dropped.

Good. I'd rather she act like who she is.

"I'll return for you tomorrow morning." And with that, she
leaves.

"Don't you even *dream* of using my washtub," Helge hisses at me
the moment the door shuts. "Your filthy skin will blacken the
wood."

Her spiteful words hit me like a punch to the gut. I suck in a
breath. I can almost feel the hatred emanating from her as she rolls
to face the wall without another word.

I guess we won't be friends either, Helge.

I crawl onto the open bed and am surprised to find that the
bench is lined with animal skins underneath the fur. There's even a
straw-stuffed pillow. I let out a sigh, trying to force myself to find
pleasure in this new comfort. But as I lie on my back, gazing at a
single star through the tiny smoke hole in the center of the shed, a
feeling I can't name creeps over me. Not regret, not anguish, but
akin to both.

I can't get Broskrap's face out of my head. The shock and rage
etched into his features. His tongue lolling open. The blood pooling
around him.

I've taken lives before today—the lives of countless animals. But never the life of another person. I've *wanted* to: I would have killed that merchant in Anfa if I'd had the chance, and the same goes for every one of the slavers. If Alvtir had let me join her army, I would have inevitably slain many soldiers in battle, or died trying.

So why do I feel this way now? I know in my heart that Broskrap deserved it. Despite what Airé said afterward, I could never have stood by and let him rape her. He acted like an animal, so I slaughtered him like one.

None of these thoughts bring relief. The feeling remains, hot and cold, heavy and hollow all at once, gummed to the inside of my skin.

Trembling, I reach for the painted wolf at my neck. As I finger the familiar grooves, I hear Mama's calm, flowing voice in my memory: *When you were a child, it was my duty to teach you balance. To teach you restraint. But you are a woman now, and it is up to you to decide who you wish to be.*

Oh Mama, I failed you. This can't be the great destiny you saw for me. I acted without thinking again, and now I can't undo what I did. Airé and Bronaugh are better off without me. And Broskrap's sons . . . Broskrap's sons are orphans now. Because of me.

I don't know how long I lie there like that, but when sleep finally opens its arms to me, I fall willingly into its embrace.

My narrow gaze focuses on a two-legged figure running through the forest. Mawu's soft light streams through the overhanging branches and creates a passage, seemingly following the figure ahead. I realize that I'm charging after him. My padded paws strike the dirt two at a time, front and back, front and back. The wind combs my fur. I'm getting closer, closer . . .

It's so much easier to hunt this way. I'll overtake him so soon, in just a few moments, and now I'm almost on him—but I'm in pain. I can't feel it, but I know somehow that I'm wounded. Badly. I glance at my shoulder. Thick, sticky blood matts my dark-gray pelt, spreading across my body from two stab wounds.

No matter. I have him now. I leap up on my hind legs just as the figure turns around and hurls another dagger at me. I know his sparse, too-pale hair, his pink skin, his furrowed brow—it's Broskrap.

The dagger sinks into my neck. My body crumples, defeated. I can't move anymore. I can only watch out of the corner of my eye as Broskrap staggers toward me. Mawu's faint light illuminates his face, but then darkness spreads inward from the edges of my vision and envelops him, and I know I am dying.

I feel him kneel by my side, and when the light emerges once again, it isn't Broskrap but me, my face, peering down at myself.

It's strange to see what I look like. It's like a reflection in a still, clear pond. The wide, full mouth reminds me of Mama, set in a somber line; the strong jaw and long eyelashes I inherited from Papa. My dark-brown hand reaches out to touch my bloodied muzzle.

Suddenly I am looking through my eyes again, looking down at the dying wolf. But it's not a wolf anymore—it's Alvtir. Or Alvtir's head on the body of the wolf. The blood trickling from her lips is a vibrant red against the bone-whiteness of her skin. I recoil, both disgusted and entranced, unable to tear my gaze from the sight.

Her jagged breath catches in her throat. "All hail the dark queen," she rasps. She flashes me a smile, her fangs covered in blood, and from the depths of my being rises a blinding panic . . .

I sit up with a start. Dread hardens like clay in my stomach. The room is unfamiliar; it takes me a moment to remember where I am. I touch my clammy forehead and squint at Helge's cot across the room. Her chest rises and falls to the slow beat of deep sleep.

It was just a dream.

I breathe a sigh of relief before falling back.

18

FREYDIS

Over the next moon, I try everything in my power to coax Yafeu out of her shell. But nothing I do or say seems to work. If I ask her about herself, she responds with a vague, clipped answer. If I offer to share in her tasks, she'll complete them more quickly just to avoid my company. I even gave her an old shift and dress of mine to replace that scratchy thrall's apron, and she wrinkled her nose and held them away from her with two fingers, as if my clothes stank like a day-old flounder and she didn't want the scent to trail her. She's like Frey before he married Gerd, always surly and brooding. My only solace is that she doesn't seem to want *any* company. She keeps her distance from the other thralls, and they do the same in return.

You think she'd be grateful to be saved from the life of a farmhand! But Aunt Alvtir's assessment that Yafeu would be suited to women's work was ... well, it doesn't seem to me that Yafeu has *ever* done a woman's task in her life. She can tend to the garden and spin yarn well enough, but the nimbler arts of sewing and weaving require a patience she clearly does not possess.

Things must be very different where she's from. It is whispered that there are great monsters in Africa, dragons that breathe fire and beasts as large as twenty men. I asked Yafeu about them once, but she merely laughed in my face again.

It seems the only response I can provoke from her is ridicule or contempt. So much for having a loyal friend and confidante, like Mother has in Helge.

I have nothing to look forward to until my wedding next spring, but every time my thoughts turn to King Hakon, a bud of panic starts blooming in my chest. All I can do is lash my mind to the tasks of the day, and try to think little of the fate the Norns have woven for me. Still, in the dark of night—when sleep eludes me, when I feel most sharply alone—I can't help but ponder their design.

Yafeu and I are doing our weaving outside this afternoon, sitting barefoot on an eiderdown in the kitchen garden and enjoying the unseasonably mild weather. At least, *I'm* enjoying it. The herbs and vegetables have mostly been harvested, but the autumn phlox are in full bloom around the edges of the plot, lending the air a fresh and powdery scent. Birdsongs mingle overhead, filling the silence between us.

We're working on a small, oblong tapestry, which I'll bring with me to Trøndelag to hang in my new longhouse. I'm adding some patterning to the scene while Yafeu sulks over my extra handloom, beating the coarse wool threads that I'll use for the trimming. Her legs are stretched out in front of her, but her back is somehow as straight as a plank of oakwood. She *never* hunches. In fact, she doesn't carry herself like any thrall I've ever known; there's no trace of deference in her bearing at all.

As usual, her thick, dark hair is woven into two tight braids. I often wonder what it looks like when it's down.

I reach over absentmindedly and touch the end of one of the

braids. She jerks back and glares at me, as though I've just struck her.

"I'm sorry," I say quickly. "I-I was just curious to know what your hair felt like."

"Why?"

"Because it's so different from mine."

"*I'm* different from you." The reply slides off her tongue with ease.

Before I can think of a response, the wooden gate swings open with a loud groan. I look over to see Mother trudging toward us, the golden brooches of her woad-blue dress glinting in the sunlight. Helge, as always, trails behind her.

I quickly pull my boots back on. Mother will scold me if there's even a trace of dirt on my feet. *You can't be running around barefoot when you're a queen,* she always says.

"Mother," I call out, "come look at the tapestry Yafeu and I are working on." I hold out the loom for her to see. "It's Odin, offering his eye to Mimir in exchange for a drink from the Well of Knowledge."

"Is that what I should tell your father?" She stops in front of us, a hand resting on her slender hip. "That you and your new maidservant are idling in the garden instead of making your wedding dress?"

Helge's eyes flit to Yafeu and she snorts, echoing Mother's disapproval.

"But the wedding isn't for many moons," I begin, confused. "I didn't think—"

"Precisely: You didn't think. Knowing you, you'd wait until the very last moment to begin, and I'd have no time to fix your mistakes."

Heat rushes to my cheeks. My stomach seems to sink to the earth, dragging my chest and shoulders inward. Mother is right: I've been putting off the dressmaking, even after Father bought me two ells of the finest silk from Bulghar. It's foolish of me.

Still, I'd rather avoid a good beating today. Even if I deserve it.

"I—I thought this could be my wedding present to King Hakon," I offer. "A tapestry to adorn his hall."

"Hakon doesn't care about *tapestries,* Freydis. He'll have your dowry as his gift. All *you* must do is bear him an heir. That's all any man ever . . ." She trails off, the color draining from her face.

"Mother," I jump in. "Perhaps it's your dress, or the way the sunlight is hitting you just now, but you look very beautiful today. Not that you don't look beautiful all the time—of course, you do. It's just—"

"Put this foolishness aside and begin working on your dress at once," she snaps.

I gaze up into her hazel eyes. I wish I could have inherited her eyes instead of Father's. They're so much lovelier, with flecks of brown and green merging like dapples of light on the forest floor. Visitors to the hall often remark that we look much alike, but I can't imagine I'm even close to as beautiful as she is. "Yes, Mother. I'm sorry. We'll start right away."

I glance at Yafeu, who is studying Mother with an odd expression. There's something about her gaze that's . . . unyielding. Nerves start to gather in the pit of my stomach.

I look back to Mother. Something like bewilderment flickers across her own proud visage; shock that a thrall would dare to look at her like that. A long, tense moment passes, and I fear she might raise a hand and strike Yafeu. But then she turns abruptly and marches off, her hands lifting her shift over the dirt. Helge makes a sour face at Yafeu before hurrying after her.

I let out a sigh at the unfinished embroidery on my handloom. I've only gotten as far as Odin's arm, holding out his eye.

"Your mother is not like mine," Yafeu says.

I look over at her, surprised. Despite Mother's orders, she resumes pummeling the threads with a vengeance, gripping the shuttle like a bludgeon. "No matter what you do, she finds fault with you."

I swallow, picking at the new row of knots on my tapestry. "It seems like no one displeases her more," I say. "Well, except Aunt Alvtir."

"What about Alvtir?" Yafeu turns to me intently. "Why does she get to be a warrior? How many women are there like her?"

"*Get* to be a warrior?" I can't believe my ears. "No one *wants* to be like Alvtir."

"I do."

I can almost feel myself pale. "You don't know what you're saying, Yafeu."

She grimaces. Yet again, I've disappointed her, and I've no idea why.

Her eyes drop to my handloom, gazing over the unfinished tapestry. "You are *nyamakalaw*."

"I'm what?"

"A maker. You have a craft."

"This? Oh. It's just something to pass the time." I search her expression for some hint of mockery, but she appears earnest.

"Who is this 'Odin'?" She taps the eye in his hand with her long forefinger.

"Odin is the Allfather, of course. The first among all the gods. And the ruler of Valhalla."

"Valhalla?"

"A magnificent hall in a world beyond our own, where the spirits of warriors go after they fall in battle. Well, only the best, most noble warriors—those chosen by Odin and the Valkyries."

"Valhalla." Yafeu repeats the word slowly, as though weighing the sound of it on her tongue. She fixes me with that strange look again. "Will Alvtir go to Valhalla?"

I frown to myself. I've never thought about that. I never give Alvtir much thought in general, other than the occasional shudder. Mother has always told me to keep my distance, lest the curse latch onto me. But Yafeu seems particularly interested in Alvtir for some reason.

Sometime soon, I'll have to warn her about the curse. But not now—not when we're finally having a real conversation. "I don't know," I admit. "I'm not sure women are allowed into Valhalla."

This seems to upset Yafeu all over again. She swings her legs in and climbs to her feet.

"B-but the Valkyries are women, so maybe she will," I blurt out, trying to salvage her interest. "And Odin himself is . . . effeminate."

She pauses. "What do you mean?"

"He is a *seidr*, a sorcerer," I explain. "And sorcery is women's work."

Her brow furrows. "So . . . a womanly man rules over all the best warriors?"

"I—I never thought about it like that!"

She smiles, revealing dimples in the hollow of her cheeks. The sight is so unexpected that I can't help but smile back. She lets out a giggle, and suddenly, I'm giggling too. How did I never realize before how *odd* that is?

When our laughter subsides, I open my mouth to tell her about Frigg, Thor, and the twins Freya and Frey as well, but at the last moment, curiosity gets the better of me. "And who is *your* supreme god?" I ask instead.

"What do you mean?"

"The . . . highest god—the one above all others."

"Well, Nana Buluku is the creator, the First One. But in my home, we worship Mawu-Lisa above all others."

"Mawooliseh," I say, trying to mimic the unfamiliar sounds. "And what is he like?"

"*Mawu-Lisa* is not a 'he,'" Yafeu corrects.

My mouth falls open. "Your supreme god is a *woman*?"

"Nana Buluku is a woman, but Mawu-Lisa is neither. They are both he *and* she. Lisa"—she points to the sun—"is the male side. And Mawu, the moon, is the female side. Together, they are one." She clasps her hands together for emphasis. "Complete. Their oneness created order in the universe, and their offspring are the many gods of sky and earth and water."

I've never heard of a being who is both male and female before. It's wondrous in its strangeness. "We have something like that—well, not like *that,* but . . . Sól is what we call the sun, and she is a 'she.' And Máni is the moon, and he is a 'he.' "

Yafeu nods, almost to herself. We sit in silence for a moment. Unbidden, my mind drifts back to Mother. I climb to my feet, brushing dirt that isn't there off my dress. "We should leave before Mother returns," I say. "She'll kill me if my wedding dress isn't finished by Skammdegí."

"Skammdegí?" Yafeu stands.

"The coldest, darkest days of the year."

A dire look crosses her face. "It gets *colder*?"

I laugh, but she doesn't join me this time. "Do you not have winter where you're from?"

"Winter?"

I explain the changing of the seasons as she follows me out of the garden and past the cookhouse, with its clang of pots and pans and the muted chatter of the kitchen thralls preparing dinner. In turn, Yafeu tells me there are only two seasons where she is from: the season with rains, and the season without. *Both* seasons are hotter than our summers, she says.

We amble past the Great Hall. "I can't imagine half the year passing without a drop of rain. Nor summer lasting all year long!"

"I never thought I would . . ." She stiffens, falling silent. It takes me a moment to realize that she's listening to the door guards' conversation around the corner. They carry on loudly, ignorant of our approach.

I recognize Orm's voice first: "Broskrap has been known to visit Old Man Ødger's farm in Nideby. They say he's probably gone there to—"

"—I know what they say and I don't believe a word of it." Now it's Gunnar, one of Father's older guards. "I've actually *been* to Nideby, lad. There's no pleasure to be had there that Broskrap's own holding lacks. It's likelier he finally drank himself in."

Yafeu looks as though she's just swallowed a beetle. I frown, confused, before remembering: Uncle Broskrap was her master before me. She must not have heard that he's gone missing.

"Drank himself in, did he!" Orm snorts. "Broskrap's no soldier, but he's no woman, either. Not when it comes to holding his ale."

"Accidents can happen when a man is oversoaked. And Broskrap is too often oversoaked. Or *was*."

They stop speaking abruptly as we round the corner, coming into view. Gunnar nods politely, but Orm turns scarlet and bows low. I wave back to them both.

When we're safely out of their earshot, I turn to Yafeu. "You must be worried about Broskrap's disappearance."

She winces. "Yes."

I'm ashamed of my own selfishness. I've been so intent on befriending her myself that I didn't even think to mention the news. "I'm sure he'll turn up soon," I say, trying to sound reassuring.

In truth, I'm as skeptical as Gunnar is. No one has seen Uncle Broskrap at the harbor since the *hird*'s return. If he'd gone to visit one of his friends among the jarls, he certainly would have been sighted leaving Skíringssal. A drunken incident is a far likelier, if sadder, story. Or worse: Uncle Broskrap *was* known for his appetites . . . perhaps a dishonored husband, or even a wronged woman . . . But no, I shouldn't let my imagination run wild. For all I know, he'll turn up soon, and then I'll feel ashamed for indulging in such speculation.

I lead Yafeu around the back of the longhouse, to the door that goes directly to my room. From the lack of guards out front, Mother is probably in the Great Hall with Father; still, I'd rather not risk another confrontation.

Just as I'm about to push the door open, a high-pitched squeal sounds from inside.

Fear grips me. I stop short, locking eyes with Yafeu. She notes my expression and nods once, letting me know she understands the situation.

An intruder. From the creaking of the floorboards, maybe more than one.

Who could have gotten past Orm and Gunnar *and* the watchtower guard? Are they so distracted, or is it someone they know?

Summoning a courage I didn't know I possessed, I push the door open just a hair. Yafeu and I peer inside through the open crack.

The fire in the hearth has gone out, but with sunlight filtering through the smoke hole, I can recognize the two figures frolicking around the room.

It's Astrid, the glass-maker's daughter, and her friend Solvi, a weaver. They were my playmates when we were young, though things changed once we grew old enough to understand the difference in our stations. They became more formal around me, more distant. We still trade pleasantries and idle gossip when we run into each other at the market, but they haven't come to visit me in years.

"That's *Princess* Freydis to you, Solvi," chirps Astrid, her voice falsely high. "Now fetch me a pail of water—and make sure it's fresh from the springs of Himinbjörg, not well-water, like you would give a common milkmaid!"

Heat crawls up my ears. My hands begin to tremble.

"Oh, *Princess,* is that how you keep your hair as golden as Sif's?" Solvi replies, matching her tone.

"The goddess only *wishes* her hair were as golden as mine!"

I feel my entire body spasm, then crumple with humiliation. I move quietly to leave, avoiding Yafeu's eyes—but she coughs loudly and swings the door wide open, revealing us.

The two girls freeze. A long, excruciating moment goes by.

"There you are, Princess Freydis," Astrid says, elbowing Solvi. They bow in unison. "We, uh ..."

"We heard the news of your engagement, and we came to pay our respects," Solvi finishes for her.

I force a smile. "How kind." But it slips as I recognize the too-tight dresses they're wearing, one of a gauzy, madder red and the other a thick, fustic yellow wool. Both girls have much ampler bosoms than I, and they look to be bursting out of my clothes. "Are those my dresses?" I blurt out—and immediately feel like an idiot for asking.

"Oh, we were just . . . entertaining ourselves, while we waited for you to return." Now Solvi is the one faltering. She shoots Astrid a stricken look.

Yafeu glances between the pair of them and me, wondering what to make of all this. My face must be redder than Orm's by now.

If only a hole would appear in the floorboard and swallow me up. I could go live with the hidden folk underground. I would never have to see Astrid and Solvi—or Yafeu—ever again.

I feign a light laugh, though it comes out more like a squeak. "They suit you far better than they suit me! Keep them, please."

I'll pay sorely for those dresses if Mother ever finds out they're missing. And if Father ever finds out . . . I'll have to say I ruined them and bear the punishment alone. He would have Astrid and Solvi executed for this. Perhaps their families too.

Their shoulders sag with blatant relief. "Thank you," Astrid mumbles, bowing again.

"You're too kind, Princess," Solvi adds.

"Come again soon, my friends! We'll celebrate properly, with a barrel of fine mead!"

Without another word, the two of them rush past us so quickly that a *whoosh* of warm air follows in their wake.

I stride into the empty room. Tears burn behind my eyes, but I desperately try to blink them away.

"Ah, here they are!" I force some brightness into my voice as I fish around my sewing basket for the ells of silk and a ball of pins. I practically throw the whole bundle into Yafeu's arms. "You can get started. I'll join you shortly." Just to give myself an excuse to turn away, I kneel at the hearth and gather the embers into a pile, poking them needlessly with the fire iron.

Please, Odin, Frigg, any god who will hear me—don't let me cry in front of Yafeu.

YAFEU

A silver armband lies on the floor of Freydis's room, dropped by one of the girls in their haste. I lean down and pick it up. After I lay the silk out on the sewing table, I take a moment to analyze the interlocking markings etched into the sides. They remind me of the markings on the doors of the Great Hall, and on the raised stone in front of them.

Why was Freydis so nice to those "friends" of hers? They were *mocking* her; we both saw it before we walked in. Even to her face, they were hardly kind.

I think of Masireh and the boys in my village. When I caught them snickering behind my back like that, I made them pay, in bruises and a broken nose.

But another memory supplants that one, sliding unbidden into my mind's eye. Masireh used to have a dog—a tall, slender thing, all skin and bones—that he and the other boys would take with them on hunts. Masireh was particularly cruel to it, often taking out the frustration of a fruitless hunt on the poor creature. I saw him kick it in the gut on more than one occasion, which the other boys found amusing and I found horrifying. Even at the best of times, Masireh seemed indifferent to its presence. I never once saw him pat its head or scratch it behind the ears.

But the dog never stopped following Masireh around. It was like his shadow. No matter how cruel Masireh was to it, no matter how brutally he beat it or how often he ignored it, it still hovered behind him everywhere he went, waiting for the pat that never came.

Freydis reminds me of that dog.

At the realization, I feel some of my hatred toward her ebbing away, like a tide receding at dawn. I slip the armband into my pocket.

With the fire crackling to life again, Freydis saunters over with a stool and an armful of clothes. She hands me one of her dresses—"for reference," she says—then takes a seat across from me.

I pin the silk around the dress in silence for a while. I debate saying nothing; silence is a welcome change from Freydis's usual mindless chatter. But a nagging sense of sympathy gets the better of me: "Who *were* those girls?"

Freydis scratches her cheek. "What do you mean? They're my friends."

Our eyes lock for a moment. She sighs and folds her hands in her lap. "It's better to have false friends than no friends at all," she says softly.

"I'm not so sure." When she doesn't respond, I put the pins down and take the silver armband from my pocket. "This reminds me of the pieces my mother used to make," I say, holding it up in the firelight. Though the markings are foreign, the overall design *is* like something Mama would come up with.

A faint smile tugs at her lips. "It's one of the first pieces I ever bought for myself. Mother usually picks out my jewelry for me; she doesn't approve of my taste. But I chose this one, and I will always cherish it." She points to one of the markings with a slender forefinger. "These are called runes. This one represents protection. And this one here"—she points to another—"represents partnership, with family, friends, or a loved one."

"So it *is* a language."

She lets her hand fall. "Your mother must be quite skilled if this reminds you of her work."

I nod. "She made this." I say, taking my necklace out from behind the shift.

Freydis leans in to inspect it. She runs her thumb reverently over the surface of the wolf. "It's beautiful."

We both gaze at Mama's necklace for a while, her studying its delicate ferocity, me lost in the memory of my last hunt, when I encountered the painted wolf.

The thought of hunting unleashes the restlessness inside me. Only this time, the restlessness blooms into possibility—an impulse to seize on this unexpected moment with Freydis. A grin steals over my face.

Freydis notices the change in me. "What is it?"

I grab her hand. "I'll work on the dress all day tomorrow. Tonight, let's do something fun."

She arches an eyebrow. "What do you have in mind?"

19

ALVTIR

The soldiers are a sorry sight. I scan their faces as they wait for me to explain why I've called them to our sparring grounds so soon after the last raid. They're huddled together like livestock in the wide clearing, eyes ringed with fatigue, wooden sparring swords limp at their sides. A brisk wind sharpens the dreariness of the cold, gray morning. It's almost as if the gods are announcing their displeasure.

At the edge of the crowd, my shield maidens—Hetha, Wisna, and young Ranveig—stand tall and proud. There's only one of them for every few dozen men, but they shine like silver amid iron.

Hetha, as always, is the first to speak: "Forgive me, Alvtir, but why have you gathered us here?"

"You're wondering why we're training so soon after the summer raid," I address all the soldiers at once.

The men shuffle awkwardly. I unsheathe Angrboda and draw it up to eye level. Even in the thin autumn sunlight, the runes seem to glimmer. The blade was made from the gods' own iron; I myself watched it hurtle down to Midgard from the stars. There are rumors among the soldiers that Odin had the dwarves Dvalin and Durin forge the sword and then sent it as a gift to me to show his favor. I always show it off when I need to bend their minds to my will.

Or to my brother's will.

"The king has ordered us to return to Iberia," I announce. "We leave tomorrow. Prepare yourselves for a long journey."

Murmurs ripple around me, and I catch many a sore glance being shared. But the good soldiers—my shield maidens, and the handful of true warriors among the men—meet my order with fire in their eyes. It makes my heart sink. I've trained them too well; they don't doubt me even when they should.

I hold up my hand, and the murmurs die down. "Pair off for sparring."

Soon the dull *thwack* of wood on wood fills the air. I weave my way around, checking their form, their vigor. Assessing who is too old or too young for the journey ahead.

"You'd be dead in an instant on the battlefield!" I snap at one of the younger men as he stumbles away from Ingmar, one of my best soldiers. "Remember your footing!"

"We're sparring, are we?" a nasally voice rings out. I grimace as Snorri emerges from behind a wide oak trunk.

Loki's damn insolence. I was hoping the little coward would be too busy searching for his missing father to join. "Some of us," I sniff.

"Tell me, cousin: Why should the king send us out to sea again so soon after the last raid? Or are you simply looking for a new thrall to warm your bed?" He smirks at his own jest and surveys the men with an air of command that makes me eager to wring his scrawny neck.

I spit on the ground at his feet. "The king's reasons are his to keep. You're welcome to join us, of course, but I thought you'd be out searching for your father."

He goes rigid, and my blood surges in triumph. I lean closer, whispering right into his ear: "Perhaps he couldn't bear what a disappointment you've become, so he leapt to his death from the cliffs."

Snorri grips the hilt of his sparring sword as a tremor of anger racks his body. "It looks like you still need a sparring partner, Alvtir."

Ah, finally.

I furrow my brow, feigning surprise. "I would be honored, Snorri, son of Broskrap."

Snorri interrupts the nearest spar and grabs a wooden sword and shield off one of the soldiers. The two men turn to watch, cheering in excitement as Snorri begins circling me.

I sheathe my sword. Hetha, as though hearing my thoughts, appears at my side and hands me her own sparring sword and shield. After all, the only wounds I need to inflict are to his pride. For now.

One by one, the *hird*men abandon their own matches and turn to watch. Their whoops and shouts create a chorus. Either I'm not the only one who wants to see Snorri receive a healthy dose of humility, or he's not the only one who wants to see me fall.

Either way, I will show them what it means to be Odin's chosen warrior.

The wind picks up to a howl as Snorri stalks around me, hatred flashing in his eyes. I allow him to believe he has an opening, knowing he won't strike until he sees the advantage. Right away he takes a quick jab. I parry it, shuffle forward, and knock my shield hard against his, sending him staggering back. Guffaws from the onlookers bounce off the trees.

Good. At least some of the men are rooting for their *stallari.*

I grin, baring my teeth. Snorri hesitates, his gaze flitting down to my mouth.

I can't help but laugh at his cowardice. It's enough to remind him of his rage and he lunges at me, sparring sword high overhead, but I sidestep the blow. It grazes my shoulder regardless. I bite my cheek against the pain. No doubt I'll have splinters to pick out later. Perhaps I've grown a little overconfident in my old age.

His sparring sword continues downward and ricochets off the ground. Taking advantage of his momentum, I stomp on the forearm of his sword hand, just hard enough to leave a nasty bruise but not break it.

He screeches, the sword falling from his grasp as his body hits the grass with a satisfying *thud*. He rolls on his side and curls around his arm like a newborn babe. Probably fighting the urge to wail like one, too.

I smirk at the agony on his face. It's an improvement from his usual snivel. Some paces away, Hetha and Wisna share an amused look, and Ranveig doesn't bother to suppress her giggle.

Good. No woman worth her salt has sympathy for Snorri Broskrapsson, and he should know it.

The *hird*men, for their part, look away in disgust. Some are pretending to be very interested in the oak leaves withering off the branches. Snorri is a captain, so they won't add insult to his injury, but I'm sure he can feel their revulsion as clearly as the pain in his forearm. I don't blame them; I'd be ashamed of any brother-in-arms who succumbed so fully to such a minor injury. They peel off one by one, resuming their own spars.

I turn around, making like I'm going to walk away, as though the match is over. Fighting his shame, Snorri tries to stand too quickly. Just the error I was counting on. I whip around and headbutt him, eliciting another shriek as he grabs his nose, now gushing blood.

"To Alvtir—" Ranveig cries out, raising her sparring sword. I silence her with a stern look. Gloating is a game for nithings. Battle has proven what needed proving; it always does.

"Enough for today," I say, raising my voice to address the men and women alike. "Go back to wherever you call home. We'll meet again at midday tomorrow."

Snorri picks his wooden sparring sword off the ground with his uninjured arm and scurries away without a word.

As I watch him disappear into the forest, I can't help but wonder if it was wise to make even more of a foe of him. I know better than anyone how destructive the enmity of weak men can be. But I needed to squash any question of allegiance in the men's hearts. It took years to earn that allegiance, and only a moment's falter would shatter it. That's the curse of being a woman who leads: They're always hungry for me to fail, for a man to best me. And just as a snake strikes when the bear lets down her guard, I know Snorri will try to take the *hird* from me as soon as he sees an opportunity.

When that day comes, I can only hope that I've proven myself worthy of their loyalty.

20

YAFEU

We hike into the northeastern woods with Lisa low at our backs. Freydis led me in a wide, confusing arc, skirting the far edge of the king's orchards before doubling back into the foothills. I assume it's so we won't be seen.

As Mawu's reign begins to take hold, the forest becomes something Other. Its *nyama* both quiets and quickens, thrumming with a different kind of life: the life of night creatures stirring from their slumber. Our dusk is their dawn.

A brook babbles in the distance. The sound carries with it the thought of Broskrap's body. That stream runs east; his corpse could be in these same woods by now. If there's anything left of it.

I shove the unsettling thought away, refocusing on my new surroundings. The trees here are old and sturdy, with fewer of the spindly, spiky-leaved trees that abounded outside the farmland. I'm no stranger to an evening spent in the bush, to letting my ears take over for my eyes as my guide. But this forest is still strange to me, with unknown animals and unknown spirits. I feel like I have the ears of a newborn baby, like I'm just getting acquainted with all the sounds of life outside the womb. There's that rhythmic chirping in the air again. The rustles of bushy-tailed rodents, or maybe a lizard, skittering through the underbrush away from our footsteps. An owl calls down from the treetops, asking *who, who* are you, to step foot in this sacred place?

Night owl. That's what Ampah used to call me, because I used to love the night. I thought that part of me had died, but I wonder if it wasn't just . . . asleep, and now it's waking up again.

The thought of Ampah should make me sad, but, somehow, it doesn't. I feel like I've fallen into a strange trance. I feel acutely present in my body, yet I sense the familiar abstraction of a dream-state. Every rustle becomes the whisper of spirits, every gnarled branch the arm of an ancestor clawing its way back to life.

A dry twig bends back, caught on the coarse fibers of my cloak. "Ow!" Freydis complains as it smacks her, drawing me from my reverie.

"Oops," I mutter. I'm not used to maneuvering with so many layers; they add an unwieldy girth to my body. Even my hunter's tunic—an item I've sorely missed—was not nearly as heavy as the clothes the *Majūs* have to wear to brave the cold.

I can't help but smirk as Freydis edges closer to my back. "You're okay," I say coolly. I can feel her *nyama* as clearly as I can hear every one of her clumsy footsteps; she's about as comfortable in the forest as I am at the loom.

Maybe we should have waited until dawn to go hunting. In Wagadu, Lisa's rise offered more safety from predators. And even though Mawu's face is supposed to be full and fat in the sky tonight, only a small portion of her light can reach us through the thick canopy; it's easy to avoid smacking into a trunk but harder to detect any tracks. But Freydis insisted we go in the evening, so we wouldn't risk running into other hunters. She sent word through Helge that she was feeling unwell and wanted to rest through dinner, so no one will be looking for us until tomorrow.

"Is this your first time outside of the city?" I ask, more to distract her than out of curiosity.

"No, but I don't get to leave very often. And I *never* go into the woods . . ." She pauses, then lowers her voice to a whisper. "Helge once told me there are trolls living in these woods."

"Trolls?"

"Monsters. Big ones. They eat human children."

I smother a laugh. "I'm guessing Helge told you this when you were a child?"

"Yes," she says soberly, completely missing my point. I'm suddenly overcome by the urge to whip around and shake her, just to frighten her further. As amusing as it would be, she'd probably scream loud enough to scatter all the prey for miles around.

And there will be prey, I think to myself with satisfaction, noting a pair of scratch marks on a trunk as we pass. Back in Wagadu, the male antelope used their antlers to scrape bark off the trees during mating season. When I described antelope to Freydis earlier, she said they were called deer and they lived in these woods too, but I almost didn't believe her, since I haven't tasted their meat or seen their hides anywhere. The sight of their tracks is as comforting as it is thrilling: Finally, I can use the skills I acquired in my old life in my new one.

"She also told me—" I cover her mouth with my hand, silencing her.

Hushed voices. And footsteps. Coming nearer.

I yank Freydis behind the scratched tree. Its trunk is far too thin to conceal us both, but we don't have time to find a better hiding spot.

". . . will see to your safety if what you claim is true, Chlothar." The voice is nasally, grating.

"I swear by your gods and mine, I have spoken only the truth, my lord," comes the timorous reply.

"*If* that is so, then all will be forgiven. But until I have proof, you will speak of this to no one. Once we are certain, I will tell the king myself. Do you understand?"

"Of course, my lord. I will keep my silence."

"Good." The footsteps stop. "If I find that you've betrayed me . . ." The nasally voice falls silent. My heart quickens.

"Lord?"

The *swish* of a sword being unsheathed. I hold my breath.

"You there, behind the tree. Reveal yourselves." A command, not a question.

"Is someone there?" Freydis steps out from behind the tree before I can stop her. "Oh, *heill,* cousin! Good evening to you, and to your companion." I scowl, but follow her lead, stepping out to join her.

The shards of Mawu's light reveal two men. The first is lanky with a beardless hatchet of a face. He looks familiar; judging by his bearing, he must be a soldier in the army. As with many other *Majūs* soldiers, his limp hair is shaved at the sides and long at the crown. His companion, however, is clearly not a soldier. Maybe not even *Majūs*. He has a corpulent build, which he covers with a loose, almost dresslike robe and an elongated hat that flops to one side. He is also beardless, and even in the darkness, I can see the outline of fear on his face.

It's not me or Freydis he fears.

Remembering his manners, the robed man offers a bow to Freydis, but Hatchet-Face narrows his eyes, keeping his sword in hand. "You're far from your bed, Princess. What are you doing out in the forest at night?"

"I'm afraid I'm suffering from an upset stomach," Freydis says smoothly. Her hand falls on my shoulder. "My maidservant and I are looking for some mugwort."

"There's none in the cookhouse?" Hatchet-Face presses.

"They ran out."

"And they couldn't send a thrall to fetch you some?"

"What are *you* doing out here?" I cut in.

His gaze flickers to me. It could be a trick of the darkness, but it seems like there's something . . . sinister in the smirk he gives me. I sense it in his *nyama,* too. "Funny you should ask. We're gathering yarrow for the journey tomorrow. It helps stop a wound from over-bleeding, as you may know. Good to have at hand in case any of my men sustain injuries during the raids." His companion quickly nods in agreement.

"What a coincidence," I say drily. "We're all picking flowers to-night."

A tense silence. Hatchet-Face stares at me like his eyes could bore a hole into my skull. I lift my chin defiantly. He would be crazy to attack the princess's thrall, but I recognize the unspoken chal-lenge in that look, and I've never been one to back down from a challenge. Even if he is a trained soldier with a sword and who knows what other weapons hidden away, and I'm just a thrall girl with some carving knives tucked into my belt, borrowed from the cookhouse.

Freydis is the first to break the silence. "Well, then. Good luck in your search."

"You as well, Princess," Hatchet-Face replies. He bows with his companion this time, then both men hasten past us.

"Will they tell your father they saw us here?" I ask when the men's footsteps have faded behind us.

"I don't think so. It didn't sound like they want the king knowing what they're up to any more than we do."

We walk in silence for a long while after that. I can tell that she's deep in thought, no doubt mulling over whatever those two men were talking about. I want to ask her who they were—she called one of them "cousin"—and if she suspects their discussion had some-thing to do with Broskrap. But I'm too afraid of turning her suspi-cions onto me.

I remind myself for the hundredth time that I don't have to

worry about her discovering the truth. Despite the nightmares that torment me every night, despite the fear that lingers at the edges of my days, there's just no reason for *anyone* but Alvtir to connect me to Broskrap's disappearance. If anything, Freydis seems especially unlikely to do so; when we overheard those two guards earlier, she completely mistook my panic for concern. Thank the gods I was so overwhelmed with shock, or I would have laughed in her face again. As if *I* would be concerned about *Broskrap's* well-being! Either she didn't know Broskrap at all, or she's even more naïve than she seems. Hopefully both, for my sake. No matter how badly she wants to be my "friend," I have no doubt that she'd turn me over to her father in the blink of an eye if she ever did find out. I wouldn't be surprised if Balli had killed a thrall for something as trivial as dropping a platter or burning a roast. For a thrall who murdered her master, death would be too merciful a fate. A shudder rolls through me at the thought.

I'm so caught up in these faraway fears, it takes me a moment to register the change in the air. I stop abruptly, letting Freydis bump into my back as I listen to our surroundings.

"What is it now?" she whispers.

More like what it *isn't*. I lift my finger to my lips. The chirps, the swishes, the rustles have all ceased. Not because of us, or any other humans. There's something else nearby. Something big. I can feel it.

A strangled squeal bounces off the trees, sending a jolt of excitement surging through me. I squint in the sound's direction. There's a wall of leaves between two intertwining trees; the animal that cried out must be right behind it. A familiar anticipation pulses in my stomach as I inch forward, sidestepping the roots and fallen branches, trying to make my footsteps as soundless as possible in these heavy leather boots.

Slow, slow, I remind myself in Papa's voice. I haven't done this in so long, I fear I'm forgetting everything he taught me. Forgetting his wisdom, the wisdom of Agé.

"Unngh!" Freydis stumbles on the fabric of her shift.

"Shh!" I hiss in annoyance, not taking my eyes off the wall of leaves.

I lower to a crouch, and we wait. After a few silent moments, I tiptoe closer and peek around the tree on the right. I get a glimpse of an antelope—at least I think it's an antelope—limp and blood-stained, being dragged by the neck across the forest floor in the mouth of another, larger animal.

The predator stops at the base of a wide tree, as wide as an old baobab, a stone's throw away from the wall of leaves. It begins to tear at the flesh of its kill. In the moonlight cutting through the trees, I can just make out its form. It's some kind of wolf—not spotted but gleaming silver and gray, much larger than any painted wolf I've ever seen in Wagadu.

Much, *much* larger.

My pulse beats in my throat like a drum. I hold my palm up behind me, hoping Freydis understands the signal and stays put. The wolf's coat shines like polished obsidian as it shifts its position, jerking the antelope to the side, completely absorbed in its kill.

I lower my hand to the carving knives. All three of them are fashioned the same way: medium-length blades with hefty bone handles, balanced well enough to throw, though not designed for hunting—and certainly not for bringing down a creature of this size.

The sound of crunching leaves is as loud as thunder as Freydis maneuvers into a crouch beside me. Instantly the wolf drops the carcass and looks over. Her growl rumbles the earth beneath our feet.

I whip around, meeting Freydis's terror-stricken face. "Run!" I whisper, reverting instinctively to my native tongue. But fear needs no translation. With a gasp, she turns and flees while I press myself against the trunk.

The wolf rears and charges after her, eager for a second kill.

I raise the knife to the side of my head and call soundlessly to Agé. I desperately hope he can hear me here, that his power extends across the great ocean and through this forest, as it does through every forest I've known before.

The wolf hurtles past my hiding spot in a flash of gray. I let the dagger fly.

Thank Agé, it sinks into her shoulder. She whips her bloodied muzzle around and lets out a howl, soon joined by a chorus of howls from all over the forest.

She's not alone.

I take off after Freydis, sprinting faster than I ever have before.

The wolf's footsteps fall in rapid succession behind us, getting closer and closer. Freydis lets out a bloodcurdling scream. With no time to aim, I turn around and desperately fling another dagger.

It lands between the wolf's front legs. She skitters to a stop and snarls, enraged, then charges at seemingly double the speed. My eyes widen in fear, and in something else—a mounting feeling that I've somehow seen this before. Maybe that's just how it feels when you're about to die, like some part of you knew it was coming.

No. This isn't how it ends.

I have only one dagger left. The wolf is almost on us now.

I stand my ground as she launches forward from her hind legs, her teeth bared, her black eyes blazing with a fire I know well. The same fire rages deep in my core, banked but never extinguished. It's the fire that would draw me out of the warmth and coziness of our hut to hunt before Lisa's rise; the fire that sustained me when the slavers dragged me across the desert; the fire that burned through the stormy nights on Alvtir's ship, when the sea threatened to swallow me whole; the fire that flared through my veins when I saw what Broskrap was doing to Airé.

Time seems to slow as I take the last dagger from my belt and raise it behind my head, aiming for the narrow space between her eyes.

FREYDIS

My heart pounds so loudly between my ears, I almost don't hear that the galloping behind me has ceased.

I'm no longer being chased. The wolf is gone.

I skid to a halt and fall forward on my knees, gasping and sputtering for air. As soon as I can breathe again, I turn around, ignoring the ache setting into my legs and chest, and scan the darkness for any sign of Yafeu.

She's turned around to face the wolf. A wolf no smaller than Fenrir himself. And I ran for my life while she faced it alone.

My every instinct is screaming at me to keep running home, but I stir up the last dregs of my courage and force my legs to jog back into the forest. I must find Yafeu. I *must*. I can't just let the wolf tear her apart. She was braver than Tyr when he put his arm in Fenrir's mouth, knowing it would be bitten off. Now I must be brave too.

Sweat slicks the gussets of my linen shift to my sides. I tear off my cloak and draw out the carving knife still tucked into my makeshift waist belt—the knife Yafeu insisted I bring. I hold it out in front of me as I run. I have no idea how to use it, but it stokes my courage to pretend that I do. My eyes scan the moonlit forest for something familiar, but I can barely distinguish one tree from another. I'll just have to trust my feet to carry me back to the point where I fled.

What was I thinking, letting Yafeu take me hunting at all, let alone at the turn of night? Helge was right: Nòtt and her daughters bring all sorts of evil to frolic in the wilderness under Máni's lenient rule. The gods must have sent that wolf to punish us for lying to my family and sneaking out of the longhouse. How arrogant we were, playing like Odin's huntsmen during the Terrifying Ride!

"I only wanted to make her happy," I whisper, hoping at least that the *dísir,* the spirits of my women ancestors, will believe me.

I barely jog a homefield's length when I stumble across Yafeu, alive and well, crouched over the fallen body of the wolf.

She killed it!

She killed the wolf!

Relief and awe wash over me like warm bathwater. My legs nearly buckle beneath me. "Yafeu!" I call out.

But she doesn't hear me. She's murmuring something in her language, one hand resting on the wolf's head, the other on its chest. Almost like she's praying to it, or offering it as a sacrifice.

I watch quietly, rooted as the trees around us, spellbound by the sight.

Maybe the wolf wasn't sent to punish us after all. Maybe it was another kind of omen. Or some kind of test? The gods are fond of such diversions.

I hang my head in shame. Whatever the Wise One intended, I can only imagine my cowardice disappointed him. I'm weak and useless, as Father loves to remind me.

But not Yafeu. Yafeu is as strong as any man, and as fearless as any of the gods—man or woman.

I can feel the last of the wolf's spirit dissipate into the air, and Yafeu falls quiet but does not move from its side. As the moments pass, I feel my body clamoring for my attention again. Every breath sends a throb to my chest; every muscle in my legs feels swollen and tender. My arms sting from dozens of tiny bramble cuts, a sensation I haven't felt since I was a child.

I look down at my shift. The arms are almost completely torn asunder. At the very least I had the foresight to change into an old one before we set out tonight. I'll have to throw it in the fire and add it to the list of garments I can only pray will go unmissed.

By the gods, I can't believe I'm thinking about my clothing right now! Only a few moments ago, I was searching for Yafeu's corpse and readying myself to fight a wolf.

Yafeu climbs to her feet, hoisting the wolf over her shoulder with a strained grunt. She turns to face me, unsurprised, as though she knew I was standing there watching her this whole time.

Well, of course she did. She hears things I can't hear. She can hear things I didn't think *any* human could hear.

"You're taking it with us?" I gawk at her. Well, looking at the wolf now, slung over her shoulders like that, I suppose it wasn't *quite* as big as I thought it was at first.

She passes me without so much as a word in response.

I came back for you, I want to say. *Doesn't that count for something?*

Instead, I turn and follow her back to the longhouse, letting the silence between us grow thicker than the trees, thicker even than the tangy scent of blood seeping into her cloak.

I've never been so grateful to be back in this dark, lonely room in my entire life. Yafeu stokes the fire high and sets the leftover water in the cauldron to boil while I change into a nightdress. The smooth cotton feels wonderfully clean and soft against my skin. I wrap a marten fur around my shoulders and take a seat by the fire, breathing in the soothing scent of burning maplewood and sending a silent thanks to Frigg for the comforts of hearth and home. The room is near sweltering, but I can't seem to warm my bones. All the excitement of the evening must have drained my body of its heat.

Across the room, Yafeu has the wolf slung over one of the empty benches along the wall. I stare at her profile as she works over the carcass. She's freed her brown hair from its braids and it juts upward in all directions, grazing the middle of her long neck, almost making a perfect circle behind her. It reminds me of a painting Father took from a Christian monastery, of a man with a golden ring around his head. The top half of the shift I gave her is caked in dried blood. Her chestnut-colored arms are thick and sinewy, her practiced hands swift and methodic as she slices the hide from the flesh with one of the same knives she used to take its life.

Now that I know what knowledge her hands carry, I feel foolish for insisting that she learn to work the loom.

Curiosity nudges me, too insistent to ignore. "What were you saying, when we were in the forest? When the wolf . . ." I trail off, suddenly unsure of what I saw.

"I was giving his spirit to Agé," she replies. "He oversees the forest for Mawu-Lisa."

I bite my cheek, thinking. I wonder if Agé is like Vidar, the Silent One, son of Odin and ruler of the wilderness. Fritjof once told me that Vidar will survive Ragnarök and avenge his father's death by slaying the wolf Fenrir. If Agé is another of his names, then perhaps it was *he* who sent the wolf, and he who took its spirit back in death.

A shiver runs up my spine. Does that mean the wolf was an omen of Ragnarök? If so, what portent does it hold for Yafeu, that she was the one to slay it?

I push the baleful thoughts away. This was only my first hunt; for all I know, everything that happened tonight could be ordinary. Except, of course, for Yafeu's prowess. Nothing about that is ordinary. "Do all the women become hunters, where you're from?"

"No."

I wait for her to say more, but she grimaces and places a hand over her neck. When she draws it away, there's fresh blood on her palm.

I gasp, noting for the first time the gash poking out from the top of her shift. I had thought all the blood was the wolf's.

"Your neck!" I jump to my feet, dropping the marten skin.

"Don't worry about it. I'll clean it later."

"Sit," I say, motioning to a seat in front of the hearth.

She sighs and heaves down in front of the fire, her legs shaking as she does. She's far more exhausted than she's been letting on.

My nausea has already returned at the sight of the wound, but I swallow it down and gather some scraps of cloth and a needle and thread from the cluttered baskets next to the sewing table. I approach her and move my hands to her shoulder cautiously, afraid she might swat me away.

When she doesn't, I pull down the neck of her shift a bit to reveal the full gash. It's as thick as the claw that made it, running from the middle of her neck down to her collarbone. A second claw mark runs parallel beside it, deep enough to blemish her dark skin but not deep enough to have drawn blood.

"You're lucky it's not worse, but it still needs stitching." My hands shake as I thread the needle. I will them silently to be still.

She snorts. " 'Lucky' is not the word I would use."

I dip an absorbent piece of cloth into the boiling water and press it onto the gash, hoping it's enough to ward off a wound-fever. Yafeu bares her teeth in silence.

"What is the name of your language?" I ask, eager both to know the answer and to distract her.

"Soninke," she says, reaching for the green gemstone hanging around her neck. It would help if she took that necklace off, but something tells me not to ask her.

"How do you say 'pain' in Soninke?" I ask instead.

"*Pain,*" Yafeu says in her tongue.

It might be a good idea for me to learn some Soninke. If we could speak in her language, she might soften to me. "Well the *pain* will be over soon." I say in Norse, swapping *pain* with the Soninke word.

She chuckles, then inhales sharply as my needle pierces her flesh. A familiar light-headedness washes over me; I bite down hard on the inside of my cheek and try to pretend that her gashed neck is no more than a torn piece of fabric I'm mending.

"If women don't hunt where you're from, then how did you learn?" I press. Now I'm trying to distract us both.

"My father taught me." Despite the agony etched across her face, she manages to hold remarkably still as I work.

"What else did he teach you?"

"How to fish. How to find ore in rocks and caves, distill it, make tools and weapons from it. How to fight, to defend myself."

I pause, surprised. "You know how to smith? And how to fight? Like a soldier?"

"Please finish," she says through gritted teeth.

I clear my throat. "Sorry . . . there." I finish the last stitch and use a clean knife to sever the thread from the spool, tying it neatly. I step back and admire my handiwork, rather pleased with myself. "It will leave less of a scar this way. But don't turn your head too much, or you'll tear the stitches."

She rolls her shoulder back. "Thank you," she says quietly.

I look around for another spare piece of cloth to wipe the blood from my hands. Oddly, I feel less queasy now that the blood has touched me.

All my life, I've been afraid of blood, of its sight and its scent. I hide every time the *hird* comes back from a raid, too terrified to see any wounds the soldiers might bear. Thinking of it now, perhaps I was afraid it was my *own* blood—I knew it wasn't, but it *felt* like it was, almost as though my blood, my life-force, could be leached out through others' injuries.

The image of Mother drenched in her own birth blood flashes in my mind's eye, bringing with it a wave of guilt.

What if Mother had seen me tonight? I know what she would say: *No king would take a woman who behaved so savagely as his queen.* And she'd be right. I should have let Yafeu go hunting by herself. She's a thrall: She can act as unwomanly as she pleases, so long as no one's around to scold me for it.

But then again . . . if I hadn't gone, I never would have seen what she can do. I doubt even Aunt Alvtir, with all her brutish ferocity, could kill a full-grown wolf with nothing but a few carving knives.

Ignorant of my turmoil, Yafeu climbs to her feet and heads back to the wolf, eager to resume her work.

As I watch her attempting to salvage the bloodstained pelt, I feel something stirring in me that has slumbered all my life. She has a kind of . . . *knowing* within her. It's what gives her that pride, that self-assuredness. I find myself oddly jealous.

My gaze drifts to my ruined shift on the ground. Seized by an impulse, I pick it up and fling it into the fire. I watch as the flames lick up the sides, curling and shriveling the fabric.

When there's nothing left of the shift but ash, I make a silent promise to myself: What happened tonight can never happen again.

Suddenly my eyelids feel like twin weights of iron. "Yafeu, I can't stay awake much longer. But please stay. I don't want to be alone." I gesture to the empty benches along the opposite wall. There're three on each side of my room, including mine and the makeshift sewing table—one for each child my parents thought they'd have. "You can put some furs there. They were supposed to be beds anyway."

She appears to give a slight nod, though it could be a trick of the firelight. Resigned, I stumble over to my bed and let my body sink down into the furs.

When I finally find slumber through the maze of thoughts, I dream of the lurid colors and sounds of the forest. They beckon me toward something that can't be found.

21

YAFEU

My hands pulse with fatigue as I finish carving a small design in the last wolf tooth. A circle with six triangles trailing its perimeter, peaks pointing outward. I lean back on Freydis's little stool, cracking my cramped neck. Framed by the smoke hole in the thatched roof, the sky is streaked with soft pinks and oranges as Lisa stretches his fingers over the land. Soon he'll rise over the green tips of the foothills we journeyed into last night, sending the night creatures to bed.

I turn back to the hearth. The stew bubbles low and thick in the pot and I give it a quick stir. I take a small taste, then add another handful of each of the assortment of herbs that I—most likely breaking one of the thousands of rules I was told—took from the cookhouse after Freydis fell asleep. But I returned two of the three knives, so I consider it a fair trade.

On a bench across from the hearth, Freydis's sleeping body undulates with each breath. I chuckle, amused at how she slept like a stone the entire night through, oblivious to my ceaseless work. She just couldn't handle the stress of the hunt.

I hang the necklace on the same post as the vest I made for Freydis from the wolf pelt. It should fall just to her hips, with claws for clasps and my new favorite finishing touch, the red-dyed sinew I found in one of her baskets.

I step back and observe my creations, feeling that same sense of regaining something I thought I'd lost—along with a sense of accomplishing something new. Mama always urged me to try my hand at more delicate and precise carving patterns, but I always resisted. Now I think I've found it: the middle ground between my natural talents and what Mama tried to teach me. After everything I've been through, I can finally embrace her knowledge.

Sorrow and gratitude congeal inside of me. I grab the green wolf. "Oh, Mama, I wish you could see this. You would be so proud," I whisper to the tiny work of art. I close my eyes, fighting back tears.

A yawn and a stirring snags my attention. Freydis's disheveled blond hair resembles a bulbul's nest as she emerges, red-faced, from a pile of furs.

FREYDIS

I wipe the sleep from the corner of my eyes, blinking them open to find Yafeu grinning at me. I startle; I'm not accustomed to waking with someone else in my room, save for Helge rousing me for breakfast on the days I oversleep. I almost ask her what she's doing here before I remember that I asked her to stay the night. In my groggy haze, I don't know which I find more peculiar—that she listened to me then, or that she's smiling at me now.

I stare at her incredulously, noting that she's changed into her old thrall's tunic. She must have disposed of the bloodied shift and overdress in the night. A tantalizing scent flows from the cauldron, wresting a groan from my empty stomach.

"Good morning," she says pleasantly.

"Morning, Yafeu," I croak.

"You slept like the dead. This morning I thought you were, and I almost escaped. But then you stirred."

I gasp, shocked and more than a little bruised at her bold words. But then she breaks into an even wider grin.

She's joking.

Relief floods through me. I grin back at her. "Sorry to disappoint."

She points to the post above the sewing table. I squint, straining to discern the unfamiliar cloth. She sets the ladle down and picks up the cloth with both hands, holding it up to the light for me to see. "For you," she says, her expression warm.

It's a shirt of some kind—no, a vest, an extraordinary vest, fashioned from the fur, tendons, and claws of the wolf.

My chest tightens. "It's been so long since I've gone on a hunt, and yesterday . . . I felt alive again."

"I felt it too," I say quietly, surprising myself.

No sooner do the words leave my mouth than I realize how true they are. I've sought Odin's wisdom in learning the runes, but last night I felt his wildness for the first time. It was terrifying, but it was also . . . exhilarating. I felt the presence of the *dísir* in every rock and branch and root. I felt them consecrate the death of the wolf, felt their solemness all around me as its spirit ascended to Asgard.

I take a deep breath, reminding myself of my promise: I can never go hunting with Yafeu again. But as I gaze into her dark-amber eyes, so animated and brimming with gratitude, I feel my resolve snapping like a twig underfoot.

"Why do you love to hunt so much?" I ask, curiosity getting the better of me, as usual. "Is it just that feeling, or is there something else?"

She cocks her head to the side, considering. "I guess it's about proving that I can rely on myself. That I don't need to depend on others to survive. It makes me feel free, even if it's just an illusion."

I feel a blush creep into my cheeks. "I've never heard a woman talk like that before."

There's a bitterness in the curve of her lip as it tilts upward. "Women aren't supposed to. But I've never let that stop me."

I can't think of anything to say to that. My gaze returns to the vest in her hands.

"My father taught me to hunt," she continues, her bitter smirk relaxing into a coy smile, "but my mother taught me how to do this." She gingerly lays the vest in my lap.

I stare down in shock at the breathtaking piece of clothing, letting my fingers roam over the unfamiliar details. It's well cut and tidily sewn. From the back, the hood appears to be of one piece with the rest of the garment, but a blind stitch on the inside reveals her skill.

And here I thought she had no patience for sewing.

"Yafeu," I begin. "I . . . I don't know what to say—"

"You can say you're starving." Yafeu cuts me off before I can babble further, grabbing a bowl from the wall. "Or your stomach can keep saying it for you." She saunters over to the hearth and ladles a hearty scoop of stew. "*Meat*," she adds in Soninke.

"*Meat*?" I enunciate carefully, wanting to get the pronunciation right.

Yafeu cracks a wide smile. She thrusts the bowl and a spoon into my hands. "Taste *meat*," she says, urging me on with a wave of her hand.

I bring a spoonful to my mouth. The very fibers that held the meat together dissolve on my tongue, giving way to an overwhelming mixture of herbs and spices. My eyes water.

"It's wonderful!" I say between bites, covering my mouth. "And very spicy."

"Your food is too bland," she says flatly. "It needs more flavor. We have *pawuda* in my homeland, but I had to guess with the other spices."

"I taste dill," I say, chewing thoughtfully. "And a bit of mustard seed. And thyme."

She shakes her head, not understanding. I'll have to go to the kitchen pantry with her to teach her the names of the herbs. She sits down beside me and waits patiently as I slurp down the rest, eating like a wild animal.

When I look up from my empty bowl, I notice the darker circles under her eyes for the first time.

I frown. "How long have you been awake?"

Yafeu glances up at the sky through the smoke hole. "It doesn't matter," she replies in Soninke with a shrug. I struggle with the meaning of her words before grasping the gist. She stares at her hands. "The sunrise was beautiful," she continues in Norse.

She stayed up *all night* to make this for me.

"Yafeu, I'm the one who should be grateful to *you*," I say. "How do you say 'grateful' in—"

The door flies open. Helge's guarded gaze falls on us. Panicking, I thrust the vest under a fur.

"Good morning, Helge," I greet her.

"Oh, there you are," she says to Yafeu. She sniffs the air and wrinkles her nose at the cauldron. "A stew? For breakfast?"

"I woke early and was starving from missing dinner, so I had Yafeu cook for me," I say quickly.

She raises a suspicious eyebrow, wrinkling her age-lined brow even further. "Your parents are taking their meal in the hall now. I'll tell them you've eaten. We will be seeing the *hird* off to the raid as soon as Sól is full in the east."

I nod eagerly, silently urging her to leave. She starts out, then stops and looks Yafeu up and down, contemptuous. "Try to look presentable," she adds before closing the door behind her.

As soon as her footsteps are out of earshot, I take out Yafeu's vest and hug it close to my chest. "I'm sorry to lie, but we have to be careful."

"What's the 'raid'?" Yafeu asks, brushing past my apology.

I relax a little at her seeming indifference to me hiding her gift from Helge. "Every summer, the *hird* journeys across the seas in search of new lands and new riches," I explain. "They bring back magnificent spoils."

"Spoils," she repeats slowly. "Am *I* 'spoils'?"

Her eyes are fathomless oceans, pulling me in. Afraid to drown in their depths, I look down at the vest. There are many questions nested within those three simple words. Questions I've never had to ponder. My people tell one story, but my deepest instincts whisper another.

I force myself to meet her hardening gaze, hating myself more and more with each silent moment. "N-no! Of course not. Y-you're my handm—"

Yafeu takes a deep, exasperated breath before interjecting: "Alvtir's warriors will be there, right?"

I choke on my half-formed words. "Where?" I manage to squeak.

"At the harbor," she says, furrowing her brow in annoyance.

"Oh." I was so lost in the depths of her words, I'd almost forgotten the matter at hand. "Yes, the entire *hird* will gather there."

"I want to come."

My eyes flit nervously to her thrall's tunic, my full stomach churning at what Mother would say if a royal maidservant came to see the *hird* off looking as Yafeu does now. "You can, but you can't wear that."

She shoots me one of her mischievous looks. "I wouldn't dream of it."

I pace back and forth outside the back door. I don't want to rush Yafeu, but any moment now, the trumpet will sound, and my parents will be annoyed if we're not ready.

I walk over to the thrall's shed and am about to knock on the door when she emerges. My breath dies in my throat at the sight of her.

She obeyed Helge—and more. Six serpentine braids stretch from the tip of her forehead to the middle of her crown, allowing her curly mane to stretch free in the back. The pressure of the braids pulls her almond-shaped eyes up at the sides, heightening their allure. Along with the green gemstone, she's wearing a fitted necklace of . . . teeth. The wolf's teeth, I realize. She must have made it last night, along with my vest. Over the dark-green dress I gave her, she's wrapped two thick leather thongs around her waist, accentuating her hips. I gulp at the sight of the carving knife she tucked into it—one of the knives from last night, cleansed and polished.

"Am I *presentable*?" She does a playful twirl. Between her free hair and the necklace, you can hardly see the stitches on her neck. At least I don't have to worry about *that*.

"You will certainly stand out—in a good way," I add hastily, studying the intricate designs carved into each tooth.

Just then, the trumpet sounds from the guard tower, one long, unbroken note. I nod at Yafeu. "It's time."

She follows me to the front of the house, where Father, Mother, Helge, and the guards are waiting for us. I look past my parents' irritated expressions, focusing instead on the vista. The whole of Skíringssal stretches out before us. Every line in the city seems to draw the eye to the commanding sight of two dozen dragon ships bobbing up and down on the Agdersfjord, the full force of Father's fleet, gathered from every town in Agder. The farmland path seethes with the bodies of farmers and shepherds and thralls alike, all marching toward the dockyard like ants to an anthill. Even from atop the hill, I can hear the cacophony of their shouts and cheers and tearful goodbyes, carried up on the breeze off the fjord. I can almost smell the barrels of smoked fish, dried meats, and freshly baked flatbread as Father's men haul as many as the ships can carry aboard the decks.

Mother purses her lips as we approach. "It is unwise to keep your elders waiting."

"I'm so sorry," I say. "It was my fault. I haven't been feeling well."

Father's lip twitches as he eyes Yafeu. Mother shares a look with Helge before casting her own sidelong glance. I blush, unsure whether it's Yafeu or my parents embarrassing me.

We pass the Great Hall, then Father's stables. The horses whinny and buck against their stalls, sensing the commotion in the air. When we reach the path to the harbor, the guards move to surround us, and I fall into step behind Mother and Father. I motion for Yafeu to walk behind with Helge; she rolls her eyes but, thankfully, does what I ask without complaint.

Mother is as lovely as ever, with her snow-fox fur draped over a gossamer red dress with a silver brocade, a string of rubies dangling between the silver brooches. But she keeps looking back at Yafeu, who, without any lavish trappings, still seems to draw every eye in Skíringssal.

I send a quick, silent prayer to the gods, praying this morning passes without incident.

YAFEU

I look past the bustling swarm of bodies to the flock of wooden dragons floating on the water. The warships' balance between brute power and supple grace strikes me like a bolt of Sogbo's lightning, same as the first time I laid eyes on them. Of course, Alvtir's ship invariably draws my gaze, with its rich, red-striped sails and the dragon prow that's somehow larger and more domineering than the rest. I swallow hard, struggling to keep my composure.

The king and queen lead us up to the shoreline, then we turn our backs to the fjord and observe as warrior after warrior files onto the ships tethered at the docks. As they pass us, I notice for the first time the disparity among the men: Some are wearing nothing but a tunic and leg-strapped trousers, while others sport gleaming byrnies, greaves, and vambraces. But every man has the same yellow shield with the black birds painted on either side, marking them as King Balli's soldiers.

Most of them nod respectfully to the king and queen and either openly gawk at or purposefully avoid looking at me. I'm not sure which bothers me more. I'm not the only foreigner in this city, but I am the only "black elf," as the king likes to call me. To the merchants and other cityfolk I'm a regular sight, both from my solo trips to the harbor and from my forays with Freydis. But many of the soldiers haven't seen me before—or at least, not since the journey from Anfa.

The hatchet-faced man arrives in a full and spotless suit of armor. In the daylight I can see his features better. Even compared with his people, his hair is too thin and too pale, reminding me, with a wave of nausea, of Broskrap. He throws me a pugnacious look as he passes.

Anger crashes like a tidal wave against the dam around my heart. I glare back at him, my fingers instinctively grazing the hilt of the knife tucked into my belt. He climbs onto one of the ships, where he immediately starts barking orders at the other men on board. I clench my teeth, staring daggers at his back. But it's not long until I feel another pair of eyes on me.

I turn back to the procession, steeling myself for another dirty look from one of the soldiers. Instead, I meet the opposite.

Blue-gray eyes, like the sea on a cloudy day, gentle and searching. They wash over me, and just like that, I feel some of the anger ebbing away. It's the same man who spoke to me here a few months ago, the one who stopped me from attempting to escape. He breaks my gaze, looking to the wharves. I study him curiously as he marches by. He's tall and leanly muscled, not quite so barrel-chested as many of the other *Majūs* men. His armor is different from the others' too. His chain-mail tunic extends down almost to his knees and is made of interlocking planks of metal instead of rings, and he wears leather vambraces over his forearms and shins. At his side rests a broad-headed ax with an elongated handle. As he leaps gracefully onto the deck of a ship—Alvtir's ship—his neatly trimmed beard catches Lisa's rays and turns from brown to auburn.

Was he on Alvtir's ship on the journey here from Anfa? As I watch him unfurl the sails with practiced hands, I wonder how he didn't draw my attention then. I guess I was too focused on the women to notice the men. "Who's that soldier?" I whisper to Freydis.

She looks over. I incline my head toward the man with the strange armor, trying to point him out without him noticing.

"*Who?*" she asks loudly.

I grimace and open my mouth to shush her when a growl of a voice rips through the din.

"March!" yells the voice, scattering the people in its way.

The crowd cleaves like stalks of grain before the scythe of Alvtir's presence. Everyone falls silent. The two women I remember from Anfa follow close behind, along with another one—a younger girl, no older than myself.

A pang of longing rips through me. I watch with a mixture of awe and envy as the four women march with thunderous strides toward Alvtir's ship, moving together as one, the strike of their boots creating a drumbeat against the wooden dock.

Alvtir's long black hair billows in the wind as she peers at us through the strands, a hint of amusement lighting up her electric eyes.

Expectation rises palpably around the king and queen as she approaches, but instead of talking to them, she stops directly in front of me.

What?

My eyes widen and my heart starts to pummel my rib cage.

She smirks at my unabashed awe, then leans in close, sending a whiff of iron to my nose as she whispers in my ear: "Soon."

FREYDIS

My mouth falls open in shock as Aunt Alvtir pulls away from Yafeu. Without so much as a word to Father, she spins around and heads for her towering warship.

What in the name of Odin could Aunt Alvtir possibly have to say to my maidservant?

I regard my father's sister with new eyes. I've seen the *hird* set sail every summer for as long as I can remember, and yet I never noticed before how the wind whips my aunt's black hair into a fury as she strides across the dock, the fluid grace in the way she leaps onto her ship, how Angrboda's silver hilt catches the rising sun as she turns, the runes there sparkling.

Alvtir waits patiently as the last girl climbs onto her ship. Then, in one fluid motion, she unsheathes her sword, whirls around, and slices the tether behind her, eliciting a gasp from the crowd. Taking it as their cue, the other captains cut their moorings, the soldiers hauling out the oars as the ships begin to drift toward the rest of the fleet. The onlookers hesitate, confused, then break into a scattered cheer.

I spare a glance at Father, who narrows his eyes at his sister's receding form. He has always been the one who gives the order to cut the tethers. Out of the corner of her eye, Mother is watching him too, no doubt wondering as I am how he will react to Alvtir's misconduct.

Normally, we would watch and cheer along with the rest of Skíringssal until the sails disappear around the bend. But this time, Father turns to Yafeu, that steely glint in his eye. She's staring after the ships so intently that she doesn't even notice him.

Fear drags my heart into my stomach. Yafeu is an outright spectacle—almost as much as the *hird* itself. *I should've made her change into normal clothes,* I chastise myself silently, though another part of me wonders if it would have made a difference.

Odin help us.

Thankfully, the Allfather answers my prayer: Father turns away from Yafeu and starts trudging up the path to the Great Hall. The guards hasten to flank him, as bewildered as the rest of us by all these unexpected breaks from ritual.

I move to follow, but a tight grip on my arm stops me short. I flinch instinctively.

"Your elf-girl thinks herself a queen," Mother hisses into my ear. Even through the shift, her nails dig painfully into the flesh of my arm. "Get her underwing or we will sacrifice her to Njord for the *hird*'s safe passage."

"No!" I blurt out, panic clawing at my chest. "I mean, let me punish her myself," I amend, adding a bite to my tone. "I will make sure she knows her place."

Mother hesitates, then releases her grip and strides past me after Father. I take it as her agreement. Helge catches my eye and shakes her head, a silent warning not to follow. She catches up to Mother and I let them go, all too glad to put some distance between us.

The rising sun blinds me momentarily as it engulfs their frames. I shield my eyes as I watch them ascend the hill. Mother's head bends toward Helge in that familiar conspiratorial angle, the embroidered hem of her dress swishing imperiously behind her. They look like Frigg and Fulla, the goddess and her most trusted maidservant and confidante, ascending the bifrost to Asgard together. My mind flashes to the image of Alvtir marching across the dock. I can't help but compare the two sights, like a pair of tapestries I might weave: Frigg and the Valkyrie, the goddess and the warrior.

Mother has all but forbidden me to interact with Alvtir, so afraid is she of the curse that has haunted my aunt since long before I was born. The same warnings were repeated over and over, like a mantra: *Alvtir is abhorrent. Alvtir is unwomanly. You must stay away from Alvtir at all costs, lest she give you her curse, or turn you into one of her kind.*

But . . . would it be so terrible to be one of Alvtir's "kind"?

For the first time in my life, it strikes me that I can't be sure which of the two, between Mother and Alvtir, truly deserves to be pitied and despised. Mother does all the things she commands me to do to be a praiseworthy woman, to be beautiful and obedient, to please men. But as I watch her trailing behind Father, giving him the same distance she always gives my aunt, it's all too evident that she cannot please him no matter what she does. He barely tolerates her, let alone loves her—and less so after every year she doesn't give him a male heir. But she remains tethered to him, regardless of his feelings or hers.

Of course, Mother could request a divorce. But Father controls the Thingmen: On what grounds could she succeed in convincing them to defy him and grant it to her? And even if she did succeed, where would she go? She was born a farmer's daughter in Alfhaimar, and her bride price was likely no sizable amount, since she married Father before he became wealthy, when he was still a jarl to the Danish king. She could go back to Alfhaimar, where her brother runs the farm with his own wife and children. But I could never imagine Mother living as a servant in her brother's house, waiting on her sister-in-law and living as a leech off whatever hospitality they would show her. That would be a fate worse than death for Mother, for whom being a royal is the highest calling.

So Mother is bound to a man who all but despises her, unable even to take a lover without risking her station. The gods know Father has strayed from Mother from time to time, as all men are wont to do. But I never heard even a whisper about a child resulting from one of those trysts. I may not have so many skills as Yafeu, but one thing I have learned to do well is to make myself so unnoticeable as to be almost invisible, to lend an unheeded ear to the whispers of king and thrall alike. What bittersweet solace for Mother, that the gods haven't granted her husband a bastard.

Meanwhile, Alvtir sails across the world. She owes no man her livelihood, her property, her body. And she isn't afraid of Father, unlike everyone else in Agder. She doesn't have to be. She leads a life of violence, to be sure. But is she truly "abhorrent"? Is she truly "unwomanly"?

Yafeu, for one, would rather be like Alvtir. Yafeu *is* like Alvtir in many respects, and from the way some of the men look at her, I know she is no less desirable than any other woman. Despite her strength and her wildness . . . or maybe because of it.

I turn back to Yafeu now. She regards me blankly. I wonder for a moment if I imagined everything that just happened, like some kind of waking dream.

Then I remember the sharpness of her ears. Even with the crowd cheering around us, she must have heard what I said to Mother.

I hang my head in shame. "I'm sorry, Yafeu," I say, and I mean it.

"I will be punished now." She states it rather than asking, as though she's already accepted her fate. I wonder if Yafeu has ever apologized for her actions, ever begged for forgiveness in all her life. I'm sure Aunt Alvtir has not.

I heave a deep sigh from the very center of my being. "No," I say weakly. "That was another lie."

I'd lied to my mother, for the second time in as many days. The thought thrills and chafes at the same time.

There's a loosening in Yafeu's face, a release of tension I didn't notice there before. She nods solemnly.

"What did my aunt say to you?" I ask, suddenly overwhelmed by curiosity.

She shrugs. "I didn't understand her words."

Now Yafeu is the one lying to me. We both know that she understands enough of our language to grasp the meaning of most things, even if she misses a word here and there. But if she doesn't want to tell me yet, then I'll just have to accept that. I still have to earn her trust.

"Yafeu," I begin, "I've saved you from a beating today, or worse. But if you don't learn our ways you're never going to"—I hesitate, taking in her chestnut skin, the wolf teeth dangling brazenly around her neck, dissent encased in her liquid eyes—"fit in."

She smirks, and again I'm reminded of Aunt Alvtir. "I don't think I'll ever fit in here, Princess."

"No, not completely," I agree. "But this is your home now, whether you like it or not. And you'll need to abide by our customs if you want to avoid my father's fury."

Yafeu scowls, as surprised as I am at my own boldness. But she doesn't reply. She knows I'm right.

"I will teach you everything you need to know to pass as a proper woman of Agder," I continue. "But I want something from you in return."

She raises an eyebrow.

"First, you have to promise me you'll be discreet in front of Mother and Father. Keep your head bowed, say nothing. Follow orders."

She makes a sound of displeasure in her throat but dips her head in acknowledgment. "All right."

"And second." I raise my chin triumphantly. "I want you to teach me how to fight."

22

YAFEU

Freydis spits dirt from her mouth and drags herself off the ground. Her rapid wheezes make little clouds in the frigid early-morning air as she wipes the beads of sweat from her brow.

I stretch my arms behind my back while I wait for her to catch her breath. The morning air is crisp, fragranced with the spindly, sticky leaves of the trees Freydis told me are called pine and spruce. The scent calms me, centers me for some reason. This little clearing in the northeastern forest has become our regular spot. Brown needles coat the earth, and I've gathered them into a kind of sparring ground, forming a soft bed for us to fall on.

Or really, for *her* to fall on.

I can't help but giggle at the thought.

"Laugh all . . . you want," she huffs. "But you still . . . haven't answered me." She balls her hands into fists and holds them up in front of her face. Freydis doesn't yet have the strength or coordination to wield a weapon, so I've been teaching her the basics of hand-to-hand combat.

If you rely on your daggers too much, they will become your weakness, Papa used to say. *Gu has blessed you with his magic, but that doesn't mean you can't defend yourself without it.*

I grin and raise my own fists, the familiar joy of muscle memory bounding back to me like a loyal dog. "The king divides the land among the jarls of Agder," I say. "And in return, they give him one-third of the land's yield as tribute and pledge their own ships and men to the king's *hird.*"

This has been our ritual for several weeks now: We wake up well before dawn and come here to practice sparring, while Freydis drills me on the ways of the *Majūs*—their laws, their customs, their gods and how they worship them. She's also been teaching me the names and uses of all the plants and animals that are new to me. I've learned that the trees with the wide trunks and the spoonlike leaves are called oaks, and the bark is used to treat skin rashes or ease a sore throat. The plants with the toothed leaves and purple, hairy stems are called mugwort and are used to cure stomachaches and stimulate a woman's moon blood. The fur Alvtir gave me is from an animal called an otter, prized for the special oils that repel water and keep the wearer dry. All this and more I've learned from Freydis. I must admit, she has more wisdom than I thought she did when we first met.

She throws a punch to my shoulder, and I let her land the blow. A self-satisfied grin lights up her birdlike face; she doesn't realize I'm going easy on her.

"But why"—I spin around and kick her fist away, wiping the grin right off her lips—"do the jarls agree to give him so much? If they have their own ships and men, couldn't they stand against him?"

"Because he swore an oath to protect them and to lead them to glory and prosperity," she replies, circling me. I rotate to face her as she goes, hopping lightly on the pads of my toes to stay agile. "In return, they swore him an oath of loyalty. And he has kept his word, so they must keep theirs. In this way, a king is bound to his people, and they to him. To break the bond of an oath is an act of grave dishonor. It is almost never done. Though Father's own *hird* is the largest—just in case."

It's hard to imagine it now, but Freydis told me that when he was young, Balli was a warrior and a hero to his people. He led the *hird* in a glorious battle that freed Agder from a foreign ruler. Among the *Majūs,* great warriors are venerated and respected above all others. The best warriors can become jarls or even kings, even if they were born with no land or title. Thus, rivalry among kings and jarls is fierce, and power comes and goes like the ebb and flow of the fjord. It is just as often snatched by a stronger man as it is passed down through kin.

But everyone, from the most powerful king to the lowliest milkmaid, follows a code of personal honor. A man—or woman—could be the greatest warrior the world had ever seen, but if they ever brought dishonor on themselves, they would lose all the power and respect they had gained.

Most important, I have learned as much about Alvtir as Freydis can tell me. Alvtir and her women warriors are called shield maidens. It's not common among *Majūs* for women to fight alongside men, but it's not unheard of either: Some of the heroes in their ancient stories—stories like the ones my parents used to tell me—were shield maidens. When Alvtir was young, she was captured by foreign soldiers, only to escape and return many moons later. But she was changed: Whatever she had gone through while she was away had made her feral and vicious. King Balli, not knowing what to do with his wild sister, allowed her to join the *hird* and recruit her own small retinue of women—the three women who, for reasons Freydis does not know, found themselves without husbands to look after them.

Freydis, for her part, is just as engrossed in her own training as I am in mine. Over the last moon, her body has lost some of its softness and gained many cuts and bruises. But she never complains about the pain, much to my surprise. It seems just yesterday that she was grumbling about a twig scraping her arm in the woods. We've had to fashion a tunic and trousers for her in secret to avoid marring her dresses with tears or stains. I'm equally surprised at how much she seems to enjoy the loose, simple clothing, given how fussy she otherwise is about looking *lady-like*.

She throws a punch at my head and I duck easily. "Loki's wiles!" Freydis swears. "How did you know I was going to do that?"

"Your eyes give you away. You need to make your move as soon as you form the idea." I swing my own fist forward and stop it right in front of her chin. She shrinks back before catching herself. "Keep your opponents off balance."

"You're *never* off balance," she mutters, leaning down to catch her breath again.

I find my thoughts returning to Balli and Alvtir. "Why doesn't your father lead the *hird* himself?" I wonder aloud. "Does Alvtir lead them because she is the better warrior?"

Freydis stiffens and colors slightly, and I suspect there's more than the exertion causing it. "It's safer for him to stay here, with the guards, in case Skíringssal is attacked. That's why he made Aunt Alvtir his *stallari,* the leader of the *hird* in his stead." She cracks a smile, adding: "You're just distracting me so I can't give you a fair fight."

I laugh, and she joins with a breathless giggle. "All right, who comes next? After the jarls?" She begins to circle me again.

"The karls: free men without titles. Farmers, artisans, traders, and soldiers."

Freydis nods, pleased. I move to strike, but she leaps aside unexpectedly, and then it's my turn to be pleased.

"And after the karls . . ." She falters. The conversation has taken a turn.

"Thralls," I spit. Before she can react, I swipe my leg out under hers. She grunts as her backside hits the ground.

"In my village, we had no *thralls*," I say forcefully as she climbs to her feet and rubs her bottom. "Everyone had to share everything equally. We survived together, as one."

Well, everyone except for my family. But I leave that part out. I don't want to tell Freydis that no one shared with us, that even though my own uncle was the chief, we still had to fend for ourselves. I don't want to tell her that everyone saw me as *jugu*.

Freydis clears her throat. "Let's go again," she says brightly, changing the subject. "This time, you'll be the one on the ground." She hops from foot to foot, mimicking me.

I crack a smile but shake my head. "That's enough for today. You need to rest."

"One more go!" she pleads like a child. Like I used to plead with Papa when he tried to end our lessons for the day. It's enough to remind me that she really *is* just a child. Even though we're about the same age, I've lived through many lifetimes of hardship compared with her. "Sól is still rising—we have time," she adds. She has that obsessive look in her eyes again, the one that makes my stomach tighten.

Despite everything her people have put me through, I find myself worrying for Freydis. She has no respect for the limits of her body. I can't help but admire her eagerness and determination, but she's pushing herself too hard; she craves abilities she hasn't yet earned.

I grit my teeth, shoving the worry aside. What do I care if Freydis gets hurt? At least training her saves me from being bored to tears at the loom. And it's getting me into fighting shape, so that when Alvtir comes for me, I'll be ready.

That's what Alvtir must have meant by "soon": that when she returns from the raid, she's going to free me and take me under her wing, just like she has with those other women warriors. I was right to trust her in Anfa after all. I just needed to prove myself to her, which I did when I killed Broskrap. She must have been there; she must have seen me do it. That's why she gave me to Freydis that same night. Soon, I won't be a thrall anymore.

Soon, I'll become the warrior I was born to be.

The thought sends a jolt of excitement through me. I spring backward on my hands, flipping my legs over my head and landing in a neat crouch.

"Now you're just showing off." Freydis grins.

I wink back at her. "All right, once more."

Her face lights up and she assumes a defensive stance. I wait for her to make the first move. She throws a jab and I dodge it easily. She stamps her foot and storms past me, frustrated.

"You're too predictable," I lecture, bending down to lace up my boots. "You have to keep your opponent off balance—"

The inside of her arm wraps around my neck, cutting off my breath. Instinct takes over. I rear forward, grabbing her forearm with both of my hands, and slam the back of my head into her nose.

Freydis lets out a shriek and stumbles back. I leap to my feet and whirl around, panicking.

She clutches her nose and turns away, shuddering in pain.

"Let me see." I try to take her arm but she recoils.

Finally, she shows me her face. Blood pours freely from her nose. Thank all the gods, it doesn't appear to be broken. "It's okay," I say calmly. "You will heal. Tilt your head back to stop the bleeding."

Gratefully, she complies. "Why would you do that?" she snuffles. "I was just trying to do what you said!"

I tear a small piece of cloth from the cuff of my own tunic and tenderly place it under her nose. She winces as I pinch her nostrils, but soon the bleeding stops.

I follow her down the makeshift path we've forged through the forest. A narrow stream flows beside us, the sound of rushing water filling the uncomfortable silence. I want to tell her that I warned her this would happen, that she can't test herself against me like that—but I hold my tongue. Pain is punishment enough. I know that from experience.

"What do I tell Helge?" she asks finally.

"You'll think of something. You always do." She doesn't like to admit it, but she's been lying to her family this whole time. Lying about where we go, about what we've been doing. What's one more lie now?

Suddenly Freydis slips on a patch of mud.

"Freydis!" I seize her by the shoulders, stopping her just before she starts sliding down the slope toward the stream. She steadies herself and straightens.

"I'm okay," she says. She meets my eyes, and we share a giggle of relief. But our laughter is cut short as a foul smell permeates the air.

"Ugh," Freydis covers her nose with her hands again. "I almost wish my nose *was* broken."

I breathe through my mouth, trying not to gag. "Let's keep going."

We resume our course, but the smell only gets sharper with each step. Fear fans out its tendrils, reaching deep into my chest and throat.

I know that smell. It's the smell of death.

And it's coming from the stream.

FREYDIS

Yafeu shoots me a nervous glance before descending the bank. My heart pulses in my throat as I follow her, stepping carefully on the muddy slope, the pain in my nose muted by the fear. Whatever that horrid smell is, it can't be good.

A conspiracy of ravens takes to the air at our approach, cawing loudly. I shiver; it seems like an ill omen.

And it is. When we reach the stream and it becomes clear what the ravens were feasting on, I nearly faint.

A corpse, its torso resting in the mud while the legs bob in the stream. It's bloated and bluish from the chill of the water, just beginning to decompose. It must have washed up recently. Scratches and tears mar the skin, along with a gash running across his neck that's far too deep for a raven to have inflicted it.

Though the eyes have been plucked out by the birds, I recognize his face:

Uncle Broskrap.

I fall to my hands and knees and empty my stomach onto the grass. I retch and retch until there's nothing left to bring up.

Who could have done this? The honorless coward didn't even have the decency to bury him.

"We have to get help," I rasp as Yafeu helps me to my feet.

"No," she says quietly.

I frown. "What do you mean, no? Your former master—Broskrap, my uncle—has been murdered!"

The muscles in her neck tense as she looks away. I draw myself up to my full height, barely reaching her chin but trying my best to look commanding nonetheless.

"Yafeu, I order you—"

"I killed him."

The order dies on my lips. I feel myself swaying on my feet as the world starts to blur. "What?"

Her inscrutable dark-amber eyes meet mine. "I killed this man."

Yafeu.

A swell of pure rage rises within me. It overwhelms me like nothing I've ever felt before. Soon I am vibrating with the sheer power of my fury.

Yafeu.

"How—how *could* you?"

Broskrap was not the best of men, but he was my kin. And he was loyal to my father. And he had two little boys to raise. Gods, what will happen to them now?

Yafeu gazes at me, saying nothing. "I've been such a fool," I continue. "This is why you want to be like Alvtir. There's something wrong with you, and I should have seen it from the start. You're a *savage*! A *monster*!"

I spit on the ground in front of her for good measure, then I fall to my knees, dizzy with rage and grief and disbelief. All my lies to my parents, all my disobedience—all for a killer. A killer who's been teaching me her ways. Another wave of nausea crashes over me. How could I have been so naïve? *I trusted you, Yafeu!*

As if she can hear my thoughts, she begins to speak: "When I was Broskrap's thrall, I lived in a barn with two other thrall girls. Broskrap worked us to the bone. He gave us little food and beat us if we tried to take any more. We were always hungry, always cold. We slept on the ground, so close to the fire that the smoke blackened our noses and mouths. One day, Broskrap followed one of the other girls into the forest. He watched her bathe, watched her enjoy one of the only pleasures we could find in the misery of our lives. But watching wasn't enough. Not for your *kinsman*. He tore her from the pond and held her down, crying and screaming, as he raped her."

Yafeu's words wash over me like ice-water. I wrap my arms around myself, as if to protect myself from the shock.

"You call me a *savage*?" she continues, her gaze darkening. "You call me a *monster*? Your kinsman was all those things—and worse. So I slit his throat. And if I could do it all over again, I would. My only regret is that I didn't make him suffer more."

I stare at the ground, ashamed to my very core. All the anger is gone, replaced by a heavy, sinking remorse.

"Now you know the truth. What you do with it is up to you. You can have your father kill me, if that is what you wish."

I muster every ounce of courage I have left to look Yafeu in the eyes. She stands tall, waiting. Waiting for me, her *owner,* to decide whether to throw away her life. The thought almost makes me retch again. "Yafeu . . . I had no idea."

Nothing.

"I'm so sorry. For everything. I won't tell anyone what you did. I promise."

Still nothing. She stares at me for a moment longer, then spins on her heel and starts climbing back to the path.

"Wait!" I call out, running to catch up with her. "We need to bury the body. Someone will—"

Yafeu claps a hand on my mouth, silencing me. Her eyes go wide.

Then I hear it too: barking. Hounds.

I suddenly remember that it's the season for moose. I was so excited to train that I completely forgot. These woods could be swarming with hunters.

Yafeu races up the bank, dragging me behind her, and pulls me behind a large oak tree. She scoops a heaping pile of dirt and rubs it on my skin and tunic before doing the same to herself. I'm so frozen with panic I don't think to ask her what she's doing. All I can do is stand there, still as a stone, as the barking draws nearer and nearer.

"Your damn dog will scare off the moose," a man's voice resounds. "He talks more than he thinks, like his slag-breathed owner."

The taunt elicits a baritone chuckle. "Your sister doesn't mind my slag-breath," the other man calls back.

It sounds like Knut and Erik, two of Father's guards. I recall with a sinking feeling that Erik is a kinsman of Broskrap on his father's side.

The barking intensifies, the hounds whipped into a frenzy.

"What's this?"

"Good gods, it's Broskrap!"

Yafeu and I exchange a terrified look. I send a silent prayer to Vidar, god of the forest, that the hounds don't find us next. That they can't hear the treacherous thumping of my heart.

Erik swears. "We must tell the king at once."

A loud whistle and the dogs race back. Soon the sounds of the two men and their hounds fade into the distance. I release a wobbly breath.

"We have to get back before they do," Yafeu hisses, panicking. "And without anyone seeing us."

I stare at the ground, my eyes darting back and forth across the crumpled brown leaves as my mind races.

Think, Freydis. Think.

Erik and Knut will use the same route we do: They'll cut through my father's orchard, the second most direct way to get to the Great Hall from here. There's only one route that'll get us there faster. One route in which we won't be seen by another living soul.

The Dead City.

Dread rakes my chest like a revenant clawing its way out of the grave. I spare a glance at Yafeu.

She reads me too easily. "You know a way."

"There is another path . . ." I shake my head vehemently. "We can't."

"Why not?"

"It's forbidden."

"It's forbidden for us to be out here in the first place! We can't worry about that now."

"You don't understand. We'd have to pass through a place of great evil. A *cursed* place. If we go there, we risk taking the curse on ourselves. And then—"

And then I might never have children of my own. And Mother could lose her unborn sons.

"—we'd be endangering the city," I finish instead.

She runs a hand over her smooth braids. "I don't have a choice, Freydis. If I'm seen coming from the same woods where Broskrap's body was found, someone might . . ." She trails off, her brow wrinkling with worry. No, with fear.

Someone might suspect the truth. That's what she doesn't say.

"I don't think anyone will suspect anything," I say. "I doubt my father remembers—"

"*Please,* Freydis! You don't know what it's been like for me. Not a moment goes by when I'm not terrified of someone finding out—let alone your *father,* of all people. You know what he'll do to me!"

I hesitate. Yafeu isn't wrong to fear my father. He wouldn't care that Broskrap beat and raped his thralls. He wouldn't care that Broskrap deserved it. He would simply kill Yafeu. And it wouldn't be a swift death—not for a thrall who kills her master, a kinsman of the king no less. He would torture her for days on end, relishing every moment of her agony.

I can't let that happen. So Yafeu was right: We have no choice.

But that does nothing to allay the dread.

I nod once. "Follow me."

Sól's chariot seems to be racing us as we sprint toward the Dead City. Yafeu follows my heels, spurring me on. My lungs begin to burn, but I force myself to keep up the pace as we round the edge of Lake Vítrir.

At the far edge of the lake, we come at last to the borders of the Dead City. Jutting out from the scorched earth is a lone tree stump, blackened and shriveled. The two stubs of branches at its side make it look like the shadow of a person. People say it's one of the spirits of the dead standing guard over their domain, protecting it from the living.

From us.

I slow to a stop and catch my breath. Yafeu halts beside me. She looks out over the ruins, littered with detritus and half-standing stone walls, all blackened by fire—the charred remains of what was once the Danish city of Geirstad.

"What is this place?" she whispers.

I take a deep breath, gathering my wits. "Twenty summers ago, after my father declared Agder an independent kingdom, King Godfred of Danmǫrk sent his entire *hird* to our shores in the middle of the night. Agder was Danmǫrk's foothold in Norveg, and Godfred wasn't going to give it up without a fight.

"We were greatly outnumbered, but Father outsmarted them.

As soon as the first Danish ships were spotted, he had Alvtir take two-thirds of his own *hird* to hide in the heart of the city, while he brought the rest of the men to the port. He told them to feign cowardice as soon as the Danes landed and retreat.

"The Danes were fooled into believing that Father commanded no more than a few dozen spineless soldiers. In their arrogance, they followed the men into the old mead hall, chasing an easy victory. Then Alvtir led her portion of the *hird* to cut them off at the back, siloing their forces.

"The Danes realized they were defeated and quickly surrendered. But my aunt wasn't interested in their surrender. She ordered the men to lock the survivors in the mead hall and set it aflame. Helge told me that the Danes begged for mercy, that their screams filled the night air as they burned alive. But Alvtir just laughed and laughed. Their suffering was her pleasure.

"Njord must have been angered by such an honorless massacre, as a mighty wind blew up from the fjord and carried the flame from house to house, burning everything between the mead hall and this lake to the ground. Many died in the great fire: not just the Danish soldiers but our own women, our own children. Burned alive in their beds.

"In the morning, Thor sent the rains to smother the flame. The *hird*men scoured the ruins, looking for the remains of the dead to give them a proper burial. But they found none. The fire had consumed even their bones. Now the spirits of the dead haunt this place, soldiers and women and children alike, unable to find their way to Niflheim. All they can do is seek vengeance on the living, by placing a terrible curse on those who would enter their territory."

Yafeu lets me finish without interruption. I fall silent, and we stand that way for a while.

I study her profile as she surveys the ruins, her mouth tight, her brow knit in concern. I've never seen her look so nervous before. Part of me is glad for it; at least she understands what we're risking by coming here.

Then, to my great surprise, she takes my hand in hers, lacing her fingers between mine. "If we believe that the curse cannot harm us, then it won't. It can't. The spirits have no reason to punish us; we're not the ones who did this to them."

I swallow. "Do you really think that's true?"

She shrugs. "What other choice do we have?"

She's right. This is the only way. Still, I clutch her hand like it's the lost hand of Tyr as we venture into the ruins.

23

FREYDIS

We move at a slow jog, careful to step around shards of earthenware and the singed spikes of fences, littered around the ruined buildings. Even with fear steadily rising in my chest, curiosity gets the better of me, and I can't help but look around. Most of what were once houses, barns, and outbuildings have been reduced to little more than piles of stone and scorched planks. The few structures still half standing are even more unsettling; you can still see the marks where the flames licked up the walls. Some even bear scratch marks. I wonder if they were made by the families trapped inside, trying desperately to claw their way out.

The air around us is eerily quiet. Not even birdsong can penetrate the realm of the dead. The land is black beneath our feet. No grass, no wildflowers, not even a weed grows anywhere in sight. Only yellow, honeycomb-like mushrooms crop up in clusters here and there. Eating just one would likely send even the strongest man to his deathbed.

Yafeu cranes her neck as we pass a stone ship. The survivors must have placed it here, in an attempt to honor the loved ones they could not bury.

Yafeu opens her mouth, no doubt to ask about the stones, then shuts it after glancing at me. I must look as scared as I feel.

Dísir, I pray silently to the spirits of my ancestors. *Let us pass safely through this wretched place. Keep the curse at bay—for Mother's sake, if not my own.*

Yafeu drops my hand and turns abruptly, drawing her knife.

Then I hear it too: footsteps.

My breath catches in my throat. I stand as still as one of the stones, watching Yafeu's reaction.

Something is following us.

Each heartbeat is like a swing of Mjölnir between my ears for a few long moments before Yafeu relaxes and puts the knife away. "It's just a deer," she says.

I risk a glance. I don't see any deer. "How do you know it's not a ghost?" I whisper.

Yafeu cuts me a look. "I know what a deer sounds like, Freydis. Ghosts don't have four hooves." She resumes our course.

"How do you know it's not *two* ghosts?" I mutter to myself.

A soft rain picks up as we jog, streaking the dirt on our skin and clothes. But we pass the last structure without further incident. It's the only building still standing: a dilapidated barn that was miraculously spared, despite being directly next to the old mead house where the fire started. Moments later, we reach the tall grasses marking the edge of the Dead City. My shoulders drop with relief. The soft *shhh* of the blades rubbing together in the wind soothes my frayed nerves.

I glance at the sky. The sun is fully visible above Mount Skagafell; my parents will have finished breakfast by now. We must get back to my room before Helge comes looking for us, if she hasn't already.

"Which way?" Yafeu asks.

"We go south to the top of the hill, then turn east at the guard tower. The guard will have his back to us—he watches the fjord and the city. As long as we stay low and stick to the grasses, we won't be seen."

The grasses bend and crunch as we step inside. We hike until the guard tower comes into view, then I drop to my hands and knees. Yafeu follows suit. Just like I did as a child, we crawl around the tower.

As expected, the guard is looking out at the fjord ahead, leaning lazily against the railing. After all, with the mountains to the north, there's no way to attack Skíringssal from behind.

And no one in their right mind would dare sneak through the Dead City.

Finally, we emerge into my family's compound. I take a quick glance around, then sprint to the longhouse, Yafeu close on my heels.

I barge through the back door to my room and collapse on my bed, utterly exhausted.

YAFEU

I shake Freydis roughly. She can't go to sleep. Not now. "We have to wash your face before Helge comes to wake us."

She says something I can't hear into the pillow.

"What?"

She swivels her neck to glare at me. "I need a moment!"

I look her up and down. Her hair is frizzed around her like a lion's mane, and her face is caked in dirt and sweat and dried nose blood. "Your hair needs brushing too."

"I'm sure it's looked worse."

"I don't think so."

That gets a smile out of her. "I can always count on you to soften the blow," she says. But a sober expression steals over her face. She draws herself up to a seat. "Yafeu, we can't go anywhere near my mother. Nor any women of childbearing age. Not until we're certain the curse hasn't passed on to us."

I take a seat next to her. "What is this curse you're so afraid of?"

She looks away, hugging her knees into her chest. When she finally speaks, her voice is barely more than a whisper: "They say that any woman who steps foot in the Dead City will no longer be able to bear a living child, and that any she touches will suffer the same fate. It began with Alvtir, as she was the one who started the fire. No woman will touch her now, lest they bring the curse on themselves. Even the men keep their distance, just to be safe."

So *that's* why no one will go near Alvtir. It all makes sense now.

"I don't know what I would do," Freydis continues, staring at the white ashes littering the hearth. "If I were the reason that Mother couldn't . . . if she lost her . . . and my own husband would never forgive me if *I* couldn't . . ." She can't even say the words. Tears spill down her cheeks. She wipes them away with the butt of her palm, then gets up and sheds her tunic, kicking it under her bed. There's an edge to her movements as she throws on a fresh linen shift and an unadorned yellow dress, fastening the shoulder straps with silver brooches.

A lump rises to my throat. I swallow and close my eyes, leaning my head against the wall. "The people in my village used to say I was cursed," I begin. "They said I was haunted by an evil spirit, which is why I acted like a boy instead of a girl. They even said my father left my family to escape it. They must not have known Papa very well. He taught me that belief itself has power— and that we can *choose* what to believe. So I chose *not* to believe in the curse."

I open my eyes to find Freydis staring at me, her expression unreadable.

"But it still hurt when they said those things," I add softly. "Every time."

Freydis waits for me to say more, but I already feel like I've revealed too much. I look away, embarrassed. After a moment, I feel her weight next to me on the bed, and suddenly her arms are around me, squeezing me tight. I have to stop myself from rearing back in surprise.

A few awkward moments pass. Then she gets up again and grabs her comb, raking it through her matted hair with a grimace.

I get up myself and rummage around for a rag. Luckily there's water left in the bucket. I wet the rag and hand it to Freydis in exchange for the comb, motioning for her to sit on a stool. She wipes her face while I finish combing her hair.

"Gentle!" she cries as I yank her head back on a snag.

"I'm sorry," I say.

She twists back to face me, her brow furrowed.

"I said I'm sorry."

"No, it's not that. It's—Yafeu, do you trust me? Do you trust that I will never tell a soul what you did?"

"I trust you enough," I say, almost under my breath.

She reaches out and clasps my forearm. "There's going to be a big commotion over Broskrap's death. He wasn't just my father's cousin; he was a man of considerable wealth and influence in his own right, so much so that Father made him a Thingman. He might have made Broskrap a jarl, but he was probably afraid that Broskrap would grow too powerful and challenge him for the throne. When word of his murder reaches the other Thingmen, they'll demand answers, fearing a threat to their own lives. Father himself might suspect that someone is trying to undermine his control over the Thing. There's a chance this will all go in our favor, that they'll cast their suspicions on one another first. But it also means their search won't end until they find whoever did this, or at least someone to blame."

I nod, feeling numb. "What should we do?"

Freydis starts picking at the loose edges of her hair. I can almost see her mind sifting through the possibilities, coming up with a plan. When she looks up, her mossy eyes are blazing with conviction. "I'm not sure. Maybe we don't need to do anything. But I do know one thing: I will earn your trust, Yafeu. Your *full* trust. No matter what it takes."

24

FREYDIS

We've barely cleaned and rested our spent bodies when Helge bursts into our room. "Broskrap has been murdered!" she shrieks. "They found his body in the woods!"

I share a glance with Yafeu. We throw on cloaks and follow Helge to the stables. A light rain starts pattering against the wooden roof. Helge rushes to Mother, who is leaning against the stable door, sobbing quietly. In all the commotion, no one seems to notice my swollen nose. The groom has taken out all four horses, who shuffle anxiously as he hastens to saddle them. Father is pacing back and forth, his red cloak billowing in the strong wind and agitating the horses even further.

Four of Father's guards approach from the other side, including Gunnar. I note that they're armed with swords and axes, even though they're dressed in plainclothes.

The saddles are secured and the guards mount. "Bring the body back to his farm," Father orders. "Search again for signs of a thief.

Question the thralls again, too. Perhaps the sight of his corpse will loosen their tongues."

"Yes, my king," Gunnar replies.

Yafeu steps forward, but I clasp her hand and pull her back beside me. "*No,*" I whisper in Soninke. "*Not yet.*"

She clenches her jaw so tightly that the tendons in her neck bulge, but she doesn't step forward again.

"*Hyaa!*" The guards dig their heels into the horse's flanks. The sound of hoofbeats striking the wet ground fills the air as they trot down the hill.

My grip tightens around Yafeu's fingers. I squeeze until the hoofbeats can no longer be heard.

I pause before entering the Great Hall and look up at the night sky. The rain has stopped; the stars are brilliant and clear, weaving a tapestry of light against the darkness. I wonder if it's a good omen from the *dísir.* I send a prayer up to the stars for another sign, one that will make my own path as clear as the night sky.

Tonight marks the beginning of the Goe month and the night of the *Dísablót.* It's normally my favorite festival in all the year, a night when women rule their husbands and all the prominent families of Agder converge at the Great Hall for feasting and music and dancing. But the curse and the murder have filled my mind with darkness; there's no room for merriment.

It's been several days since the guards set out to Uncle Broskrap's farm, and they still haven't returned. Yafeu and I have gone about our chores with barely a word spoken between us. I know she is afraid for those two thrall girls, but I'm more afraid for Yafeu herself.

What if they tell the guards the truth: that Yafeu is the one who killed him? Father will take her from me and . . . and worse. Panic squeezes my throat at the thought. I couldn't live with myself if that were to happen.

With a heavy sigh, I join the stream of young women trickling into the Great Hall. The hall is splendidly decorated, with wreaths nailed to the beams and extra candles on the tables. In front of the hearth, a stone altar to Freya sits on a special wooden table inlaid with gold serpents, and on the wall behind the dais hangs a colorful new tapestry of Freya opening her arms over Folkvang.

Yafeu and I and the other unwed women shuffle to the northern side of the hall. The men enter next, filling the southern side. Then Fritjof strikes up the lute, and we all turn to watch as my mother, and the other mothers behind her, enter in one long procession. Their footsteps strike the wooden floor in time with the solemn melody. Each lays a gift before Freya's alter, a jug of mead or some honeyed ginger cakes. Mother's hair is loose, cascading down her back in the style of the goddess herself, and around her neck lies a copy of the Brísingamen, Freya's dwarf-forged necklace of seven thick braids of gold.

The last offering is made, and the music dies down.

"Hail, Freya, and all the *dísir* who watch over our family and the families of Agder. We make these offerings to you in thanks for your many gifts. May you continue to guide us all to great deeds and good fortune." Mother's clear, strong voice echoes around the hall, and even the men bow their heads in reverence.

Yafeu leans over and whispers in my ear. "Why is your mother leading the ceremony, and not the king?"

"The *Dísablót* is a celebration to honor the *dísir,* the women spirits and ancestors, who watch over us and guide our fates. It is Mother's right to lead." My chest swells with pride as I add, "And when I am queen of my own hall, I will lead the ceremony there."

Yafeu nods solemnly and bows her head. Of course the *Dísablót* would be the one night she shows some genuine respect for our customs.

After the prayer, the real celebration begins. Everyone finds a seat as the tables are laden with platters of salted ox tongue, walnut bread and buttermilk cheese, and jugs of mead to wash it all down while a fragrant stew from a dozen slaughtered lambs boils over the hearth. Fritjof sings a more cheerful song, barely audible over the chatter of the Thingmen and their families. Yafeu leaves to assist Helge and the other thralls with the food and drink, leaving me to dine with my parents.

I'm too nervous to eat, so I push the food around my plate to make it look like I'm enjoying it. I want more than anything to trust what Yafeu said—that the curse of the Dead City isn't real, that it's all in our minds—but I made sure not to sit too close to Mother, just in case. Father grumbles over the expense of the feast, even more than he usually does, but Mother is so lavishly adorned in her costume as Freya, so much more so than any of the jarls' wives, that he perks up a little—if only to take a selfish pride in this reflection of his own wealth, like a farmer parading a prized sow in front of his rivals.

Still, the specter of Broskrap's death casts a noticeable pall over the festivities. While their wives trade pleasantries, the Thingmen cluster at the far end of their tables. From their low voices and grim expressions, I know they're discussing Broskrap, much to Father's chagrin.

As the feast wanes, the thralls take to the farthest table and quickly scarf down their own meals. I watch them, noting how little the other thralls talk to Yafeu, and how little she speaks to them in return. I used to think Yafeu avoided them because she didn't want any company. Now I wonder if it doesn't have something to do with Broskrap's thralls, and what she did to protect them from him. Maybe she's afraid that she'd do something like that again.

After she's had some time to eat her fill, I signal her to join me. She meets me at the near corner, where Fritjof is now entertaining the younger children with some story or another. His exaggerated gestures entrance the children, who watch his every movement with wide eyes, their little mouths hanging open or grinning widely.

Adults tend to regard Fritjof warily, as though his eccentricities might rub off on them. Even Father, who leans heavily on his counsel as a seer, keeps him at arm's length. But children are drawn to him like moths to a flame. I myself spent hours at his side during the winters of my girlhood, begging him to tell me stories about the gods. I coveted Fritjof's gift back then; I yearned to explore the roots and branches of Yggdrasil, to converse with the gods and see into the Well of Fate. As I got older and saw what the Sight did to him, I contented myself with learning herblore and the magic of the runes, thinking it better to be stuck in Midgard with all my wits.

Fritjof shoots me a lopsided grin, though it feels, as usual, like he's grinning past me. Or through me. With Fritjof, I can never be sure what he does intentionally and what is one of his tics. Yafeu stands at my side as we listen to his tale.

"So Odin and his brothers fashioned the oceans from Ymir's blood, the soil from his skin and muscles, the plants and trees and flowers from his hair, the sky from his skull, and clouds from his brains." He jerkily mimics pulling the brains from his own skull, eliciting a chorus of "ews" and "yucks" from the children, in turn making him cackle loudly. Fritjof is nothing if not a performer.

"Finally, Odin got around to forming the first man and woman, though their names escape me for the moment..."

"Ask and Embla!" I chime in.

"Oh yes! Ask and Embla." He winks at me before continuing. "Odin made Ask and Embla from the trunks of two oak trees. And he saw that Ask and Embla needed protection from the giants, so he built a fence around their dwelling place, Midgard. That is the name of our world, you know."

"This is your griot?" Yafeu whispers to me.

"Griot?" I try out the unfamiliar word.

"The keeper of stories."

I nod. "He is a skald: a poet and a storyteller."

"Skald," she repeats.

"The best skald in all the land," I add. "And the best seer as well. He sees into other realms, even into the hall of the Norns, who show him glimpses of the future. But the Sight has cost him much of his sanity. I want to ask him if he knows how the search for Broskrap's murderer will end. He may not have seen, or he may not be able to tell us, but it's worth a try."

"What is the story he tells now?"

"It's the story of how our world came to be."

Yafeu scratches the faint scar that remains on her neck, thinking. "In Wagadu, they say that Mawu-Lisa journeyed around on the back of a great rainbow serpent named Aido Hwedo. First, they created the earth. The different terrains were shaped by the winding movements of Aido Hwedo's body. The mountains were formed from Aido Hwedo's excrement wherever they stopped to rest, leaving gold and other precious stones inside. When Mawu-Lisa was finished, they asked Aido Hwedo to encircle the earth and rest underneath it to support its heavy weight."

"Aido Hwedo reminds me, somewhat, of Jörmungand," I say. "Jörmungand is the great serpent who encircles the oceans around Midgard. He is the child of Loki and the giantess Angrboda."

"Hmm," Yafeu says absently, still watching Fritjof.

I open my mouth to say more when the doors swing open with a resounding echo, revealing the four guards. Instantly my heart jumps into my throat.

The chatter dies down as everyone swivels their heads, watching them approach Father's table. Yafeu's stare is hard, her jaw clenched tight as they pass. Thankfully, they stride right by us without so much as a glance.

Father's glare sweeps over the hall, and everyone quickly resumes their conversations, pretending all is well, though their furtive glances over to Father's table betray their curiosity.

As Father motions for the guards to sit, my mind starts to race. I turn to Yafeu. "Quickly," I whisper. "Serve them mead, so you can hear what they're saying."

YAFEU

I grab several horns and a flagon of mead and walk as casually as I can over to the king's table. Werian, Balli's serving boy, furrows his brow, but I cut him a hard look and he quickly ducks away.

". . . questioned them thoroughly," I hear one of the guards saying as I approach. I hand the horn to another guard, who accepts it without looking. "They all told the same tale as before: They assumed he had gone to visit a friend in another town. It wasn't the first time he had left without warning, so they didn't concern themselves over it."

"So, you've learned nothing," King Balli says drily.

My heart begins to race. I keep my eyes trained on the ground as I make my way around the table, handing the horns to the guards and refilling Yngvild's and Balli's horns from the flagon.

The color drains from the guard's weathered face. "We *did* learn something from the body, my king. The wound on his neck was not wide enough to fit an ax, nor deep enough for a dagger. It looks to have been made by a woman's knife. That's why we haven't returned until now: We tortured the two thrall girls day and night. But their story did not change."

I stand frozen behind the king's chair, gripping the flagon with both hands.

They *tortured* Bronaugh and Airé. Still, neither one of them gave me up. Not even to spare themselves from suffering.

Oh, Airé, I'm so sorry! You were right all along.

King Balli sighs in frustration, pinching the bridge of his nose. "Even a dimwit like you, Gunnar, should be able to see that they're only protecting each other. Broskrap's wife is dead. If a woman killed him, it was almost certainly one of them. Bring them here, and I'll question them myself. If they still won't talk, then we'll execute them both."

My mouth goes dry. The hall seems to tilt.

I lose my grip on the flagon but catch it just before it crashes to the ground.

The king looks over his shoulder, peeved. "Excuse me," I murmur. I bow and make my way back to Freydis, who is pretending not to watch me as she chats with a girl I don't recognize, likely some Thingman's daughter.

Freydis's demeanor shifts as soon as she sees my expression. She sends the girl off with a nod and threads her arm through mine. We start walking around the room arm in arm, like a pair of old friends, except that she's subtly leading me away from the heart of the festivities.

My mind flashes to the memory of Ampah and I walking down the road to Koumbi Saleh, the day I provoked those men at the market. The men who turned out to be slavers, who came for my village that very night.

Ampah died because of me. Because I couldn't control my rage. *I won't let it happen again.*

As soon as we're out of earshot, I shrug Freydis's arm off mine. "The guards are going to bring Bronaugh and Airé to your father," I say, keeping my voice low. "They know from the wound that it was a woman who killed Broskrap. He thinks it's one of them."

Freydis goes white as a sheet. I don't even need to tell her the rest: She knows what that means. She knows what will happen. "I'm sorry," she whispers.

I feel empty, detached. "I'm going to tell him it was me."

She looks at me sharply. "No."

"I have no choice."

I turn back to the king's table, but she grabs my shoulder. "Yafeu, *no*! This won't solve anything! You shouldn't have to die for what you did. You were only doing what was right!"

"And I *still* have to do what is right." I lift her hand from my shoulder, gently clasping it between mine. "I didn't save Airé just to let her die in my place."

"Please . . ." Her voice starts to waver, her wide, lichen-colored eyes glistening in the torchlight. "I just need more time. I'll think of something. I'll find a way to save them *and* you."

"It's too late. I'm sorry." I start toward the royal table again, but she seizes my arm.

"Wait! I have an idea!"

I pause, following her dogged gaze to the closest longtable, where a handful of her father's guards are drinking and carousing. Her eyes alight on a heavily built man with long, braided orange hair and a matching beard. Orange fuzz covers his arms—arms that encircle a squirming young thrall, a girl at least several winters younger than me. She tries to climb out of his lap, but he pulls her back with a growl of a chuckle, nuzzling his head into her neck.

My hands ball reflexively into fists. But my anger is quickly chased away by confusion as Freydis makes her way over to the table, motioning for me to stay behind. "Erik," she calls out to the man.

Erik looks over and inclines his head respectfully. The thrall girl wisely takes the opportunity to slip away. He says something I can't make out over the cacophony of voices, but I recognize his voice: It's one of the hunters who found Broskrap's body.

Freydis converses with him for a short while, then she places a hand on his arm and leans down to whisper something in his ear. Instantly, Erik's expression hardens. When Freydis leaves, he stands and trudges off.

"What did you say to him?" I ask as Freydis resumes her place beside me.

"What I had to."

Barely a moment passes before shouts start to rise above the din.

"Murderer!" thunders Erik. "You honorless nithing!"

A deathly hush falls over the feast.

"Quit your prattling, Erik. You've had too much to drink." I recognize the baritone voice as that of his hunting partner.

"How could you, Knut? How could you kill him over your *whore* of a sister?"

It dawns on me what Freydis has done.

The other man leaps to his feet, towering over his accuser. Erik is bulkier, but Knut has at least a head on him, his pale face scrunched with fury. Both men are poised as though they would tear the other limb from limb right now, were they not in the Great Hall on a sacred night.

"I killed no one, you cow-milking oaf!" Knut roars.

King Balli stands, and all the eyes in the room turn to him. "This is a grave accusation, Erik," he calls out. "Do you have any proof?"

Erik shifts his weight from foot to foot. "I know it in my heart of hearts!" he calls back.

"This matter has troubled us all greatly," the king says evenly. "But if there is no proof, then I cannot lay the guilt on Knut—"

"I challenge Knut to a *holmgang*!" Erik shouts.

An eager murmur racks the crowd at this sudden turn. A woman cowers against the far wall, weeping quietly to herself. From the way no one will comfort her, I gather she's Knut's sister.

But a grin spreads over Knut's face. He looks like a hyena that has just cornered his prey. "I accept."

The king ponders for a moment, then nods. "So be it."

Immediately, the crowd erupts in a cheer. All except for Knut's sister, who bawls loudly until two women lead her away, sharing a look of distaste even as they do so.

"What's happening?" I ask Freydis, overcome by a mixture of relief and confusion.

"Erik has challenged Knut to a *holmgang* over the murder of Broskrap," Freydis replies, her tone strangely vacant. "It means they will fight to the death."

25

YAFEU

Lisa rises and sets three times, and on the fourth day we set out for Leidholm. It's a tiny wisp of an island only a short row down the bend of the fjord, surprisingly close to Skíringssal but invisible from its shores thanks to the mainland's mountainous ridge.

I steer a small rowboat with Freydis through the quickening currents of the fjord. It's a cold day today, and the sea air blows even colder across the water. Rowing soothes the chill in my bones a bit, but Freydis shivers and pulls her own otter cloak closer around her shoulders.

"So anyone can challenge anyone else to a *holmgang*?" I ask, my teeth chattering.

Freydis grimaces as the wind picks up, whipping the fine strands of her hair out of its braid. "Only if the challenger has been greatly wronged by the challenged. It's how a man can seek justice, outside of a trial."

"Can't the other man refuse?"

She shakes her head. "He would be decreed an outcast, a coward with no honor. To us, it's a fate worse than death. He would be chased out of Skíringssal and forbidden from ever returning. And he would find no welcome elsewhere: No one in all the kingdoms of Norveg would give food or shelter to an outcast. Not even passage on a ship may be granted him, according to our laws."

"Then where do they go? What happens to them?"

"I don't know. It is said that some outlaws try to survive deep in the woods. But if the beasts don't take them, the winter will. Even a man of little honor would rather die in battle."

What strange laws her people have. I round the bend and row for a while in silence. Leidholm looms larger and larger ahead of us, and soon we reach the shore. I drag the rowboat into the tall grass, falling behind Freydis. The islet is all weeds, untamed grasses, and wildflowers, dotted with the occasional cluster of birch trees and ax-marked stumps.

Freydis leads me to a clearing in the center of the islet, where the grasses have been cut short. Yngvild and Balli, Erik, the guards, and a small contingent of Thingmen are already there, all wrapped in thick furs against the biting cold. One of the king's men has brought a goat, which paces nervously back and forth on its tether.

Erik paces much the same way. He holds a simple short sword in one hand and a yellow shield in the other, and he wears a metal helmet that sits so low on his nose it barely leaves room for his eyes. I wonder how he can see well enough to fight for his life.

The king looks annoyed to see his daughter in attendance, but he doesn't say anything. It's my fault we're here: I told Freydis that it was my duty to at least bear witness to the duel, since I am Broskrap's true killer. She gave me a puzzled look but didn't protest.

Soon Knut pulls onto shore and joins the group, bearing his

own short sword, finely made though covered with scratches, and a heavily worn leather chest plate. Erik's chest plate is spotless, his helmet gleaming—but Knut's armor has actually seen battle.

I had assumed that Balli's guards were the best of the *hird*men, but apparently the opposite is closer to true. According to Freydis, they all get the same share of the spoils from the raids, and though it's much safer to remain in Skíringssal and guard the king, it's also much duller, and much less glorious. And most *Majūs* value glory and adventure over safety, especially since the warriors who die in battle have a chance to go to Valhalla. By comparison, dying of old age is almost dishonorable. It explains why they fight with such abandon too.

The *hird*men often mock the guards as cowards, but occasionally a soldier will decide he's had enough glory and adventure for one lifetime and ask to join the guard. Usually the man has taken a wife and had several children by then, and he's ready for a less dangerous way to put food in their bellies.

Clearly Knut is one of those. Now his reaction to the challenge makes more sense. He's itching for a good fight; I can sense it in the tensing of his arms, in the eagerness of his *nyama*. The warrior energy thickens the air like an invisible mist, setting everyone on edge.

When everyone has taken their place, Balli gestures and two of the guards stake animal hides into the soft earth, marking the battleground. He begins stating the rules.

The list of rules goes on and on, to my surprise. No dispute in my uncle's village would ever be settled in such a brutal manner, but it has its own kind of logic. The *Majūs* are a violent people, savage even, but they have their warrior's creed, and every warrior respects it. If nothing else, I admire them for that.

Finally, Balli raises his arms, and the duel begins.

It doesn't take long for Knut to strike. He thrusts his sword forward, aiming for Erik's side, but Erik blocks it and swings his sword back wildly. Knut dances easily out of reach.

As I watch them trade blows, blocks, and dodges, I feel a strange thrill come over me. I've never seen two *Majūs* fight each other before, and it delights me to study their form and technique. But there's more beyond their tactics that captivates me: They fight as if in a trance, reminding me of the shaman in my village, the way his *nyama* would almost shimmer after consuming the root bark of the iboga plant. Like him, their bodies are in our world, but their spirits are in a higher realm.

It quickly becomes clear that while Erik is the stronger of the two, Knut has more stamina, moving with a fluid, well-trained grace. Soon Erik is heaving in ragged breaths, his anger no longer enough to sustain the pace of his frenzied blows.

Erik staggers backward, and Knut is on him in an instant, like a wolf leaping on fallen prey. He knocks the shield out of Erik's hands with his own and plunges his sword deep into Erik's chest.

A cheer rises from the spectators as Erik falls to his knees. My stomach lurches as he takes his last breath, then crumples, his blood pooling out onto the hides.

Knut is proclaimed the winner. He immediately places a large bowl under the goat and slits its throat. It dies quickly, without bleating, to the approval of all. Knut lets the blood both collect in the bowl and spill out onto the wet earth. "To the king, and victory!" he says, holding up the bowl. A sacrifice of some kind.

I look to Freydis to explain, but she says nothing. Her wide eyes are glued to Erik's corpse, her face a shade too pale.

And with that, it is done. Blood repaid with blood.

That night, as I stare at the ceiling in Freydis's room, my body wrapped in warm furs on the makeshift bed, my belly filled to bursting with leftover scraps of goat meat, I pray to the gods. I beg Mawu-Lisa for forgiveness for allowing another to fall in my place. No matter what kind of man he was in life, Erik didn't deserve to die for my crime.

But he did, because of Freydis. Because she wanted to earn my trust. She didn't save just my life, but Bronaugh's and Àirè's too—knowing full well it would cost the life of one of her own people. She manipulated two grown men into fighting to the death over a lie.

How sorely I've underestimated her. It scares me to think that she's capable of that, but it impresses me just as much. And I feel as grateful to her as I do guilty. The conflicting feelings swirl and clash in a storm of confusion.

"Freydis?" I roll to face her, the wooden frame squeaking under my weight.

She does the same. "Yes?"

I will earn your trust, Yafeu. Your full trust. No matter what it takes.

I want to tell her what Alvtir said to me at the docks. That I'm not going with her to Trøndelag. But at the last moment, I think better of it. I turn back to the ceiling. "Never mind. Good night."

I can trust Freydis to save my life, but that doesn't mean I can trust her to let me go.

Lisa is setting as I trot across the rolling green hills. I move toward the sound of water in the distance, pacing myself to the rhythm of the earth.

I approach a pool fed by a small waterfall and stop to take a drink. The water coats my parched throat and sweeps through my body. It feels like the sensation of chewing peppermint. I breathe deeply and open my eyes.

As I gaze at my reflection in the water, I realize that instead of two legs, I have four, all covered in fur—and yet my upper body is still the same. The silver fur shines with the unnatural glimmer of the spirit world. I tremble with awe as I look into my human eyes and down my marula-colored arms. My bare chest sways lightly as I shift my hindquarters to get a better look at my reflection.

"She's over there!" I hear Freydis's voice call from a distance.

Panic floods me. I race away from the sound of her voice, but it feels like my legs are moving through molasses . . .

26

YAFEU

I t's too cold to venture outside the next morning, so Freydis decides to spend the morning teaching me the runes. She says that the runes hold all the magic of her people, and to learn them is to learn how to call on the gods.

I still don't know what to think about her gods. Some of them are not so different from mine, and I've often wondered if they're not one and the same, with different names in different lands. The antics of Loki the Trickster are like those of the mischievous Legba; Thor, god of thunder and lightning, sounds a lot like Sogbo.

But her gods don't *behave* like gods at all. They welcome chaos over order, always testing themselves against one another, always acting on the strangest whims. The stories she tells me about them are laughably absurd: In one, Thor must dress like a woman to pass as Freya at her wedding; in another, Loki fathers a horse with eight legs. I doubt that all the stories are true—if the gods themselves are even true gods.

But learning the runes is as good a way to pass the morning as any, and better than most alternatives Freydis could come up with. So we sit cross-legged on cushions in front of the fire as Freydis carves each rune into a piece of firewood and explains the meaning it holds. Her eyes are alight with a familiar mischievous glint, the same spark I often see in them when we are training.

"This is *fe*," she says, carving a long line with two smaller ones jutting upward at an angle from the center. "It stands for the sound *fffff.*"

"Like your name," I say, stifling a yawn. I didn't sleep well last night, and it's difficult to pay attention to Freydis's lesson.

She nods excitedly, ignoring my fatigue. "Exactly! And for that reason, it is used to invoke Frigg, Freya, and Frey. It is from the mysterious fire of *fehu*—a fire that was born of water—that Frigg and Freya derive their power as seeresses. Hence, *fehu* is also the source of a rune-caster's ability to harness the magic of the runes. Fritjof says that such power lies hidden in all of us, like a wolf in the forest. But to draw on that power, one must face the darkest parts of oneself."

A wolf in the forest. The dream from last night flits through my mind. "I dreamed last night that I was a wolf in a forest," I say idly.

Freydis straightens. "What happened in the dream?"

I shrug and squint into the fire, sifting through the dregs of the vague memory. The wind groans outside, rattling the walls. "I remember I was . . . looking in a pool at the base of a waterfall. And my reflection was strange. The bottom half of me was a wolf, I think. But the top of me was the same."

The blood drains from her face. "Your *fylgja*," she whispers. "Your *fylgja* appeared to you."

I frown. "What's a *fylgja*?"

"A companion, of sorts. A spirit who accompanies you, who guards you throughout your life."

Mama's voice echoes in my head: *The painted wolf was howling, the night you were born . . . she is with you, always . . .*

"What does it mean?" I ask.

She looks down. The knife and log are quaking in her trembling hands. She puts them down and clasps her palms together. "I-I can't say for certain. When your *fylgja* appears to you as an animal, it's usually a sign of good fortune to come. But seeing *yourself* as a *fylgja* . . ." She meets my eyes, lowering her voice to barely more than a whisper: "It's an omen of death."

I suppress a smirk. After everything we've been through, Freydis is still so superstitious.

I make a show of weighing her words, until I realize I really am considering them; it *was* a very disturbing dream. "Maybe it means that I am poised between two fates," I say finally.

She leans over and seizes my hands in her own, her green eyes alight once again. "That must be it! We should cast a spell." She leaps to her feet and rummages through her assorted baskets, tossing out their contents in her impatience. I roll my eyes, knowing I'll be the one to clean this mess up later.

"Aha!" she says triumphantly, holding up a bone. "It's a thigh-bone from the wolf you killed!"

"Have you done this before?" I ask curiously. I never thought of Freydis as a sorceress, but now that I have seen the depth of her knowledge of these magical markings, I wonder . . .

"Yes," she says simply. She curls her legs underneath her and picks up the knife, setting her focus on the bone. "Now, we will start with *perthro* . . ."

Her brow furrows in concentration as she carves the first rune with the finesse of practiced fingers. "You have more skill than you let on," I say carefully. "You are not only a weaver. You know things. Useful things."

She snorts. "My parents always said that I was useless, so I guess I looked for ways to prove them wrong. Not that it ever changed their minds." Her tone is light, but there's pain in her expression. "Anyway, they wouldn't approve of this particular skill. Father would beat me senseless if he knew I was a rune-caster."

I study Freydis appraisingly, remembering another of Papa's

lessons: *There are many kinds of strength in the world, as many as the people who possess them.* I never understood what he meant by that, but I'm starting to now.

"I don't know who I would have become if my family treated me that way," I confess. "My father must have known that the things he was teaching me were not proper for a girl to learn. But he never seemed to care. And when he left us in the village, my mother and my brothers were the only people who didn't hate me for who I was. And Ampah."

"Ampah? I don't think you've mentioned her before. Is she in your family too?"

A lump rises to my throat. I hug my legs into my chest. "She was my only friend. She died in the desert."

Freydis pauses, her knife hand stilling on the bone. "You must miss her very much," she says tenderly.

"I do." I swallow. Freydis lays a hand on my forearm. We sit for a moment in silence. I'm the first to break it, not wanting to sink any deeper into my grief. "So, what is this spell we're casting?"

An eerie grin lights up her face, half shadowed in the dim light of the fire beside us. She leans in, eyes glittering. Outside, the wind screams. "We're invoking the Norns. To sway the tides of your destiny."

27

YAFEU

At first, winter filled me with delight.

Freydis walked with me outside when the first flakes of white fell from the sky. She couldn't believe I'd never seen this "snow" before, and she laughed at my awed expression as I spread the fine substance across my reddening fingers. I laughed back at the sight of the flakes clinging to her eyelashes. We spent that afternoon bunching the snow into balls and throwing them at each other, laughing even as our skin stung.

But the charm wore off quickly; now the whole city is buried. The one trip we've been able to make was to check in on Fritjof in the city, and only because Freydis wanted to ensure he had everything he needed to outlast the winter. Blankets upon blankets of snowfall stretched that otherwise quick excursion into a long and grueling journey.

And the snow is nothing compared with the cold—the brutal, unrelenting cold that turns the snow into ice, covering the trees in glittering shards of hoarfrost that remind me of Alvtir, making me long even more for her speedy return. The fjord does not freeze over, but everything else does. It's dangerous now to go outside: We could slip and fall on the ice, or get so cold that our fingers and toes could turn black and have to be cut off. So we've been stuck inside for one moon after another. How anyone lives like this year after year is beyond me.

Lisa travels faster and faster across the sky, until his daily journeys are as swift and fleeting as they were long and leisurely in the summer. The enduring darkness seeps into my mood, infecting it. A restless energy has begun to keep me awake because I can't tire my body during the day. My arms have lost some of the strength they'd regained, and it makes me angry at no one in particular.

Yngvild has announced that she is with child, and though the baby hasn't even quickened yet, there's a great fuss and fawning over her among Helge and the other thralls. The upside is that Freydis and I are mostly left to our own devices. We've begun taking most of our meals alone in her room. I'm relieved, even though I have to do all the cooking; I don't cherish any moment spent in Yngvild and Balli's presence. Aside from their obvious contempt for me, there's something wrong with Balli's *nyama,* something that leaves an acrid taste in my mouth. I would be glad to go with Freydis to Trøndelag just to escape them, if it weren't for Alvtir's promise. *Soon, soon, soon . . .* I hear her voice echoing in my head every day.

There isn't much to do, at least not while the snow persists, to prepare for Freydis's wedding, which is to take place as soon as the last of the frost has melted. So we set about finishing Freydis's wedding dress. It shouldn't have taken us longer than a few days, but nothing ever seems to satisfy her, even the work by her own hand; she'll finish lacing a brocade along the hemline and then immediately exclaim that the design isn't quite right, and we must take out the silver thread with extreme care. We went through eight different pairs of brooches before she found one suitable. Every time we pick up the thimble and thread she sighs heavily, and her shoulders fold inward. I've been wondering if it's more than the restlessness that I too am feeling, if instead she's trying to prolong the task—as though she won't have to get married if she doesn't have a dress ready in time. In fact, whenever I mention King Hakon, her husband-to-be, she shrinks back down and changes the subject.

The last time she did this, I finally asked her why she doesn't want to talk about him, and she told me that she was first betrothed to someone else. Another king named Harald. She met him when they were children, and she found that she liked him. She was happy enough when her father picked him, even though she herself had no say in the matter. Now she doesn't know what to feel: She's never even *met* Hakon. She will marry a stranger, a man who's just as likely to be cruel to her as kind.

I can't say I envy her fate, even with all the power and respect that comes with it. Likewise, I can't help but feel guilty whenever she talks about us going to Trøndelag together. But I figure it's better to let her hold on to that illusion for now. She'll be upset enough when Alvtir returns and reveals her plan for me. If I tell her before it's too late, she might even find a way to stop me. So I keep my future to myself and do my best to keep her mind off hers.

We often spend the evening telling each other stories. I tell her the ones I would beg Mama and Papa to tell again and again when I was little. Like the story of Amanirenas, the one-eyed warrior-queen of the East, who leads her army to victory against the foreigners who had conquered her land. After Amanirenas captures their forts and drives them away, she knocks off the head of a statue that bore a resemblance to the evil foreign king, and she buries it beneath one of her people's sacred temples to honor her triumph. And the story of Ogiso Emose, the first woman to rule Igodomigodo, where Mama is from. Emose's mother was a great trader, renowned across the kingdom for her beautiful beads and clothes. She dies giving birth to Emose, but Emose inherits her wealth, fame, and mind for trade—and her abiding love of beautiful things—

and becomes one of the greatest Ogisos to ever rule. Freydis likes this story the best, of course. In return, Freydis shares with me the stories Fritjof and Helge would tell her as a child. My favorite is the bear's son—a story about a warrior with a bear's strength and courage, who fights a ferocious monster that had killed his companions and terrorized his king's hall.

Finally, the snow begins to melt. It isn't even close to warm, but winter is releasing the land from her claws. The city stirs slowly, as if waking from a great slumber. The brook beside the hill has cracked and thawed into a slow trickle. Everything smells wet and new.

"I wonder how long it will take for the farmers to rise up against my father," Freydis says one night. We're both in our beds and I was beginning to drift off to sleep, lulled by the crackling sound of the fire. Freydis asked me to stay with her night after night, until it became clear without her having to say so that I was to share this room with her and move the skins out of the shed. I was grateful to get away from Helge's permanent scowl, so I sleep here without complaint.

"What do you mean?" I ask thickly, my head heavy with the promise of sleep.

She rolls to face me. "This is the longest, coldest winter I can remember, and the farmers feel the effects of the cold well after it's passed. It hardens the soil, which weakens the seeds. In Hvitbjorg this past summer, the harvest was so low that the jarl feared the farmers wouldn't have enough to feed their families over the winter. But Father still demanded the same share of the crop." She sighs and pulls the fur up to her chin. "I've been wondering how those families are faring now. If they've lost any children. If they're angry with Father for ignoring their plight."

Of course they're angry, I wish I could say. *I feel angry on their behalf. Don't you?* Instead, I say nothing, and soon sleep overtakes us.

I haven't seen the *fylgja* again, and Freydis says this is good. Instead, my dreams—the ones I remember—are of my family, or

Alvtir, or the curious soldier who caught my gaze before the war-ships left.

I wake this morning before the first light, wrenched from a cozy dream of Mama rocking me in her arms by a sense of wrongness coiling in my gut. I wipe the sleep from my eyes, roll out of bed, and throw on my boots and one of Freydis's cloaks, not bothering to wake her to ask her permission.

As if compelled, my feet carry me outside and over to the front of the hill, past the Great Hall. I turn my gaze to the fjord, pulling the cloak closer around my shoulders against the freezing predawn air. Lisa has just begun to lighten the sky, and I can just make out the blurry shapes gliding across the dark waters . . .

The ships!

Alvtir.

I race down the hill, not caring who sees me or how suspicious it looks that the princess's "black elf" is running around alone before dawn. The trumpet sounds in three lengthy blasts from the guard tower, alerting the slumbering city to the *hird*'s return.

Soon. Alvtir's promise runs circles in my head, growing louder and louder. But when I finally reach the harbor, I see only green-and-white sails rounding the bend.

Where is Alvtir's ship?

The first ships dock and the weary soldiers disembark to an equally muted reception from the growing cluster of cold, tired cityfolk. Noticeably fewer men climb off the ships than got on them that day they left. Wherever they went, they took significant losses.

The knots in my stomach tighten as the hatchet-faced man hops onto the dock. He shoots me a menacing smile, like he's happy I've come.

Soon I see why: The last of his soldiers disembarks, dragging nearly a dozen people, bound to one another with rope, behind him. People with skin the color of roots and bark and the earth.

He's taken more of us. My heart sinks with the weight of a new anchor, a new despair. I flash back to the caravan, to when I was bound to a chain of bodies like this one.

"They were a gift from the gods, you know."

I whirl on the hatchet-faced man, narrowing my eyes. He folds his arms across his chest with a triumphant smile.

"The ship carrying them to Iberia must've docked just before ours," he continues. "We found them tied to the deck, just like that, waiting for us to take them." He winks.

I clench my jaw as I hold his mocking gaze, digging my finger-nails into my palms until I draw blood. But I don't lash out. Because that's exactly what he wants.

Instead, I force myself to turn back to the new thralls. The sunken eyes of an elder lock with mine. He makes a noise and the others look my way. I can see the last embers of hope sparking back to life in their irises as they take in my skin, dark like theirs, and my healthy, groomed appearance.

But I have no hope to offer this man. Nor any for the others.

The elder opens his mouth, but before he can speak and earn himself a beating, I turn away and sprint up the hill.

I run as fast as I can all the way back to the royal longhouse, ig-noring the scorching ache in my legs. Freydis snores away as I hang up her cloak and climb back into bed with my pulse hammering in my ears. She sleeps like nothing has happened. Like everything is normal, because for her, it is.

I have no doubt that that wretched man brought those people here just to deepen my suffering. But in the workings of another realm, I wonder if this isn't my retribution from the gods, a twist of justice for letting an innocent man die for my crime.

The thought makes my chest ache. I make a promise to Mawu-Lisa to help the new thralls however I can.

Still, the skins beneath me grow wet with tears.

Over breakfast, Freydis tells me that Hatchet-Face's name is Snorri, and he's Broskrap's oldest son. I should have known. As we put the final touches on her wedding dress, I keep my guilt at bay by imagining all the different ways I could kill the pale-haired snake. The neckline becomes his throat as my fingers close in on it, squeezing the life out of him. Then my knitting needle becomes a dagger to the jugular. He bleeds out slowly, like his father. The images get more and more detailed, until I realize I'm frightening myself with my lurid thoughts.

"We have to find the new thralls," I say as Freydis tries on the dress.

"Why?" she asks absently, running her hands over her waist. "Do you think it's too tight here?"

I stamp my foot in frustration, startling her. "Because! You don't know what it was like for me when I first came here. I have to help them, however I can."

"All right," she says, though her expression is quizzical.

"You don't have to come with me. Just give me the afternoon off."

"I want to help. And it will go easier for you if I'm there."

By the time we've dressed and made our way down to the city, it's late in the afternoon. We go from stall to stall, then house to house, asking everyone from the traders and the artisans to the fishermen whether they've seen thralls with skin the color of mine. I'm reminded of when I made these same rounds asking for my father, back when I was Broskrap's thrall. Only this time, with the princess at my side, the people are far more respectful—and helpful. Most of them know who I'm talking about: Even if the color of their skin didn't stand out, Snorri apparently paraded them around before auctioning them off to the highest bidders. But no one remembers exactly who those bidders were. Until we come to a house Freydis remembers as belonging to a carpenter and his family.

A heavyset woman answers the door wearing a scowl, which disappears from her red face when she sees who it is. "Princess Freydis! How can I help you?"

Freydis searches her memory. "It's Thurid, right? You are Skarde's wife?"

The woman looks pleased as a peach. "You have quite the memory, Princess!"

"We're looking for the thralls who arrived this morning," I jump in. "The ones who have dark skin, like mine."

She wrinkles her nose, but Freydis gives her a cloying smile. "If you know where any of them are, I would be *most* grateful."

The woman hesitates. "We bought two of them, a boy and an old man. I think they call themselves"—she furrows her brow—"Na-he-roh and Ma-ba-noh. All the others were taken to the farms."

Through her terrible pronunciation, I recognize the names Nyeru and Mbaneh. Soninke names.

My heart leaps into my throat. Freydis and I share a look. Of all the slaves Snorri could have brought back to Skíringssal, what are the chances that they too would be Soninke? It seems too far-fetched to be a coincidence.

"I don't know if we'll keep the elder one much longer," the woman adds. "Snorri offered us a good price to take him with the boy, since neither would be suited for hard labor, but he's worse for wear. He might be too feeble to be of much help to us. Not to mention he doesn't speak a lick of our language, and the old don't learn so quickly as the young."

"I can help him—and you," I say. "I come from the same kingdom they do. I speak their tongue. I can teach them yours. Even the elder."

She considers for a moment, her eyes darting back and forth between me and Freydis. "I suppose it can't hurt. If that's all right with you, Princess."

Freydis nods. "Where are they now?"

She points us to an outbuilding, then disappears inside her house.

We head to the outbuilding, but Freydis leaves me at the door.

"You're not coming in?"

She shakes her head and looks up at the sky, pink with Lisa's descent. "There's nothing more I can do. You're free to stay here for the evening."

That word: *free*. Can someone truly be *free* if it's only for an evening?

"Thank you," I say anyway, and part of me means it—not for letting me stay, but for continuing to track down the others.

I open the door and step into the muggy gloom. Two dark-skinned figures sit by a crackling firepit, one child and one man. I recognize the man immediately as the elder I noticed on Snorri's ship. He's washed since I saw him this morning, but it hasn't helped his appearance much. The woman was not wrong: He's too frail, even for an elder. But his *nyama* is vigorous, his large brown eyes lively under a thin line of coiled gray hair. He studies me as I get closer, tilting his wizened face to one side. Next to him, a young boy—seven or eight years old, at most—stares up at me fearfully. I'm reminded with a pang of how Kamo and Goleh looked at his age.

"You see, Mbaneh? Kinswoman has come for us," the old man says in Soninke, slinging his arm around the boy reassuringly.

The rapture of hearing the silky flow of Soninke for the first time in so long is quickly replaced by a surge of guilt.

"I'm sorry I ran from you earlier, kinsman," I say, addressing him using the same term of familial endearment that he so generously used for me. "I didn't know you were from Wagadu until I heard your name."

"Are we not all the children of the gods, whether we are Soninke or no?"

I hesitate, wondering at the meaning of such piercing words. "I'm Yafeu," I say without thinking. When did it become so natural for me to give my father's name as my own?

"I am Nyeru. And this is Mbaneh."

The boy hides behind Nyeru's sullied tunic. I smile awkwardly.

Interacting with young children was never something I did well. I always felt they were more of a nuisance than anything else, and the mothers in my village were all too glad to keep their babies away from the *jugu* girl. "It's a blessing to meet you, Mbaneh," I say.

"I sense that you've had a long journey, Yafeu," Nyeru says. "Even longer than ours." His gaze is soft and full of mourning. There is a sense of the divine in his *nyama,* much like the diviners of Koumbi Saleh, and yet he seems so much . . . *warmer* than any priest I've ever met. It's as though he feels no need to hide his own hardships, and so I shouldn't feel the need to hide mine.

I feel a momentous uncoiling of the tightness in my chest. Tears well behind my eyes as I nod.

"Tell me," he says gently, patting the empty seat at his side.

I sit on my knees and start at the very beginning. I tell him of my capture in my village, of my mother getting Kamo and Goleh to safety as I fell, of the long caravan through the desert, Ampah's death, the merchant at Anfa, the indescribable connection I felt with Alvtir, the betrayal I felt when she left me with Broskrap, the terrible rage when I saw him hurting Airé, killing him in the grips of that rage, then being given to Freydis that very night, Alvtir's cryptic promise, growing closer with Freydis, how she lied to spare me from being punished for Broskrap's murder. As the words tumble out, I grow more and more emboldened. I realize I've never spoken my full story aloud before. I've told bits and pieces of it to Freydis— but with her, I'm always holding something back. Somehow, the compassion I feel in Nyeru's gaze compels the full truth out of me. Maybe it's also the telling of my story in my own language; it feels harder to hide behind than the slippery tongue of the *Majūs.* When I choke up at certain parts, overwhelmed with grief or despair, Nyeru reaches out and clasps my hand. Eventually Mbaneh does the same, trusting me because his elder does. I grasp his tiny hand in my own, letting the ache for my brothers fill me instead of pushing away the pain like I usually do. Finally, I come to the *hird*'s return. "And you are the first ones I've found," I finish. I fall silent, feeling a wonderful sense of lightness, as though the weight of all those memories was somehow lessened by sharing them.

Nyeru leans back. Something about his expression, kind yet solemn, reminds me of Mama. "Your spirit knows where you're going, and how to get there, Yafeu. Do not question that."

I struggle to digest his words. "Who were you back in your home village?" I ask, mystified. "Where do you come from?"

"I too was taken by slavers," he says. Nyeru tells me of his village, only half a day's walk from mine along the route to Koumbi Saleh. He is a shaman of one of the *Maghan* clans, the direct descendants of Diabe Cissé, the first Soninke. To be a shaman from such a line—he must have been highly respected, revered even. He had a family, he tells me; he was content with what the gods had provided for him.

Then the gods changed their minds. The slavers came and destroyed their village and captured as many as they could, just the same as they did to mine. His wife and children were slaughtered in the scuffle. He and Mbaneh, the grandchild of his younger brother, were the only ones from his family who survived the grueling journey across the desert. The slavers sold them and the rest of the survivors to a foreign merchant, who took them to al-Andalus. That's where they were taken by Snorri.

Eventually Mbaneh nods off to sleep. Nyeru and I stay up conversing, sharing stories of our past lives.

"Nyeru," I say softly, remembering my promise to Thurid. "You must learn the language here, as I have. The *Majūs* are not a forgiving people. If you're not useful to them, they will sacrifice you to their strange gods. But I can teach you and Mbaneh how to survive here."

Nyeru nods solemnly and clasps my hand in his. "Thank you, kinswoman. I knew from the moment I saw you that you were sent to us by the gods."

I smile weakly, feeling the twinge of guilt yet again. Snorri said *they* were sent to *him* by the gods. I wonder if there's any truth to either claim. Maybe Snorri's gods sent them to him, and then my gods sent me to them. Or maybe my gods sent them here, but not to punish me: Maybe they didn't want me to be alone anymore. I wonder if I'll ever know. I wonder if it even matters.

I'll fall asleep here if I don't go back to the longhouse now, so I reluctantly climb to my feet. "I'll return as soon as I can—with food—and we can begin our lessons."

Nyeru clasps my hand. "Yafeu," he begins, his vibrant gaze darkening.

Before he can say more, Mbaneh lets out a bloodcurdling scream. He begins thrashing around, his limbs flailing wildly against the furs. Nyeru scoops him into his arms.

"No!" Mbaneh screams, his hands clawing at Nyeru in blind terror. I help restrain him, my heart pounding in alarm.

"It's been happening every night since we were taken," Nyeru explains. "I'm grateful he doesn't remember in the morning."

My heart sinks at that. He's too young. Too young to have experienced so much suffering. "He may not remember, but he will bear the scars forever," I murmur.

"Nothing lasts forever, Yafeu," Nyeru replies. "Sogbo transforms the earth from dry and barren to wet and fertile, and back again. The waters are calm when Agbe and Naete are at peace, and chaotic when they are arguing with each other. Agé takes the spirit of the antelope felled by the hunter, and sends more antelope to be born. Even Mawu and Lisa must take turns ruling the sky. Change is the one thing we can always rely on."

Again, I'm reminded of Mama. She used to say the same thing, whenever I'd start to feel hopeless about my plight in the village: Nothing lasts forever.

Eventually Mbaneh stills, and I take my leave. I walk back to Freydis's room under the dim light of Mawu's crescent, my feet following their own memory while my mind leafs through images of the flooded banks of the White River, of golden fields of millet, of

Papa swinging down from his camel and Mama painting beads in her workshop.

Nothing lasts forever.

Alvtir's ship is the last to arrive, over a week later. I'm already in the city, perusing the stalls in the market with Freydis after my second lesson with Nyeru and Mbaneh, when I hear the triple bellow of the trumpet. My heart thunders. I push my way to the front of the crowd gathering at the harbor.

The women-warriors hop out first and tether her ship to the open dock. It feels like an eternity until Alvtir herself disembarks.

"Alvtir!" I call out, jubilant.

But she brushes past me without so much as a glance.

I am dumbstruck, rooted in place, watching mutely as she ascends the hill to the royal compound.

I feel slimy and hot all over, like my skin is covered in tar. Around me, the cityfolk continue to reunite with their loved ones, catching them up on all the tumult they've missed: the finding of Broskrap's body, the trial, the *holmgang*. Their voices fade to a dull hum as I rejoin Freydis in the market.

"There you are! Why did you . . ." She trails off when she sees the expression on my face. I follow her in silence as she mills around, eventually purchasing some beads from a glass-maker.

How could Alvtir ignore me like that? She made me a promise before she left: *Soon.* How much longer will I have to wait?

Or did she change her mind while she was gone?

I do my best to wave the doubts away like buzzing flies, but they nip at me throughout the rest of the day. If Freydis notices my mood, she wisely doesn't ask me about it.

All this time, I've been waiting for Alvtir to welcome me into her company of women-warriors. But if she's changed her mind—if I am truly no one to her—then that means I'm going to Trøndelag with Freydis. That means I'll live the rest of my life as her slave.

No. I won't resign myself to that fate. I must join Alvtir and become the warrior I was born to be. I *chose* that destiny in Anfa, and I choose it now. No matter what.

As I lie awake in bed that night, I make another promise to myself: If she doesn't recruit me before Freydis's wedding, then I'll find a way to free myself. And then I'll convince Alvtir that I'm worthy of becoming one of her warriors.

It's just like Papa said: The gods will save me, but first I must save myself.

ALVTIR

A thick warmth envelops me as I enter the Great Hall. The coppery scent of blood fills my nostrils. My brother must've made another one of his "sacrifices" last night. Or maybe it's just the spirits of the slaughtered that haunt the place, the stench of their despair on the long road to Niflheim.

I never like being in the Great Hall during the day. During the nighttime feasts, the hall of light is worthy of its moniker, glowing from the light of hundreds of soft candles and torches. But in the day the same hall transforms into a prison, dark and confining. Even now, after braving the winter elements for weeks on end, the shelter it provides is suffocating.

My brother is speaking in low tones with Snorri by the hearth. They fall silent at the sight of me.

As I approach, Balli turns away and takes a seat on the throne. Snorri folds his arms across his chest and composes his weaselly face into a toothy grin.

Something is wrong.

"*Heill,* brother." I stop next to Snorri, my shoulder brushing against his with a silent threat as we both wait for the king to speak.

My brother fixes me with a look of accusation. "Why did you separate from the rest of the fleet?"

"I took my ship to Lisbon," I reply readily. I'd prepared the excuse before we even left these shores. "The city is walled and heavily guarded, but it is said that some of the wealthiest Saracen nobles reside within. I deemed the risk too great for an open attack; instead, I made landfall out of sight of the city's harbor and went alone to the wall on foot. I waited, hidden, until the dead of night, then searched for their vulnerabilities. I had hoped to find a crack in their defenses that my crew and I could exploit for a clandestine attack. Unfortunately, we found the city to be impenetrable. There were no openings in the wall, and the Saracen patrol was organized and disciplined. It was worth the diversion, though—if only to bring this knowledge to you."

A hint of disappointment flickers across my brother's face, but Snorri's smile is that of a man who has just won a very long game of *tafl*. "Oh?" he drawls. "Did you go to Lisbon seeking riches for your king? Or did you seek an audience with the *Saracen* king?"

By Loki's misbegotten children! How did he know?

In answer, Snorri takes something from a pouch at his belt and tosses it on the ground.

A fat hand, severed at the wrist, its fingers adorned with thick rings bearing exotic gemstones.

Chlothar. The poor Frank. I wonder how long my brother drew out his torture. I'm sure it was needless; if I know Snorri, he offered to double my pay, then had Balli kill him just to get out of the deal.

Balli clucks at my silence, taking it for guilt. "Were you hoping the brute would make you his queen?"

I can almost feel Snorri preening beside me. That insult came from his forked tongue. What other poison has he whispered in my brother's ear in my absence?

"Brother," I entreat him, ignoring Snorri and approaching the throne. I take a knee, clasping Balli's right hand with both of mine. I can tell from the furrow in his brow that my sudden earnestness has caught him off guard. "The Saracens of al-Andalus would make formidable allies. For centuries, they've kept the Christians at bay."

He lets out a mirthless laugh, snatching his hand away. "Perhaps my memory is failing. Did I *order* you to go looking for allies? Was that the mission I entrusted to my *stallari*?"

His mockery snaps the last tether of my restraint. "You refuse to acknowledge the threat the Christians pose, but you cannot deny that this land grows colder every year, and the harvests are thinning. You heard Jarl Tófi: His farmers may starve before winter's end. What will happen when the other jarls fall short on the tax? I'll tell you: You will be forced to accept what they can give, or they will be forced to rebel against you. Either way, you won't be able to sustain a *hird* of this size. Your soldiers can't live on fish alone; when the grain runs out and the flow of silver dries, they will break their oaths and flee. We will be more vulnerable than ever before. An alliance with Trøndelag will not protect our people; the soil in the North has always been poor, and the frost lasts even longer than it does here. We *need* allies from the South."

"How dare you tell me how to run my kingdom?" Balli roars, slamming on the arm of the throne. "I'm the one who freed us from the Danes! I'm the one who brought might and prosperity to Agder! You'd be nothing but a ruined woman with a *cursed womb* if it weren't for my mercy!"

His words strike me like a thunderous blow from Mjölnir. I flinch, despite myself. "I do not question your wisdom as king. I see only the battlefield, but there I see what you cannot. As your *stallari,* I must beg you to at least consider—"

"You are *not* my *stallari,* Alvtir."

My ears have been jinxed by Loki himself. "Brother—"

"You've left me with no choice. Snorri will take over as leader of the *hird* in my stead. You will be a captain under his command. I leave you the shield maidens, and the men of your ship."

No.

"Brother—my king—" Words abandon me, just as the gods have abandoned me. I grasp at straws. "What of all the years past? Have I served you so poorly that you would strip me of my honor?"

"I warned you" is all he says. He flicks his fingers in dismissal.

My feet are rooted to the floor, my mind still reeling in shock.

"I look forward to seeing you in training," Snorri adds.

In an instant my hand is around Snorri's throat. "I should slit you open from nose to navel, snake!"

He gurgles and flails helplessly in response. I tighten my grip, reveling in the blue tinge that seeps into his sharp cheeks.

"Guards!" I hear my brother shout, his voice laced with panic. Then four pairs of arms are prying my own from Snorri's neck, binding them tightly behind my back.

"You can't do this to me!" I scream at Balli as the men drag me to the doors. "You can't turn your back on the will of the gods! I am a *berserker,* chosen by Odin *himself*!"

A wave of remorse crashes upon his face. Then he shuts his eyes and looks away.

Coward.

The guards haul me outside and throw me onto the cold, hard ground.

"I am the glory of—" I'm cut off by the doors slamming shut in my face.

I gaze up at the hoary sky, breathing heavily as rage cools to ice beneath my breast.

In a way, I am almost glad. Now I will feel no remorse for what I've done. I suppose blessings come in many guises, just as the All-father walks the earth wearing many faces.

The four guards remain outside, blocking the entrance with their bodies. The eyes that peer down at me from under their helmets are full of fear. Even one on four, I could slaughter them in a heartbeat. They know that as well as I do.

And their relief is palpable when I don't. Instead, I grunt and climb to my feet, brushing the snow and ice off my bottom. But the moment I turn to leave, some passing thrall crashes right into me.

Rage flares within me again, blasting through the ice. "Idiot—"

Then I notice the snow-fox fur around her shoulders, the ring of blond braids streaked with gray. That's no thrall.

Yngvild whips around and recoils as she recognizes me in turn. Her hand flies to her lower belly.

My jaw falls open.

It can't be.

She drops her hand instantly, her expression full of remorse. Then she whirls back around and rushes off without so much as a word of greeting.

It was just a moment. But it was enough.

By Thor Odinsson's large, hairy bottom!

My sister-in-law is pregnant again.

My mind races as I march down the hill, leaving the Great Hall behind me. Was that milksop of a skald right after all? Or does Freya send yet more false hope? But *why*?

Foolish woman, I chastise myself. It doesn't matter one way or the other. Yngvild is no more deserving of mercy than Balli is; an unborn babe changes nothing.

Wise One, I will serve you unto the end.

28

YAFEU

"He should be here by now!" Freydis stomps and throws yet another dress to the floor.

I roll my eyes and bend down to pick it up. From the moment she woke this morning, Freydis has been whipping through her room like a sandstorm in the desert. She's lucky her longhouse has a wooden floor, unlike the barn, or the thralls' shed I used to share with Helge. Or rather, *I'm* lucky, as *I'm* the one who washes her clothes.

"I'm sure he's on his way," I say, laying the dress on her bed with the others.

Freydis is already wriggling into yet another dress, her back to me. I walk over and tie the straps behind her shoulders. She gnaws on the nail of her forefinger as I do.

"Freydis." I turn her to face me. "What's *really* bothering you?"

She looks away. "What if his ship is damaged and sinking? Or— or blown off course by some wind or storm?"

"Is that what you want?"

A silent moment passes. Freydis sighs and turns to the door. "Of course not."

I grab one of her cloaks and follow her outside. Lisa is high and bright overhead. The sky is the faintest blue a sky could be, the clouds as white. The breeze is warmer than it has been, carrying the sweet promise of summer, though the dreadful winter still won't release its grip, visible in the ice and mud piled against the walls of the hall. It's almost a beautiful day, this day that is supposed to bring Freydis's husband-to-be to Skíringssal's shores.

For the hundredth time today, Freydis scans the fjord for his ship.

"Helge will fetch us when Hakon has arrived," I say, also for the hundredth time.

I watch her chew her bottom lip and fight the urge to offer any further word of comfort. She still doesn't know that I have no intention of going with her to Trøndelag. That when the wedding is over, our friendship—if I can even call it that—will be over as well. Still, I can't stop worrying about what will become of her in Hakon's hall. I asked Freydis what he's like, and all she knows is that he's older than she is. But will he tolerate her curiosity? Will he let her grow into the woman she wants to be? Or will she end up like her mother, yoked to a man who only values her for her potential as a broodmare?

My mind drifts to old memories of Mama and Papa together. How they laughed together. How they always seemed to be touching each other—a hand on the shoulder, an arm around the waist. I am the fruit of a union of love; I can't imagine how it must feel to have no choice in a mate.

Finally, the small dot of a ship appears at the bend of the fjord. Far from lighting up with joy, Freydis's face seems to harden into stone. She spins on her heel and beelines back to her room without a word. I follow, closing the door behind us.

"I think this is the best one yet," I say loudly, playfully ruffling the folds of her dress.

She gives me an empty smile and plops down on a cushion near the hearth. "You said that about the green one."

I study her as she stares absently into the fire, picking at the corners of the braid I wove this morning. Her fine, slippery hair is already frizzing out of it.

I grab a brush and a few strands of dyed sinew. I stand behind her and undo the braid, smoothing the strands into submission. "Whenever I was upset," I begin, "my friend Ampah would sit me down and braid my hair while I talked about whatever was bothering me."

"That sounds nice," she says. But she doesn't offer more.

I arrange her hair in one big circular braid around her head, emulating the shape of a crown, as she requested. As I'm pinning it down, the door opens with a groan. Freydis rises with a start, nervously rubbing the creases of her dress.

"King Hakon of Trøndelag has arrived," Helge says, using her most diplomatic tone. "Your father is in the Great Hall awaiting his entrance."

The short walk to the Great Hall has never seemed longer. When we arrive, Helge and I step aside to let Freydis in first.

We find King Balli drumming his fingers on the arms of the throne. Freydis glances around, likely looking for Yngvild, who is curiously absent.

"Father." She bows her head as we approach, but he doesn't acknowledge her presence. I feel a bitter hatred bubbling up inside me, but I shove it back down. I have nothing to gain by mouthing off to King Balli, and plenty to lose.

Freydis stops just behind the throne and turns to face the door. Normally I would stand with the other thralls behind the guards at the side of the room, but Freydis grabs my hand before I can leave her side, squeezing hard. We wait in silence together as the sound of footsteps grows louder and louder. The two colossal doors heave a sigh as they're pushed open, revealing half a dozen soldiers.

"King Hakon of Trøndelag," announces one of the men before stepping to the side.

An old man with a large gut spilling over his leather belt enters the hall and strides toward us. His face is pink and crusty, creasing in the way that *Majūs* skin does when it has endured many winters. His beard is long and thick, but his wispy gray hair clings to his scalp for dear life. Trailing behind him is a thin, raven-haired girl with a flat face and shifty eyes, dressed in a formfitting linen shift and a gossamer blue dress. She looks to be about my and Freydis's age, give or take a few years.

I frown as the man approaches us. "Princess Freydis," he says in a deep, throaty voice before engulfing her delicate hand in his pink paw.

Freydis flashes something between a smile and a grimace. "King Hakon. We welcome you to Agder."

It's all I can do to keep the shock from twisting my face. This *elder* is King Hakon? He's as old as Balli—at least!

"My messenger gave word of your great beauty," he continues, "but words do not do you justice." He brings her hand to his lips and gives it a loud, wet smooch. Freydis flinches, then catches herself. She lowers her chin demurely as he raises his head from her hand. His rich-brown eyes harden as they shift to the king.

"Balli!" Hakon exclaims, smiling like a boar baring his tusks.

Balli smirks down his nose. "King Hakon."

"It's been a long time, my friend. Allow me to present my own daughter, Asé."

The raven-haired girl bows briefly. "It is an honor to meet you, King Balli," she says. Her voice is treacly, like old syrup. Instantly, I don't trust her. She turns to Freydis with a too-bright smile. "And you, Princess Freydis. Is it too soon to call you Mother?"

Freydis blanches. This girl her own age is to be her daughter by marriage.

"Speaking of mothers, where is your lovely wife?" asks Hakon.

260 WILLOW SMITH & JESS HENDEL

"She is resting," Balli replies. "She has been unwell. I didn't want to tax her health before the ceremony."

"I suppose she is getting on in years," Hakon quips.

Balli's lips twitch, then break into a joyless smile. "Aren't we all, Hakon. Aren't we all."

Freydis stares at the ground in front of her. A lump rises to my throat at the sheer misery in her expression. As the two kings exchange backhanded pleasantries, I lean over and whisper into her ear in Soninke: "You said Hakon was an older man, but words don't do his wrinkles justice."

Freydis's hand flies to her mouth as she stifles a laugh.

"Stop," she says playfully in Soninke.

"I've never seen so large a belly on a man before. He looks more pregnant than your mother—"

The screech of the king's throne scraping on the floor jolts us back to the present. He steps down from the platform to stand in front of us, staring daggers at me. I meet his hard gaze, unflinching.

Before I can blink, he slaps me hard across the face.

My head ricochets to the side, but my feet don't betray me by stumbling back. I slowly turn my head back to him, meeting his eyes once again. Rage springs to life within me, matched by his own furious expression. He raises his hand to strike another time.

Hit me again. See what it gets you.

"I'm sorry, Father," Freydis cuts in. "Yafeu was . . . calling upon her people's gods to bless my marriage with Hakon."

Balli's face contorts into an unsettling smile. He lets his hand fall. "You would call on your *African* gods *here*? In this hall that is blessed by Odin himself?"

I say nothing.

"I should slaughter you like the animal you are for such blasphemy."

"Father—"

"*But* . . . " He holds up a hand to silence Freydis. "I'm feeling rather generous today. The arrival of my old friend Hakon has set me in good humor." His grin is almost inhuman now. "Bow before me, and I will ask the Allfather to forgive you."

Silence stretches out. Gritting my teeth, I give a clipped bow, never taking my eyes from Balli's.

He clucks disapprovingly. "Is that how you bowed to your black elf king?" He steps back, gesturing to the ground. "Bow before me like you would bow before him."

I know what he wants to see. Behind Balli and Hakon, Asé's thin lips curl into a satisfied sneer. I dig my fingers into my palms. Rage howls inside me.

But I don't want to die. Not today.

So I fall to my knees, then my hands. Then I lower my forehead to the dirt. I stay like that, prostrated before him, for the span of a single breath. The longest breath of my life. And when it is done, I climb back to my feet.

"*Much* better," Balli says triumphantly.

Hakon's laugh is booming. "Such girlish nonsense! That will go away when I put a little prince in her belly." He pokes Freydis's stomach with a fat finger and winks.

"You must be tired from your travels." Balli turns to Hakon and his men. "We've prepared several houses for your stay. I'll show you the way."

He throws me one last menacing glare over his shoulder as he leads Hakon and Asé from the hall.

29

FREYDIS

I shift uncomfortably in the steamy water, trying to avoid burning my backside on the hot stones in the washbasin. My skin is red all over from the heat, and my fingers and toes have pruned. But I must endure awhile longer.

The Thingmen's wives have been flitting in and out all morning, paying their respects to Frigg and adding reinrose essence to the water, kneeling with knowing smiles to whisper the secrets of intimate wifely duties in my ear. If they notice the dread I feel, they don't seem concerned.

When I finally have a moment alone, I lean back and submerge myself in the perfumed waters, taking comfort in the sensation of floating. I pray this will work, this ritual of cleansing myself of my old life. What I wouldn't give to emerge from a bath and find myself transformed into a new woman, a better woman—one who can face her fate with the grace and courage of a true queen.

More than anything, I wish Yafeu could be with me now. But only married women are allowed to attend me during the sequestration. To allow a maid into the bath chamber would be an affront to Frigg on the day of my wedding. And I'll need all the favor Frigg can give me, if there's even a sliver of happiness to be found in my marriage to King Hakon.

At least Solvi and Astrid can't attend me either. I'm sure they're beside themselves with delight. *Beautiful Princess Freydis, marrying an old man in the bloom of her youth.*

Far worse than Hakon's age or appearance is the way he reacted to my father's brutality toward Yafeu. The sight of his great belly jiggling with laughter is seared into my mind like a cauterized wound. He seems more suited for Aunt Alvtir than for me.

Maybe he was making a show of it for Father's sake, I tell myself. *He's probably much gentler than he was in his youth, as old men tend to be.*

Still, the thought of fulfilling my "wifely duties" after the wedding feast tonight brings fresh bile to my throat.

"Wipe that sour look from your face." Mother's sharp voice bounces off the walls of the bath chamber. "Men like Hakon have no stomach for a woman's bitterness."

I jerk upright, splashing bathwater everywhere and scalding my bottom on a stone. I didn't even hear her enter.

She takes a seat on the edge of the basin, placing a hand on her swollen belly. Her eyes sweep over my naked form, appraising. I draw my knees into my chest, suddenly shy.

Her expression softens. She tentatively reaches a hand to the back of my head. I flinch instinctively, but her touch is gentle. She strokes my wet hair, crown to neck. "I know what plagues your thoughts," she says quietly.

Tears form behind my eyes, blurring my vision. I can't remember the last time she stroked me like this.

"King Hakon is not a great man," she continues. "But he is not your father. And for that, at least, you can be grateful."

I nod at my knees. "Will I ever love him?" My voice is barely a whisper.

She sighs heavily, and in her exhale, I hear all the suffering she's endured at Father's side. "Such love is uncommon in a marriage. And rarer still for a queen. But you will love your sons, should the Norns see fit to give you them. And"—she pauses—"and you will love your daughters too."

I look up at her in surprise. Her usually tight, drawn face is glowing with pride, adding to my sense of wonderment.

Will I look down at my own daughter like this one day? If the Norns will it, then maybe I will find happiness after all . . .

Mother stands abruptly, her face slipping back into its usual mask of flinty disdain. I watch her long braid swing back and forth imperiously behind her as she marches out of the bath chamber, and then I am alone once again.

YAFEU

I've never seen the Great Hall look more magnificent than it does tonight. The king has spared no expense: The floors have been swept clean, the columns shimmer with a new coat of wax polish, spotless white sheepskins have been draped across the benches and slung over the beams. Barrels of sweet mead flow freely, and the tables are laden with all kinds of meats, fish, cheeses, fruits, and breads. I feel like I've walked into Valhalla itself, as Freydis describes it; all that's missing are the golden shields on the ceiling. Instead, hundreds of candles burn bright on iron chandeliers hanging from the rafters. They cast a cozy glow on the crowd of guests, some hundred or more who've come from all across Agder and Trøndelag to celebrate the wedding. I stand with Helge and the other thralls of the royal family at the side, squinting through the gaps in the crowd to see the ceremony.

Freydis stands next to Hakon. Asé and the dozens of men Hakon arrived with stand to their left; Queen Yngvild, King Balli, and Alvtir stand to their right.

The queen wears a thick, loose woad-blue dress—one that's far too big for her, even with her newly protruding belly. Is she trying to hide her pregnancy? But why? She normally courts the attention.

A wisp of smoke coils around her, emanating from Alvtir, who wears a simple black tunic with gold trim and trousers, puffing brazenly on a bone pipe. Yngvild swipes the air in front of her and shoots Alvtir a look of disgust. If Alvtir notices, she pays her no mind.

I stare daggers at Alvtir, hoping she'll feel my gaze and remember her promise to me before the night is done. But she doesn't notice me either.

Unlike her, I was forced to wear a dress tonight. Before we parted last night, Freydis pressed one of her nice dresses against me along with a pair of sandals and begged me to wear both to the wedding. It's a relatively simple flax dress, dyed a deep-burgundy color, and I'm grateful that it doesn't make me stand out even more than I already do. Though it is a little tighter on me than I'd like.

Freydis's eyes never leave the ground as she turns to face Hakon. She truly looks like a queen tonight. *She is a queen now,* I realize with a shock. Her golden hair cascades freely down her back, and her green eyes are lined with kohl, which makes them look less innocent. The silk dress we spent so long making clings to her soft curves. On her head sits a garland of wildflowers.

Asé watches with her hands clasped together in front of her, as though she's savoring the sweetness of the moment. A wave of hatred washes over me at the sight. Her wide smile doesn't quite reach her eyes. Even from here, I can tell they're glittering with smugness.

I've learned that Hakon was married once before in his youth, but his wife died last winter. Of her children, only Asé survived. That's why he's taking a young second wife—the need to bear heirs. What I can't understand is why Balli would choose Hakon for Freydis instead of the man she was supposed to marry.

Hakon hands Freydis a rusted old sword. "The sword of my ancestors is yours, until you bear me a son," he proclaims loudly. *Maybe she can use it to fend off his advances,* I think to myself with a smirk.

To my surprise, Balli steps forward and offers Hakon a sword in return, one equally as weathered. "With this sword of my ancestors, you accept your duty to protect my daughter henceforth," Balli intones. He seems as bored as Freydis is downcast.

"I accept." Hakon bares his teeth in a lascivious grin. In unison, he and Freydis take something off the hilts of each other's swords—a pair of rings, I think—and the hall erupts in cheers.

Balli raises his arms to the crowd. "Let the feast begin!"

I lean on the far wall, waiting for the feast to wane. We thralls aren't allowed to eat until the last guest has had his fill.

I'm not even hungry. Something else has been steadily filling my stomach tonight: panic. Panic that my time to come up with a plan is almost over.

Tomorrow, Freydis sails for Jómssal in Trøndelag. Unless I can think of some way to get out of her service between now and then, I'll be going with her. Just like the rest of her *things*.

For the thousandth time tonight, my eyes search for Alvtir's. She sits at the edge of the royal table, still languorously puffing her pipe. She's been ignoring me all evening, despite my many attempts to catch her eye.

How many times does she have to betray me before I learn my lesson?

I'm on my own.

Freydis gives me a faint smile. She thinks I'm looking at her. Someone places a hammer in her lap—yet another of the *Majūs'* strange wedding rituals. At this, Hakon lets out a boorish laugh that resounds even in the din of the crowded room, setting my teeth on edge. If I don't do something, that old bull will be as much my master as Freydis is.

I grit my teeth and turn to study the carousing guests. Everyone looks their finest for the occasion. The women wear richly dyed dresses held up with silver and copper brooches, the crowns of their heads ringed with garlands similar to Freydis's. The men sport patterned tunics, some with intricate detailing embroidered into the sides. Already they're leaving their seats at the table to dance with their women or paw at the other thrall girls in the shadows. Both women and men wear a great deal of jewelry: rings, bracelets, necklaces, and armbands, made of everything from gold to glass to amber. I wish I could steal the jewels off their bodies and use them to buy my freedom.

Hakon's people stare back at me with naked curiosity. I assume they've never seen someone with my complexion before. Freydis said Jómssal is much smaller and more isolated than Skíringssal; they don't get many foreigners there, even from lands far closer than Wagadu. I wonder if they also think I'm a "black elf."

I'm leveling a hard stare at a particularly leery man in Hakon's retinue when I feel someone approach me from the side. I tense instinctively, my hand flying to the side of my thigh, where one of the carving knives is strapped, hidden beneath my shift. Thralls are forbidden to carry weapons at any time, but not even a soldier in the king's *hird* would be allowed one on a feast night. So many armed, drunk men all crammed into a hall would be asking for disaster, Freydis said. But that's exactly why I couldn't bear to be defenseless.

I glance at the man out of the corner of my eye, noting the blade of brown hair brushing his angular jaw, a jaw that begins where the top of my head ends. It's the soldier I met that day at the harbor.

"Should I ask him to stop staring at you?" He inclines his head toward Hakon's man, a subtle smile tugging at the corner of his lips.

"You can ask, or I can break his nose," I reply. Oblivious, Hakon's man cracks another lewd smile. I'm speaking of him, but I hope I sound menacing enough that the soldier beside me won't try anything himself.

"Why not try your words before your fists?"

The annoyance tumbles out of me before I can stop it. "Has that worked against your enemies, warrior?"

He turns to face me, the red flecks in his beard glinting in the candlelight. He's dressed in a plain blue tunic, which makes his gray-blue eyes look even more like a gentle river, as though they're somehow in motion, somehow flowing. "The times I've chosen to speak instead of fight are the only times I don't regret," he says softly. "Many quarrels can be solved without bloodshed."

"Not all of us have the *privilege* of being heard when we speak."

His eyes widen in surprise, and I smile inwardly at the victory. But why does it feel like a victory? What is this match that we're in? I take an uncertain step back.

"I didn't realize . . ." He trails off.

"I'm a thrall, and a woman. And an elf—or so your people say."

"And yet, your fire burns too brightly to ignore. They can't put it out, no matter how hard they try."

Now it's my turn to be surprised.

"Ingmar!" A slurred voice rings out from among the king's men. One of them waves him over with a horn, sloshing mead on the ground.

Ingmar.

I whisper the name in my mind, turning it over as I would turn over a fine dagger in my hands.

Ingmar.

Ingmar looks over at the group, then back at me. "I'm sad we won't be seeing more of each other . . ."

I hesitate, but the water of his eyes washes over me. I relax, despite myself. "Yafeu."

"Yafeu. May the gods grant you good fortune in Trøndelag."

I stare up at him, unable to think of a reply. He bows his head respectfully, then starts off toward his comrades.

As I watch him take his seat, I become sharply aware, for the first time tonight, of my aloneness. Everyone here drinks and laughs with their families or friends. Even the other thralls have one another to share whispers with, in between setting out plates of food and refilling horns with mead. Freydis told me to enjoy myself, but I almost wish I were working too, so I wasn't just standing around being a spectacle. If only someone would stop staring and come speak with me instead, as Ingmar did.

I'm grateful when Fritjof picks up an instrument—a long wooden box with strings stretched across the front—and approaches the royals' table. The other musicians stop playing and the room stills, everyone turning to watch. The instrument looks like a *ngoni*, but where the griots play the *ngoni* with their fingers, Fritjof drags a brush of some kind across the strings. It makes for a flowing, mesmerizing sound. When he reaches the table, he begins to sing:

Erik the Red and his men of might
Forsook the old gods and hailed the White Christ.
They found a new land on a fell winter's day,
And to the White Christ did they give their thanks.

And yet the men could find nothing to eat
The fish had failed, and so had the meat.
Thrice did Sól ascend to her height;
Thrice did Máni sail through the night.

Finally, dizzy with hunger, they saw
That Thorhall, the right hand of Erik, had gone.
They set out to search for the man in a skiff,
Till Thorhall they found on the edge of a cliff.

His arms were wide, his gaze to the sky,
He mumbled and hissed and whirled and writhed,
And the men were frightened, for they had forgot
The look of a man in talks with the gods.

Pleaded, they did, but he would not relent,
So they went down alone to the beach where they camped.
And there on the shore, they saw with surprise
A whale had strayed to the shallows and died.

The men rejoiced and boiled the flesh,
But a sickness arose and gave them the sweat.
Then Thorhall came down from the cliff and said:
"Look what you've wrought, old Erik the Red,

Your men cannot eat, for they have not
Made offerings to the old sea god."
Erik most wisely turned to his wards
And bade them burn the whale for Njord.

When dawn arose, the air was sweet,
The fish returned, the birds in fleet,
And the land was ripe with hare and deer
For the men had remembered to praise the Vanir.

I can barely hear the thunderous applause of the audience over the sound of my heart beating between my ears. The world spins around me, even though I've had no mead tonight. I grab the wolf at my neck.

That was Mama's story. The one she used to tell me about Papa when I couldn't sleep. There were several variations in the song, but the core of the story is the same—the starving travelers, the whale, the illness, the prayer to the gods.

How could Fritjof possibly know it?

I push my way through the drunken revelers laughing and belching; it seems like the entire crowd stands between me and Fritjof.

I'm about to reach him when someone pushes past me, and I catch a flash of metal emerging from their cloak. A moment later I remember: Weapons weren't allowed tonight.

I pause to watch the cloaked man as he weaves through the crowd. He makes for the royals' table, moving too swiftly, too deftly.

There's something wrong. His *nyama* is fixed on someone.

On Freydis.

The world grinds to a halt. A single moment stretches into eternity.

In the next, Freydis will be dead, and I will be free.

"In the name of Christ!" the man shouts. He lifts the blade above his head, poised to strike.

30

YAFEU

My knife sinks into his eye as if into butter. A strangled grunt escapes the would-be assassin as he crumples to the ground.

Freydis and Hakon twist in their chairs. Their mouths fall open as they take in the sight of the dead man with a dagger in his hand and murder in his one good eye.

Asé turns to stare at me, and then everyone is staring at me, and I realize—I'm the one who threw the knife.

Bewildered, I look down at my hands; they made the choice for me.

Suddenly, all across the hall, a dozen men leap to their feet. Still others emerge from the corners or step out from behind the columns. They sprint toward the royal table, blades glinting in the firelight as they draw daggers and axes and other weapons they're not supposed to have.

Chaos descends.

The screams of women fill the air. "Protect the king!" someone shouts, though I can't tell who, nor which king they mean. All the fighting men around the royal table are on their feet just in time to meet the first wave of attackers with whatever they can grab, drinking horns and carving knives for weapons and serving platters for shields.

Several of the guards go down right away. Balli stumbles back onto the dais before he's quickly enveloped by a wall of men. Yngvild and Asé have disappeared under the table.

I race over to Freydis, who's still gaping at the assassin's body, frozen in shock. "Get under the table!" I shout. She flinches and stares at me, eyes wide and uncomprehending. With a grunt of frustration, I roll across the table, grab her arm and yank her forcefully to the ground. I pull the carving knife from the dead man's eye before turning to face the other assailants.

The hammer falls from Freydis's lap with a thud. As if woken by the sound, King Hakon grabs it off the floor and roars to his feet. He spins and smashes the head of the assailant who had just reached his side.

The attacker's skull shatters with a sickening crunch.

But the attacker wasn't interested in him—he was coming for Freydis.

To our right, Alvtir lets out an inhuman shriek and charges headfirst into a group of attackers. The few dozen *hird*men in attendance push their way through the fleeing crowd; in all the panic, they couldn't possibly get here in time to save us. I grab the useless fabric at the bottom of my dress and rip it off, freeing my legs.

Another attacker sidesteps the fray and tries to approach us from behind. I leap on him. All thoughts flee my mind as instinct takes over. A thrilling focus floods my veins, sharp and pure and ancient as the roots of the first baobab. I slash his throat with the knife and wrestle his own dagger out of his grasp as he falls.

A feral cry escapes my mouth as I whirl to face the next attacker. I see the flash of an ax, but my knife slices across his torso before he can strike. Blood pools around his fingers as he clutches his side. I waste no time sinking the dagger into his shoulder, slicing downward, aiming for the heart.

The dam has broken again. The rage flows freely, pouring into my muscles, imbuing my movements with speed and precision. I don't know these men. I don't know what they want. But it doesn't matter. These *Majūs* or those *Majūs,* it's all the same to me now. I don't even know myself anymore. I know nothing but the need to kill.

This is what I was born to do. This is the fire the gods breathed into me when they created me.

Now, at last, I will let it burn.

All too soon, every assailant near me is down. I scan the room, hungry for more. I watch Ingmar dealing an expert blow to the temple, sending his opponent crashing to the floor. Alvtir whips around, her hair undulating around her like black water. She cackles like a rabid hyena as she plunges a dagger into a man's gut.

I spot two more attackers fighting the wall of men around Balli. One of them falls, but the other hacks a hole in the line, taking down one guard, then another. He's on the verge of getting through.

I hesitate. My gaze flickers to the dagger in my right hand.

Should I stop him? Or should I let him kill Balli?

Before I can decide, Freydis grabs the kitchen knife out of my other hand. She rushes over and plunges it into the man's back. He falls face-first onto the floor.

Silence fills the hall. Freydis steps back from the body. She looks down at the blood spattered across her dress with wide eyes.

My mind returns with a sudden force. I blink and shake my head, feeling dazed. A putrid stench fills my nose. My mouth is dry. My arms pulse, my fingers cramping.

I look around, letting the dagger slip from my grasp. All the attackers are dead, as are many of Balli's and Hakon's soldiers. Most of the women and children have fled, along with a number of Thingmen.

A sob sounds from under the table. Balli's guards grab Yngvild by the elbows and lift her up onto the bench. Others do the same for Asé. Yngvild clutches her belly with both hands, whimpering and wide-eyed. Asé looks equally as stricken.

A wet feeling between my toes grabs my attention. I look down.

Three bodies. Their blood pools around my feet, leaking into my sandals, painting my toes red.

I killed them all.

Without even questioning it, I sent these men to their death. These men who were probably no more my enemy than anyone in Skíringssal.

And I *enjoyed* it.

Twin waves of horror and shame crash over me. Unsure what else to do, I drop to a crouch and murmur the blessing for fallen game in Soninke. A small gesture. Meaningless. But it will have to do.

I feel every eye in the room on me as I stand. One of Balli's guards, a fresh-faced younger man, steps forward, pointing to my necklace. "*Úlfheðinn,*" he whispers. Reflexively, I tuck the green wolf into the collar of my dress.

"*Úlfheðinn.*" The whisper echoes across the hall.

For the first time since she'd returned, Alvtir looks me in the eyes, her icy gaze boring into mine.

But then she looks down, crouching next to the body of one of the attackers. She rips something from his neck—a necklace—and lifts it to the light.

Meanwhile, Ingmar kicks the body in front of him with his boot, rolling the dead man onto his back. He pulls up the man's sleeve and pulls something off his arm.

"These bands bear the mark of King Hakon," he calls out.

"And they are wearing the sign of the Christians around their necks," Alvtir adds, holding out the necklace for all to see.

I squint. The pendant looks like *nauthiz,* the rune of necessity. A short horizontal line crisscrossing a longer vertical one.

From the gasps that rip through the hall, I know it is not *nauthiz.*

I look to Freydis, who recoils from the man she just married, her face frozen in horror.

"That's ridiculous!" Hakon says. "This is my wedding! Why would I kill my own bride?"

"Perhaps you never meant to marry her," Balli says, his eyes narrowing. He sits on the throne now, flanked by the surviving guards.

"Perhaps the wedding was a ruse," Snorri finishes for him. "Perhaps your real aim was to kill King Balli's line in one fell swoop, so you can claim Agder in the name of your Christ god!"

"Blasphemy!" Hakon booms. "I am Thor's man to the bone!"

"You're a cross-worshipper in disguise!" Balli shoots back.

More insults are shouted back and forth across the room. Both Hakon's and Balli's men reach for their makeshift weapons, but Alvtir holds up her hands.

"Enough!" she proclaims loudly. "No more blood should be spilled tonight."

Silence falls again.

King Balli is the first to break it. "My sister is right," he says, keeping his gaze hard on Hakon. "However, I cannot allow this marriage to go forward. Not until your innocence has been proven."

Hakon looks as though it's taking every ounce of his restraint not to leap over and throttle Balli in his throne. "Freydis is *already* my wife," he growls.

"You haven't bedded her," Balli says bluntly. "The marriage is unconsummated, and therefore void. Until the truth is known."

Hakon thinks for a long, tense moment, then heaves a great sigh. "I will accept this—but only because I *am* innocent."

"The feast is over," Balli announces needlessly.

Hakon storms out of the hall, his men in close pursuit. The remaining guests start filtering out, murmuring among themselves.

Exhaustion gnaws at my bones. I want nothing more than to go back to Freydis's room, or even to Helge's shed. Wherever I can curl up under a fur and be alone. But I'll have to take care of Freydis first.

I glance over at her. She's shaking violently, looking down at the body of the man she stabbed.

"There is one more thing." Alvtir's harsh voice rings out.

Balli shoots her a look edged with warning.

To my shock, she turns to me. "The princess's thrall has acted with both honor and valor. It is thanks to *her* that the princess still breathes."

Everyone is staring at me again. My face grows hot.

"As Orm said, she has revealed herself to be *Úlfheðinn*," Alvtir continues. "The Wise One must have sent her to protect us. I ask that she be placed under my guardianship, so that she may serve you in the *hird*."

It takes a few moments for me to grasp the meaning of her words. I look to Balli in silent desperation, studying every small variance in his expression as he scrutinizes me.

"Do you swear on your honor to be loyal to your king?" he says at last. "Will you follow my orders and lay down your life for me, should the need arise?"

I pause. It's no small thing to swear such an oath. But when I look to Alvtir, who gazes upon me, icy eyes laden with an intent I can't quite determine, I realize that this is my chance. My only chance.

"Yes," I reply. Remembering Freydis's lessons, I add: "On my honor."

"Then it is done," Balli says. "She will be a valuable warrior—*if* she continues to act with honor."

I don't miss the warning behind his words. I'm sure he doesn't want me in the *hird* at all, but from what Freydis has taught me, he has little choice himself. My intention was only to save Freydis; nonetheless, the men I fought were Balli's enemies as much as hers. And I fought well. Woman or no, he must acknowledge me as a warrior, or risk losing his own honor in the eyes of his people.

Tonight, that is. He is still the king, and he could always have me killed for even a hint of disloyalty.

With that in mind, I bow deeply, composing my face into a mask of humbled gratitude. But when I stand, my eyes meet Snorri's burning glare, and I can't help but throw him the tiniest smirk.

Alvtir nods and strides out of the hall without another word. "Ready Hakon's ship," Balli orders one of his guards, who nods and hurries out after her.

The few thralls who didn't flee in the chaos begin clearing the tables. Freydis snaps out of her daze. Still trembling, she takes my hand. We walk in silence together back to the longhouse.

FREYDIS

When we reach my room, I melt stomach-first onto my bed.

"You'll stain your furs," Yafeu says, lifting me gently. I sit up and let her slip the dress over my head. I watch numbly as she tosses it into the fire. So many dresses have gone up in flames lately; too many to be a coincidence.

The garland has caught on a tangle of my hair. I rip it off and toss it in with the dress, grateful to be rid of it.

Yafeu and I sit side by side on my bed in our shifts, and I realize she's waiting for me to speak first.

"I killed a man tonight," I say finally.

"You saved your father's life."

"And you saved mine."

She doesn't respond.

"You're leaving me," I add. My voice cracks and my eyes well up against my will.

"I belong with the shield maidens," she says softly.

"I suppose I've always known you weren't meant to be a thrall," I muse aloud.

Suddenly Yafeu's eyes are deep dark oceans, roiling and bottom-less. "*No one* is meant to be a thrall."

Her words sink deeper than any weapon. My cheeks burn in shame, but I force myself to hold her gaze. "You're right," I say. She always has been. "But *you* were meant to be a warrior," I add, hoping she'll think better of me for it.

Yafeu takes both of my hands in hers. "You have strength inside you too, Freydis. *Believe* it."

A wave of gratitude washes over me. I squeeze her hands tightly, blinking back tears.

"Are you sad you'll have to wait longer to become a queen?" Yafeu asks.

"I didn't want to marry Hakon," I confess. My chest clenches; again, saying it aloud makes the truth impossible to deny. "But I didn't want it to happen like . . . *that.*"

Yafeu gives me a strange look.

Before I can respond, the door swings open.

Aunt Alvtir. You can barely see the blood against the black of her tunic. I force my shoulders down from my ears.

"It's time," she says to Yafeu, not sparing so much as a glance my way before shutting the door again.

I let out a mirthless chuckle. "How kind of you to check on me, Aunt Alvtir. I'll be all right, but I thank you for your concern."

Yafeu gives me that look again. For some reason, it makes the trembling start back up. I wish I could control myself. I wish I wasn't such a weak, useless, frightened little girl.

Yafeu reaches a tentative hand to my shoulder, but I pull away. Once I've collected myself, I remember. "I was waiting for the right time to give this to you."

It takes a great deal of effort to stand and walk to my chest. I unbolt it and take out what I've been hiding: an indigo-blue cloak for Yafeu, held up by a silver brooch. I'm particularly proud of the design I had welded into the center by one of the best metalworkers in the city: It's a combination of our two tongues—or at least, how I wrote her tongue using the runes—joined together to create an abstract pattern, so none but the two of us could know its import. "I thought you might need it in Trøndelag. But even a shield maiden could use a proper cloak from time to time."

Yafeu's eyes widen, and I swell with pride. "It's beautiful," she says.

"I designed the brooch myself," I continue. "It's a mix of my language and yours. This," I say, pointing to the first set of runes, *fe* and *íss*, joined together at the points with *fe* turned upside down, "is for our two names. The runes are joined to represent our friendship. And this"—I point to the second pair of joined runes below—

"Are *maðr* and *lögr*," she finishes. "*M* and *L*. For Mawu-Lisa."

I nod, pleased as ever at her sharp memory. "In the old times, they were called *mannaz* and *laguz*—the mind of humanity, and the energy that runs through all living things. So it is also like the *nyama* that you told me about, in a way."

Yafeu throws the cloak around her broad shoulders. It fits perfectly. She beams, showing off her white teeth. It might be the biggest smile I've ever seen from her.

"Will you visit me?" I ask, my voice breaking again.

"As much as I can."

"You promise?"

"Yes."

I know she won't like it, but I can't help myself: I jump into her arms.

She hugs me back, and I let the tears spill out into sobs.

Of course the Norns would rip Yafeu away from me at the very moment she finally becomes my true friend.

When the tears subside, she lets me go. I scrub my face and watch her gather her few possessions. She gives me one last smile before turning to the door. The beautiful cloak billows around her as she walks out of my quarters, for the first time not as my thrall but as a shield maiden.

And once again I am alone.

YAFEU

I feel the cool night air moving through my nostrils, down into my chest and expanding my stomach.

I am free. At least, as free as any of the shield maidens under Alvtir's guardianship.

She leads me down the path into the city, setting a brisk pace. If she notices my new cloak, she says nothing of it.

I want to thank her for what she's done for me, but something about her demeanor lets me know to remain silent. We pass the empty market stalls, the longhouses for the prominent artisan families and their collection of sheds and outhouses, stark silhouettes against the moonlight with their roofs nearly meeting across the narrow wooden walkway. I can hear men shouting down at the fjord—King Hakon's men, readying to sail back to Trøndelag. The cloak keeps me warm despite the chill of the night, and I feel another stab of gratitude for Freydis.

We walk for ages and ages, past the westernmost house on the edge of town and into the bordering forest. I've never been into these woods before.

We follow a narrow trail through birches and evergreens and over a small, babbling brook. Mawu's face is close, her glow luminous through the budding branches overhead. It almost feels like she's giving us her blessing.

Finally, we emerge into a glade, in the center of which lies a relatively small longhouse.

A pack of hulking creatures bounds toward us. I reach for a knife reflexively, but Alvtir kneels down and spreads her arms wide. Three massive dogs barrel into her, barking and whimpering and leaping all over. Even in the moonlight, I can see the striations of their muscles under their short fur.

I almost fall over myself when Alvtir coos to them: "Yes, I'm home! Yes I am, my brave girls!"

I'm grateful for the darkness; otherwise she might see my eyes popping out of my head. She takes scraps of food out of a pouch on her belt and tosses them to the beasts, who gobble them up hastily.

"This is Yafeu." She pronounces it correctly this time. "Go say hello!"

And then they're on me, wet noses pressing against my toes and poking inside my cloak. I reach a hand out to pat their heads and I get it back covered in slobber.

They trot after Alvtir as she walks ahead. I squint for a better view of her homestead in the moonlight. A small barn and an out-house sit a few paces behind the longhouse, followed by a little fenced-in plot, maybe a garden. I can just make out another shed beyond that. Maybe it's where her thralls sleep, though it looks too small to house more than one.

She pushes open the wooden door and I follow her into the gloom. The only light is a weak red glow from a few dying embers in the hearth. Alvtir tosses in some kindling and picks up a piece of flint, striking the firesteel until the wood picks up the sparks and becomes a flame.

I glance around. Columns divide the room into three aisles, raised wooden benches running along the entire length—simple spaces for eating and sleeping. The central aisle boasts a modest stone hearth with a large cauldron hanging over it, and a tiny smoke hole overhead. In place of furs or tapestries, an impressive selection of axes, daggers, and the yellow shield with the two ravens line the walls. Hugin and Munin, Freydis said the ravens were called. Thought and memory.

The memory of the first time I saw Alvtir flashes in my mind. How she leapt down from the balcony onto the square, how she threw her sword in the air. As if its *nyama* is calling to me, my eyes are drawn to the sheathed sword lying on one of the benches.

Alvtir leads me past it to another bench lined with fur. "This hasn't been used in some time," she says gruffly. Her irises look like salt crystals in the firelight. "You will sleep here."

I nod and set what few possessions I call my own down at the foot of the bed, sending a layer of dust into the air. It's no grand collection: the otter fur, a pair of boots, my thrall's tunic and trousers from Broskrap, the dress and shift I wore as Freydis's thrall, the nightdress she gave me to sleep in, and the wolf's-teeth necklace I made. I take off the new cloak and hang it on a nearby post. The carving knife from the king's cookhouse—which, after tonight, I figured I deserved to keep—I shove under the pillow.

I turn to Alvtir. She clears her throat and shifts her weight from foot to foot. The floor creaks loudly, filling the silence between us. She runs a hand through her hair. "Well . . . we'll need to make you some armor."

"Thank you," I reply.

She nods once and turns away to undress. Unbidden, the strange image of Alvtir sleeping in a full suit of armor pops into my head, and I have to suppress a laugh. A delirious thought from a tired mind.

I crawl under the furs and my exhaustion hits me with brute force. No sooner does my head touch the pillow than I fall into a dark nothingness.

My paws strike the earth with wild abandon. The forest is a tangled mess of shadow and light, folding and unfolding ahead of me.

Is she still behind me? Have I lost her?

I use the last of my fading energy to duck into a bush. The brambles scrape my arms and snag my fur. I try to quiet my heavy breathing, sending a silent prayer to Agé: Please don't let her find me, please don't let her find me.

Just as my heart begins to settle, someone reaches through the brush and yanks me up by the hair on my head. I scream, clawing at the figure with all my might. I hit the ground with a thud and scramble to my feet.

Freydis stares at me with an eerie expression, as though she were looking through me rather than at me. Tears of blood flow down her cheeks, dripping onto her green silk dress. "I'll never let you go," she says.

Panic seizes me as she steps closer. I rear onto my hind legs and try to scratch her, but no matter how many times I slash at her face, I keep missing her skin. Confused, I look down at my paws and realize that my pelt has changed. One of my paws has the spots of a painted wolf and my other paw is the plain gray of a wolf of Norveg.

My eyes widen in horror. I look up at Freydis, but she's no longer there.

31

YAFEU

I wake with a twinge in my head and a heaviness in my bones. Lisa's light slants down through the smoke hole, illuminating my strange surroundings. Panic surges through me and I bolt upright, whipping the knife out from under my pillow—but then I remember: This is Alvtir's home.

My home, now.

Sleep beckons me to return, but I sit up and stretch my limbs, fighting the urge to close my eyes.

"Alvtir?" I call out hoarsely.

No response. In fact, no sounds of human life at all. No guards bantering outside, no clang of crockery from the cookhouse. I hear only birdsong and the swaying of trees in a gentle wind, and the air smells of citrus and resin. It soothes me. I could get used to waking up here.

As I swing my legs over the edge of the bed, I notice that I'm still in my shift from last night. I tear it off, hoping to tear the memory from my mind along with it. Gratefully, I note an extra set of clothing waiting for me on the floor. I was dreading throwing on my thrall's tunic after all this time, but the thought of wearing my other dress wasn't appealing either.

I buckle the leather belt over the light-gray tunic and run my hand over the wrinkled linen, fingering the rope-like pattern at the neckline, little interlocking diamonds of yellow and pink. It's plain but well made. I'm surprised by how well it fits me, hugging my curves, falling just above my knees and past my wrists. For some reason, I thought Alvtir was much taller than I am.

I spot some flatbread, a hunk of cheese, and an assortment of dried fruits waiting for me on a platter by the hearth, along with a jug of water and a bowl filled to the brim with fresh cherries. The sight of food makes my stomach spasm. I hadn't realized how ravenous I was. But I know I should find my host first. I ignore my hunger and walk outside.

"Alvtir?" I call again, shielding my eyes from Lisa's glare. He is already a full orb in the eastern sky; I slept late.

Again, no response from Alvtir. She must have gone to the city. The three dogs race over to me, tongues lolling. They whine and nuzzle their cheeks into my outstretched palms.

Her holding seems even smaller in the light of day. The land is unevenly shaped—like a natural clearing that was built upon, rather than land that was intentionally cleared for a homestead. The bending, red-speckled branches of a cherry tree arc over the small garden I noticed last night, each row lined with tightly coiled green buds. A few chickens roam around in front of the little barn, scratching and pecking the ground. It's just a henhouse, I realize; that's why I don't hear the familiar lowing of cattle or bleating of sheep in their stalls. I suppose it doesn't make sense to keep livestock when you live in the forest.

But where are Alvtir's thralls? Certainly Alvtir, as the king's sister and the leader of his army, is rich enough to own more than a few thralls. Perhaps, with a home this size, she has no need. Or no want.

She lives here all alone. Or she did, before yesterday.

I wonder with a jolt of anxiety if there's something I'm supposed to do in her absence. But if that were so, she would have woken me before she left. The chickens have been fed; the garden looks well tended and free of weeds. For the first time since I stepped foot on these shores, I have a day to myself.

For once, I have no excuse for why I can't see Bronaugh and Airé.

I told myself I couldn't go see them after the *holmgang* because I couldn't risk arousing suspicion, even though the Thingmen considered the matter settled. When spring came, I hid behind my chores taking precedence, or my lessons with Nyeru and Mbaneh. But the truth is, I was ashamed. Ashamed that my actions caused them to suffer.

Now, with no duty to hide behind, that shame hits me with full force. It's time for me to face them. I'll never forgive myself for causing them pain, but the least I can do is tell them how sorry I am.

I head back into the longhouse with newfound purpose. I could finish the entire meal Alvtir has laid out for me, but instead I eat a moderate amount of bread and cheese, enough to take the edge off my hunger, and pack the rest into a spare basket. At least I'll have something to bring the two of them. I tuck the kitchen knife into my belt for good measure and set out into the trees.

By the time I've found my way back into the city and trekked up the long path to Broskrap's holding, Lisa is past his peak. My heart quickens at the sound of children laughing. Broskrap's two boys play at the edge of the barley field, their wooden toy swords discarded at their sides.

One of them jumps up and slaps the head of a barley stalk. "You can't reach it!" he taunts his brother.

The shorter one jumps up after him. "I can too! I touched it with my fingertips!"

"Liar!"

"I did! Look, see?"

Shame and sorrow rise like bile to my throat. *They'll grow up without a father because of me.*

I shove the thought away. If anything, they'll grow up to be better men without Broskrap's influence. Airé and Bronaugh will bring them up right.

They glance at me as I pass. I wave awkwardly, but they're already back to their game. To them I'm just another thrall that came and went, if they remember me at all. They'll never know I'm the one who took their father from them.

I spot the familiar forms of Bronaugh and Airé bent over in the garden. Dread crests inside me as I approach. I pause, waiting a stone's throw away for Bronaugh to look up.

As soon as we lock eyes, her face lights up with joy. I smile back, feeling the wave of dread receding. She opens her mouth to speak, then closes it again, shooting a surreptitious look at Airé, who remains in a crouch, her gaze firmly planted on the weeds she's pulling from the soil.

The dread swells again. I raise the basket and incline my head toward the barn. Bronaugh nods and climbs with effort to her feet. My heart breaks at the wince on her face as she hobbles over.

Inside the barn, Bronaugh throws her arms around me. "Yafeu came back!" she exclaims.

I hug her fiercely. I hadn't realized how much I'd missed her. Her body feels full in my arms and it gladdens me. She's no longer a waif living on the scraps of a cruel master. She flutters my new cloak as she pulls away. "Look at Yafeu!" she says admiringly.

"Are you hurt, Bronaugh?" I ask.

The pained look returns to her face. "The guards . . . but I am healing."

The lump in my throat thickens. I look away, unable to meet her eyes. "It's all my fault," I whisper. "I'm so sorry. Airé was right all along."

"No!" She squeezes my hands tightly. "You set us free. Life is much better. And look!" A coy smile dances on her lips as she drops my hands and spreads her arms wide. "Bronaugh is fat now!"

I smile despite myself. Bronaugh always knew how to lighten my mood. "Then I guess you and Airé don't need this." I hold up the basket.

"From your new master?" she asks, her eyes wide. She must be nervous about accepting anything that would earn me a beating later.

I wonder: Who *is* Alvtir to me now? Not my new master, exactly. My guardian? My teacher?

"From my new home," I reply.

"We had a big meal this morning. You eat, you eat!" she tuts, shooing me toward the basket like a mother would a stubborn child. "Yafeu is too skinny!"

I refuse to eat until she at least agrees to share the cherries with me, and finally she relents. Over the makeshift meal, Bronaugh tells me all about how life has changed on the farm since Broskrap's death. To my great surprise, she tells me that Alvtir came back for them shortly after she took me away; Alvtir gave them twenty silver ingots and told them to run the farm as they always have, and to stick to the story that Broskrap was visiting another town if anyone came asking. And here I didn't think Alvtir cared at all. I realize with a shock how little I truly know her.

All the thralls share the money and the yield of the land and animals among themselves. Airé continues to look after Broskrap's two young sons. After the *hird* first returned, Snorri would come from time to time to check up on the farm, but once he saw that they were keeping up the usual work, he left them to their own devices.

It hits me that *Snorri* is Bronaugh and Airé's master now, as the eldest of Broskrap's sons. I don't know why I hadn't thought of that before. What will happen to them if he decides to move onto the farm? Or if he sells it to someone even worse than Broskrap? It chills my blood to even consider that possibility.

Bronaugh tells me that, on his very first visit, the young boys begged him to take them with him to his own homestead in the city, but he claimed he couldn't take care of them with his duties in the *hird,* and that they were better off staying put. Of course, Snorri wouldn't stoop so low as to *care* for his own brothers.

I nibble on the bread and let my eyes wander around the room as Bronaugh devours the last of the dried fruits. It feels strange to be in the barn again after so much has happened. It's smaller than I remember it being.

A form darkens the doorway. Airé slams the door behind her, ushering all the daylight from the barn.

My heart clenches at the sight of her. Her tunic hangs off her skeletal frame. Even in the scant light from the smoke hole, I can tell that her skin is pallid, her hair clumpy and unkempt. How has she lost so much weight since I left? Bronaugh said they were eating well!

I shoot Airé a hopeful smile. She doesn't return it.

"Did anyone see you?" she asks, her sunken eyes darting around nervously.

"No, Airé," I reply. "I wanted to come back before, but I couldn't. Alvtir gave me to the princess, but I'm free now." I glance back and forth between her and Bronaugh excitedly. "I'm not a thrall anymore!"

Airé flops down on a fur and rolls away from us without another word. It occurs to me that she might still be sleeping here, even though Broskrap's house must have a spare bed. I guess I wouldn't want to sleep in that house if I were Airé.

Bronaugh ignores her and plies me with questions about my time with Freydis. She listens with wide eyes as I tell her of the attack at the wedding. Throughout our exchange, I can't help but notice the newfound distance between Bronaugh and me. We strain to keep the conversation flowing smoothly, careful to avoid any treacherous topics, like a pair of explorers hopping from rock to rock above rapid waters. But the rapids are still there, just below us.

We *are* different now, I realize: Bronaugh's master may not live here, but that doesn't make her free.

I decide to leave much sooner than I'd planned. I promise to come back and visit again, and Bronaugh makes a show of looking pleased. But we both know it would be better if I stayed away.

I desperately want to ask why Airé is so thin and sickly, but I'm afraid to ask in front of her, and when I stand up to take my leave, Bronaugh gives me a warm hug goodbye but doesn't walk me out.

"I'm glad that you're well," I whisper into her ear as we embrace.

"Thanks to Yafeu," she whispers back.

My heart is heavy as I leave the barn behind.

I try to shake it off, remembering the fact that I'm finally getting what I've wanted since Anfa—no, what I've wanted my whole life: to become a warrior. A childish excitement mounts in my core at the thought. This time, I don't try to suppress it.

As my feet carry me down the familiar path to the city, I realize that I don't know what else to do with myself for the day. I was expecting to spend it with Bronaugh and Airé. Since I'm already in the farmland, I could start looking for the other thralls ... but something inside me rebels at the idea. Just for today, no more obligations, no more responsibilities. Just for today, I will do as I please.

There's still plenty of Lisa's light ahead, and the smattering of clouds in the sky are the white of a bone-dry day. I decide to seize Sogbo's rare slumber and take a walk along the fjord to clear my head.

This time, when I reach the edge of the city, I veer off the path, keeping to the outskirts of Skíringssal. After last night, I'd rather avoid the prying eyes and hushed whispers. I wish I weren't the object of so much attention all the time. I wish, just for this afternoon, I could appear to be a *Majūs* woman myself.

I reach the fjord and turn east along the shoreline. My mind relaxes into the calm blue expanse of the fjord. The damp, salty breeze feels pleasant against the warmth of my cloak. It is good to be near the water. Agbe and Naete are tempestuous spirits. Some days they roil, striking fear into the hearts of all who cross them; today they are placid, sowing peace in the harrowed loam of souls like mine. Maybe Papa, wherever he is, is finding his own peace on this same body of water.

Papa!

With all that happened after, I had forgotten about Fritjof's song. The man in the song had a different name, but that doesn't mean it isn't Papa. After all, the *Majūs* know me by a different name—his name. Maybe Papa is still out there, exploring new lands with this "Erik the Red." Who knows . . . the *hird* sails far and wide as well; maybe our paths will cross someday. Maybe *that's* the "great destiny" Mama saw for me.

But I won't hold my breath waiting for that day to come. I'm no longer the little girl who needed her papa to save her. I saved my-self, just as he always taught me.

Pride swells in my chest, soothing the frayed edges of my heart.

I amble by a few fishermen casting long lines from the shore, hoping their sea god will be generous even though the hour is wrong. They look away when they see me, inching closer to the shore as I pass. It's a different kind of reaction than what my pres-ence usually elicits from the cityfolk, tinged with fear rather than fascination. I swallow hard, trying to ignore them.

My shadow becomes a long-limbed giant as I walk and walk. I've never been this far east of the city before. The shoreline disappears and I have to climb a few paces up a hill into the forest to keep going. The grass is thin and slippery, the branches mostly spare.

On the other side of the hill, I come across a kind of encamp-ment. A dozen or so longhouses are strewn about between the trees. Men are everywhere—wrestling, playing *tafl* and tug-of-war, shooting arrows at a painted board and insulting one another's aim. This must be where most of the *hird*men live. The ones who don't live on the farms.

Nerves coil in my gut; I wasn't prepared to run into them today.

I keep my gaze straight ahead, but I can feel their prying stares as I march by.

I become aware of the soft pad of boots on the grass behind me, following me.

My heart begins to race. I stop in my tracks and draw my knife.

When the footsteps are near enough, I whirl around and lunge, pressing the knife against the neck of . . .

Ingmar?

"Easy," he says, throwing his hands up.

"Why are you following me?" I ask. Fear still flickers inside me, and I hold the pressure on the knife at his throat.

"I'm not—I only meant to catch up with you. I saw you pass, and I thought I'd ask you if you wanted some company."

Sincerity shines through his blue-gray eyes. I tuck the knife into my belt with an exasperated sigh. "You should know better than to sneak up on me," I say, resuming my pace to hide my embarrassment.

"I do now!" Ingmar retorts, catching up to my side. "Believe me, I don't want to give you any reason to use that knife."

For some reason, I burst into laughter at that. Surprised, he starts laughing too, and the wave of laughter crashes over us both. I smile at him as it ebbs, but he falters. "It's all right if you want to be alone." He looks at his feet. "I don't want to be a bother."

"I would like some company," I admit. "Though I should be heading back to Alvtir's now."

"I'll walk with you."

"It's a long way."

He shrugs good-naturedly. "I've been meaning to visit the market."

We reverse our course and fall into step side by side. A strange shyness overcomes me, and I find I don't know what to say to him. "You're dirty," I blurt out finally, noting the green stains on his plain brown tunic, the gritty soil underneath his fingernails.

"I was clearing some land near my tent when you walked by. There's no hope for a proper garden out here, of course. But I'd at least like to plant a few herbs. A rosemary bush, maybe some dill."

He was toiling in the dirt when he saw me pass by, so he stopped and ran after me? Strange man. I wonder if he really needs to go to the market after all. I wonder what Ampah would think about all this. "You didn't strike me as a gardener," I say.

He smiles, his eyes wrinkling lightly at the seams. He has the kind of grooves around his eyes that only come from smiling often. "A green thumb makes every supper a feast."

Supper. Ingmar talks like Bronaugh does. He even pronounces his words the same way, with that waver around the vowels. I smile back at him. "Sounds like good sense to me."

"Truth be told," he adds, his smile fading, "I'd much prefer to be a gardener than a soldier."

I cock an eyebrow. "Oh?"

He nods. "I'm saving up my silver. Someday I'll leave Skíringssal and start my own farm. Build a house, plant some oats. Get a cow, maybe a few sheep."

I don't bother hiding my surprise. "That's the life you dream of? Milking cows? Working the plow?"

He shrugs again. "Everyone deserves a home of their own."

"I'm not sure I ever had a home," I say, looking out over the fjord. Mama, Kamo, and Goleh are out there somewhere, across many seas. I've wondered so often where they are, how they're faring now that the village is gone. Their absence is a weight that never lifts. But I spent six years longing to escape that village, and I can't bring myself to miss it—no matter how much I miss them.

"The *hird* is a kind of home, perhaps," he says thoughtfully. "*You,* for one, don't strike me as a woman who will tire of the fighting life."

"Maybe someday," I admit, meeting his eyes. Today they look more gray than blue. "But not anytime soon. I've waited too long for my chance to become a warrior."

"Yafeu," Ingmar begins, hesitant. "I've never seen someone fight like you fought last night. Not even Alvtir."

Oh. So *that's* why he wanted to talk. Disappointed, I tear my gaze from his and fix it on the granite cliffs jutting out over the fjord in the distance.

"You were . . ." He pauses, searching for words. "Inspiring. It's all any of us can talk about."

"Even Snorri?"

He surprises me with a hearty laugh. "No. But Snorri's not much of a warrior. Though if you tell him I said so, I'll swear by all the gods that you're lying."

I chuckle, relaxing somewhat. "You fought well too."

"That's a great honor, coming from you."

I feel my cheeks grow warm as my stomach does an excited little flip. I fiddle nervously with the edges of my cloak. What's *happening* to me?

"Where did you learn to fight like that?"

"My father taught me," I reply, grateful for the slight change in topic. "He's a skilled fighter—and a better hunter."

I find myself slowing our pace back to the city as Ingmar continues to inquire about my life before Skíringssal. I tell him all about Wagadu, how the land is showered with rain for many months and then dry as a bone for many more, but there's no winter like there is here. I tell him about life on the road with Papa before he left us, about Mama and Kamo and Goleh, about our monthly pilgrimages to Koumbi Saleh, a city a thousand times more grand than Skíringssal. I surprise myself with how much spills out of me. I find myself telling him things that I never even told Freydis. He listens intently, understanding intuitively when I don't want to say more, never pushing me, exhibiting only a gentle curiosity. It's a welcome change from the prying fixation I'm used to feeling from the *Majūs;* the difference is subtle but palpable, like the difference between silver and polished iron.

"What about *your* family?" I ask, realizing how much I've spoken and how little he has.

As I suspected, Ingmar is from Ireland, like Bronaugh, from a kingdom called Connaught. His father was a Northman he never knew—the man raped his mother on a raid while her village was plundered. She was left with nothing but a baby in her belly. After Ingmar was born, she started selling her body to survive. They made their way to a city called Dublin, but she died of an illness when Ingmar was still a young child. Another Northman, one of the men who had frequented his mother's bed, took pity on him and raised him as his own, renaming him Ingmar. He was a soldier, and he trained Ingmar in combat. The two eventually traveled south to join the army of the Roman emperor. But another emperor usurped the throne, as always happens with rulers, and the pay for sell-swords wavered with the empire. After Ingmar's foster father died in battle, he left the guard and traveled north. He wanted to serve a chief who would share the spoils with his loyal warriors, as is the Northmen's way. And it was better to pillage for gold and silver, he reasoned, than to fight another long, drawn-out war in the name of some distant ruler.

"Was your mother a Christ-worshipper?" I ask, remembering how the first assassin invoked the god last night.

"She was a Christian in name more than anything else. Life was too hard for her to believe that Jesus watched over her."

"And you?"

"I pay homage to the gods of whatever land I'm in," he replies. "But in my heart, I don't know if I believe any of them are watching over me either."

I nod my understanding. "My father believed that the gods save those who save themselves."

"Your father sounds like a wise man."

"Aren't you afraid of becoming like *your* father?" I blurt out before I can stop myself.

He looks away, and immediately I regret asking. I can tell I've struck at the core of his burden.

"That's why I chose to come here," he says, "to follow Alvtir. She doesn't allow us to rape the women of the lands we raid. The men grumble about it, but we have more honor than any other *Víkingar*. And we always get what we came for."

I feel doubly grateful to be Alvtir's ward.

"To be honest," he adds softly, "I never wanted to fight at all. I have the skill for it, but not the taste. If there are such goddesses as the Norns, they must have seen fit to weave me this fate. They made me an orphan, gave me neither property nor a good name. So I must earn those things for myself. There is no other way."

I nod, feeling his burden as if weighed on my own heart.

Just as we're about to turn out toward the growing shoreline, my skin begins to prickle.

A strange and vibrant *nyama* ripples out from the forest. I peer in and spot a scraggly, white-haired man crouching at the foot of an oak tree. He looks more creature than human, squatting on the ground in an unnatural position and poking the dirt with a stick.

The little hairs on my arms raise instinctively. Is this one of the "hidden folk" Freydis spoke of? I always thought she was imagining things.

If Ingmar notices the creature, he doesn't pay it any mind. We draw closer and I realize that the man is mumbling to himself, drawing something in the dirt with a fallen branch.

It's the skald! I realize with a start. *Fritjof!*

"You!" I shout.

I take off in a sprint. Fritjof stands quickly. He has a wild look in his eye, like he's frightened of me. Apparently everyone is frightened of me. Abashed, I slow my pace and give a small, polite bow, just to show him I mean no harm.

"You're the king's skald." I stop in front of him.

"Balli's skald, now," he mutters.

Fritjof looks just as odd as he sounds. The *Majūs,* for all their lack of taste, are at least a very tidy people. They love to bathe and are meticulous about grooming their beards and hair. But the skald's skin is covered in dirt, his long hair and beard matted and unruly. In his craggy face sit two mismatched eyes, one blue and one gray with a milky sheen. He feels both familiar and strange to me at once.

"I'm Yafeu," I say, gathering my thoughts.

"They call me Fritjof," he replies, suddenly lucid.

"I know. I met you once before, when I was the princess's thrall."

He cackles, a tinkling, silvery sound that sets my teeth on edge. "My name, she knows my name, the dark queen."

Queen? I have to suppress my own laugh. Freydis said Fritjof has one eye in the realm of their gods—I don't know how long I'll have before he's blind to this world again. "Yes, I know your name. But tell me: How does Fritjof know my mother's bedtime story, the one about the whale?"

He squats and picks the stick off the ground. "Even babes know the legend of Erik the Red."

I lean back against the coarse bark of the oak tree. "Tell it to me," I say with authority. As long as he thinks I'm some kind of queen, I might as well command him.

"Erik Thorvaldsson, the explorer, the exile. He sailed west, more west than any before him ever dared, and discovered an untouched land of natural splendor. Vinland, he named it, and sent for others to join. They say the Huntsman, his closest companion, was swarthier than you." He gestures to me with a fitful motion.

"Thorhall," I say, remembering the poem. "And you say this story is known by many?"

"By all," he confirms. "The myth travels the ocean in Erik the Red's wake."

My heart sinks. If the story is a well-known myth, then Mama must have heard it from Papa, who would have heard it from some merchant or other on one of his many travels. She made him the hero, instead of this Thorhall, to make me feel better. To comfort me. So I could keep worshipping Papa, keep thinking of him as a hero, even after he left. I should have guessed it before; it's just like Mama to do something like that.

Fritjof turns to me, a faraway look in his eyes. He drops the stick and seizes both of my hands. I rear back, alarmed, but he grips me tightly and starts chanting:

All hail the dark queen
Her crown is forged in iron and blood
All hail the dark queen
The Norns will weave her victory!

He finishes and lets out a cackle that becomes a fit of coughs. I wrench my hands from his grasp. My blood has turned to ice in my veins. I grab him by the neck of his raggedy tunic and yank him up to face me.

"Where did you hear that? What song is it from?" I demand.

"It comes when they will it." He points to the sky. I look up, confused, prompting another bout of maniacal laughter.

Dismayed, I let him go. I won't get a straight answer from him now. He's too far gone.

Immediately he crouches back down and feels around for his stick. That's when I see what he's been tracing in the dirt.

It's the runes on the brooch of my cloak. The same ones—exactly as Freydis arranged them, upside down and interlocking. A shiver coils around my spine, constricting each vertebra with icy tendrils.

It doesn't mean anything, I tell myself. He taught Freydis the runes; she must have sought his help with the design.

I walk back toward the fjord, leaving him to his drawing. "Her crown is forged in iron and blood . . ." he mutters behind me.

Ingmar is gone. I cringe at myself for running away so suddenly; he probably thinks I'm the rudest woman he's ever met.

I pick up a jog toward the city. Lisa sinks lower in the sky, sending streaks of pink over the harbor in the distance. Fritjof's strange chant still echoes in my head.

My mind flashes unwillingly to the Dead City. *If we pass through it, we risk taking the curse on ourselves,* Freydis said. Of course, I don't believe in the curse.

Nonetheless, I find myself picking up my pace, as if trying to outrun anything that might be haunting me.

ALVTIR

Sól drives her chariot through the sky as gaily as ever. Lake Vítrir shimmers back at the cloudless sky, rippling faintly in the gentle breeze. On such a serene day, it would be easy to put my worries aside for a while. I could bring the dogs to the lake, have a swim.

Were it not for the fact that I'm standing behind my brother, watching him beat the few remaining wits out of his pitiful skald-seer. That Snorri tagged along doesn't help matters either. My brother's new *stallari* is more like his shadow these days.

"Why did this happen?" Balli presses Fritjof. "Are the gods punishing me for breaking my oath to Harald?"

Fritjof looks one way, then the other, confusion making his worn face look even older. It looks as though two gods are speaking to him at the same time, and he doesn't know which one he should heed.

What I wouldn't give to know which gods they are, and what they're saying to him.

Do I still have Odin's blessing? Or has the Allfather forsaken his chosen warrior?

As if hearing my thoughts, Fritjof looks me square in the eye.

I've faced legions of bloodthirsty soldiers without fear, but this strange look from the skald-seer is enough to make my heart quicken.

"The oath was broken in poisoned blood," he says cryptically.

"What does that mean?" Balli asks. Fritjof grins maniacally but says nothing, prompting Balli to send a swift kick to his gut. I grimace as Fritjof lets out a cry of pain and doubles over.

"You will answer your king, Skald!" Snorri adds needlessly. I roll my eyes so hard I nearly catch sight of my brain.

Fritjof coughs and grabs the hem of Balli's cloak. "The oath was broken in poisoned blood," he repeats. "Slaughter the sheep and the blood is restored. Slaughter the flock and the blood is lost."

I stand very still, my hand resting on Angrboda's hilt, my face a mask of disinterest.

My brother sighs. "That's all we'll get from him," he announces to no one in particular. "Go now."

Fritjof scrambles away. His howling cackle echoes through the trees as he disappears into the forest.

Balli turns to Snorri. "One thing is clear, at least: Freydis should not marry that cross-worshipper Hakon." He spits on the ground. "Send a messenger to Harald and tell him we wish to honor the pledge and begin the negotiations. And make haste. We should hold the ceremony before Yngvild's condition can no longer be denied."

A familiar heaviness sets into my bones.

Snorri bows. "At once, my king." He shoots me a snivel and lets his shoulder brush mine as he saunters off.

Finally, my brother turns to me. I'm surprised to see an uncharacteristically rueful look in his eye. "You were right about the Christians," he says.

How big of you, brother. But it's far too little, too late.

I nod anyway, twisting my expression into one of grim humility. "If the Christ god could turn the heart of a man like Hakon, anyone can fall prey to his power."

"All the more reason to join forces with Harald," he says, half to himself. "Together, we can easily overpower Hakon's *hird*. We will purge Trøndelag of its Christian plague and carve up the land between us. We'll do the same to any kingdom that has forsaken the true gods." He grabs my shoulder and squeezes, the sight of conquest lighting up his eyes once more, as it hasn't done since our youth. "Think of it, sister. Together, Vestfold and Agder are powerful enough to unite all of Norveg under our rule. There will be many a glorious battle with the Allfather at our side. Once it is done, you will take care of that little peacock Harald, of course. After that, there will be no one left to stop us. The White Christ himself will bow to the one true king of Norveg!"

I smother a sigh as my heart, or what little is left of it after all these long years, crumbles into dust. Loki himself must have clouded my brother's mind. Or perhaps the Christ.

No. The truth is that there is no god to blame: My brother's sickness is all his own. Where I see annihilation, he sees only acquisition. The "Christian plague" is simply another excuse.

"You are wise, brother," I murmur.

A moment of doubt flickers across his eyes before they harden to a stony resolve. He lets his hand fall from my shoulder.

"Do you need me for any further interrogations?" I ask dutifully.

"The skald has told us everything we need to hear." He signals his guards and turns back toward Skíringssal.

I wasn't expecting to have the rest of the day to myself. Good. I'll need all the time I can get now; the preparations will span a moon or more.

"Enjoy your new ward," Balli calls over his shoulder.

That I will, brother. That I will.

32

YAFEU

A thud jolts me awake. In one motion, I sit and grab the knife from under my pillow. My eyes land on a round wooden shield and matching wooden sword resting at the foot of my bed.

"She's an ugly thing, not much charm to her. But she'll do."

I look up at Alvtir's severe face, surprised to see a touch of warmth lighting up her eyes. She hands me yet another set of clothes—this one undyed, much like my thrall's tunic, though a little thicker in my grasp. "You start today," she says.

I leap out of bed and dress quickly. Nerves and excitement flutter in my stomach, but I force myself to scarf down a bowl of honeyed porridge anyway.

The dogs race toward us as soon as we're outside. "Head east along the shoreline," Alvtir says, kneeling down to let them lick her face. "You'll hear them before you see them."

I frown. "You're not coming?"

She pushes the dogs away and grabs an ax, not meeting my eyes.

Her thin lips are pursed into an even thinner line as she sets a log on the chopping stump. "I'm no longer in command of the *hird*. Snorri Broskrapsson is the new *stallari*."

Dread floods through me, rooting me in place. "Snorri leads the *hird*?"

She gives a swift nod as she raises the ax above her head. The whack of her blade splitting the log in two rattles my bones.

Snorri is my commander. The porridge threatens to come up and I clench my teeth, fighting the urge to retch.

Alvtir looks up sharply. "Well, what are you waiting for?"

The words tumble out. "I can't train under Snorri. I hate him. And he hates me even more. He'll try to kill me the first chance he gets."

She grabs the split piece of wood and places it back on the stump. "Would you rather go back to being the princess's thrall?"

She's right. I don't have a choice. I grit my teeth and force my feet to carry me to the trail. When I reach the edge of the clearing, I spare a brief look back. The striations in Alvtir's arms writhe as she yanks the ax out of the stump.

The buzz of male voices grows louder as I cross the encampment and approach the wide clearing where the *hird*men are gathered. The field is a swirling mixture of mire and weeds. I reach the edge and dozens of pale men turn to stare at me.

"*That's* the *Úlfheðinn*?" someone says.

Úlfheðinn. The mysterious word echoes in my mind.

"I didn't know she was an elf," someone else whispers.

I glance around, searching for a break in the throng of men. All men. My breath quickens. Where are the shield maidens?

"Yafeu!" A clear voice breaks through the buzz. I'm relieved to meet Ingmar's cool gaze a moment later. He takes my arm and leads me through the crowd to the other side of the field. Once we've put a little distance between us and the rest of the men, my anxiety begins to subside.

"I believe you're looking for these two." He leads me over to two women and a large man conversing in front of a wide oak tree near the field's edge. As we draw near, I realize it's the same two women from the boat—the willowy, mouse-haired one, who tended to my wound, and her quiet companion, who reads water like Freydis reads the runes.

"Ah, the woman of the hour," the first says, turning to me. "Welcome. I'm Hetha, and this is Wisna." She gestures to the sturdy woman with short blond hair leaning against the tree trunk, who nods in greeting. Their postures are relaxed, their smiles easy. I feel my shoulders drop an inch as I nod back.

"And I'm Dag." The large man reaches out and grasps my forearm in a firm shake. His playful green eyes and plump cheeks give his face a boyish look, despite his thick black beard and hair. It's a face that hardly matches his enormous stature. His *nyama* is also friendly, and despite him being a full two heads taller than me, I can tell he poses no threat. "We're honored to have an *Úlfheðinn* join our little band of nithings," he says.

That word again. I frown. "I'm Yafeu—not *Úlfheðinn*."

They laugh heartily at that, leaving me even more confused.

"Here comes Ranveig," Hetha adds. I follow her sight line to the wiry girl approaching us with quick, bouncy steps. It's the same girl I saw with them when the *hird* left for the last raid. Bright-red hair engulfs her head, flitting in the breeze like flames. Her body is all angles, from her knees to her face, which is folded into a scowl. She looks around my age, give or take a year. She stops in front of me and looks me up and down with obvious disdain. I can't help but stare at the intricate patterns tattooed on her arms as she folds them across her chest and spits on the ground.

"Ranveig," Hetha begins, "this is—"

"We have a saying here, *Úlfheðinn*," Ranveig cuts in. "Where wolf's ears are, wolf's teeth are near."

I meet her scowl with one of my own. "And what's that supposed to mean?"

"It means you're the ears—and *I'm* the teeth."

I open my mouth to reply, but a voice much sharper than my own pierces the early-morning haze instead.

"*Heill, Víkingar!*" Snorri's voice.

"*Heill!*" The *hird*men respond in unison.

Snorri steps in front of the crowd. A white-hot hatred floods me at the sight of him. Instead of the simple training clothes we all wear, he's dressed in his full suit of armor. It's as if he wants the men to know he's ready for battle at any moment.

He fixes me with a smug grin. I return the expression, doing my best to put all the venom I feel in my heart into my gaze.

He wastes no time. "As some of you may have heard, Alvtir has been stripped of her command," he calls out. "The king has chosen me to be his new *stallari*."

Murmurs rip through the *hird*men. Hetha and Wisna share a look of shock. Ranveig bites her lip and glowers at the mud. I can feel the waves of rage flowing from her *nyama*.

I scan the faces of the men around me, searching for the limits of their loyalty. Some look pleased, but many of them, especially the older men, seem clouded with confusion. Perhaps they don't know what to feel; I wouldn't either if I had grown to manhood with Alvtir as my *stallari*.

Snorri frowns. Clearly, he was expecting a bigger reaction. "Things will be different from now on," he continues. "For too long, we have chomped at the bit, suffering under a woman who forbade us to act like men. She called herself Odin's chosen warrior, but we are Thor's men, one and all!" He grabs the hammer around his neck and holds it up for emphasis.

The response swells. Cries of agreement fill the air, egging Snorri on.

"Would Odin put reins on Thor, the mighty protector of Asgard? Would he deny his own son his warrior nature?"

"No!" the men bellow. The ground begins to tremble with the force of their stomping.

"So why should we, the protectors of Agder, be denied our warrior natures?" Snorri challenges. "Alvtir had us following her woman's code, but I say, no more! We men deserve to *take* what we want! We've earned that right by serving our king in battle!"

My throat constricts as cheers erupt from the *hird*men. They raise their sparring swords in the air and shout their glee to the gods. I turn to Hetha and Wisna. A look of foreboding passes between them, and then to me.

Snorri raises his hands for the men to settle. He may not be a great warrior, but I can see now that he does have skill. He's almost like a griot, the way he plays on the men's emotions, inciting their indignation along with their lust for violence. He controls them masterfully.

All the worse for me.

His eyes find mine, and he shoots me an ominous smile. The clamor dies down. He lets the eager silence stretch out. The men are like fish on a hook, waiting for him to reel them in.

"We have a new shield maiden today," he says at last. "You should know that everything you've heard about her is true."

Murmurs go up around me. I narrow my eyes at Snorri. What game is he playing now?

"I was there at the princess's wedding. She killed ten men with only a dull kitchen knife." He gesticulates theatrically. "No doubt she'll be the one training *us* today."

A fire sparks to life in my core.

That's not true. He's setting me up to fail. I can't live up to that story—no one could. I figured Snorri would try to have me killed, but he's cleverer than I thought. First, he'll let me die under the weight of my own reputation.

"Bet *I* could take her!" someone calls out.

My hands curl into fists at my side. I clench my jaw so forcefully that my cheeks begin to ache.

Snorri chuckles under his breath. "Today, we'll start with sword practice," he says decisively. "Pair up!"

Of course, Snorri would choose to start with sword practice. Swords are far costlier than daggers or axes, which is why you only see them in the hands of a rich king's army. He figures I don't have any familiarity with the weapon—and he's right.

I turn to the women, desperate to avoid sparring with one of the *hird*men, who look a little too eager to test their mettle against the new shield maiden. Hetha and Wisna have already found an open space and squared off. I look at Ranveig, but before I can open my mouth, Dag appears out of nowhere and taps her on the shoulder.

"Spar with me?" he asks.

"Some other time," Ranveig replies coolly. Dag's round cheeks flush pink, making him look even more boyish. She catches my eye. "*Úlfheðinn,* let's go."

"My name is *Yafeu.*"

Ranveig's scowl contorts into a wicked grin. "*Yafeu,* then. Shall we begin?"

She tosses her shield to the ground, and I follow suit. I brandish my sparring sword in front of me, trying to remember how Alvtir held hers back in Anfa all those moons ago. The long weapon is top-heavy and clumsy in my unskilled grasp.

Before I can blink, Ranveig leaps forward with her sparring sword raised high above her head. I raise my own sparring sword instinctively to block, but the force of her blow is too strong. The sword is knocked from my awkward grasp. She stays the wooden shaft a hair's breadth away from my neck and holds it there for a long moment, her chin lifting in silent triumph. Then she backs off and readies herself to go again. I grab my weapon from the mud, my face hot.

Ranveig steps forward abruptly and jabs the tip of her sword toward my abdomen. I jump to the right, dodging the blow, and slice at her side. The wood scrapes her biceps then collides with her sword with a dull thud. Our eyes lock as we push the edges together with all our might. My arms begin to burn from the inside out. I grit my teeth and push harder, ignoring the pain.

Ranveig grins again, then leaps back. My feet slip on the mud and I fall forward, dropping the sparring sword and breaking my fall with both hands.

A chorus of snickers sends the heat back to my cheeks. I try to push myself up, but the acute pressure of a boot pressing into my back stops me short. Rage flares up inside me, spilling over the dam. The laughter grows louder before Ranveig lets up.

I pick up the sparring sword and jump to my feet, not bothering to wipe the sweat from my brow or the mud from my tunic. I notice the *hird*men forming a circle around us, amusement writ large on their faces, as though they were watching a particularly entertaining chicken fight. If Snorri cares that they've ceased their training, he doesn't bother to tell them. I glare at him as he leans against the trunk of an elm with his arms folded across his chest, a smug smile painted across his face.

This is exactly what he planned. He wanted them to watch me be bested so easily, to erase any semblance of respect they might've had for me.

I focus on Ranveig, struggling to keep my composure. Was she in on this plan with Snorri, or does she have her own reason for humiliating me? I don't know what I could have done to earn her contempt.

If only we could spar without this useless weight of a weapon!

But I can't. Not until Snorri decides I've been humiliated enough for one day.

This time, I focus on dodging Ranveig's blows, instead of trying to beat her at her own game. I keep my sparring sword up defensively, staying light on my toes. The girl is in much better shape than I am, and is extraordinarily nimble, much to my dismay. She gets several good *thwack*s in with the flat of her sword, and the men burst into laughter every time. I don't know which hurts more, but at least I don't fall on my face again.

Finally, after my sparring sword and my pride have been whittled down to a toothpick, Snorri relents. "Move to hand-to-hand combat!" he shouts.

I drop the wooden sword with relief. My arm is sore from finger to shoulder, and I can already feel the bruises blossoming across my torso.

Ranveig tosses her own sparring sword and immediately raises her fists. I smile and return the gesture, eager to give her what she's asking for.

Ranveig may be handy with a sword, but I'll be teaching her a few things about the weapon of the body.

Just as she starts to approach, Ingmar steps between us, facing me.

"Pair up?" he asks, his liquid eyes hopeful. "That is, if you can find another partner, Ranveig."

I grimace, frustrated. He wants to spar *now*? Now that it's finally my turn to throw that preening flamingo of a girl into the mud?

You're not saving me from anything, I want to scream. But I know he thinks he's doing me a kindness.

"She's all yours—whatever's *left* of her," Ranveig spits. She spins around triumphantly, crashing right into Dag's barrel of a chest.

"I see you need a partner!" Dag says eagerly.

Ranveig groans, annoyance sharpening her features even further. "Fine," she says through gritted teeth.

Dag looks as happy as a hippo in a mud-bath. Ingmar shoots me a knowing smirk, and I feel my frustration ease. Maybe Ranveig is getting what she deserves after all.

We move to a patch of dry, weedy grass, less slippery than where Ranveig and I sparred.

"Don't go easy on me," I say as we face off.

"Don't go easy on *me*," Ingmar retorts.

I open my mouth to argue with him further, but the playful glimmer in his eyes stops me short. "I won't," I say instead.

"Good."

Then he lunges.

I sidestep his attack with ease, then feign a punch that fools him into a defensive posture. I put the real force into the second jab, exactly as Papa taught me. I stop my fist at his side so as not to hit him with any real force.

Ingmar's eyes widen as he takes in the position of my fist, hovering right at his kidney. He'd be rolling on the ground in agony if I had followed through with the blow. He breaks into a wide smile that meets my own, his eyes alight with exhilaration.

I celebrated too soon. Immediately he grabs my fist and twists me into a hold with my arms behind my back. I can't break free—if anything, the more I struggle, the more it seems to secure his grip. The firmness of his chest against my back sends a tingle down my spine. He smells like resin and salt, the woods and the sea rolled into one.

"You'll have to teach me that sometime," I say breathlessly.

"Anytime," he pants.

Ranveig's grunts fill the air. I glance over as she rains her frustration down on poor Dag. Other than them and Hetha and Wisna, the rest of the soldiers drop all pretense of sparring and push in around Ingmar and me, itching to see how this new match plays out.

We face off again, and soon we're trading blows and parries in equal measure. The *hird*men murmur and cheer, this time with approval.

Their calls morph into a song, and it starts to feel like we're dancing. I throw a high kick that he ducks with ease. He whirls around to strike, and I use his own force to shuffle him to my other side, but he regains his footing immediately and sends his fist toward my cheek. I recover quickly. In one swift movement, I throw a spinning back kick, grabbing his neck with the back of my knee and twisting his body to the ground. Ingmar hits the grass with a grunt and I thread his arm between my legs and press the back of my legs to his chest, raising my hips and pushing the inside of his elbow toward the sky. I give him a look that says I could break his arm if I wanted.

"That's enough for today." Snorri's voice rings out from somewhere beyond the circle of riveted onlookers.

I release Ingmar and jump up, still buzzing with energy. I offer him a hand. "You'll have to teach *me* that sometime," he says as he takes it, pulling himself to a stand in front of me. His blue eyes gleam, reminding me of the way the light hits the fjord in the early morning. I gaze up into them, a full head above my own, feeling a warm sensation spread from my core.

It takes me a second to realize that I'm still clasping his hand. I drop it quickly and look away, releasing a breathy giggle. "Of course."

"Until anytime, then," Ingmar says, bowing politely.

"Well done, Shield-Breaker." Dag claps him on the shoulder. "And you, *Úlfheðinn*! Anyone who knocks Ingmar on his ass is a friend of mine!"

Ingmar laughs, and I can't help but join. Then I can't help but sneak a glance at said part of Ingmar's body as he walks away.

After a moment, it occurs to me that Dag said *anyone*, not *any woman*. I decide I like this Dag very much.

The men gather their sparring weapons and chatter among themselves as they disperse, casting curious glances my way. At least I haven't made a *total* fool of myself today. "She teach you a lesson, Ingmar?" one of them quips to Ingmar as he passes.

"Just as Snorri said she would," Ingmar retorts.

A chorus of guffaws rises up from the men. I look around for Snorri, eager to see his hatchet face turn red at this twist of his words. But he's nowhere to be found.

With a sigh, I reach for my own sword and shield. My back aches as I bend over, and I let myself fold into a stretch. For once I welcome the cool breeze drying the sweat on my skin. I'm sore from head to toe already, and it will only be worse tomorrow. But it's a welcome soreness. It's the feeling of growing stronger, more intoxicating than any ale.

"Yafeu!" Wisna calls out.

I stand as she and Hetha approach.

"We usually eat dinner with Alvtir after training," Hetha says.

"Oh." I search for Ranveig behind them, but she's nowhere to be found.

"Ranveig's not coming," Hetha states coolly, reading my thoughts.

Hmm. I wonder if she has a family of her own to eat with, or if she's simply avoiding me.

On the walk back to Alvtir's, I find myself opening up to Hetha and Wisna as easily as I did to Ingmar yesterday. Gradually, the trials of the day ebb from my mind like the tide of the fjord, replaced by a feeling that is warm, expansive, and altogether new.

By the time we reach Alvtir's longhouse, the long fingers of sunset are reaching in through the open door. Stillness greets us. The fire has long since snuffed out, the ashes turning white on the hearth. The henhouse is shut, the garden empty. Even the dogs are gone, presumably out with their owner, wherever she is.

Her absence doesn't seem to trouble Hetha or Wisna. Wisna disappears to gather firewood while Hetha sets a pot above the hearth. They move with the ease of familiarity, and it strikes me that they must have done this a hundred times before.

I clear my throat. I'm not used to this feeling of idleness. "I'll look for something to eat," I say, heading to the storage vats at the back of the longhouse.

"There should be some salt fish soaking in a barrel back there. We'll boil it with whatever else you can find."

I change into my thrall's tunic, resolving to wash the training clothes before bed, then gather the fish, some greens, and an assortment of dried herbs. I insist on cooking the stew, noting that Hetha and Wisna are my own guests in Alvtir's absence.

"She doesn't have many spices, but I tried my best," I say apologetically as they take the steaming bowls from my hands. I watch intently as Hetha takes her first sip, closing her eyes and furrowing her brow as she weighs the flavors on her tongue.

"Is it all right?" I ask.

"All right?" She slurps down another spoonful. "You've spoiled us, Yafeu!"

"It'll be even harder to choke down Alvtir's cooking after this," Wisna adds.

I grin delightedly as they scarf down the rest of their bowls. I take some time to savor my own meal, feeling particularly pleased with myself.

"How long have you known Alvtir?" I ask when they begin to slow.

"Almost eight years," Hetha says, ladling extra chunks of fish into Wisna's bowl.

"And you've been in the *hird* that long as well?"

Wisna nods. "Neither of us could stand the thought of a husband," she says between bites.

"Or of being away from each other," Hetha chimes in, placing a hand on Wisna's knee. With a rush of understanding, I remember observing their tenderness toward each other on the journey here. They really are only for each other.

"It's not an easy way, but it's our own," Wisna says.

I can't help but smile at the sentiment. "It sounds like a good life."

"And you?" asks Hetha.

"Me?" I echo, confused.

She gives me a sly smile. "You and Ingmar are well matched. Perhaps in more ways than one."

My cheeks grow warm, and I feel grateful for my dark skin.

"Oh, don't pester the poor girl," Wisna gruffs between bites.

"He's just a friend," I say quickly. I sit up straighter, trying to assume an air of maturity. "I ... respect his zeal for battle."

Neither of them looks convinced. I try to change the subject. "Has Alvtir ever ... had a companion? In that way?"

A silent moment passes. "War is Alvtir's only companion," Wisna says finally. "At least, as far as we know."

"You're the first person to get past her guard," Hetha adds.

A sudden nervousness writhes like a snake in the pit of my stomach. "What do you mean?" I ask, slightly defensive.

"She's generous with us, and we know she cares, in her own way," Wisna says. "But she's never shared her *home* before. Not even with a thrall."

"No wonder Ranveig is so jealous of you," Hetha adds.

I frown. Ranveig—*jealous* of me? Two days ago, I was nothing but a maidservant. A lowly thrall. And now I've earned the jealousy of a shield maiden?

I choose my words carefully. "I don't know why Alvtir would care about me any more than the women she's fought beside for years."

Hetha and Wisna take that in with amused expressions. "I do," Hetha replies. A slight smile rests on her lips as though inscribed there, and I wonder if I'll ever see her without it.

I've just slipped into bed when the door swings open. I sit up, meeting Alvtir's stoic gaze. "How'd it go?" she asks nonchalantly, running a dirty hand through her dark hair. There are black smudges all over her clothes.

"Why aren't there more of us?" I ask, ignoring her question. "Why aren't there more women in the *hird*?"

She sighs and removes a worn pouch from her belt. "After I took on my last ward, Ranveig, my brother forbade me to recruit any more women."

She tosses the pouch into my lap, then takes a seat on the bench across the hearth. I blink down at the pouch, uncomprehending.

"Balli didn't want his *hird* filled with women on account of his *feral* sister," she continues, her voice dripping with sarcasm. "He told me I was spoiling too many ripe young women. That their place was in the bedroom, not the battlefield. In truth, he was embarrassed." Alvtir scoffs as she reaches for her pipe and starts packing it with herbs.

316 WILLOW SMITH & JESS HENDEL

So that's why she didn't make me her ward until now. I'm almost grateful for the assassins—if they hadn't tried to kill Freydis, I wouldn't have had the chance to prove myself in front of the king.

I look down at the pouch and unwrap the cords of dyed sinew that hold the soft skins in place. A glimpse of iron emerges from within the folds.

I inhale sharply as Gu's magic flows through me from the smooth, dark blade, filling me like a drinking horn. I raise the dagger tenderly and hold it up to the fire. The heavy antler hilt is carved into the outline of a wolf. There are no runes or inlays on the blade; just perfect precision. Tears threaten at the bottom of my eyes. The sheer quality of this forged blade is far more captivating than if it had some ornate design etched into the metal, like so many of the weapons and tools sold at the market.

Speechless, I lift my eyes to Alvtir's. She takes a puff of her pipe, the corners of her lips twitching up at my reaction.

A storm of rage and confusion starts up inside me. "But . . . you didn't have to abandon me." The words spill out, words I've been holding back ever since Broskrap's barn. "You didn't have to leave me with that vile man. You didn't have to make me a thrall at all. So why? Why do that to me? Was it some kind of sadistic test?"

Alvtir's expression betrays nothing. She lets out a cloud of smoke and speaks slowly as it clears. "I do not take a ward lightly, Yafeu. When I led the raids, I fought under a code: I do not harm women or children. I saved you from that man in Anfa for one simple reason: because I could. And that was more than anyone else would have done. You were no one to me, just some foreign thrall girl. I sold you to a man I thought I could control—a man I believed wouldn't harm you, at least not in the way that the man I killed would have. Again, that was more than another would have done. You were nothing to me, until I happened to see you take Broskrap's life. That's when I saw your true potential. Only then did I realize that Odin had led me to you in Anfa, just as he led me to that very pond so that I might witness your bravery and prowess. So I gave you to Freydis to keep you safe, to bide the time until I could think of a way to convince my brother to go back on his decree. But you are much more than I realized, even then. You are *Úlfheðinn,* a warrior inhabited by the spirit of the wolf, capable of feats no ordinary soldier can achieve. I am a *berserker*—a bear-warrior. Odin chose you, as he chose me, to triumph over our enemies and carry out his will."

I find myself speechless again, reeling at her harsh candor.

Úlfheðinn. So that's what that word means. Alvtir believes I am blessed by the highest of the *Majūs'* gods . . . *now.* But before I had taken a life, I was nothing to her. I was nothing to any of them.

"If you're as close with the gods as you think you are, you would treat all their creations with respect. Regardless of their *use* to you," I retort.

"My gods don't show such compassion to those they cannot use." She takes a puff from the pipe and leans forward, resting her forearms on her knees as she blows out another cloud of smoke. "Before I made myself Odin's vessel, I was nothing."

"That's no excuse."

Alvtir only nods, gazing at the fire as if into another realm.

I want to tell her that she doesn't have the right to say who chose me, or for what. I want to tell her that I don't believe in her "Odin," that I give thanks to Gu, Agé, and Mawu-Lisa for my gifts. But then Mama's words bloom in my mind: *The spirit of the painted wolf remains by your side. Remember to honor her, and she will guide you on your path.*

It doesn't matter what Alvtir or the others believe, then or now. What matters is that I am honoring the spirit of the wolf by finding my own way, as best as I can. That's something my parents might agree on, for once.

"You've a dangerous path ahead," Alvtir continues. "Every shield maiden had to prove that she was worth five *hird*men to gain half the respect of one. With Snorri in command, you'll have to be worth ten."

"You don't have to tell *me*," I bite back, thinking of Snorri's deception today, carefully designed to undermine that very respect. I consider telling Alvtir about it, but I'm sure she won't spare any pity. She was the very first woman to join the *hird*—not just as a soldier, but as a leader of men.

I study her as she stares at the dying flames, and for the first time I notice the weariness in the lines of her face.

"Where did you make it?" I ask, motioning to the blade in my lap.

She cocks an eyebrow. "How do you know *I* made it?"

"You're covered in soot."

She looks down as if noticing her dirty clothes for the first time. "Ah, so I am." She jerks her head toward the door. "Why don't I show you?"

The cold air bites my cheeks as I follow her past the henhouse and into the forest, staying close to the small aura of light from her soapstone candle. The hounds paddle happily behind us, the sound of their pants chasing our footsteps in the darkness. We come to a shed and she kicks the door open.

I step inside, instantly recognizing the crunch of hammersmith flakes under my boots, the sharp scents of coal and slag. As my eyes adjust, I take in the tools hanging from the beams, the bellows pointing to a stone table covered with ash, the anvil beside it.

My heart swells to bursting.

A forge!

"This is *yours*?"

"Built it fifteen years ago," Alvtir replies. "Angrboda was forged here by my own hand." She unsheathes her sword and holds out the flawless blade for me to admire. The runes carved down the center almost glitter in the candlelight. "She was made from the gods' own iron, sent down in a ball of fire from Asgard."

Iron from the skies! "I knew I sensed Gu's magic in the sword," I murmur.

"Gu?"

"The god of iron," I explain. "My people are blacksmiths. My ancestors learned the craft from Gu himself, and my father passed the sacred knowledge on to me."

"You surprise me yet again, Yafeu." She spreads her arms wide. "You can use the smithy whenever you please. I'll buy some iron at the market."

Elated, I look around the forge with a new sense of purpose. "You won't be disappointed."

She flashes a mischievous grin. The points of her teeth look strangely sharp in the candlelight. "I know."

33

YAFEU

The days pass like the beat of a griot's drum. Wake, eat, train, eat, sleep. Repeat. The air gets warmer, the leaves unfurl on the trees, and soon there are wild berries to pick and veal for sale at the butchers' stalls. Meanwhile, the soft padding my body amassed over the long, cramped winter is slowly replaced with hard, sinewy muscle. It pleases me to see it bulge and flex as I move.

I don't have as much time for the forge as I'd like, but the routine offers its own small delights. Dag's oblivious antics, Hetha's easy laughter, Wisna's understated wisdom—they all sweeten the long hours of training, like molasses stirred into porridge. Snorri finds every excuse to undermine me, but the more I improve, the less it bothers me. Even Ranveig and I have come to an unspoken truce. After I bested her a few times in hand-to-hand combat, the field between us leveled off. Now we both have the bruises to prove the other's skill. We're far from friends, but she respects me enough to leave me alone, and I'm happy to return the favor.

Through our sparring matches, I've come to know them all as warriors. Dag has all the strength and relentlessness of a bull, which inevitably wears his opponent down. Ranveig also prefers to be on the offensive, but she's too small to throw her body around the way Dag does, so she relies on agility and resourcefulness, using every part of the battleground to her advantage. She once threw dirt in my eyes after I knocked her down; we didn't speak for a week after that.

Hetha, on the other hand, fights defensively, wielding her shield as its own weapon, waiting for an opening before she strikes with her sword. When that opening comes, she never misses. Facing her has made me aware of all the ways I leave myself vulnerable. Caution doesn't exactly come naturally to me, but I'm learning.

Wisna doesn't use a shield at all. When I asked, she told me that she was stabbed in her left shoulder on a raid in Northumbria. "Barely missed my heart," she said with a lopsided grin. The wound never fully healed, and she now can't bear the weight of a shield for long. She can block most blows with her axes, but an observant opponent can see that she favors her right side too much. Luckily, in the chaos of battle, no enemy would notice.

Most of all, I look forward to sparring with Ingmar. Hetha was right: We *are* evenly matched in battle. We trade wins and losses, then teach each other the moves we used. He's better with a sword, but I'm better with daggers. He's stronger, but I'm faster. I want to ask Hetha and Wisna if he's as good a man as he seems, but I don't want to encourage any further speculation. They already assume too much as it is.

They've all taken many wounds over the years, and they all bear the scars with pride. It puts me to shame, because I have so few of my own. I thought myself strong, but these men and women are battle-hardened warriors. They've gone on many different raids, fought many different enemies. And they've survived. I've gotten into my fair share of scrapes, but only three "battles," if I can even call them that: when the slavers came to my village, Anfa, and Freydis's wedding. The first two times, I was *running* for my life more than *fighting* for it. And even at Freydis's wedding, the assassins weren't really a threat to me. I could have hidden or fled if I'd wanted to. So the raid this summer will be my first real test.

The raid.

It's constantly lurking in the back of my mind, the dread growing with each day it draws nearer. I was so focused on becoming the warrior I always wanted to be that I never stopped to consider what it entails, what it would cost me. It won't be like fighting the slavers, or the guards in Anfa, or the assassins at Freydis's wedding. The *hird* plunders entire villages, entire cities, even. Villages like Airé's. Like Bronaugh's. Filled with people who've done nothing to harm me or mine. But I will be forced to harm them.

And I will do it under Snorri's command—for Balli's gain. That's the oath I swore.

Worse still is knowing what *I'm* capable of. I killed three men at the wedding—and I enjoyed it. I *reveled* in it. With Snorri leading the *hird* and Balli controlling from afar, I can no longer deny the possibility that great evil will be done through the *Úlfheðinn.* Through me.

Then again, isn't that the fate of every warrior?

I picture the Ghāna's soldiers training on the grounds outside Koumbi Saleh. How I longed to join them, to be one of them! Now I wonder: When the Ghāna orders them to attack his enemies, do they ever weigh the justice of it? And if they find it wrong—if they despise the order they've been given—do they still find virtue, even glory, in seeing it through? Or do they simply follow the order and think nothing of it? After all, most soldiers don't get to choose which king to serve, nor which commander to follow into battle. They probably don't waste their time brooding over things they cannot control.

I wish I could be like them: unthinking, unquestioning. But I can't. Not after everything I've survived. I know what it means to be a victim—and I know what it means to be a killer.

At the very least, I've promised myself that I'll fight under Alvtir's code, no matter what Snorri commands. I won't harm women or children. What's more, I'll use my earnings to buy Mbaneh and Nyeru's freedom. And the other Soninke thralls as well—eventually, I'll save up enough to buy all their freedom. That alone is worth whatever I must do on the raids.

Sometimes you must cause suffering to end suffering. It sounds like something Papa would say.

I try to visit Nyeru and Mbaneh at least once a week, usually on the way back from training. Both have already learned a great deal of the *Majūs'* tongue, but I can see the toll that life as a thrall is taking on them both. It eases my worries about the raids to promise them that I will free them from the carpenter as soon as I can.

All in all, I've never been so exhausted, but underneath the exhaustion there's something new, something good. Instead of just *being,* just *surviving,* the feeling of finally . . . *becoming.* It's a current that is unfamiliar to me, and I am all too willing to let it sweep me away. Even Snorri's constant goading can't pull me upstream.

Every four days, the *hird* gets a reprieve—or at least everyone else does, but Alvtir insists on using those days to train me one-on-one. She says we won't take a break until I can ably wield a sword and shield. "Snorri the Snake is worthy of his name," she explained before our first lesson. "He doesn't chase his prey. He lies in wait and watches it move, studying its strengths, its weaknesses. Then he strikes without warning, hitting the most vulnerable point and putting every ounce of his poison into the bite. If you don't want to become his prey, then you can't show any weakness."

As much as I hate filling my precious free days with yet more exertion, I have to admit that her grueling regime is working. Snorri is none too pleased by my progress; he'll have to find some other way to embarrass me soon enough. The thought keeps me from complaining too much.

I try to remember that debt as she jabs her sword toward my chest and I fail to block it with my shield, momentarily blinded by

Lisa's descent. Seizing on the distraction, Alvtir knocks the shield off of my arm with her own. The blow ricochets up my shoulder and I bite down a yelp of pain.

"*Never* drop your shield-arm!" she barks. "Your shield is the only barrier between you and Valhalla. Again!"

"*You* don't even *use* a shield," I hurl back, frustrated. "Besides, isn't it every warrior's dream to go to Valhalla?"

"Oh, but you're not a warrior yet," she says, raising her sword. "The golden hall will have to wait for you. *Again!*"

I fling myself at her with abandon. Again, she knocks me back with irritating ease. "You're letting your anger get the best of you," she scolds.

I lean on my knees, catching my breath. Now I know how Freydis felt when I was training her. "I'm the *Úlfheðinn*," I grumble. "Anger is the source of my strength, *remember*?"

She gives me a strange look. I straighten, thrown by the sudden shift in her demeanor. "Take it from me, Yafeu: There's only so much water in that well."

I swallow hard, feeling the dryness of my throat in sharp contrast with the sweat soaking my tunic. Her words make me uneasy, laden as they are with a meaning I can't discern. "I'm just tired," I say.

She sighs and turns away, wiping her brow with the back of her arm. "That's enough for today. Do your stretches, then get a good rest. Maybe you won't fight like a puppy next time." She twirls her sword around her hand and stabs it into its sheath with practiced precision, punctuating her disappointment.

I roll my eyes behind her back. *I don't fight like a puppy when I train with the* hird, I think to myself.

I drag my spent limbs toward the longhouse, but Alvtir veers off, striding purposefully toward the trail to the city.

"Where are you going now?" I yell after her, though I already know her answer.

"I have business," she says, at the same time as I mouth the words, flattening my face into an impression of her deadpan.

She always has *business,* at all hours of the day and night. I hardly even see her outside of these sessions. When I wake in the morning, she's already gone. Sometimes she doesn't return until long after I've gotten in bed for the night, if she even returns at all. Since I joined the *hird,* Mawu has fattened and shrunk and fattened again, and she hasn't once come to train with the rest of us. Hetha and Wisna continue to take dinners with me afterward, and when Alvtir does show up, they converse with her like everything is as it always was. But I can feel the edge of uncertainty in the silence between their words. I know they're wondering if she's still part of the *hird* at all. I've thought about asking her myself, but I'm afraid of what the answer might be.

Even if I did ask, I'm not sure she would tell me. She won't even tell me what her "business" is. So I choose to believe that she spends her days working on a plan to get rid of Snorri and reclaim her position as *stallari,* that she doesn't tell me or the others what she's up to because she's protecting us. It's the only explanation I can think of for all the secretiveness.

"Right," I say tartly. "I'll leave dinner out for you. Again."

Without so much as a glance in reply, she disappears into the forest.

34

FREYDIS

"Not there!" I snap at the two boys carrying the midsummer pole. "It should go in the *center* of the field, so everyone can dance around it. This is too close to the fence."

The boys nod hastily and struggle to unearth the garlanded pole. I turn to the thrall girls placing stones around the bonfire pit. "Help them."

I watch the group haul the pole over to the middle of the field and drive it into the summer-soft earth. I already regret my tone; it's not their fault that I'm on edge. This morning seems to stretch into eternity—and not only because it's the solstice. At least setting up for the midsummer festival gives me something to pass the time until Harald arrives.

Tonight, this field will be full to the brim with revelers. Thingmen and farmers and thralls alike will feast on smoked pig and celebrate together, shouting their prayers to Frey for a bountiful harvest to come. Boys will pick wildflowers to give to their sweethearts. Lovers will sneak into the woods or jump the fence into Father's barley fields, taking cover under the tall stalks. Many babes will be born next spring.

And Harald and I will preside over it all. Thingmen will lay gifts at our feet, proclaiming our wedding blessed for falling on such a sacred time of year. Even the thralls will toast to our union. Perhaps we'll take a turn around the midsummer pole together, laughing and singing and forgetting our station for a few precious hours. I smile at the thought.

I can hardly believe, after everything that's happened, that my dream is really coming true. I nearly had to lose my life to gain it back, but now Harald will finally be mine.

And yet, the warm spring of excitement I should be bathing in is chilled by worry. Worries I didn't have with Hakon. What if Harald finds me unattractive? Rumors of his handsomeness have run so wild, I can only imagine he's the image of Frey himself. Or even if my form appeals to him, what about my mind? What if he finds me dull? What if we have nothing to say to each other? What if he's already fallen in love with someone else?

I close my eyes, trying to think of yet another prayer to offer my namesake. But over the last moon I've made every sacrifice I could think of, cast every spell Fritjof ever taught me. There is no prayer I haven't already uttered. So I whisper simply: "I place my trust in you, Freya."

If only Yafeu were with me. What was it she said to me last time?

Whenever I was upset, my friend Ampah would sit me down and braid my hair while I talked about whatever was bothering me.

The thought of Yafeu brings a pang to my heart. Father offered to buy a new handmaiden for me after she left with Alvtir, but I found I couldn't stomach the thought of taking another thrall. I told him it would cost more than it was worth to send a new girl on the long journey to Vestfold with me, that I might as well wait until I arrived to find a new handmaiden, one who could accustom me to the ways of Harald's hall—and whose cost would be his burden. Father seemed pleased by my reasoning. It's probably the only time I've ever spoken wisely in his eyes.

Almost two full moons have waxed and waned, and Yafeu hasn't once come to see me. Of course, I'm happy for her; she deserves to walk her own path. But I had hoped our paths would cross from time to time.

I can't visit her myself; it would surely get back to Mother. I no longer believe in the curse—not since Father announced my marriage to Harald. If anything, the gods have been conspiring in my favor all this time. Nevertheless, Mother believes. She would punish me for going to Alvtir's house even if she wasn't with child. She might even have me placed under guard.

Which means, if Yafeu comes to my wedding tomorrow, it could be the last time I ever see her. After that, I'll be leaving for Vestfold, for Harald's storied hall.

Just like I've always wanted, I remind myself earnestly. I can make new friends in Vestfold. Friends who will see me as the queen I was raised to be, poised and generous and blessed by the gods. No longer will girls like Astrid and Solvi mock me behind my back. No longer will I be known as the timid, foolish daughter of a pitiless king.

The exultant blast of the trumpet in the distance interrupts my thoughts.

He's here!

I almost trip over my shift in my haste to get to the Great Hall. I'm wearing my finest dress—at least, the finest one that remains untarnished. It's made of silk from Miklagard, with delicate silver embellishments at the hemline. I've fastened it with a pair of gleaming silver brooches over a linen shift. Harald has accumulated significant wealth with the kingdoms he's added to his own; I know Father will be eager to make his own fortune seem just as large. I've braided some buttercups into my hair for the festival, but I wonder now if it looks jarringly childish against such regal attire.

It seems like half the day passes until Father emerges from the hall, but finally, he does.

"Let's go," he says brusquely.

"Without Mother?" I ask, hesitant.

"She's not coming," he snaps. "If Harald knows she's with child he will demand a higher dowry. Do you want that, girl?"

I shake my head quickly. He's in one of his moods, but at least he looks clear-eyed on this most important of days. No henbane.

My eagerness bounds in front of me like a dog as we make for the harbor.

The last time I was to be married, the guards brought Hakon up to meet us at the Great Hall. It was a show of power on Father's part, that we would not descend from our high hill to greet him ourselves. But he was a lesser king than Harald, and Father has been strangely superstitious since the disaster at the wedding, leaning more than usual on custom and ceremony. He must not want to risk any offense to the gods.

By the time we approach, the boatmen have already secured Harald's ship to the dock. The dark maple stem is the shape of a man's head instead of a dragon's, and soon its likeness emerges beside it, on the face of a golden-haired man striding across the dock.

Harald.

My heart skitters to a stop as I take him in. He *is* the picture of Frey: tall and broad-shouldered, with curly hair the color of spun gold flowing freely down to his neck, framing a sharp jawline and full, bowstring lips. A purple cloak lined with fur as white as snow brushes his heels. He has the upright bearing and lithe, graceful figure of a seasoned warrior. No wonder Sól has come out from the clouds to shine upon him.

An older man catches up to him, and the two approach us side by side. The elder's short hair is graying with age, but he has the gait of a much younger man, with a grizzled face and an aura of stern authority. This must be Harald's uncle, Guthorm. He served as regent when Harald was a boy.

"King Harald," Father greets him. "Welcome to the shores of Skíringssal."

"We are honored to be your guests for this joyous event, King Balli," Harald replies in a voice as silky as my dress. "This is my uncle, Guthorm Nialsson."

Father acknowledges the older man with a nod, then gestures to me. "My daughter, Princess Freydis."

Harald eyes me up and down approvingly. I blush and look to my feet, both shocked at his brazenness and thrilled that I seem to please him.

"You are the image of your namesake, Princess Freydis." A shudder of delight runs through me as he breaks into a sweeping bow.

"You flatter me, King Harald," I say, daring to lift my gaze to his sun-kissed face. His hazel eyes linger on my bosom, sending another flush to my cheeks.

Guthorm clears his throat. "There is much to discuss before tomorrow, King Balli," he says gruffly. "Your messenger gave us the terms of the dowry. Some of those terms we cannot accept."

Father narrows his eyes at the man, but Harald throws his head back and lets out a braying laugh. It's an oddly abrasive sound coming from such a beautiful man. "My uncle, always focused on politics!" He claps Guthorm on the shoulder. "He tends to spoil the mood, but he has my best interests at heart."

"A commendable quality for the warden of a king," I offer amiably, trying to smooth over the tension.

"Indeed," Harald says, nodding. "It frees me to follow more . . . *interesting* pursuits." His eyes return to my bosom.

Again, I am startled by his boldness. I wonder if all the men in Vestfold are so forward.

"Don't we all wish we had an Uncle Guthorm in our lives," Father says drily.

"Uncle," Harald continues, ignoring him. "Why don't you speak with King Balli on my behalf while Freydis gives me a tour of this

famed city? We can all meet again at the midsummer festival tonight."

"A fine idea," Father cuts in before Guthorm can reply. He must
think he'll have the upper hand without Harald present for the negotiations. But one look at Guthorm tells me that won't be the case.
He's as protective over Harald as a mother bear over her cub.

"Wonderful," Harald exclaims.

Guthorm and Father turn to the hill and immediately launch
into an argument about my dowry. But Harald smiles widely and
offers his arm, and it's as if they don't exist.

"You're not weary from the journey?" I ask, tucking my hand
around his elbow. The skin of my palm tingles where it meets his
jet-black tunic.

"It takes more than a little boat ride to make me weary, my
queen."

My queen. My heart skips a beat at the sound of that phrase on
his lips. This man could be the son of the Aesir, and *I* will be his
queen! Skalds will compose poems about our love, sagas that will
outlast the ages.

Oh, thank you, thank you, thank you, Freya! And thank you, dísir
*of my line, for guiding me true! And thank you to the Norns for weav-
ing our fates together! Thanks to all the gods across all the realms;
even the frost giants of Jötunheim!*

"Then I'll gladly show you all you wish to see," I say. "Shall we
start with the market? Our craftsmen are known for their fine work,
and traders frequent us from far and wide with a great variety—"

"I've seen enough markets to last me ten lifetimes. Take me to a
place only you can show me. Somewhere special, where we can be
alone."

I match his mischievous smile with one of my own. "I know just
the place, *my king.*"

"Where are we?" Harald asks, glancing around the little glade. Sól
has driven her chariot past the arch of the sky, sending a slanting

light that stretches our shadows across the grass. The evergreens sway in the soft breeze and I breathe deeply, savoring their clean, woodsy fragrance. I hope they have evergreens in Vestfold.

"A training ground, of sorts. I used to come here with my hand-maiden. She's a skilled warrior." I lift my chin proudly, meeting his searing gaze. I'm getting used to these little challenges in his eyes; he should know that his queen isn't as meek as she looks. "She taught me how to fight."

He cocks an eyebrow at me. "Is Princess Freydis a fearsome shield maiden, like her infamous aunt?"

"Hardly," I chuckle.

"And no one comes here now?"

I shake my head. "Can you imagine what my father would do if he knew my thrall girl was training me in combat? He'd box me silly—"

Harald spins me toward him and presses his lips against mine, silencing me.

I freeze, stunned, then force myself to relax into the kiss. His lips are warm and insistent. I let out a soft moan. I feel his hands gripping my bottom and I pull away, breaking the kiss as gently as I can.

"We should be getting back," I say, taking a step backward. "The festival will begin at nightfall."

"I know you want this," he murmurs. I take another step back, but he closes the gap between us. My back scrapes against bark as he crashes into me, nipping at my neck.

"Stop!" I cry out. "Please, we must wait for the wedding!" I try to push him away, but he grabs my wrists and spins me around. He slams me so hard into the trunk the air is knocked out of my chest. I can't cry out as he twists my arms painfully behind my back, holding them in one hand while the other snakes up my dress.

"I want to know what I'm getting first," he whispers in my ear as I gasp for air. "After all, your father isn't known for honoring his agreements."

I hear my undergarments rip as he tears them off. Panic floods me, freezing my mind.

Think, Freydis. *Think.*

Yafeu. What would Yafeu do? I remember the last time we were here. I attacked her from behind and she nearly broke my nose with the back of her head.

I stop struggling and sink down in his grasp, hoping he thinks I've surrendered. His belt clinks as he unbuckles it. He lowers down slightly—

Now. I launch myself up and back. My head connects hard with some part of his face. We crash into the grass, me landing on his chest.

"You little bitch!" he screams, dropping my arms.

I waste no time. I scramble to my feet and break into a sprint, ignoring the pounding in my chest and head.

I sprint the whole way back, nearly collapsing at the door of the Great Hall.

"Princess!" I hear Gunnar say, though his voice is distorted, as though I'm listening to him from underwater. The ground sways, and the current pulls my legs out from under me. I catch his arm and hold it to keep from sinking.

Then the world rights itself, and the pain returns with my breath. Everything aches.

"Thank you," I say, releasing the guard. But as I reach for the door, he moves to block me.

"I'm sorry, Princess Freydis. The king said not to let anyone disturb them."

"He didn't mean *me!*" I step around him and shove open the door before he can stop me.

Laughter peals across the hall. Father's throne is empty. Instead, I find him sitting at our table across from Guthorm. From the amused looks on their faces and the sight of several pitchers of ale on the table, I take it they've come to an agreement.

My heart sinks into my stomach. I'm too late.

"Freydis," Father says, scowling at me through glazed eyes. "I told the guards not to let anyone in."

"Father, I must speak with you at once."

He sighs and reaches for a pitcher. "What is it now?"

"I wish to speak *alone*," I say forcefully.

Guthorm arches an eyebrow at me.

"Guthorm will be your kinsman soon, girl-child," Father drawls, refilling his horn. "Speak freely."

I take a deep breath and close my eyes. "Harald has tried to . . . force himself . . . on me."

Silence. I open my eyes to see Father and Guthorm exchanging a smirk.

". . . And?"

"And, I didn't—we—we're not m-married . . ." My voice trembles, buckling under the weight of despair. "The gods haven't blessed our union—it isn't—"

Father's horn hits the ground with a loud clang, wrenching the words from my mouth. "Foolish girl!" he explodes, surging to his feet. "You will give Harald whatever he wishes to take. You belong to him now, to do with as he sees fit. And you will be *grateful* for the honor."

I stare at my father in disbelief. I start to feel a strange sense of detachment, like I'm seeing him through someone else's eyes. His bony hand sits on the gold buckle of his belt, his sunken chest heaving labored breaths against the gold brooch of his blood-red cloak. So much gold, as if such finery would make up for the body that withers underneath it. His sagging face is as red as a beet, his lips twitching in rage.

"I will not," I whisper.

He snorts. "What did you say?"

"You don't care about me. You never have." I walk toward him slowly, feeling courage mounting inside me with each step. "You don't care about *anyone* at all. Not my mother, not your people," I continue, louder. "You're just a vain, greedy, wretched old man, not worthy of the life Odin breathed into you."

I stop right in front of him, a hair's breadth from his face, drawing myself up to my full height. He glares at me through bloodshot eyes—eyes that have always stared me down, cowing me, making me mistrust my own mind, my own heart.

All my life, I've feared him so. And he's not even taller than I am.

"I am *ashamed* to be your daughter," I spit.

His palm connects with my cheek. Hard. I am falling to the floor before I can blink.

My head slams against the floorboard. Pain blossoms before my eyes. I struggle to look up at Father—two of him, now three of him—before the darkness swallows me whole.

35

FREYDIS

Grainy oak walls come into focus. There's a plush fur beneath me instead of the hard floor. I'm in my room, in my bed.

My head is throbbing. I lift my fingers to my cheek and wince at the tenderness there.

How long have I been asleep? I force myself to sit up, fighting a rush of dizziness and nausea. I gulp down the rest of the water in the flagon beside my bed. The dizziness subsides a little, but I need more.

I force myself to stand and hobble over to the door. I push it, but it doesn't open.

Panic floods me yet again. The throbbing in my head intensifies as I throw my weight against the door, pushing with everything I have.

"Princess Freydis!" Orm's voice sounds from outside. "We're under orders from the king to make sure you don't leave your room. It's for your own safety."

I back away from the door in disbelief.

I am a prisoner. A prisoner in my own home.

The weight of the truth crashes down on me. I sink to the floor, tears welling in my eyes.

What I said to my father was all too true. To him, I'm a prize to be bartered away at best, a constant reminder of his lack of a son at worst. Mother is little better. And Harald . . . gods, how could I have been so naïve?

Yafeu is the only person who has ever seen me for more than the role I'm supposed to play. She's the only one who's ever seen me for who I am. Or at least, who I *could* be. Who I *want* to be.

Oh, Yafeu, where are you when I need you the most? Did you ever truly care about me?

Is there *anyone* in the world who truly cares about me?

The sobs rip through me, violent and wild. I lie on the floor as they rack my body, ravaging my pounding head. I feel a terrible unfurling, like a vicious bird trapped inside me that's desperate to stretch its wings. I twist and writhe. I squeeze my fingers and toes. I pound the floor until my fists are splintered and bloody, and then I pound my own thighs. From somewhere low in my belly, a sound between a cry and a scream pours out of me. I don't care that Orm can hear me on the other side of the door. I don't care about anything except relieving the pressure.

When the purge ends, I'm hollow.

At first. But then a memory emerges from the void, something Yafeu said to me:

You aren't so different, Freydis. You have strength inside you. Believe it.

What would Yafeu do if she were in my place?

Slowly but surely, the hollowness fills with resolve. I drag myself off the floor and change into the plainest dress I own. I reach for my cloak—then, on second thought, I choose the old, worn cloak I would let Yafeu wear. I grab the iron pan hanging from the wall and take it with me to the door.

"Orm," I call out. "I need to use the outhouse."

"I'm sorry, Princess, but the king said—"

"It's urgent," I insist. "Please, Orm. Don't let me suffer. You can accompany me there and back."

Silence. I hold my breath. Just as I think he's going to ignore me, I hear him sigh. "All right."

When he opens the door, I'm ready.

I whack him on the head with the pan and he crumples to the ground, unconscious.

"Sorry, Orm."

It takes more strength than I knew I possessed to drag him inside. I unbuckle his belt where his sword is sheathed and strap it around my hips. The presence of the sword steels my nerves somewhat; now I know why Yafeu always insisted on having a weapon on her body.

I peek out the door, glancing around. The compound is empty tonight, thank the gods. Sól has dipped under the mountains— everyone must be at the bonfire by now.

Maybe Yafeu will be there as well; I can only pray that I'll find her before someone recognizes me.

Pulling the hood low over my head, I set out on my way.

Gods, dísir, *if you watch over me at all, guide me now to Yafeu.*

36

YAFEU

"Have you seen her?" Dag wrings his hands, nearly crushing the bouquet of wildflowers he spent the afternoon picking.

Hetha slings an arm around his shoulder. "Ranveig isn't one for celebrations, dear Dag. Why don't you relax and have a horn of mead?"

"I never thought I'd see the night that *we* have to coax *you* to drink," Ingmar adds, patting Dag's stomach.

"I'll have none of your flak tonight, Shield-Breaker." Dag swats at him with his flower hand, further crumpling the pitiful bouquet. No one has yet had the heart to tell him that half the flowers are weeds.

"I can't believe how much *all* of you drink," I say drily. All around us, the *hird*men are in various states of intoxication. Lisa has barely set, and some have already passed out facedown in the field. The rest are dancing rowdily or chasing squealing girls around the midsummer pole, or jostling one another in line for the mead table.

The evening air is thick with a heady mix of yeast and smoke and roasting pig.

"Oh, come off it, Yafeu," Hetha says, slapping my back good-naturedly. "It's the midsummer festival! They say if you wake up with a clear head tomorrow, you didn't celebrate properly."

"At least *we'll* have hangovers, my love." Wisna raises her horn to Hetha's.

"If we wake up at all," Hetha adds.

I roll my eyes as they guzzle the contents down in one fell swoop, but I take a hearty gulp from my own horn. Maybe it *would* be good to drink a little more than usual tonight: I've had knots coiling in my stomach all day at the prospect of seeing Freydis again.

I told her I would visit her, but between training with the *hird* and Alvtir, plus looking after Nyeru and Mbaneh, I haven't had the time. Or at least, that's what I tell myself. I wonder now if I haven't been avoiding her out of guilt.

I know I shouldn't feel that way. Freydis is getting exactly what she wanted all along: to marry Harald of Vestfold. If all the gossip is true, he's the man of her dreams, and this wedding will be one for the ages. I'm sure when I see her tonight, she'll be rosy with joy. And she'll understand that I've been busy. After all, we're both living the lives we were fated to live. Just not together.

I take another sip from my horn and glance around nervously. But instead of Freydis's wispy, honey-colored locks, I catch a flash of a wild auburn mane. It's Ranveig all right, standing with her arms folded across her chest and staring moodily into the raging bonfire. All by herself, of course.

"There's your sweetheart." I point her out to Dag, who gulps. He tries in vain to smooth the cowlicks of his unruly black hair before heading over.

"This should be entertaining," Ingmar whispers to me.

The two of us trail behind as Dag approaches Ranveig. "For you, my lady." He bows low and holds out the bouquet.

"Will you just leave me alone, you oaf?" Ranveig smacks the bouquet out of his hand. Dag watches her stomp off with eyes as round as the moon will be tonight.

Ingmar and I share an amused look. "Sorry, Dag." Ingmar pats his shoulder. "Better luck next year."

"She burns more brightly than the bonfire." Dag sighs. "I think I will have that drink now." He saunters off to the mead table, barreling through groups of revelers as he goes.

"Nothing fazes him, does it?" I shake my head and turn to Ingmar with a smile. Instead, I meet his uncertain gaze.

"I wanted to pick some for you." He scratches the back of his head. "But I didn't think . . . I wasn't sure that you'd like that."

"Oh." I look away, unsure what else to say.

"There will be time for flower picking later, Ingmar." Alvtir emerges from the shadows. A wave of relief washes over me at the sight of her. I hadn't seen her since yesterday, and I was beginning to worry. "I've been looking for you."

"Which one of us?" I ask playfully.

"Both," she says, her expression solemn. "Round up Hetha and Wisna, Ranveig and Dag. Tell them to gather their possessions, but don't call attention to yourselves. Come in groups of two, no more. Meet me back at the house. And come armed."

She turns and disappears into the darkness. Ingmar and I share a look of confusion.

"What do you think that's about?" he asks.

"I don't know," I reply. "But it can't be good."

Mawu is full and low in the sky by the time Ingmar and I emerge from the narrow trail into Alvtir's holding, making the irksome summer twilight even brighter than it usually is. We find Alvtir stoking a roaring fire in the pit outside her longhouse, a smaller version of the bonfire at the midsummer festival. The other four stand to the side, waiting for us.

As we approach, I note that Alvtir has changed into the fearsome bearskin vest she wore in Anfa, Angrboda in its sheath at her hip.

"*There* they are." Ranveig folds her arms across her chest and turns to Alvtir. "Now, are we here to play dress up? Because I have better things to do."

Alvtir cuts her a look. "Better than listening to the woman who saved you from a life of *whoring*?"

My mouth falls open. Alvtir *saved* Ranveig? Where? When? I look to Hetha and Wisna, but they pointedly avoid meeting my gaze.

Ranveig glares at Alvtir. She spits on the ground but doesn't utter another word.

"What's going on, Alvtir?" Hetha asks.

Alvtir stands, facing the group from across the bonfire. I can't help but imagine her walking into the gates of Valhalla looking exactly as she does now, with Mawu at her back and flames in her cobalt eyes.

Then she lets out a deep, shaky breath that makes my heart quicken. She almost seems . . . *nervous.* From the shift in the others, I can tell they feel it too.

She looks each of us in the eye in turn, turning last to me. Her gaze is keen and searching, as though the fire is a torch she's using to peer into the darkness of my heart.

Finally, when she is satisfied with whatever she has seen, she begins: "The six of you are the only people alive whom I would trust with my own life. You are the best of the *hird* not only in skill, but in honor. You have never questioned my leadership, nor have I doubted your loyalty. So I will share with you now the secrets I have kept."

Her eyes still hold mine. "Yafeu, you are new to us, so you do not know: On our return from the last raid, I took my ship to the Saracen city of Lisbon. I left the others on a beach far outside the city and went alone to its walls, on the pretense of scouting for a weakness in their defenses."

She looks now to the others. "I could not speak of my true mission then, but it was not that. Before we left Skíringssal, I paid a Frankish trader who frequents Iberia to find a way to get me an audience with the emir of al-Andalus. The emir did not come himself, but he sent two of his advisers to meet me on his behalf. I offered them a truce: an end to the raids in exchange for joining our forces against the Christians when the need arises for either of our kingdoms. I did all this without my brother's knowledge. When Balli discovered it, he stripped me of my position as *stallari*."

She pauses, letting the shock settle over us.

So that's why Alvtir no longer leads the *hird*. Even before the attack at Freydis's wedding, she knew the Christians were dangerous. So dangerous that she went behind Balli's back to form an alliance against them.

"For many years, I believed it was my duty to save this kingdom from the Christians: not only our people, but our gods, our very way of life. But I could not get my brother to see reason. So great is his greed that it has blinded him to this threat. Even after it came to his own hall, he still would not open his eyes. He would rather throw your lives away on an endless quest for more gold than use your might to defend his people. And he would rather bleed his own people dry than accept any less from them than what he believes he is due. He does this all in the name of our gods, hiding behind false declarations of their will."

She shakes her head ruefully. "He is not the only one at fault. When he decided to wed his daughter to that conqueror King Harald, I realized: I too have been blinded by arrogance and self-righteousness. I wanted to believe the Christians were the enemy. But I was wrong. My *brother* is the true enemy. At least the Christians fight for their god; year after year, we fight only for my brother's greed. We pillage innocent towns and slaughter innocent men for his greed. And Harald and the other kings of Norveg are no better. Like Balli, they pay tribute to the gods with their words, but they act only for their own gain. There's not a whiff of honor left among them. They aren't worth saving, and neither are the people who follow them. Let the Christians tear them apart—if they don't tear one another apart first."

She pauses again. No one speaks a word. The silence is so complete that when the fire pops, it sounds like thunder.

"At first, I sought the Saracens of al-Andalus as allies because they've been fighting their own war against the Christians. Thus, when the emir's advisers brought me into Lisbon, I was expecting to see a city hardened by centuries of battle. What I saw was quite the opposite.

"I saw a city that far surpasses our own, in which all different people—people from different lands, with different gods—were living together without violence. The Christians and Saracens and so many others had found a way to coexist in peace.

"I believe I could live there in peace as well. So I'm leaving Agder, and Norveg, to its fate. I plan to ask the emir for a small plot of fertile land in exchange for training his soldiers in our arts. I'm leaving this very night, while Balli's men are too drunk to notice, let alone stop me. I asked you here to give you the choice to join me.

"I won't lie: It won't be a glorious life, not compared with the life you know. We will be farmers first, and soldiers second. We'll be building our own homes, cultivating the land ourselves. It will be backbreaking work, and it will earn you no renown. And you'll be leaving everyone you know behind.

"Worst of all, you'll be breaking your oath to your king. You'll be branded an oath-breaker, a nithing. But I have come to believe that it is more dishonorable to serve a king like Balli than to break the oath that binds us to him.

"Still, I know it's too much to ask of you—so I don't ask. I only offer you the choice. You may stay here if you wish. But know this: War will come for this land. Either at the hands of King Harald, or at the hands of the Christians."

The heavy silence stretches out. Apprehension is palpable in the cool night air.

A whole host of emotions rolls through me at once. I'm far too overwhelmed to think clearly.

I know part of me is relieved not to be forced to kill innocent people for Balli's gain—and, of course, to be free of Snorri Broskrapsson. But another part of me never wanted to become a farmer. Though I guess I never really considered it before. And we would still be soldiers . . .

Then my mind conjures up the memories of the slavers. I have no love for Balli or his people, but how can Alvtir be so sure that this emir is any better? How does she know that life among the Saracens would be any different than staying here and fighting the Christians, or Harald?

Wisna breaks the silence before I can ask. "Alvtir, you should know by now that you'll never be able to get rid of us."

Hetha takes Wisna's hand. "I only regret that we won't get to gut Snorri Broskrapsson first."

"You're still my *stallari*, Alvtir. I too will go with you." Ingmar's smooth voice rings out.

"You've all lost your minds!" Dag says gruffly. "So . . . I'll be in good company."

Alvtir nods, her gaze pregnant with emotion. She turns to Ranveig. "Still have somewhere better to be?"

Ranveig shakes her head. "I am with you," she replies in the most genuine tone I've ever heard escape her lips.

Alvtir's gaze shifts to me. I gaze into her pale-blue eyes, eyes that seem to be brimming with tears. Silence hangs in the air between us, and in that silence, so much unsaid. We both know that, somehow, our bond has become unbreakable.

A rustling sounds from the forest, drawing our attention. Hands fly to weapons as a cloaked figure staggers out of the darkness.

"Take me with you!" the figure says.

My heart drops at the voice. I hold up a hand to stay Alvtir and the others. "Freydis, what are you *doing* here?"

She takes a deep breath and removes her cloak.

My chest clenches at the sight of the bruise blossoming on her cheek. I inhale sharply. "What happened to you?"

She stops at my side, but turns instead to Alvtir. "I saw Yafeu leave the bonfire and followed her here. I've come to escape my marriage to Harald. I can only believe that the gods led me here for a reason. Please, Aunt, take me with you."

Alvtir says nothing. Her face is as hard as stone.

Freydis sweeps her pleading gaze across the group, but Ranveig doubles over and bursts into laughter. "*She* wants to join *us*?" she says between fits.

Freydis flinches, struggling to keep her composure. "Yes, I do."

"You don't understand, Freydis," I say gently. "There's no place for a princess h—"

"I'd rather die than live another day as *Princess* Freydis!" A tear streams down her swelling cheek. She wipes it away furiously. "I've lived my whole life in a cage of fear. Fear of my father's anger, fear of my mother's disappointment. I let them decide my fate because I was too afraid to question them, and even more afraid to think for myself. All I could do was pray to the gods for a scrap of happiness in my future. Then Harald . . ." Her fingertips brush her cheek. She shakes her head sadly. "Harald only proved how wrong my parents have always been. I want more than the life they've chosen for me. I want to be free to make my own fate." She wheels on her aunt. "Just as you do. Just as *all of you* do."

Her words cut the heavy silence. I know all too well the pain of feeling trapped in a life I never wanted. But to walk away from the life of a princess is different from walking away from the life of a slave, or even the life of a soldier.

"I am moved by your plight, but you are not ready for the trials that lie ahead of us, child," Alvtir says. "I'm sorry. There is no place for you on this journey."

Freydis hangs her head, wilting. The hopelessness in her eyes touches some nameless, soul-deep suffering inside me, a suffering that will always recognize its reflection in another. I know I can't turn her away.

So I turn to Alvtir instead. "We would lose our own honor if we left her here."

The others balk at my words. Even Freydis draws back from me in surprise. But Alvtir's gaze is flinty as it meets mine.

My heart picks up instinctively as she stalks toward the two of us. She grabs Freydis's hand and wrenches it open, eliciting a squeal of protest from Freydis.

"Look at her hands," Alvtir says, her voice tight. "No calluses, no scars. She won't last a day in Iberia, if she even makes it that far."

It takes every ounce of my strength to hold my head up against the gale of her disapproval, but I do. "She may not be like us, Alvtir, but that doesn't mean she has nothing to offer. For one, she's a rune-caster." Alvtir's eyebrows rise at that, but I press on. "And a good seamstress. She can stitch a wound"—I point to the scar on my neck—"as well as mend clothing. She knows which plants heal different wounds and ailments. And she thinks on her feet, like the queen she was raised to be: She sees into the minds and hearts of others, and she knows how to bend them to her will. She saved my life that way, at a time when the strength of an *Úlfheðinn* was useless."

"I don't claim to be as worthy as any of you," Freydis says, jumping in to address the group. "But I will do whatever it takes—suffer whatever I must—to earn my place among you."

Alvtir's furious gaze holds my own for a long moment. My breath is hitched in my throat. No one so much as bats an eyelash as we wait for her reply.

Finally, she lets out an exasperated sigh. "She's your responsibility," she grunts.

"I understand," I say.

And I do understand. Even as part of me rejoices for Freydis, I can already feel the weight of that responsibility settling on my shoulders like the heaviest cloak. A cloak I'll never be able to take off.

Not until one of us dies.

FREYDIS

I feel lighter than I have in years. Buoyant, even.

They're taking me with them. I'm leaving Skíringssal.

I'm *free*.

I turn to Yafeu, searching for a way to express my gratitude. But the feeble words die on my lips when I see the haunted look on her face.

She's your responsibility. That's what Alvtir said to her. Not so long ago, she was *my* responsibility. It's hard to believe that only a few moons have passed since then.

Guilt forms a strangling grip around my heart. But there's nothing I can do now. This is the only path ahead; I have no other choice but to walk it.

I throw my arms around Yafeu. "I won't be a burden," I whisper fiercely. "I swear it."

But even as I say the words, tears spring unbidden to my eyes, and before I know it, I am weeping and shaking like a child in her arms.

I'm clinging to Yafeu for dear life. And I hate myself for it.

She strokes my back. "It's okay. You're here now. You made it out." She steps back, gently cupping my cheeks in her hands. "See? I told you: You're strong."

I draw in a deep breath and exhale slowly, trying to settle myself. "I believe it," I say. "I believe it."

I feel another hand on my back and turn to see one of the shield maidens—the tall, willowy one with kind eyes. "Everyone has their own battle to fight. But we don't have to fight them alone."

"Welcome to our band of nithings!" her blond companion adds, eliciting chuckles from the group. I chuckle myself, relieved at their kindness.

"Breaking our oath? Kidnapping the princess?" the barrel-chested man booms. "I think it's time we shared a drink!"

"Hear, hear!" adds the leaner man, the one with short brown hair and eyes that remind me of Lake Vítrir on a mild summer day.

Yafeu cocks an eyebrow at me and grabs my hand. "Come. I'll introduce you to the others."

The towering fire swims in my vision, as do the pairs of legs stretched out around it. I have no idea how much I've had to drink, only that Hetha keeps refilling my horn with ale.

Look at me, drunk in Aunt Alvtir's holding with a coterie of traitors. If the girl I was only a year ago could see me now, she'd be shocked silly. She'd probably scold me even worse than Helge would if she caught me in such company.

And yet I've never felt so happy to be exactly where I am. Not since I was a little girl tramping fearlessly through the woods around Skíringssal. That was the last time I felt this free.

I was nervous at first when Alvtir took Yafeu aside to speak in private, leaving me here with the rest of the group, but the others have been nothing but kind and welcoming. All except for that sullen redheaded girl, Ranveig. Even through my drunken haze, I catch her shooting me accusing looks across the licks of flame as she sharpens her sword. I suppose it will take more than Yafeu's assurance to earn her respect.

"So you never had *any* say *at all* in who you'd marry? Not even to approve of the man?" Hetha asks, pouring me yet more ale. I try to wave it away but she places the horn firmly in my hand.

"My marriage was always a matter of forging an alliance that would benefit Agder." I take a small sip. "In my father's *tafl* game, it doesn't matter if the pawn disagrees with his move."

"I don't blame you for running," Hetha says. "I would have too. Especially with a father like King Balli."

"At least we're free to choose who we love," Dag adds, casting a hesitant glance at Ranveig.

"Thank the gods for small mercies," Ranveig mutters.

I stifle a giggle, which escapes as a hiccup. I clap my hand over my mouth, embarrassed.

Ranveig narrows her eyes at me. "*Princess* can't hold her ale." She drags her blade across the whetstone, producing an earsplitting scrape. "Probably can't hold a *sword* either."

Silence falls over the group. She's right: I don't know how to wield a sword. Yafeu never taught me that. But she did train me in other ways. I open my mouth to say so when Ingmar jumps to his feet, drawing his own sword from its sheath.

"Worried you don't have the grace of a princess, Ranveig?"

Ranveig grins like a dog baring its teeth and stands, tossing her own sword from palm to palm. "I'll show you grace, you Irish bastard!"

I recoil at her words, but Ingmar lets out a guttural laugh. "Have at me, then!"

They begin to fight, their movements deft despite the ale in their bellies. I glance around the fire anxiously, but at the amusement on everyone's faces, I relax. I suppose the line between a real fight and a playful one is thinner when you're a warrior.

I take another sip of ale and let my eyes rest on the dancing flames. One of my aunt's hounds lays its head on my lap, and I scratch it behind the ears absentmindedly. The clink of blade on blade swirls with laughter in the smoky night air. Soon enough, I'll be able to banter and jest and spar with everyone else. Soon enough, they'll embrace me as one of their own. Even Ranveig.

A thump pulls me back to the moment. Ingmar has knocked the sword out of Ranveig's grasp. She throws her hands up. "Well fought, Ingmar Shield-Breaker," she says, a tad breathless as she plunks back down by the fire. "Were you defending the princess's honor—or her maidservant's?"

She means Yafeu. Even through the orange glow of the flames, Ingmar clearly reddens.

"Oh, don't bait the man just because he bested you," Wisna says gruffly.

Bait him? With Yafeu's honor?

Where *is* Yafeu? Has she been speaking with Alvtir this whole time? I hope it's not me they're discussing. I squint over at the shed now, but I can't see anything in the darkness.

A voice rings out in song. I turn back to the group and am shocked to find that it's coming from Dag. There's a softness to his voice, an evenness of tremor as he belts out the words to a tune that seems familiar:

From frost-kissed peaks to churning seas,
O'er leagues of land and ocean's breeze,
In maiden's sigh and poet's song,
I've roved and reaved the wide world long.

It's an old feast-song, I remember now. Something the *hirdmen* sing from time to time after returning from a raid. Helge would sometimes hum the tune while she bathed me or brushed my hair, when I was a child.

Oh, weary now this heart of mine,
For Valhalla's hall and mead so fine,
To feast 'neath Odin's watchful gaze,
And end my days in golden haze.

Wisna joins in, and her voice too has a beautiful timbre, low and honeyed. Ingmar reaches a hand out to Hetha with a graceful bow. She grins and takes it. They dance around the fire as the others sing:

Fierce battles fought in lands afar,
Under the glow of the guiding star.
I've split the shield-wall, broke the line,
In glory's name, the blood-wine's brine.

Yet, call me now to Heimdall's horn,
To rise with dawn of the endless morn,
Where Einherjar in joy shall meet,
And friend and foe again I'll greet.

I've seen the dragon-ships set sail,
I've felt the bite of winter's gale.
I've heard the raven's victory call,
And witnessed kings and jarls fall.

Now Norns have spun, my thread grows thin,
And long for ending to begin.
Take heed, ye young ones, of my tale,
For life is but a fleeting gale.

I gaze into the fire, wishing I were a seeress who could divine our fates in the dance of the flames. At the start of the last verse, I begin to sing, and find myself surprised at the steadiness in my own voice:

Strike me down, O kinsman brave,
Send me off on final wave.
Valhalla waits, its gates stand wide,
And there, at last, shall I abide.
There, at last, shall I abide.

37

ALVTIR

You will be the first to know my story, Yafeu. The world knows me as Alvtir the *Berserker,* but that is only a mask. Behind that mask, there is a woman. At least, there *used* to be a woman. In truth, when I was young, I was not so different from Freydis. Like her, I was but a bargaining chip in the hands of callous men. Like her, I longed for love and freedom.

Unlike her, I found both.

His name was Aonghas. He was everything I wanted in a mate: staunch, honorable, and kind to his core. He was alive to the beauty of the world but didn't flinch at its ugliness. He accepted both in his heart, as he accepted me for all that I was.

This city was Geirstad before my brother renamed it Skíringssal. None of the men in Geirstad had ever noticed me—ever truly *saw* me—outside of my appeal as the jarl's daughter. I was never beautiful; I was only strong, smart, and able. Aonghas valued those qualities in me. He saw me as an equal. From the moment I met him, I longed for him with a passion I'd never known I was capable of feeling.

But Aonghas was a Pictish warrior, just passing through Skíringssal with a lord of northern descent before returning to Skotland to build his home in the Norðreyjar. He spoke with great fervor about those wind-whipped islands, of all the different kinds of people there, people who had traveled from far and wide to make their home in a place of peace. The youngest of many sons, he'd served all his life as a mercenary, fighting wars that were not his to fight and finally earning enough to buy his own plot of land.

The last night of his stay, I sneaked out of my family's house and we spent the night together in my father's barn, lying next to the animals like thralls, but with more happiness in our hearts than any royals. Father would have beaten me if he'd caught us—and had Aonghas executed for dishonoring his daughter. But we were young and in love. We would have defied the gods just to be in each other's arms.

"There's nothing for you here," he whispered as we clung to each other in the darkness. "Come with me and I'll make you my wife. We can start a new life together."

I said yes at once. He was right; there was nothing for me here. I was my brother's better in every way, but even though I outshone him, I would never take his birthright. By the simple virtue of his maleness, he would become the jarl when our father passed, while I would be married off to the highest bidder. Before Aonghas came along, the best I could hope for was a husband who wasn't cruel.

We stole a merchant's *knarr* that night and set sail before Sól could drive her chariot into the sky. The winds were with us all the way, a sign of the rightness of our course. On the very next sunrise, we landed on his island in the Norðreyjar, and before the same sun set, we were married by the laws of his people—a Pictish wedding. It wasn't legitimate according to my people's customs, but it was more than enough for me.

The island had been settled only a few years earlier. One could hardly even call the settlement a village. There was much to be done: The land needed clearing, tilling, and sowing; houses and wells and cairns needed to be built. It was more labor than I ever imagined, starting a new farm from raw land. We toiled from sunup to sundown every day, collapsing from exhaustion every night. We went to bed hungry more often than not.

But I have always been strong. I have always been a survivor.

Besides, our love kept us nourished and content. And the island was exactly like Aonghas had promised. Our neighbors were good, like-minded folk. They'd come from Ireland and Dal Riata and Northumbria and beyond. We welcomed one and all to our village with open arms. Picts, Norse, Sami—it didn't matter who you were, what gods you worshipped. So long as you came in peace and were ready to work hard, you were welcome. I didn't miss my jealous, hateful brother or my indifferent parents. I doubt they missed me either.

After many moons, we finally got the farm up and running. We built altars to Njord and Frey and Odin, and placed stones for the worship of his own gods, which were both different from and the same as mine. All was well, save for the fact that I couldn't seem to conceive a child; I assumed the dearth of food and the strenuous labor were to blame, and that as soon as the farm bore its first true harvest, my body too would be ready for the bounty of motherhood.

Before the first harvest came, our village was destroyed.

Not by *Víkingar*. By a new Christian king from Skotland, driven by Christ to force the Picts into his worship—and to slaughter all those who refused.

I watched in horror as the king's soldiers slit my husband's throat. I watched as his blood spilled onto the soil we'd worked so hard to nurture.

Then the soldiers turned to me. By then I would have welcomed death, but death was not what they had in mind. They took their turns on me, over and over again. Beating me profusely. Finally, when they'd had their fun, I was left to die.

But I have always been strong. I have always been a survivor.

When I came back to consciousness, the village—my home—was charred and empty. All were dead or captured.

For a time, I simply lay on the ground of our house, hoping Hel would claim me soon so I wouldn't have to endure the pain. I moved only to nibble on our meager rations or drink the rainwater that fell into a bucket outside. I don't know how many days and nights I passed in this way, waiting for death. But the gods had other plans for me. Gradually my body healed, and I realized I had no choice but to find my way back to Geirstad and pray that my father would take me back.

As soon as I was strong enough, I buried Aonghas and took the handful of coins he had hidden. By Njord's mercy, I found an old skiff that the soldiers hadn't burned. It wouldn't survive the journey to Norveg, but I used it to make my way to the mainland. After several long, luckless days, I was finally able to trade the coins for a ride on a merchant's ship back to Geirstad.

On that journey, I missed my moonblood. It was too early for me to show; the babe hadn't even quickened yet. But I knew, in the way a woman knows, that I was pregnant. My greatest agony was not knowing if the babe was sired by Aonghas or one of my attackers.

I returned to Skíringssal to find that my parents had died, taken by a plague that swept the land after I left. So I fell to my knees before my brother, who now called himself a king. I begged him to take me back. It pained me to do it, but I lied and told him that Aonghas was secretly a Christian spy in league with the Scottish king. I said he had taken me captive that night and was planning to use me for ransom, but I eventually escaped and made my way home.

Balli accepted this without question, likely because he knew he could use me to his advantage. He had declared Agder's independence from King Godfred of Danmǫrk, and he needed a *stallari* to lead his army. He never once asked of my life in the many months I was gone. In turn I told him nothing. It was a mutual understanding that we were simply to pretend it hadn't happened.

Not long after, Godfred's men came to our shores to reclaim Agder. They had us outnumbered three men to one, but I came up with a plan to level the playing field between us. As soon as the first Danish ships were sighted, I took two-thirds of the *hird* into the forest. I ordered the rest of the men to act like nithings when the ships came to shore and retreat to my family's holding in the heart of the city. The Danes were fooled into believing that we had no more than a few dozen sell-swords at our call, men with neither courage nor loyalty. In their arrogance, they followed our men into the old mead hall, chasing what they believed to be an easy victory. I led the rest of the men to cut them off, trapping their forces.

We fought hard, and it wasn't long before the surviving Danes threw down their swords and surrendered.

But I didn't want their surrender. I wanted their blood.

I locked the Danes in the mead hall and had our men set it aflame. But the fire grew, burning everything between the mead hall and Lake Vítrir to the ground. Half the city was lost: not just the Danish soldiers but our own women, our own children. Burned alive in their beds. Thanks to me.

I had won our freedom, but the people feared and despised me for it. My brother took credit for the brilliance of my plan, but he had no trouble letting me bear the disgrace for the violence. He let the people say whatever they wished about me, so long as they revered him. He built a new hall for himself atop the hill, much grander than the hall of our forebears, and called it Skíringssal, hall of light. He expanded the port and welcomed merchants and artisans to our shores. He was the city's savior; I was its curse.

As the months went on, my pregnancy began to show. Disgusted, my brother sent me to live with my widowed aunt. She had no children of her own and was kind enough to me, but I was regarded as disgraced by everyone else. They all assumed I'd been ruined during my "slavery" in Skotland. I couldn't tell the truth without giving away my betrayal—and in truth, I didn't much care what they thought. All that mattered was my child. My only hope was that the babe would bear a semblance to Aonghas, so I could be sure he was the father. It was that hope that kept me going.

I would never find out. The babe came too early. My aunt wouldn't let me look at his face. She wouldn't even let me hold him. She said women went mad when they held their stillborns and refused to believe they were dead.

My heartbreak was complete. I had nothing left to live for.

Women whispered that my womb was cursed by the gods as a punishment for burning our own people alive. A rumor spread that any woman who touched me would take on the curse and bear only dead babes.

I often wondered if the people were right. Maybe I *was* cursed by what I had done. Then again, bad luck had found me long before the battle began, and it would continue long after it ended.

My aunt was old and frail, and she died shortly after my son. I found myself with no one to look after me, and nothing to offer the world but a woman's rage.

But I have always been strong. I have always been a survivor.

I resolved to train twice as hard as I trained the men, lest any one of them accuse me of weakness. I would *prove* to them that I deserved my place as their leader. And soon I became the best warrior among them, a *berserker* renowned across Norveg. I thought I knew, then, why the gods had spared my life, when they'd taken everything else: I believed I was chosen by the Allfather to save my people from annihilation at the hands of the Christians.

The Battle of Geirstad was over, but the battle for the old ways was just beginning. I let my brother think I served him as his *stallari,* but Odin was my one and only king. He protected me as I took my revenge on the Christians. Even as hatred consumed me, I was convinced I would be remembered in the poems as Alvtir the Vanquisher. The skalds would sing of how I alone prevented Ragnarök from coming to pass.

What a fool I was.

Summer after summer we raided the Christian shores. A thousand of them died by my hand alone, and still I thirsted for their blood. There is an old curse among our people: "May you find that which you seek." Indeed, there were always more Christians to kill—more, and more, and more. No matter how many Christians we slaughtered, no matter how many of their villages we burned to the ground, I could not stem the tide.

When I learned that Godfred's son Rollo had become one of them, I realized I was failing. Ragnarök was upon us; I was sure of it.

But I couldn't convince my brother. I had to take matters into my own hands. There was no other way: I had to get rid of my brother to save his people. I had to take the throne for myself. So I hired assassins to pose as King Hakon's men and infiltrate my niece's wedding. They were to kill my brother in Christ's name, along with Yngvild and Freydis.

It may seem ruthless of me, but as long as a child of Balli lived, my rule would be questioned. And with Balli out of the way, Hakon might have used his marriage to Freydis as an excuse to claim Agder for himself. Hence, I seized the chance to wipe out my brother's line *and* show the people I was right about the Christian threat, all in one fell swoop.

But *you* stopped me. You could have stood by and let Freydis be killed—after all, she was your master. Instead, you chose to save her. And in doing so, you revealed yourself to be *Úlfheðinn*.

I couldn't understand it at first. I thought Odin was guiding my hand, but if that were true, he would have guided yours to aid me, not stop me.

Then, when I came to get you from Freydis later that night, I heard her tell you of the way she had joined your language and hers. I saw the two of you embrace in true friendship.

And I realized I was wrong. About everything.

I had Odin's strength in me, but not his wisdom. I thought I alone could save our people from the White Christ and prevent Ragnarök from coming to pass. I thought if I could do this, it would mean that I was blessed, not cursed. Now I realize that *neither* is true. All that I've done, all that I've suffered, and all the suffering I've brought to others was for a greater purpose. But not the purpose I had conceived.

No, Odin's plan was never for me to stop Ragnarök. Ragnarök is inevitable.

Odin's plan was for me to save *you*.

38

YAFEU

"My last task is to take you somewhere safe, where you can weather the coming storm. Along with the best of my people, the few who still have honor." Alvtir gestures to the rest of our group, a stone's throw from the stumps we're perched on in front of the garden. They're singing and dancing by the fire, celebrating their last night in Skíringssal. The meat of a dozen slaughtered chickens is perched high above the flames to smoke. No one pays any mind to the two of us.

I'm at a loss for words, reeling from Alvtir's many revelations. She waits patiently for me to form my thoughts.

"Why would Odin want you to save me?" I ask finally. "I have my own gods. I don't worship him."

Alvtir leans in close, her gaze intent. "Because Ragnarök is not the end: It is a new beginning. And new beginnings call for new ways, and new leaders. Leaders like the one I see in you."

Mama's forewarning echoes in my mind: *You have a great destiny. Great and terrible.*

"A great flood is coming," Alvtir continues. "The Christians are part of it, but you are part of it too. Once the old ways have been washed away, the world will resurface, cleansed of evils like my brother. It is in this world that you must plant the seeds of your truth. You may not believe in Odin, but the Wise One believes in you. It is your blessing *and* your curse."

"Why not you?" I counter. "We follow wherever you lead. Others will do the same."

She shakes her head, smiling sadly. "I was only ever good at burning things down. You have the fire in you, just as I do. But fire won't be enough. Burning won't be enough. You will have to be good at building, too."

I can see there's no use in arguing with her. But something more urgent nags at my thoughts.

"Alvtir, how can you be sure that the people of al-Andalus will leave us in peace? War is everywhere; people will find an excuse to harm others, if it suits their ends to do so. Could there ever be a land that is truly immune?"

"I had the same doubt at first. But the emir is said by all to be a man of honor. He appoints his advisers by merit instead of kinship, and I sensed both honor and merit in the men I met with. They had even learned our tongue, so that we could speak directly without the aid of a translator. They were eager to distinguish themselves, as young men often are, but their desire for peace was sincere. I saw the proof with my own eyes in Lisbon. I've been wrong many times in my life, but rarely do my instincts lead me astray when it comes to judging someone's heart."

I return her smile. "If you trust them, then I trust them too."

But her expression turns solemn. She reaches out tentatively, as though asking permission. When I don't flinch or recoil, she grasps my hand in hers. It's not the first time I've felt her skin against mine, but it's the first time I've ever really *noticed* her touch. It's callused but gentle.

"Do not make the same mistakes I've made, Yafeu. There is more to life than serving the gods, and more to peace than serving the same gods. People can do the wrong thing in the name of the right god, and the right thing in the name of the wrong one. It's who you are beneath it all that matters."

I watch the others, pondering her words. On the surface, we have almost nothing in common. But Alvtir is right: In our hearts, we are more alike than different.

Maybe that's what Papa was trying to teach me all along. The gods are one thing, but this world is another. There's something the eight of us see, a vision we all share—and through *living* it together, we make it real.

"Go, join them." Alvtir waves me away. "Have fun."

"Aren't you coming?"

"I'd like to say goodbye to my pups before I send them into the wild." She climbs to her feet and whistles for the dogs, who come bounding. "You know, there's another old saying," she adds, her smile sad as she strokes their heads. "You can't teach an old hound a new trick."

She leaves me to ponder the meaning of her words. "Alvtir," I call out. She turns back, her gaze glittering like rime in the twilight. "Thank you."

She nods once and turns away. I watch her disappear with her dogs into the woods.

"You have that look again."

Ingmar approaches me, several loose blades of hair bouncing against his cheekbones. "What look?"

"Like your mind is wrestling with itself." He takes Alvtir's seat beside me. "What were the two of you talking about for so long?"

I shake my head. "I don't know where to begin."

We sit in companionable silence and watch the others as they sing some rowdy drinking song. Ranveig kicks an empty plate into the fire, to the great amusement of all.

I turn to Ingmar, seized by a sudden sense of urgency. "Let's go somewhere—just the two of us."

He smiles. "I know a place." He offers a hand, pulling me to my feet.

We stand facing each other for a moment, just as we did that first day of training. The clear blue water of his eyes washes over me. Only instead of cooling me down, it sets me on fire.

Then we slip quietly into the woods.

We emerge into another glade, smaller than the one where Alvtir makes her homestead. Two boulders part the grass in the center. I hear the trickle of running water coming from somewhere nearby. The air is warm even with no fire, and Mawu is so close, I wonder if we're feeling her warmth as we feel Lisa's during the day.

Ingmar leads me between the boulders. We lie on our backs and gaze up at the blue-black sky, sprinkled with stars that were once strange to me, stars I've somehow grown accustomed to over the last year. To my surprise, a few new stars appear, wink out, and then appear again in a different spot. I gasp at the sight.

"They're fireflies," Ingmar explains. "We call this place Tyr's grove. I come here sometimes to be alone with my thoughts."

"Thank you for sharing it with me," I say, squeezing his hand.

I hear him swallow and see the apple of his throat bobbing up and down out of the corner of my eye. "There's no one else I'd rather share it with," he says softly.

I turn to face him. He does the same. I place my hand on his chest. His heart hammers against my touch, his eyes darkening into twin sapphires.

"Yafeu . . ." he whispers.

Slowly, I press my lips against his. He grasps my upper arm and pulls me closer. I open my mouth and let his tongue dance against mine. A moan escapes my lips and I roll over, straddling him, lost in the flow of my desire.

He cups my face with his hands and plants a trail of kisses along my neck. I let my hands roam up his tunic, feeling the firm ripples of his stomach, his chest, his shoulders. He slips his tunic over his head and reaches, tentatively, under mine. His lips find mine again. The kiss deepens, growing rapturous. It's not enough.

Then it's all too much.

I flinch as his hands trace up my sides. I curse myself inwardly at the involuntary reaction. Ingmar stops immediately and searches my face.

"Are you okay?" he asks. His brow is furrowed, concern clearing the hunger from his gaze.

"Yes. No? I'm not sure."

He takes my hand in his, bringing it to his lips for a gentle, reassuring kiss.

"Ingmar, I've never . . ."

"Don't worry, there's no rush," he says tenderly.

Relief washes over me. Ingmar gently turns me over and drapes his cloak over my body. He gazes down, the soft blue of his irises soothing every aching part of me.

"But there's something else I can do—just for you—if you'd like . . ." A mischievous gleam appears in those irises now, like the glimmer of moonlight on the fjord.

The corner of my lips curve up. I start to nod a little too fast, then catch myself. "That would be acceptable," I say as casually as I can.

He lets out a low chuckle. Slowly, he lowers his head and disappears under the cloak, kissing the middle of my chest, my navel, and then each hip bone tenderly. The sensation of his soft lips sends shock waves through me, rippling outward from my lower abdomen. A moan escapes my parted lips. I feel his steady fingers reaching under my tunic and untying the knots of my pants with ease before . . .

Shivers of ecstasy race through my body as his warm mouth envelops me. I gasp. He teases me further, painting shapes and patterns with his tongue. My body is his canvas. Soon my hands are groping the soft tufts of his hair under the cloak. The pressure inside of me builds like Djo thickening the air before a storm. Ingmar grips my thighs, responding to the rhythm of my yearning. I squirm at the will of his skilled tongue, fully opening myself to him.

The pressure becomes too much to bear and I throw back the cloak, needing to meet his eyes. The cool night air does nothing to put out the fire raging beneath my skin. His eyes, illuminated by Mawu's rays, languidly connect with mine, guiding me into an ocean of unknown pleasure.

After the last wave recedes, Ingmar tenderly rolls me on top of him again. I let my head rest on his chest, breathing in his scent of sea salt and resin and a lingering hint of smoke. "Was that acceptable?" he says playfully.

I laugh. "More than acceptable."

"I've been thinking about doing that since the first time you bested me at training."

I feel the heat rush to my cheeks as I remember that moment, with my legs around his shoulders, the attraction between us crackling in the heat of combat.

His fingers trace lazy patterns on my cheek and I nuzzle into him, savoring the moment.

But even through the haze of this newfound euphoria, I find my thoughts drifting inexorably into the future.

"Your face feels somber," Ingmar whispers. "Shall we go again?"

I poke his ribs, suppressing a grin. "I'm thinking about tomorrow and . . . Every day after that."

I feel his chest expand as he takes in a breath. "Do you wish we were staying?"

I hesitate, considering. "In truth, I'm relieved that I don't have to go on the raids. I tried to tell myself otherwise, but I know in my heart that I could never attack innocent people. Not for Balli's or Snorri's sake—but not for Alvtir's either. No matter who gives the order, if I carried it out, I would be no better than a slaver." No sooner do the words leave my mouth than I realize just how true they are.

"Alvtir won't ask that of us. Not anymore."

"I know. And I also know that al-Andalus is much closer to Wagadu. I ache for my homeland, and I would give anything to see Mama and Kamo and Goleh again."

"But?"

But.

"But I haven't found my father."

I never wanted to admit it to myself, but from the moment I arrived in Skíringssal, a part of me has been clinging to the hope that Papa is somewhere nearby. That any day now, I'll find him—or he'll find me. Now I have to leave that hope on these shores. It feels like leaving *him*.

The thought drags my heart into my stomach, and new tears start to burn behind my eyes.

"I'm so sorry, Yafeu," Ingmar says softly.

For some reason, his compassion only makes the feeling worse. I try to think of something to say to lighten the mood, but I find I can't think of anything. Reluctantly, I climb to my feet. "We should go back."

We walk hand in hand back to Alvtir's, as ready as we'll ever be to greet the unknown.

39

YAFEU

None of us sleep. Instead, we spend the night preparing.

I finally find out what Alvtir's "business" has been all along: She's been stockpiling supplies, gathering everything a group of seven might need for a journey with no return. We find surprise after surprise waiting for us in the henhouse: a large tent, extra furs, another bow and heaps of arrows, shoulder packs made of woven birch bark to carry everything. What she couldn't purchase, she says, she made herself.

We fill the packs to the brim, tucking Alvtir's extra weapons beside ours in our belts. With Alvtir's permission, I take a dagger from her wall. It gives me a satisfying sense of wholeness to carry two. We fill every waterskin at her well and stuff as much dried fruit and flatbread as we can carry into extra satchels, leaving room for the chicken meat. Hopefully it will be enough to sustain us; Alvtir won't risk making landfall before al-Andalus unless we have no other choice.

After my own packing is done, I throw on my cloak and head outside to check on the woman who gave it to me, who should be finished wrapping the chicken meat by now. Freydis didn't bring anything but the sword she stole and the clothes on her body. We'll both be relying on Alvtir's generosity to get by.

I find her poking the embers of the dying fire, looking morose. Large clumps of hair have fallen out of the braid at the top of her head; she hasn't bothered to fix it. "There's something I should have asked you much earlier, Freydis." She gives me a questioning look as I take a seat by her side. "How are you?"

Her smile is thin. "I don't know," she concedes. "I left to find you, and to escape Harald and my father. The *dísir* guided me to both. It's just . . . it's all happening so fast."

Nyeru's enigmatic words come unbidden to my mind. "Your spirit knows where you're going, and how to get there," I say softly, feeling a pang of guilt. I wish I could take him and Mbaneh with us, but there's no way Alvtir would condone it—it was hard enough to convince her to bring Freydis. And even if she did, it wouldn't matter: Neither Nyeru nor Mbaneh is strong enough to survive the journey. I hope they don't think I abandoned them. I hope they forgive me.

Freydis nods absently. My eyes wander to the sword she brought with her, propped up in its sheath against the log bench on her other side. I squeeze her shoulder gently. "I'm glad you're coming with us."

She meets my eyes and smiles, genuinely this time. "I am too."

With our minds and backs equally laden, our group makes for the harbor.

As soon as we emerge from the western woods into the city, the tension among us rises palpably. The sky is unsettlingly bright for the dead of night, but the city is empty: Alvtir picked the night of the midsummer festival for this very reason. We tread as quietly as desert mice as we skirt the edge of the market. Dag kicks over a bucket next to a smoking shed, and we all freeze. Ranveig glares daggers at him.

But no one comes to check on the noise, and we quickly resume our course. The fjord is eerily calm, the ripples of high tide lapping gently at the sliver of shoreline, indifferent to our approach. The shadowy outlines of the docks stretch like long wooden fingers into the fjord. Even in the twilight, Alvtir's ship, the *Jörmungand,* stands out from the other sleeping dragons like gold among bronze. It bobs against its tether now, waiting to be set free.

My heart quickens as we draw near. The long necks of the dragons arc ahead of us.

We're so close, so close to our freedom—but I can't shake the feeling that something isn't right. Our careful footsteps on the rocky sand are the only sounds I hear, but my skin is crawling. Even with the whole of Skíringssal at the bonfire, it's too quiet for comfort.

A strange *nyama* emanates from the ship. A restlessness greater than our own.

The group picks up their pace, their eagerness bounding ahead of them. Ranveig and Dag pass Alvtir, taking the lead. I hear them hop quietly onto the dock.

"Wait," I whisper. But no one stops.

Panic floods my veins all at once.

"*Wait!*" I raise my voice to a hiss. "Something's wrong!"

No sooner do the words escape my lips than a dozen soldiers leap up from the deck of the *Jörmungand.*

Ranveig and Dag skid to a halt.

We all watch in horror as more and more men jump from the decks of the other ships. They draw their weapons and charge onto the docks.

It's the *hird.*

They knew. Balli knew.

I catch up to Alvtir as Ranveig and Dag drop back. "I should've known you wouldn't let me go so easily, brother," Alvtir mutters. Freydis's hooded figure stands frozen at her other side.

The *hird*men break into a run.

"What do we do?" Ranveig asks breathlessly.

Alvtir looks to me. Dread is a riptide, threatening to pull me under. But I stand tall and give her a slight nod.

If her gods can face their own death with honor, then so can I.

There's a sibilant *whoosh* as Freydis unsheathes her stolen sword, her lips pressed into a grim, determined line.

Alvtir glances at her, surprised. Freydis's eyes betray no fear as she meets Alvtir's questioning gaze.

Alvtir turns back to the onslaught of soldiers and draws her own sword. "For Valhalla!" she screams, thrusting Angrboda into the air.

"For Valhalla!" the rest of us roar back in unison.

And then they are upon us.

The only sounds I hear are my heartbeat and my breath.

The chaos around me is eerily muted as one of the soldiers slashes the air in front of me. I parry his attack and kick him hard in the groin. He stumbles and falls to the ground, and I plunge Alvtir's dagger into the soft spot between his shoulder and neck. I take advantage of the lull to look around, searching frantically for Freydis.

I can't see her, but I do see my other friends, each fighting off a handful of their former brothers-in-arms.

In this moment, I understand why Alvtir chose them.

Ranveig slides through the legs of a soldier, slicing his ankle with her sword as she does. He drops to one knee, and she leaps up and thrusts her sword into his back. A feral scream escapes her lips as she whirls and slams into another soldier, taking him by surprise and plucking an ax from his belt. He falls, and she hurls the ax at the next soldier coming at her. A clean hit between the eyes.

Where wolf's ears are, wolf's teeth are near.

Another soldier runs for me, ax in hand, drawing my attention. I drop down and grab the shield from the man I killed, raising it just in time to catch the blow. My arm vibrates with the force of it, but the shield holds. I toss the shield with his ax lodged in it aside and thrust my dagger into his throat. Blood spatters across my face and tunic as he falls.

I wipe my eyes and catch sight of Freydis. She's a dozen paces away, trying to fend off two soldiers. Thankfully, they look like they're trying to disarm her rather than hurt her. She screams in frustration and flails her sword, but they block her easily.

I'm making my way over when a hard blow to the back of my head stops me short.

I fall to the ground, spots clouding my vision. I blink them away and look up at the man who hit me.

A weaponless soldier lifts his fists above my head, fury writ large across his face.

Wisna intersects him before he can strike. She brings her ax down on his back. He gurgles, spitting blood onto the sand.

I reach for my dagger and drag myself to my feet. Freydis slashes at the soldiers, who leap out of the way, waiting for their opening.

"Freydis!" I yell to her through the chaos. "I can't protect you! You have to run!"

"They won't hurt me!" she calls back, swinging the sword wildly again.

Three soldiers close in on me, obscuring my view.

Freydis lets out a bloodcurdling scream. Fear crashes into my gut like a boulder falling from a cliff. *"Freydis!"*

A heavy hand grabs the back of my neck and pushes my face into the shingle. Knees dig into my spine, pinning me in place.

Alvtir's harsh laugh cuts through the air. I lift my head, straining to look around. The soldiers have pinned her to the ground as well. And Hetha, Wisna, Dag, and Ingmar.

They've won.

Freydis lies in an unmoving heap. Three soldiers stand around her, blocking her from my view.

No, no, no . . .

The knees on my back let up as the soldiers grab me by the hair and yank me to my knees. I grit my teeth against the pain as they twist my arms behind my back, holding me in place.

As the sky lightens, signaling Lisa's impending ascent, four figures emerge from the city. It's Balli, Snorri, a tall, richly dressed blond man—most likely Harald—and a graying man beside him.

Alvtir's laugh grows sharper as they approach, then skids to a cough as she takes in haggard breaths. "Brother," she wheezes. "How did you know?"

Balli takes a step forward. "My daughter, if I can still call her that, led my guards straight to you," he says smugly.

The others look to Freydis, their expressions contorted in shock and betrayal. But Alvtir says nothing. She looks up at the reddening sky, a cryptic smile spreading across her face.

"It's one thing to poison them with your cowardice," Balli continues, gesturing to us. "But *my daughter,* Alvtir? You would steal the princess from her own husband?"

"Oh, I won't marry her like this, Balli. She's ruined." Harald kneels in front of Freydis. He grabs her, pulling her out of the semicircle of guards by her hair. Her knees buckle and sway as he inspects her, turning her head from side to side.

My heart stops.

A deep gash runs from her right eyebrow down to the edge of her lips. Blood pours from it onto the front of her dress.

Harald wrinkles his nose in disgust. "What a shame," he murmurs, loudly enough for all to hear. He releases Freydis's hair, letting her collapse onto the sand.

Rage screams inside me. I strain against the soldiers' vise-like grips.

"A good beating might fix her weakness of mind, Balli. But her face ..." The older man trails off.

Balli's jaw tightens for a moment, then he sighs. "Then she will die with the rest of them," he announces. His tone is as matter-of-fact as if he were announcing that it's going to rain in the afternoon.

"They were only following my orders," Alvtir says, her expression sobering. "I offer my life in exchange for theirs."

Snorri starts toward her, drawing his sword. "And why should we not take your life *and* theirs? You're all oath-breakers—traitors to your king!" His voice burns with wrath, but the look on his face is pure glee.

Rage rears its head inside me again, but Alvtir's expression doesn't change, her gaze locked on her brother.

"The oath was broken in poisoned blood." The strange words roll seamlessly off her tongue. "Slaughter the sheep, and the blood is restored. Slaughter the flock and the blood is lost."

The color drains from Balli's face. He regards Alvtir with wide, disbelieving eyes. Snorri starts to say something, but the king holds up his hand, stopping him. "It was you," he breathes.

Alvtir bares her teeth. A drop of blood falls from her lips.

The two siblings stare at each other in silence for a long moment. When Balli finally speaks, it is with a cold decisiveness that chills me to the bone: "They will live as outcasts, without honor. Neither human nor god will take them in. Not in this life, not in the next."

Alvtir nods once.

With that, Balli approaches his sister. As he draws near, I notice his eyes are brimming with tears. If I could move, I would shake my head in disbelief.

He stops in front of her, and one of the soldiers hands him Angrboda.

"So be it," Alvtir says softly. She holds Balli's gaze for a long, agonizing moment. Then the soldiers push her head down.

My throat tightens, my heart thrashing wildly against my rib cage. Balli raises Angrboda in the air, gripping the hilt with both hands. The blade gleams as it catches Lisa's first rays.

A flapping of wings sounds from somewhere in the distance, followed by the piercing cry of ravens.

Alvtir swivels her head, her eyes catching mine. She grins through a mouthful of blood. "All hail the dark queen," she says.

Then Balli brings the sword down on her neck.

Ranveig screams at the top of her lungs as Alvtir's head rolls toward her. She thrashes violently against the soldiers holding her back.

"Release them," Balli croaks. He looks up, as though addressing the sky: "To the traitors who followed her: From this time forth, you are outcasts. You have until midday to leave Skíringssal, or your life is forfeit. As Alvtir's ship belongs to me now, I suggest you make for the woods." He spins on his heel and marches back up the hill.

Harald and the elder share an indecipherable look. "It's time we took our leave as well," the elder says. "There's nothing left for us here."

Harald nods in agreement. "Gather the men. We sail within the hour."

The elder turns and follows Balli up the hill while Harald strides purposefully to the far dock. He doesn't spare so much as a glance at Freydis as he passes.

The soldiers release their grasps and move to form a wall, blocking the dock where Alvtir's ship is tethered.

No—not Alvtir's ship. It's Balli's ship now.

I stagger to my feet as a wild-eyed Ranveig collapses near Alvtir's head, unleashing more earsplitting screams. Nausea washes over me at the sight. Thankfully Hetha and Wisna wrench her away.

I race over to Freydis, who's lying unconscious in the sand. I turn her on her side, inspecting her cheek. The slash is thicker than a finger and deep enough to show fat and muscle. Blood pours from it at an alarming rate. Her right eye is swollen shut. Ingmar helps me lift her up.

"I'll carry her," he says quickly. I help him drape Freydis over his back, then I hastily pick up his fallen pack, along with my own and Alvtir's, slinging them all across my shoulders. Wherever we go now, we'll need these with us more than ever.

Hetha and Wisna grab their own packs and Ranveig's as they drag her kicking and screaming toward the western woods. "Bring her to Alvtir's," Wisna calls back. Somehow, Hetha manages to get Ranveig to stop screaming and run on her own two feet.

I'm relieved to see no other injuries among us. We fall into a single line, jogging up the narrow trail for a small eternity before reaching the clearing. Alvtir's homestead is unchanged, indifferent to all that has passed since we left. But the forest surrounding it is alive with the hollers and whoops of the soldiers on our tail.

"Why are they following us?" I ask Ingmar as he emerges from the trail behind me, still carrying Freydis on his back. His breath comes in ragged, heaving gasps.

"So they can kill us if we don't make it out in time," Dag replies before kicking open the door to Alvtir's longhouse.

We hurry inside. Ingmar sets Freydis down near the unlit hearth. She stirs half awake, groaning and writhing fitfully on the floor.

"This is her fault," Ranveig hisses. "We should leave her to die!"

Everyone ignores her. Wisna drops to her knees next to Freydis's head. "We need to cauterize the wound," she says quietly. "It will stop the bleeding."

A long moment passes. Everyone, including Wisna, is looking at me expectantly. My blood runs cold as I realize they're all waiting for me to tell them what to do.

I take a deep, jagged breath. "Dag, find something for Freydis to bite down on. Wisna, get a fire going. I'll get something to wrap her face."

As they carry out my orders, I cut a long strip of cloth from my old thrall's tunic. When I return the fire is raging, and so is Freydis. I kneel in front of her and hold my dagger out to the flames.

Wisna pours water over Freydis's cheek, doing her best to wash away the sand before sprinkling some herbs from her pack onto the wound. Freydis howls and flails, but Ingmar takes hold of her arms and pins her to the ground. Dag moves to her feet, engulfing them in his broad arms.

"*No!*" Freydis growls as Hetha jams a thick leather strap in her mouth. Wisna moves to Freydis's other side and helps Ingmar hold her down.

When the blade glows, I remove it from the fire and kneel next to Freydis. Water mixes with blood on her face. She looks at me with one wild, unrecognizing eye. My mind flashes to the memory of examining Ampah's wound, that very first night in the desert.

Hetha holds her head steady. I gently stroke her hair. "By all the gods, my own and yours: I swear that you will make it through this," I say, trying to sound reassuring despite the thickness in my throat. I switch to my language: "You're going to live."

Then I press the searing blade against the gash. A scream rips through her as the acrid stench of burning flesh fills the room.

I take the blade away and she falls silent, her eyes fluttering shut. The others release their grip as her body goes slack.

I set the dagger down and wrap the cloth around her face, doing my best to cover the long wound. My fingers graze her other cheek, hot and slick with her sweat.

Ingmar peers out at the woods through the doorway. "I doubt we'll have until noon," he says ominously. "We should leave as soon as we can."

"Does anyone know these woods?" I ask the group. "Is there anywhere we'll be safe for the night?"

"There's a place I used to go with my father," Dag offers. "A cliff overlooking the fjord. It's west from here—hopefully out of Skíringssal's bounds, but I can't be sure. I haven't been there since I was a boy. If we leave now, we might make it by nightfall."

I square my shoulders. "Show us the way."

40

YAFEU

It's a steep, winding climb up to the granite-and-gneiss cliff. We have to bind Freydis, still unconscious, to Dag's back, but everyone makes it up in one piece.

The ledge is unusually flat and level, just long and wide enough to hold a camp for the seven of us. I walk to the edge. The orange-and-pink sunset stretches over a sweeping, dizzying view of the fjord winding through the hills. The sheer beauty stands in stark contrast with the anguish condensing in my chest.

I turn and survey the group. Their expressions are haggard as they set down their packs and help untie Freydis, their faces covered in dirt and sweat and blood that isn't theirs.

"My father called it Völund's Anvil," Dag says after he's caught his breath. "We camped here on hunting trips from time to time. It's too high up for bears or wolves, and the soldiers won't see or hear us from the ground. But if someone did get it in their head to climb up, we'd have the advantage."

"You did well, Dag," I say gratefully. "We'll make camp here for the night."

As Hetha and Wisna build a fire, using the flint and wood they wisely packed from Alvtir's, Ingmar, Dag, and I set up the tent. Ranveig sits with her back against a boulder, silently refusing to help.

The breeze is stronger than below. Much stronger. It moans in our ears, tearing at any shred of uncovered skin as we work. It strikes me that, up here, this tent is our only protection from the wind blowing off the fjord.

"We'll have to take turns," I think out loud as I drop my pack on one of the stakes. "It looks like five, maybe six can fit inside."

"The other two can keep watch," Ingmar finishes.

There's no dirt to drive the stakes into, so we weigh down the edges of the tent with any rocks we can find that are light enough to carry but heavy enough not to blow away. When the tent is reasonably secure, we carry Freydis inside. I wrap her in her cloak for warmth. Her chest rises and falls so slightly that it's nearly imperceptible.

I sit by her side for a while, whispering prayers to her ancestors, to Mawu-Lisa, even to Freya, the *Majūs* goddess for whom she is named. It is the first time I have prayed to one of their gods, but I fear it won't be the last.

When I can't think of anyone else to pray to, I whisper to her in Soninke: "I'm sorry I didn't protect you. You were my responsibility, and I failed you. But you *must* live, or else you'll make me a liar. Okay? Be strong." Tears well behind my eyes, but I swallow them back down. I have to be strong too. If not for myself, then for the others.

Night falls quickly. Everyone but Ranveig gathers around the modest fire. The wind whips our hair around our heads. Mawu is full in the sky for the second and final night, casting an eerie silver glow over the ridge. The same glow I found so beautiful last night in Tyr's grove now makes our faces seem pale and drawn.

My stomach roars. I feel the full force of hunger return, no lon-

ger kept at bay by the shock of the day. I take a small loaf of flatbread and one of the smoked chickens from a satchel, carving them
both into meager slabs. I pass them around without a word. It's not
much of a meal, but we need to ration. No one complains. No one
says anything at all.

I walk over to Ranveig with her piece. She's already curled up
against the boulder under a fur. Her eyes are shut, but I can tell
she's not asleep from the way she's shivering. "Move closer to the
fire," I say, trying to sound commanding. "You don't have to eat
with us, but you'll freeze if you stay out here."

Ranveig opens her eyes and scowls, but she gets up nonetheless
and shuffles over to the fire. She settles next to Hetha, who is now
weeping softly in Wisna's arms.

I take my own seat again. Next to me, Ingmar eats his share in an
equally weighty silence. Even Dag can't think of anything to say to
lighten the mood.

"We need to come up with a plan," I say finally.

"A *plan*?" Dag snorts. "We're outcasts. There is no plan."

I frown. "What do you mean?"

"She doesn't understand," Ingmar says. "Yafeu, to be an outcast
is to live with dishonor. Even if we could find another village
through these woods, no one would take us in."

"Some would argue that it's better to die than live such a life,"
Dag mutters.

"And you're one of them?" I challenge.

"I'm an oath-breaker," he growls. "Death is better than I deserve."

"That's not true!" I say firmly. "You were loyal to Alvtir. She was
our *true* leader."

"And now she's dead," Ranveig cuts in. I flinch at the harshness
in her tone.

No one responds.

For the first time, it truly hits me:

Alvtir is dead.

Alvtir—who rescued me from the merchant in Anfa, who took me into her home, who gave me a life I never dreamed I could have—Alvtir is dead. And so is our future.

The anchor sinks further than ever before, dragging my heart into a dark, yawning chasm at the bottom of my chest. It should drown me, but I find that I've already drowned.

I never realized that in all the times I felt the anchor before, there was always some small part of me that refused to yield, that kept crawling forward despite its crippling weight. Maybe it was the part of me that trusted what Papa taught me: that if I just *believed* in myself, everything would be all right in the end.

Now I almost welcome the heaviness. At least it's something I know I deserve.

Somewhere in the forest below, a wolf howls. I reach for the green wolf at my neck, but touching it brings no comfort this time. As I stare hopelessly into the fire, Mama's words once again come unbidden to my mind: *You have a great destiny. Great and terrible.*

You were wrong too, Mama.

My shoulders begin to tremble. I don't want the others to see the film of tears in my eyes, so I look up and watch the smoke. It curls and writhes in its death throes before disappearing into the night, taking with it Alvtir's dream.

41

YAFEU

The days crawl by with little to do but survive.

The wind blew out the fire several times that first night, so we started making camp at the base of the cliff, close enough that we could start the climb at a moment's notice if we heard anyone approaching, but less exposed to Agbe and Naete's powers. We argued bitterly that morning whether it was worth the added danger from predators and soldiers, with Ingmar and Ranveig in favor of taking the risk, and Hetha, Wisna, and Dag countering that it was safer to stay put. I finally jumped in, reasoning that even though the ledge was safe, the climb up wasn't: It was only a matter of time until one of us, weakened and exhausted as we already were, slipped and fell to our death.

That put an end to the argument, though I could tell Hetha and Wisna were angry with me, and I wondered if I should have stayed quiet. I hadn't meant to be the final word on the matter, only to give my opinion along with the rest. The incident gnawed at me for the rest of the morning.

Freydis remained unconscious for the entire day, caught in the throes of the blood-fever. With nothing to do but watch her suffer and wallow in my own remorse, I was grateful when, that afternoon, Ingmar suggested we hold a funeral in honor of Alvtir. It gave us all a much-needed purpose.

We had no body to bury, but we gathered stones and arranged them in the shape of a ship, an ancient custom among the *Majūs*. We stood around the stone ship and honored her the only way we could: with our words.

It turns out every one of us owed a debt to Alvtir. Hetha and Wisna spoke tearfully of how she saved them from loveless marriages with men, giving them the opportunity to stay together and fight for their keep. She took them under her wing and trained them from the time they were my own age. Ingmar said that even though he was always ashamed of the violence and killing that comes with the life of a soldier, following Alvtir's code taught him that there is honor in being a warrior too. Dag spoke of a hungry childhood as the youngest of a poor farmer's many sons. Despite his brother's protests, he left the farm as soon as he was old enough and joined the *hird* under Alvtir, seeking a better life. And he found it: Even after everything that happened, he still considered himself luckier than any of his brothers.

I spoke last, telling the others of how Alvtir protected me in Anfa and allowed me to come with her to Skíringssal. How she fed me, clothed me, and forced me to train with a sword and shield so that Snorri couldn't tear me down. Though the feelings clawed at my throat, I didn't speak of how betrayed I felt by her for so many moons, how angry I was. How hurt I still am. Only after I finished did I let myself cry.

Ranveig was the only one who didn't speak at all. No one blamed her. She spent most of the day in a state little better than Freydis's.

That night, I found myself praying again to my gods and the gods of the *Majūs*. Not just for Freydis, but for Ranveig, that she wouldn't go mad with grief.

I don't know which god to thank, but by the grace of one or another, Freydis woke from the fever the next morning. When she emerged from the tent at the end of my watch, I was so relieved I almost cried. Then she asked me and Ingmar where we were and what happened, and I almost cried for a very different reason. In the retelling, it was like I was hearing her agonizing screams, then watching Alvtir die, all over again.

I left out the part where Harald called her "ruined," but I didn't spare her from the knowledge that her father almost condemned her to die with the rest of us. She deserved to hear that truth, whether she was ready for it or not. If it shocked her to hear it, she didn't let it show. In fact, she bore the whole story a little *too* well. Better than any of us would have in her shoes.

As Freydis recuperated, the rest of us spent the next few days exploring our surroundings. Dag led us to a shallow freshwater pond, a brisk quarter day's walk from the cliff. We have to boil the water before we can drink it, but it's better than nothing. The six of us go there each morning to bathe and refill the waterskins, and to pick ripe strawberries from the bushes we found nearby. Beyond that, we discovered little of immediate use to us, save for some hedge nettle, which Freydis made into a salve for her wound.

We spent another day making a lean-to from a pine tree. It won't be enough shelter when winter comes along, but we can't build anything permanent here. It's a miracle we haven't already been found; maybe Agé hasn't abandoned me after all.

I know we'll need to go farther out eventually, to put some real distance between us and Skíringssal. But I don't know which direction we should take.

There are two real choices. First, if we wanted to reach another town, our best hope would be to hug the coastline. We can't head east—even circumventing Skíringssal, we'd still be at risk of running into the *hird*men. And it doesn't make sense to go deeper into Agder anyway. But we could head west toward Rogaland, following the Agdersfjord until it hits the sea, then turning north along the shore. Eventually, we would come upon some sort of settlement.

The second option is to attempt to cross the mountains. No one knows for certain what lies on the other side—or if there even *is* an "other side."

The coast is more immediately dangerous: Balli would ensure that word of our status spread quickly, and any *Majūs* would be more likely to kill us than open their arms to a band of outcasts. That's apparently true even in Rogaland. I'm beginning to understand what Dag meant when he said some *Majūs* would choose death over the life of an outcast.

But the mountains pose a different set of perils. Wisna thinks if we make it across, with some luck, we might eventually reach the Sami villages—Airé's people. But that could take many moons, and I remember from my time at Broskrap's farm that those mountains were capped with snow even before winter began. We could freeze to death if we're caught in the mountains when the season turns. Not to mention the possibility of running out of food.

So I don't have the heart to ask everyone to leave the cliff. Not yet. Not until someone can decide one way or the other.

Or better yet, come up with a better plan than either.

The season for deer has passed, but Wisna brought some netting with her, and she and I have managed to catch a few fat squirrels and hares here and there. The meat is tasteless without any seasoning, but it fills our bellies for now. What worries me more is how plump the rodents are; Wisna says it means a cold winter is coming.

At night, we take turns keeping watch while the others sleep, two at a time: Ingmar and I, Hetha and Wisna, and Dag and Ranveig. Freydis wants to take a watch herself, but I insist she sleep the night until she's fully recovered.

I wonder, sometimes, if she will ever fully recover. The scar is as thick as a grown man's finger, and twice as long, extending from her eyebrow to her lip. Her eye is likely shut forever. But the injury has cost her much more than an eye. She rarely leaves the tent, and when she does, she says very little, except to protest when anyone tries to help her with something. Then again, the rest of us don't talk much either. Though our wounds are less visible than hers, we've all lost our spirits.

To occupy ourselves during the long summer days, we play games of *tafl* with Alvtir's set, which we discovered in her pack on the second day. Otherwise, it's not always easy to stay busy. We set the traps, we check the traps. We walk to the pond and back. We gather roots and mushrooms and chop wood for fires. We cook, we eat, we sleep. In between, we try not to give in to despair.

One week passes like this. Then another. And another.

Our fourth week in the forest, things take a turn for the worse. I can feel the others growing restless, agitated. Quarrels break out over imagined slights—someone taking too short a watch, or someone else hogging space in the tent. Everyone is on edge.

I'm not surprised when Ranveig is the first to snap. She's sharpening a knife on a stone one idle afternoon when she suddenly throws both aside with an exasperated grunt. "I'm sick of waiting around!" she exclaims, leaping to her feet.

Hetha and Ingmar look up from their *tafl* game. Dag is out with Wisna foraging for food. I'm practicing carving the runes Freydis taught me on a spare log of firewood; I'm hoping it will lift her spirits to see how many of them I remember. "Then go find them," I say readily. "They can't have gotten far."

Ranveig scoffs. "You know that's not what I mean, Yafeu. I'm sick of this damn cliff. I'm sick of these damn trees. I'm sick of the whole damn forest!" She kicks the tent for emphasis.

"Hey!" I'm on my feet in a flash, as are Ingmar and Hetha.

"Why don't you take a walk, Ranveig?" Hetha intervenes.

"Why don't we *all* take a walk, Hetha?" Ranveig counters, her voice rising.

A startled Freydis emerges from the tent a moment later, swaddled in a fur like a newborn. "What's going on?" she asks sleepily.

"What's going on, *Princess,* is that we're tired of waiting for you to recover from that little scratch. We need to get going."

Freydis looks at me sharply. "What's she talking about? Am I the one keeping us here?"

"No!" I say quickly. "We're only staying here until we figure out our next move."

"And when is that going to be? Hmm?" Ranveig spreads her arms wide. "Are you waiting for a sign from one of your African gods? Do you even have a *clue* what to do next?"

Ingmar steps forward. "You're out of line—" he begins, but I hold up a hand.

"If you have an idea, let's hear it," I say.

"Fine." She straightens, squaring her shoulders. "I think we should go east, to Tønsberg in Vestfold. It's two days' sail from Skíringssal with a good wind, so it won't take many moons by foot, so long as we follow the sea. We can ask King Harald for refuge."

If it weren't for Freydis's mouth falling open in shock, I would think I didn't hear Ranveig correctly. "You want us to go to Harald's hall," I say anyway, just to be sure.

"Why not? He can't be too fond of Balli after what happened. We could offer him a bargain: knowledge of Skíringssal's vulnerabilities in exchange for restoring our honor and positions in his *hird.*"

I let out a mirthless laugh. "He may not be a friend of Balli's, but that doesn't make him a friend of ours. He's certainly no friend to Freydis."

"And what of Freydis? What has she done to earn her place in our ranks, besides getting herself maimed?"

"Ranveig," I growl in warning, but I can't think of anything to say in response.

"She defied her own father to join us," Ingmar offers, but Freydis has already wilted, crumpling in on herself.

"Ranveig is right," she says weakly. "You shouldn't avoid Vestfold for my sake."

"It's out of the question," I snap. "Freydis, even if he hadn't hurt you, Alvtir herself didn't trust him. We all heard her say so. And we didn't break our oaths to one cruel king just to swear allegiance to another."

"Then what's the alternative, Yafeu?" Ranveig demands.

I falter. This time, no one steps in on my behalf.

Ranveig crosses her arms. "Well? We're all waiting!"

"We stay put until we can agree on our course," I say finally. "*All* of us."

"Right. You don't have one."

Ranveig storms off, leaving her words to echo in my head.

"Don't let her get to you," Ingmar says during our watch that night. "Lashing out is just her way of grieving."

We're perched on stones in front of the fire, staring at the dancing shadows of spruce trees. Mawu is hidden somewhere behind the canopy. The crackle of the fire mingles in the cool night air with the crickets' song and Dag's lengthy snores. We've stopped expecting the *hird*men to come for us in the dead of night, but the danger from bears and other scavengers is real, so we've kept up the watch just to be safe.

"But she's right, Ingmar," I say. "Not about Harald, but about me."

It strikes me that I've been avoiding opening up to Ingmar about this, even though we've grown much closer these last few weeks. We've spent a lot of time alone together on these watches. At some point—I don't remember exactly when, or which one of us initiated it—we started sharing a fur, curling up together in our sleep. I wake each morning to find his arms wrapped around me, his legs entwined with mine. But it feels less like romance and more like . . . comfort. Maybe even a survival instinct. The same instinct that has stopped me from sharing my doubts.

That instinct rears its head in me now, but I choose to fight it. I can't bear this burden alone any longer; I have to confide in someone.

I unsheathe the dagger Alvtir made me and turn it over in my hands, swallowing hard before I speak.

"You asked me what Alvtir and I had been talking about, the night of the midsummer festival. She told me that she thought I would become a leader someday. But she was wrong to believe in me." I turn to face him, meeting his cool, steady gaze. "Everyone is looking to me for answers, but I . . . I can't save us, Ingmar. I *can't*. I know we need to plan for the winter, to stockpile food and build shelters against the cold. And I also know we can't do that here. But I don't know where else to go. There's no path forward that isn't fraught with danger. If only Alvtir were here . . ." I look away, shoving the dagger back into its sheath. "Well, if Alvtir were here, we wouldn't be."

The fire burns low before us. I let out a sigh from the depths of that chasm in my chest. The weight *has* lifted a little, but the hollowness in its wake feels even worse.

Out of the corner of my eye, I watch Ingmar lean forward, putting his elbows on his knees. He cocks his head to the side, thinking. "Alvtir was a good leader," he says at last. "But she was not perfect. She saw the world in black and white. She never leaned on anyone, never asked for help. And she took matters into her own hands when she should have trusted us enough to consult us first. Those weaknesses are what got her killed, and got the rest of us into the mess we're in now. No one wants to admit it, but it's true."

I say nothing as he gets up and tosses a log into the fire. Then, instead of taking his seat again, he crouches down in front of me, taking my hands in his.

I stare at my lap, afraid at what I might see on his face. Afraid that if I look into his eyes, I'll know he's lost his faith in me.

He continues anyway: "Maybe the leader we need now is one who doesn't pretend she has all the answers. One who *does* lean on those around her. One who sees what even the weakest among us has to offer—and finds a way to use their gifts. That is something you do better than anyone. I know because I've seen it myself. And Alvtir saw it too."

I look up, surprised. His sea-gray eyes are ringed with dark circles. The angles of his face are even sharper from eating so little, and his cheeks are smudged with dirt and ash, his brown hair falling in a tangled mess around them. But he's every bit as dazzling to me as he was at the harbor so many moons ago, the day I first laid eyes on him.

I lean down and plant a soft kiss on his cracked lips. "Thank you," I whisper.

I don't know if I believe what he said—but I know *he* believes it. For tonight, that's enough.

42

YAFEU

When I wake early the next morning, Freydis is gone. The cloth I used to wrap her wound—which she still uses to protect it from the elements—lies discarded on the empty fur.

"Where's Freydis?" I whisper to Dag and Ranveig as soon as I emerge from the tent. The sky is streaked with pink and orange. Hetha and Ingmar are still asleep.

They swivel their heads in my direction. "She wanted to bathe," Ranveig replies. "We told her how to get to the pond."

With a grunt of frustration, I throw my boots on. I grab the piece of firewood with the runes carved into it, abandoned beside the pile. I never got the chance to show Freydis yesterday: she shut herself in the tent after Ranveig left and didn't come out again, not even to eat. I tuck it under my arm and set out in the direction of the pond at a jog, leaving Ranveig and Dag bewildered behind me.

Lisa is low in the sky by the time I arrive. I find Freydis standing knee-deep in the water, fully clothed and head bowed. The bottom of her dress is drenched.

"Freydis!" I call out. "Thank Agbe. I was worried about you!"

She doesn't reply. She doesn't even look up at my approach.

"What's—" Before I can say "wrong," I realize what she's staring at.

Her reflection.

My heart sinks. I knew she was going to find out eventually, but I was hoping to delay it for a little while longer. At least until she'd regained more of her strength.

"You know why all of this happened, don't you?" Her tone is as bitter as a blackthorn berry.

I set down the firewood and fold into a seat at the edge of the grassy bank. She stands in profile; I can only see the unmarred side of her face. Her shadow extends toward me, long in the early-morning light. "Things happen in battle," I say gently. "I should have protected you."

"There's nothing you could have done. It was already too late."

"Freydis—"

"Don't you see?" She whirls to face me, shattering her reflection in the water. "It's the curse. It all began the day we passed through the Dead City. Hakon's betrayal, Harald's violence, now *this*!" She points to her scar, staring me down with her one good eye. I've never seen her this furious before. Not even when we found Broskrap's corpse in the stream.

I resist the urge to look away. "I told you. I don't believe in the curse. I believe in *you*."

"How much more proof do you need?" She spreads her arms, just like Ranveig did yesterday. "Look around, Yafeu. We're outcasts. We have nothing. When winter falls, we're as good as dead. And you know it. You *know* it!"

My throat constricts. Her scarred face blurs as tears spring to my eyes.

I shake my head vehemently. "I watched my village burn to the ground. I was ripped away from my family, dragged across the desert, and forced to watch the life drain out of my only friend, and I couldn't do anything to stop it. And then Alvtir rescued me—only to give me to *Broskrap* as a thrall. All that before I *ever* set foot in your *Dead City*." The tears spill out, but I force myself to continue. "I don't know why the gods let me suffer so much. I don't know why they let *you* suffer so much. Maybe you're right, maybe we are cursed. But even if we are, it doesn't matter. I'm not giving up. I'm not going to lie down and let death take me. And neither are you."

"I have nothing left, Yafeu!" she says angrily. "I used to be a princess. I used to be beautiful. Now I'm neither. I'm *nothing*." She kicks the water, sending violent ripples across the pond. Then she falls to her hands and knees, her long braid dropping into the water, her face inches from the surface.

I climb to my feet, picking up the log of firewood. I trudge into the pond, not even bothering to take my boots off. The frigid water is a shock where it hits my skin, but I don't stop until I'm right in front of her. I tuck the log under my arm and grab her under the shoulders, lifting her as gently as I can to her feet.

Her mossy-green eye is empty when it meets mine. I hand her the log. She looks at it dully.

"Freydis," I begin. "You are so much more than you know. You have a wisdom all your own, something no blade can take away. And you have me. I'm your friend, and I *need* you." As the words tumble out, the staggering truth of them pierces my chest. I grab my heart reflexively, my fingers digging into the skin beneath the tunic. My voice cracks. "I don't know what to do. I need your help to save everyone. So help me. *Please*."

Freydis blinks at the log, her jaw flexing. Her eye glistens. She scrubs at it with the butt of her palm. "You messed up *uruz*," she says after a moment. "The top is supposed to be slanted, like the roof of a house. Not flat."

"Well, at least the gods can't be any angrier with me."

She chuckles softly at that, and my shoulders sag with relief. I follow as she wades to the bank and gets out, tossing the log aside. We drip water onto the grass, shivering despite the warmth from Lisa's rays.

I watch quietly as she picks at the edge of her braid, her eye darting back and forth. I know she's turning everything over in her mind, trying, as I have, to come up with a plan.

"There's only one path forward," she says finally. "The one that leads back to Skíringssal."

"We'll be killed," I say. "I've thought about it myself. At best, we could stay at Broskrap's farm, but even that would be too risky. We'd have to spend our days shut in the barn, hidden even from Broskrap's boys, living off the labor of the thralls." I couldn't live that way; nor could I burden Bronaugh and Airé like that.

"Not if I make a claim to the throne. We'll kill my father and take Skíringssal for ourselves."

My eyes go wide. I gape at her, speechless. Her stone-cold tone is more of a shock than if I'd jumped in this pond in the dead of winter.

Kill Balli, and claim Agder for herself?

I might think Freydis was joking—or had lost her mind—if I didn't know her better. She can't marry a king anymore, but that doesn't mean she's given up on becoming a queen. I remember how passionately she always spoke of presiding over her own hall someday. It's what she's wanted more than anything, all her life.

An uneasy feeling sweeps over me; not so long ago, Alvtir was talking about killing *her* and taking the throne with the same icy indifference.

"The problem is," she continues, "we're outnumbered. Greatly. We're six—seven if you count me, which I don't advise—against nearly a hundred."

I smirk. "That's the *biggest* problem with that plan, yes."

"But there's no shortage of people in Agder who are fed up with their king. Some might even be angry enough to stand with us against him. Certainly the farmers in the outer provinces have been pushed too far. I know at least one young jarl who wouldn't hesitate to rally his men against my father, if given a proper chance. Once we had enough support from around Agder to pose a threat, some within Skíringssal might grow emboldened enough to join us. Maybe even some of the *hird*men. Then we'd actually stand a chance—presuming the gods are with us, after all."

I consider for a moment. "But how could we arrange to meet with the jarls without risking our lives? Do we go by foot, or do we risk sending someone into Skíringssal, to plead with one of the merchants or traders to make the case for us? Either way, all it takes is one person loyal enough to Balli to turn us in, and we're done for. Even if that didn't happen—even if people are as ready to turn on their king as you claim—it would take a long time to gather the support we need to challenge him. Years, even. How do we survive until then?"

"I don't know. I guess we'd have to find supporters within the city itself first." She exhales, chewing the inside of her cheek. "If only we knew who would fight with us against Balli. And if only we had a way to get the word to those people, to rally them somehow."

Out of nowhere, an idea pops into my head.

A grin spreads slowly across my face. It's almost as if Mawu-Lisa themselves just whispered in my ear. Or, rather, Legba—because this is a plan that smacks of his cunning.

I seize Freydis's hand. "Maybe we do."

43

YAFEU

I t's ironic how quickly a refuge becomes a prison, and a prison becomes a refuge. When I was a thrall, the forest was my only escape, the closest I came to truly feeling free. Now, as I creep silently into Broskrap's compound in the dead of night, leaving the forest behind, it feels again like I'm making an escape.

Only this time, I really am.

Triple-checking that I'm alone, I steal a moment to savor the wide-open sky. After more than a month of peering up through the dense foliage, it almost makes me dizzy to see it in its fullness. Mawu is absent, making the stars seem even more dazzling, like thousands of tiny candles bobbing in a dark sea.

My eyes fall to the barn ahead of me. My heart hammers in my chest, and it's not from the long and arduous trek here. Doubts needle at the fore of my mind. Doubts that I already mulled over with the others, debating and deliberating until we all agreed it was worth the many risks. Risks like: Will they help us? Am I asking too much of them? Even if they find others who are willing, will it be enough in the end?

It reminds me of something Mama used to say: *You can put your fears to bed, but you can't make them fall asleep.*

I take a deep, shaky breath, my hands poised on the rough surface of the barn door. This is my last chance to turn back, to call the whole thing off. But Freydis was right: This is our only path forward.

I open the door and step inside. A darkness darker than the night outside engulfs me. I blink as my eyes adjust. The air is close, tinged with the hint of a foul scent, like something rotting. "Bronaugh? Airé?" I whisper.

"Yafeu? Is that you?" Bronaugh says sleepily.

"It's me."

I hear scraping, then the dying embers flare to life, illuminating her face. "Yafeu!" She rushes over and throws her arms around me. I hug her back, scanning the room for Airé over her shoulder. But I don't see her anywhere.

"Where's Airé?" I ask as Bronaugh pulls back, clasping my hands.

"Sleeping in the house tonight. But what is Yafeu doing here? We heard what happened. We thought we lost you."

Even in the dim firelight, it's good to see her face again. It makes my chest clench, remembering what I came here to ask of her. "Bronaugh, I need your help."

She nods readily. "Anything."

"Are you sure this is a good idea?" Ingmar says, keeping his voice low. The dark, moonless night has long since fallen, but the seven of us have been waiting at the edge of Lake Vítrir, to give the whole of Skíringssal enough time to fall asleep.

"There's no turning back now" is all I can say in response.

In truth, I know how he feels. Despite what I told Freydis—and myself—about choosing not to believe in the curse, part of me *was* nervous the first time she brought me here. Now I'm more than nervous. I'm truly afraid. The spirit world is always closer to ours at night, and there's definitely something *jugu* about this place. Something that makes my skin crawl and sparks a burning instinct to flee, to get as far away as I can.

"Don't worry, Ingmar. What awaits us in Skíringssal a fortnight from now will be much, *much* worse than some angry spirits," Hetha says cheerfully. I smirk; only Hetha would make a joke at a time like this.

"I'm with Shield-Breaker," Dag chimes in, shifting from foot to foot. "We're soldiers, not seers. We can't protect ourselves against spirits and shades."

Freydis is the first to step forward. She whirls on the two men, her stolen sword bobbing in its sheath at her side. "If you can't walk among spirits, then perhaps you shouldn't release them from the living."

My eyebrows nearly hit my hairline.

Freydis is right, of course: Every one of us has taken lives. If we can't brazen out the dead, who can? But I'm surprised at her boldness, and more than a little proud. Last time, *I* was the one urging *her* to keep going. Her courage is enough to make me remember my own.

So I square my shoulders and follow. Ingmar quickly catches up to me, then Hetha and Wisna. "Gird your loins, brother!" Wisna calls back. Dag groans, but soon enough I hear his hurried footsteps behind ours.

So it is that Freydis Ballisdottir, former princess of Skíringssal, leads the six best soldiers in Norveg into the heart of the Dead City.

The stump that marks the threshold looks unsettlingly like another figure in the darkness. As we pass it, the sounds of the night are suddenly muted, as though we've crossed through an invisible wall. The air grows sharp with disquiet. We keep our eyes on the ground, watching out for the shards of wood and clay that litter the blackened earth. It makes it easier not to look at the collapsed buildings, or the monstrous shadows they cast.

Soon we're jogging past the oval of rocks. I stare at the arrangement with new eyes, knowing now that it's a stone ship. It must have been placed here after the battle, to honor those who died in the fire.

The people of Skíringssal believe that the souls of the dead are trapped here, unable to find peace. If that's true, is Alvtir unable to find peace either? Or is it enough that we honored her in the best way we could, as the survivors of the Battle of Geirstad honored their lost loved ones?

Just then, I notice that our footsteps have increased in number. I stop and look around, holding up a hand to the others.

Freydis falls back beside me. "What is it?" she whispers, a hint of fear tarnishing her resolute expression.

My lips curve into a smile as I see the answer. "Look!" I whisper back, pointing to the stone ship behind us.

Everyone turns. In the faint light of the stars, I can just make out the outline of a deer in the center of the stone ship, its long neck bowed to the ground. We watch in awe as it nibbles on the mushrooms that grow there. The mushrooms I thought must be poisonous to live where nothing else can.

I'd forgotten one of Papa's earliest lessons, the one he told me after I killed my first antelope: *All things must die, but death, in turn, supports life.*

Ragnarök is not the end, Alvtir had said. *It's a new beginning.*

Odds are, we'll all be dead before Lisa's rise. But maybe our efforts will inspire others. Maybe change is just as inevitable as Alvtir came to believe.

"It's a sign from the gods," Wisna says quietly.

I share a promising look with Freydis. "Maybe they're with us after all," I say, holding out my hand.

She takes it. "I hope so."

Heartened, we resume our course, Freydis and I holding hands all the while. Just before the tall grasses, we stop again at the last structure: a barn not unlike Broskrap's. It's the only building that survived the fire, standing beside the rubble of what used to be the old mead hall, though its walls are charred and peeling. A thin wisp of smoke rises from the smoke hole now, gray against the black of the sky.

We reach the door. Hushed voices filter out.

The others turn to me, waiting. Freydis drops her hand and gives me an encouraging nod. This is the part where I take the lead.

I feel a familiar nervous tightening in my stomach, though the sensation is so much more intense than I remember it ever being before. I run through the plan I hatched with Freydis in my mind. It now seems impossibly tenuous. Was Bronaugh able to pass our message on to other thralls over the last moon? Could they understand her well enough? Did they tell any others?

I push the door open slowly, nearly paralyzed with dread.

But the barn is full to the brim.

My heart leaps in my chest. From the looks of it, every one of the Soninke thralls has come. And not just them, but many others as well. At least three dozen solemn faces turn to us as we enter. Some have the same hooded eyes and warm skin as Airé; others are freckled like Bronaugh and Ingmar. Men and women, young and old, brown-skinned and ivory-skinned—all gathered here to answer our call. Even some of the royal thralls have come, including Werian, Balli's pockmarked serving boy.

I nearly bleat from the heady mixture of shock, relief, and amazement at the sight. From the look on her face, Freydis feels much the same.

Bronaugh walks over to greet us. I clasp her hands, overcome. "I did good, no?" she asks, her brown eyes twinkling in the light of the blazing fire.

"Better than good, Bronaugh. I don't know how I'll ever thank you."

"You thank me by winning." She faces the crowd, waiting until they fall silent. "This is Yafeu, the woman I told you about." She gestures to me. "She was a thrall once, just like us. She fought for her freedom, and now she wants us to fight for ours."

At the same time, Nyeru emerges from the cluster of Soninke thralls. "Nyeru!" I switch to Soninke. "What are you doing here?" He's too old to fight with us, though I don't say that out loud.

He places a hand on my shoulder. "We all fight in our own way, kinswoman." He turns, addressing our people. "This is Yafeu," he says in Soninke, echoing Bronaugh's introduction.

No one says a word. They wait for me to speak. Their hands clasp whatever weapons they could pilfer from their owners: shovels, scythes, drawknives, chisels, hammers. Weapons that are hardly a match for swords and battle-axes.

I take a deep breath and try to look every one of them in the eyes.

"You were brave to come here tonight," I begin in Soninke, trying desperately to control the tremor in my voice. Nyeru repeats my words in Norse. "There is so much I wish to say to all of you, but we don't have time. I know you've all suffered greatly. I've suffered too." My throat constricts. I swallow, struggling to gather my thoughts. "I want to tell you that your suffering was not in vain, because it led you here tonight. That all our gods, though they are as different from one another as we are, are standing beside us now. That they believe in us. But what matters most is not what the gods believe. What matters most is what *we* believe."

I feel a powerful *nyama* begin to bloom inside me. I pause, letting it fill me with its strength. When I speak again, it is from my very core. "Here is what I believe. I believe that every one of you should be free. I believe the thieves who stole your freedom should pay for it with their lives. And I believe that we can only defeat them together.

"Nevertheless, we will not force you to fight. Each of you is free to make your own choice. I won't lie about our odds: Most of you are not trained warriors, and even if you were, we are still greatly outnumbered. It is likelier than not that we go to our deaths.

"But whether you join us or not, whether you fight with us or not, I swear to you that if we win, you will be free under Queen Freydis's rule."

I lock eyes with Freydis. Everyone looks to her to affirm my words. She places her hand on the hilt of her stolen sword and bows to me without a word. Murmurs of approval ripple through the crowd.

"I am no seeress," I continue, repeating myself again in the Norse tongue. "I cannot predict our fate, nor do I know the will of the gods. I can only offer you a chance, and I won't judge anyone who turns that chance down. But I, for one, would rather die fighting for what I believe than live a lie." The flow of words ceases abruptly. I stand in silence, my breath hitched in my throat.

A lithe Soninke girl with umber-brown skin and eyes takes a step forward. She plunges her scythe into the dirt. "I am with you, Yafeu," she says in Soninke.

I nod to her, my heart swelling with gratitude. Then another steps forward, plunges her makeshift weapon in the dirt, and echoes her words, this time in stilted Norse: "I am with you, Yafeu."

Then another: "I am with you, Yafeu."

And another: "I am with you, Yafeu."

Soon, every thrall in the barn has come forward. It's all I can do to hold back the tears.

"Thank you all," I manage to say in both tongues, my voice thick with everything I can't put into words.

"Ademola." Nyeru motions to a tall, young man around my age at the front of the crowd. His gait is graceful as he approaches, and I can't help but notice the sinewy striations of his arms. "This is Ademola," Nyeru continues in Soninke. "He is the son of the great chief Jawuru and a seasoned warrior. He can lead our people into battle."

Ademola places his hand over his heart in greeting, observing me intently. The strength of his *nyama* fills the space between us. His eyes shine like polished smoky quartz. "I am in your service," he says in our native tongue, bowing his head in respect.

I bow back to him. "No, kinsman. I am in *yours.*"

Ademola's serious expression blooms into a rapturous smile.

Out of the corner of my eye, I see Freydis pull Balli's serving boy aside. "We have a special task for you, Werian, if you're up for it."

I turn back to the expectant faces of the others. "Here's our plan."

44

YAFEU

The night sky is black as tar. Mawu is a sliver, her face turned away from us. Like she can't bear to watch what will happen next. The still, frigid air carries the promise of autumn, but I left the cloak Freydis gave me behind. I'd rather be cold than encumbered tonight. And I won't be cold for long.

I did decide to wear both my necklaces. "Hey, Ranveig," I'd said when I put on the teeth earlier today. "What was it you said about where wolf's teeth are?"

Her answering grin reminded me of Alvtir.

She sticks close to me now as the seven of us crawl on our bellies out of the tall grasses and into the royal compound. We reach the Great Hall and straighten one by one, prowling quietly around the back like the predators we are. We don't want to alert the guard at the watchtower to our presence. Not until the last possible moment.

Fear has been steadily swelling inside me all day, and now it's a tidal wave poised to crash. But I feel something else, too: the *Úlf-*

heðinn stirring awake. My heartbeat roars between my ears, from terror or fervor or both.

When I was training with the *hird,* I thought a raid would be my first test as a shield maiden.

Instead, I'm leading a coup.

I reach the front edge of the hall and raise my fist behind me, signaling the others to halt. The door guards' conversation rises above the music and merriment filtering out from the hall.

"...be *our* turn to raise our horns and enjoy some of King Balli's generosity?"

"Kjartan, you old mare, you'd be lucky to get a thrall girl's table scraps."

"If he gets the scraps, I'll take the girl!"

I risk a quick peek. Six guards slouch in front of the doors, illuminated by torches on either side. One for each of us, save Freydis.

It's the night of the *Freysblot,* the feast celebrating the harvest and honoring the god Frey. According to Freydis, in addition to Skíringssal's farmers, Balli's guards and the captains of the *hird* should all be in attendance. Was it only a year ago that Broskrap left for this very same feast, leaving me to visit the harbor and dream of escape? It's hard to believe.

I lock eyes with the others. First Ranveig, then Ingmar, then Dag, Hetha, Wisna, and finally Freydis. Each of them nods back. Lightning cracks open the sky. In the flash of white, with mud on their ragged armor and vengeance in their eyes, they are more than soldiers. They are the stuff of nightmares.

Even Freydis looks more ferocious than I've ever seen her. She wears Alvtir's oversized, little-used leather cuirass under the wolf vest I made her. The sword she stole from the guard rests at her hip. We trained her to wield it over the last few weeks. Mostly to defend herself, but also to attack, if needed. I can only hope it will be enough to keep her alive. Either way, I know her aunt would be proud of her. She would be proud of all of us.

I leap out into the open, jolting the six guards from their complacency.

"Hey! Remember me?"

The guards chase me around the corner. Fools. My companions are on the guards before they can even unsheathe their swords. Ranveig slices the first man's head clean off his shoulders as Hetha buries her ax in the chest of another. Ingmar, Dag, and Wisna take down their companions just as easily. The *Úlfheðinn* rears its head within me, smelling blood. No sooner does the last guard round the corner than I plunge a dagger into that vulnerable spot between the neck and shoulder. His mouth opens and closes like a fish as he falls.

"No thrall girls for you tonight," Ranveig growls, the gleam in her eye turning savage in the dim torchlight.

Thunder rumbles in the distance as the seven of us step out from the shadows. A droplet of rain taps my head. Then another. Suddenly the rain is pouring down in buckets. I let Freydis take the lead when we reach the door, positioning myself behind her shoulder.

The trumpet sounds from the watchtower in a series of fitful spurts. The signal for an attack.

Good. We're done hiding.

The sky flashes and booms: the war-cry of the gods. Whether they're with us or against us, we'll know soon enough.

For now, it doesn't matter.

For now, we fight for ourselves.

Freydis throws open the doors of the Great Hall, and we charge inside with the storm.

Inside the Great Hall, the music has stopped. Empty horns and platters line the tables. The closest tables are for the farmers and their families. They are already shrinking back from us, their panicked murmurs filling the air. But those at the far tables—the captains of the *hird*, Balli's guards, and finally Balli, Yngvild, and Snorri themselves—stay seated. They swivel their heads at us as we enter, their expressions befuddled. There are forty, maybe fifty in total.

"Freydis." Balli's voice is slurred.

Freydis ignores him, addressing the farmers instead. "If you wish to live, go home. Now." We move to the side, freeing up the doorway so the farmers can escape.

In the days leading up to our gathering with the thralls in the Dead City, the seven of us hotly debated the plan. To my shock and dismay, Freydis wanted to set fire to the Great Hall, blocking the doors from the outside. So did Ranveig. It was the first time the two have ever been in agreement. Dag and even Wisna took their side, arguing that we were too severely outnumbered to stand a chance. But I couldn't just overlook the fact that the farmers and their families are innocent. Not to mention the thralls, not all of whom could be warned.

Freydis and the others believed their lives were a necessary sacrifice for our cause, but I ultimately won them over by pointing out that there's no honor in killing without showing your face. If Freydis was truly to become queen of Agder, it wouldn't be enough for Balli to die. He must die in the right way, at the right time. Freydis would stand no chance against him in a *holmgang;* he may be old and out of fighting shape, but he was once a warrior. Still, she needed to challenge him publicly and face his forces with honor—to *prove* to the people that she deserved to succeed him by more than blood alone. Otherwise, one of the jarls would simply take his place. Even Freydis couldn't deny my reasoning there.

So we decided to fight, even though we would be only seven against dozens of soldiers and guards. We could only pray that Bronaugh's help would be enough to tip the scales, that the thralls would come to our aid.

That is, until we saw Werian at the barn in the Dead City. Then we thought of another way to level the playing field.

We also gambled that the farmers wouldn't take up arms against us. That they'd rather flee with their wives and children than risk their necks defending their king, even against so few as seven.

And we were right. The farmers don't need to be told twice. They stampede past us, as do most of the serving thralls, leaving the hall half empty. Dag quickly closes the doors.

That's when I see the thrall slumped against the column next to the hearth, bound with his hands behind his back. He lifts his head.

My heart stops as I take in his rich brown skin, his lined face and short gray hair.

Nyeru.

He smiles faintly, but rage overwhelms me.

What were they planning to do to him?

I glare hotly at Snorri, my blood boiling at his exultant sneer. I want to scream. I want to throw a dagger at his head, even though he's almost certainly too far away for even my aim to hit its mark. I want to kill everyone in this hall, innocent or no.

But Freydis's voice rings out strong and clear, stopping me. As she speaks, Dag, Ingmar, Hetha, and Wisna drag the nearest table over to the doors and block them.

"King Balli of Skíringssal, you have broken your oath to protect the people and ruled without honor. Now I have come to claim what is mine. Before the sun rises, you will be dead. I will take your place as queen of Agder."

A long, silent moment passes. The hall seems frozen, until Helge steps forward toward Yngvild, who sits gaping at her daughter. She says something I can't hear, struggling to help Yngvild out of her seat.

Helge—who is too old, too long enslaved to even dream of freedom—is the first to protect her master.

Then Snorri begins to laugh. I hold his mocking gaze without blinking.

"Kill them," Balli orders. Snorri quiets as the king struggles to his feet. "I said, *kill them!*"

The captains rush us, followed by the guards. Or rather, they try to. Their legs seem to be failing them. They're bouncing off one another and running into columns, their movements sluggish and uncoordinated, their sense of balance skewed from more than just a few horns of ale.

I lock eyes with Werian, Balli's serving boy and the key to our plan. He stands a few paces behind the royals with the handful of thralls, girls and boys and Helge, who stayed. His smile is triumphant. Mine is too.

Werian knows where Balli keeps his supply of henbane. His job was to pour the potion into certain pitchers of ale: only the pitchers that would be served to the royals, the *hird*men, and the guards. He could recruit any other thralls he was absolutely certain he could trust to help him.

From the looks of the soldiers, he has done his task perfectly.

According to Freydis, henbane relieves pain in the body and calms the mind. But only if you have a little. In higher amounts, it has the opposite effect, causing the drinker to become agitated and clumsy, even delirious, like a fever from an infected wound. It can even cause death, though it doesn't look as if we'll be so lucky tonight. The guards and *hird*men are largely out of their wits, but they'll still put up a fight.

The *Úlfheðinn* howls with delight. I let it suffuse me as I line up shoulder-to-shoulder with my friends. My warriors. Ingmar moves to my right, Dag to his. Ranveig moves to my left, followed by Wisna, then Hetha. Freydis drops behind us, as we'd agreed.

I raise my daggers above my head and strike them together. The clang echoes around the hall. *"For Valhalla!"* I shout.

"For Valhalla!" comes the response.

Before we can charge, Werian shouts something in a language I don't know. He makes a mad dash for Balli, holding a carving knife in his right hand.

"Werian—no!" I shout.

But I'm too late. Snorri's sword is already buried in his gut.

A look of pure hatred passes between Snorri and me. It takes me a moment to realize that Snorri was too quick, his blow too precise. My eyes flicker to the horn in front of him.

It's full.

For all his many vices, Snorri Broskrapsson is not like his father. He didn't drink his ale.

Werian clutches his stomach, an expression of agony twisting his young face. Then he falls.

The dam bursts. A feral cry rips through me. My warriors echo it.

Screaming like demons, we race forward and crash into the first wave of Balli's men.

The *Úlfheðinn* takes over. Still screaming, I parry one captain's attack and stab him in the heart. The blade sinks in easily; he wears neither cuirass nor chain mail. Another approaches—a guard. He is wearing a full suit of armor, so I throw my other dagger into his thigh, where he's unprotected, retrieving it as he tumbles past me. Blood from the artery spatters my arm.

I glance around. It looks like Balli did learn a thing or two from the attack at Freydis's wedding: He had his guards come in full armor tonight. But the *hird*men appear to have only their weapons, leaving them vulnerable in their drugged state.

This might just work.

The thought invigorates me as another woozy guard tries to rush me. He's not even holding his sword correctly. I knock it out of his hand before kicking him in the kneecap with all my strength. He shrieks in agony as it dislodges, which I cut short with a slice to the jugular.

I whirl around, looking for the next man to kill. But none are coming for me. My friends are sickles, and their former brothers are ripe for harvesting.

Ranveig is laughing—*laughing*—as she chops an arm off one of the captains. Arinbjorn, I think his name was. She kicks him into a table so hard it's knocked over. The empty platters shatter on the floor. A weaponless guard lunges for her, and she slaps him in the face like an insolent child. Which is what he is, compared with her. She picks up one of the clay shards and uses it to puncture his eye, cackling all the while as he screams in anguish.

I would vomit if I weren't in awe. I was right about Ranveig: She must be a *berserker,* like Alvtir. Frey will get his blood tonight after all.

And then I remember: *Nyeru.*

Ingmar is closest to me, still at my right, ripping his long ax out of a soldier's neck. "Ingmar!" I shout. "Cover me!" He watches my back as I sprint to the column where Nyeru is tied.

"I knew you would save me again," Nyeru says weakly as I slice through the ropes binding his wrists. Freed, he stumbles forward but quickly regains his balance.

"Hide, kinsman."

I help Nyeru under one of the few tables still upright. I launch my dagger at the closest captain before he can come for us. He goes down. That one's name I never learned.

But there is a captain whose name I know all too well. And he's still alive.

"Snorri Broskrapsson!" the *Úlfheðinn* screams through me as I turn to Balli's table. But I can't see him or Balli. On the dais, the guards have interlocked their shields, forming a barrier, with spears protruding from the gaps. I remember this formation from training: a shield wall. It can be used offensively to break through an enemy's line, or defensively to protect something—or someone. Balli and Snorri must be hiding just behind.

I fight my way to the dais, leaping over the bodies of the dead. But the barrier is already moving. They reach the side wall and turn, reassembling with the wall covering their backs before I arrive.

Now I can see what was concealed behind them on the dais. The few serving thralls who stayed behind are all bleeding out on the ground. I recognize the thrall girl who had been sitting on Erik's lap at the *Dísablót* staring lifelessly up at the ceiling, an ax buried in her skull.

Rage bursts through me again. I lunge and bang fruitlessly on the shields, trying to hack my way to an opening. A spear comes at my stomach, nearly skewering me. I spin out of the way in time, but it still grazes my side. Stings, but I'll live. The opening closes as quickly as it appeared. I clutch the wound, backing away in disbelief.

"Cowards! Honorless nithings!" the *Úlfheðinn* shouts.

My friends finish off what's left of the guards and captains while I fling insults at the shields, as if my words could break through when my daggers could not. "Fight me, Snorri Broskrapsson! Fight for the life of your king!"

But the barrier doesn't break. The shield wall advances like nothing happened, shuffling closer and closer to the door, taking Balli and Snorri with them.

"Want to know why they call me Shield-Breaker?"

Ingmar's bloodstained hand falls on my shoulder. I answer with a smile. There's blood on his face, too. And I feel the blood on mine.

It's not over yet.

The rest of us gather behind Ingmar. The hall is a mess of shards of clay pots, slabs of meat, smashed fruits, ripped sheepskins, overturned tables, benches cracked in two. And many, many bodies. And blood. Blood everywhere, on everything. I scan for Nyeru and am relieved to find him crouching against the far wall, terrified but alive.

Freydis is the last to join us. Sweat pours down her face, clumping the strands of hair that have fallen from her braid. I look her over. She doesn't seem to have any injuries. She gives me a brief nod; she's all right.

Ingmar races forward, hooks his long ax around one of the shields, and yanks it back, creating an opening. We crowd around the hole. But more swords and spears come out from the gap, and the shield wall closes in the span of a heartbeat.

Ingmar grunts in pain. I wheel around as he falls back, clutching his arm.

Panic swells in me as blood streams from his wound. "Back up!" I shout to the others.

Thank the gods, Ingmar hefts his sword and regroups. We match the shield wall's movement toward the door but keep our distance. "I'll go in again," he says, panting.

"No!" I grab his uninjured arm. "It's too dangerous."

"We have no choice."

"Wait until they reach the doors. They'll have to break formation when they get to the barricade."

No sooner do the words leave my mouth than an earsplitting boom sounds from the doors. The table shakes, scooting back.

"It's the rest of the *hird,*" Hetha says needlessly.

No. Not yet.

Another boom, and the table scrapes back.

"Get ready!" I shout, also needlessly.

We line up facing the door. Freydis again drops behind us, taking cover.

One last boom, and the doors fly open. The *hird*men pour into the hall like ants into an anthill.

These are the lower-ranking soldiers. The ones who weren't invited to the feast. Who didn't help themselves to horn after horn of the king's ale.

The ones who weren't drugged.

They slam into us. "Hold your ground!" Dag shouts.

And we hold our ground. We are still their betters. We are still Alvtir's chosen warriors. And the open doors still silo the *hird*men, so they can't hit us with their full force.

We fight them back steadily, ignoring the exhaustion. Ignoring the blood on our faces, in our hair, on our armor, and now streaming from our wounds. Dag roars like something inhuman as he picks up a bench and tosses it into the onslaught of *hird*men, taking five down all at once. Ranveig picks up a bowl and chucks it at the next man's head.

Suddenly there's a lull. The stream thins to a trickle; fewer and fewer *hird*men are coming at us. We press forward, regaining some ground. Then the shield wall disappears out the door. Ingmar hurls his ax with all his might, but it hits a shield and bounces off harmlessly.

"They're getting away!" I shout as the *hird*men resume rushing in around them.

"Soldiers!" Freydis calls out from behind us. "I beg you: Drop your weapons, or turn them around! The king you fight for is not worthy of your lives!"

They don't listen. There are too many of them. They force us back. And back.

We're trapped now. There's no way we can take all of them. There's no way out.

Hetha stumbles over a fallen body. "Hetha!" I cry. But I'm fending off two *hird*men; I can't help her.

Wisna steps forward, parrying the soldier's killing blow just in time. Hetha staggers back to her feet, meeting the next soldier's sword with her shield.

My heart falls. We can't keep this up. We have minutes, maybe seconds, until Balli's soldiers gut us one by one.

We're going to die. And it's all my fault.

Papa was wrong. I believed in this crazy, reckless plan. I believed with all my heart. But believing didn't give it power. It only made me lead my friends to their deaths.

Mawu-Lisa . . . Odin . . . Freya . . . Gu . . . if any of you are with us in this, let us find a way out of here alive.

"Kyaaaahh!"

A voice from outside. The *hird*men stop their assault. A moment of confusion. We pause, catching our breath.

Then they're falling back.

Outside, through the doors, lightning flashes, revealing a whirl of brown skin—skin the color of mine.

My heart leaps in my chest.

It's Ademola, leading the thralls. His undyed tunic is ripped at the sleeves, revealing his muscular arms as he leaps in the air, gripping a scythe with both hands.

"Kyaaaahh!" he cries again. The thralls slam into the *hird* from both sides. The soldiers falter and wheel around, confused by this new attack.

"Now!" I shout.

The seven of us charge the door, killing the retreating *hird*men as we go. The fire in our hearts has sparked anew, and now everyone in our path is kindling. Wisna spins like a tornado, flinging soldiers this way and that. Ranveig falls to the ground, scoops up a spear, and jams it into a soldier's stomach as she slides between his legs. Ingmar takes that soldier's sword as he falls and uses it to cleave another in two.

There're only two more *hird*men left in the hall. Dag runs headlong into them. They turn around, panicking, but he tramples them like a bull loosed in a chicken coop. Hetha and I finish them off.

We reach the door. We should be free now, but there's a barricade of bodies just outside. Thrall and soldier clashing, pressing together in a writhing mass, blocking our exit.

The shield wall is gone, dissipated in the chaos. The rain has stopped, but the sky flashes again, and I catch the flutter of a red cloak before it disappears down the hill. It's Balli, leaving the battle like the coward he is, making for the safety of his fields. Escaping.

The *Úlfheðinn* howls its wrath. "I need out—now!"

Wisna interlocks her fingers and reaches down. I step in and springboard up from her hands.

I land smack in the center of the core of *hird*men, knocking one down as I land. I take advantage of the momentary confusion and slash out wildly.

"For Alvtir!" I hear Ranveig cry out overhead. She lands next to me and plunges her sword into the chest of one of the soldiers. Dag is next, then Ingmar. All four of us slash and hack our way out.

I look back at Ingmar, who twirls his ax above his head and brings it down onto the skull of a soldier, cracking it in half like a melon.

"Go!" he shouts. "We'll hold!"

I spin back around and make a break for it. "Cover Yafeu!" Dag shouts. Ademola and another thrall step in front of me, fighting off the soldiers as I make my way out of the fray.

The night air hits my burning skin. I nearly fall over myself as I sprint through the darkness down the hill. I leap over the fence into the barley field, now barren after the harvest, save for a handful of dark figures on the other side. One of them wheels around.

"Stop her!" Snorri's voice.

Two other figures, guards or *hird*men, move toward me.

But the *Úlfheðinn* won't be stopped.

I charge them, slicing their necks in an instant, one with each dagger. I hear them gurgling as they die layered over the gentle chirp of crickets, the groan of trees in the forest just ahead, bending in the wind that always blows so angrily off the fjord.

Snorri and the king vanish into the forest. I race toward the tree line as fast as my legs will carry me.

I slow as I enter the darkness, sheathing one of my daggers. My hunting instincts take over. I've learned how to walk in these boots, and I make myself silent as I stalk through the trees. Sight becomes secondary to sound as I listen for the snap of a twig that will show me to the creature that doesn't belong here.

It's not long before I hear it: a crunch from behind the low branches of a large birch. I stalk over to the trunk and yank the king out from behind it.

He brandishes a sword, and even in the darkness, its *nyama* is unmistakable. It's Alvtir's sword, Angrboda. Yet more rage courses through me at the sight of such a cowardly man wielding the weapon of a true warrior.

Before he can so much as blink, I slice off his sword-hand.

He screams as I thrust him up against the birch trunk, shrinking in my grasp. His blood is warm against my chest. I never realized before how small Balli is.

Mawu shines down through a gap in the canopy, illuminating his terror-stricken face. I gaze, exultant, into his frenzied eyes as the realization of his impending doom seeps into them.

"Look at me, King Balli, and know that Yafeu is the one who will *end* you."

"I should have killed you when I had the chance," he snarls.

"For Alvtir." I echo Ranveig, raising my dagger high.

I can just make out the gleam of Mawu's light on his teeth. I squint: He's *smiling* at me. No, not at me. Over my shoulder.

I spin around just in time to dodge a crushing blow from—Snorri. *"Heill, Úlfheðinn."*

The king leaps on me from behind, wrapping his arms around my neck. I slam my head back into his and he ricochets off the trunk of the tree. He lets go and falls to the ground, unconscious. It gives me just enough time to dodge Snorri's next blow and regain my footing.

"I've dreamed of this moment for a long time," Snorri says, flourishing his sword eagerly.

"So have I." I unsheathe the second dagger, twirling both around my hands.

He lunges. I cross the daggers and catch it, but the force of his blow ricochets through my bones.

I toss him to the side, scraping the daggers down his arm. He shrieks and slashes back at me. This time I'm not quick enough—I leap away but he slices a deep gash into my thigh.

The burning pain overwhelms my senses for a moment. He takes advantage, lunging again.

I roll to the side and jump back up, fighting through the pain, but I feel myself growing dizzier and dizzier. My thigh is slick with my own blood. The *Úlfheðinn* is bleeding out of me.

Snorri kicks the daggers out of my hands. My grip fails me. I'm weaponless. Hopeless.

He chuckles as I fall to my knees. Mawu's light seems to disappear. Darkness creeps in around me.

Snorri leans down and whispers in my ear: "You're nothing more than a black elf whore, pretending to be someone you're not and could never be. It's time to end this little game." He raises his sword above his head.

"And you're nothing more than a man." I grab the carving knife—hidden in a small sheath strapped to my calf—and slice the tendon above his right heel.

Snorri screams and collapses, dropping his sword.

I climb unsteadily to my feet, trading places with him. He whimpers as he crawls backward on his elbows, propping himself up against the nearest tree.

Summoning the *Úlfheðinn's* last ounce of strength, I drive the knife through his left shoulder, pinning him to the tree. He screams again, and the sound brings a smile to my lips.

The desire to make him suffer enlivens me. I bring my foot down hard on his nether regions. He shrieks and coughs blood, which joins the blood from his shoulder as it soils his tunic.

I bend down and whisper in his ear, just like he did to me. "You squeal just like your father did before I took his life."

His breath is raspy, wheezing. Even through his pain, his fingers inch toward his sword, just beyond his grasp. I kick it away.

"No—for Valhalla!" he begs. "You have to give me my sword!"

"Valhalla doesn't want you." I wrench the knife from his shoulder. "For Alvtir," I say again, looking deep into his eyes as I drag the knife across his neck.

Snorri gurgles and moans as the blood spills out of his body. I stand over him, watching the life drain from him. Finally, his head falls to the side, his eyes lolled open.

A wave of triumph crashes over me.

Snorri is dead.

I killed him.

But when the elation recedes, it leaves nothing behind.

I fall to the ground, the last of the fire leaving my body with the blood from the gash in my leg. I feel dizzy again.

A shadow looms over me. Have my ancestors come for me already?

Through the haze, I suddenly remember: the king.

I look up to see him towering over me, holding Snorri's sword in his left hand. I try to roll away, but I can barely move. It's all I can do to stare up at him with every ounce of defiance I still have. At the man who will succeed, at last, in ending my life.

So be it.

His lips turn up into a sneer, and then—

A sword bursts through his chest.

The bloody runes glitter in the moonlight. Angrboda.

His blood splatters onto my face, just like the merchant's blood in Anfa. Balli looks down at it in shock, then stumbles forward and plummets face-forward onto the ground beside me. Dead.

I look up at the figure looming behind him. Her face is shrouded in darkness.

"Alvtir?" I murmur.

But she morphs into another: Freydis. Covered in the blood of her father.

And then all is black.

45

YAFEU

I wake up to eyes like a glistening pool of water in a sunlit glade.

I blink. Ingmar's face leans over mine, his forehead creased in concern. There's an orange glow around his head, and I wonder for a moment if I'm dead.

But the next life wouldn't begin with a pounding in my head and a throbbing in my leg.

"She's okay," I hear him say. He helps me up to a seat, and I realize I'm in a bed. Freydis's bed, to be exact. And it's daytime.

"You gave us quite a scare," a deep voice grumbles: Wisna. I look up to see her, Hetha, and Freydis hovering nearby. Their clothes are fresh, their faces clean and smooth with relief.

I lift the fur to get a look at my thigh: The wound has been wrapped tightly.

Hetha hands me a pitcher of water. Thirst hits me with overwhelming urgency. I drink the whole thing down in one gulp.

Freydis offers me a plate of cheese and a chunk of old, hard flatbread. I'm still not used to the scar on her face, and it jars me back to reality even more. I'm definitely still alive. "It's all I could find, I was rushing..." She trails off as I tear into it ravenously, as if it were the most fragrant, hearty feast.

"How long was I asleep?" I ask once I've finished my meal.

"A day," answers Hetha.

Memory floods back to me, fragmented and jumbled. I tense. "The king?"

"Dead, along with Snorri," Freydis says quickly.

My whole body goes slack with relief. Thank the gods. Thank every god, *Majūs* or mine.

It feels like it must be a dream, but it's not. It's real. "We did it," I manage to croak. "We won."

"We won," Ingmar affirms, cupping my cheek with his palm.

His eyes are soft and tender, but my gaze flickers to his upper arm. The gash has stopped bleeding, though it will certainly scar.

What would I do if he'd fallen?

I reach for my cheek and clasp my hand over his, hoping it's enough to convey what I can't say out loud in front of the others. "So *that's* why they call you Shield-Breaker?" I ask instead, remembering how he used his ax to rip a hole in the shield wall. I'd never seen anyone do anything like that before.

"It is."

"You'll have to teach me that sometime."

He smirks. "Anytime."

I catch Freydis's eye. "Freydis..." I trail off, noticing the sheath at her hip. That isn't the sword she stole from the guard. I would know the hilt anywhere: It's Angrboda, Alvtir's sword. My mind flashes to the image of the blade sticking out of Balli's chest. How he fell to the side, revealing Freydis behind him. "You saved my life," I finish.

Hetha and Wisna glance at her sharply. Didn't she tell them?

"I owed you one," she says sheepishly, though a hint of darkness passes over her face. "Well, more than one."

"Consider us even." I throw off the furs, not caring that I'm not wearing any trousers. Ingmar tries to help me to my feet, but I wave him away. "I can walk on my own."

He snorts as I take a wobbly step forward. "Always so stubborn."

"No one will think less of you for it. Not after the battle," says Hetha.

"What do you mean?"

She cocks an eyebrow. "You're a hero, Yafeu."

"*We* are heroes," I say firmly. I limp halfway to the post where my trousers are hanging before giving up and letting Ingmar support me. "What have I missed?" I wince as I pull the trousers over my injured thigh.

Freydis answers: "The moment I told them Balli had been killed, the *hird*men threw down their weapons. There's no honor in fighting for a dead man."

"Not much silver in it either," Ingmar quips.

"We spent most of yesterday tending to the wounded and burying the dead," Freydis continues. My chest clenches, thinking of Werian and all the other thralls who lost their lives in the battle. "And getting word to all the farmers and cityfolk of our victory. My mother and Helge have been placed under guard in Helge's house. And we took my father's body to the harbor. We found Alvtir there. My father had her head displayed on a spike. So we replaced it with his."

She put her father's head on a spike?

Once again, I'm surprised at her brutal ruthlessness. What happened to the girl I met a year ago?

"The farmers and the cityfolk have all but bowed to Freydis already," Ingmar adds. "But the surviving *hird*men are another story. They had little love for Balli in their hearts, but whether they will pledge themselves freely to Freydis is still unclear. Many left in the night. They took most of the ships."

I grimace, and not from the pain in my leg. It's a blow to lose those soldiers, and those ships. But with Balli dead, they're free to do as they please.

I'm sure if Freydis were a man, they wouldn't have any problem offering her their allegiance.

"What about the thralls? Did you free them?"

Freydis nods. "They are free. All of them, as we agreed—even those who had no part in our actions. But . . ." She exchanges a look with the others.

I stiffen. "But?"

"But their former masters are no longer required to feed or house them. For the most part, they've been kicked out of their homes. They've been wandering the city, sleeping under stalls at the market, or on the remaining ships. I'm not sure what to do with them."

I stare at Freydis, incredulous. "You let them sleep outside? What about the encampment—those houses are at least half empty now. Why can't they stay there?"

She falters. "I . . . I honestly hadn't thought of that."

"There won't be enough room for all of them. They should start clearing the forest and building more houses now."

Freydis chews her lip, then nods.

"Where are they now?" I ask.

"Ademola and some of the others are cleaning out the Great Hall," Wisna says.

"With Dag and Ranveig," Freydis says, jumping in. "I didn't order them to clean up our mess."

But that's just what they're doing, whether she ordered it or not. I shoot her a look. "Come with me? We'll tell them together that they can start building a new house in this compound." I turn to the others. "Nyeru used to be a carpenter's thrall. Can you find the man? The others will need his guidance during the construction."

The three of them nod and take their leave. Freydis helps me get my boots on, oddly refusing to meet my eyes as she does. I briefly wonder if it's uncomfortable for her to assist me as I once assisted her. But I dismiss the thought; she has a lot on her mind.

I lean on her as we walk to the Great Hall. It's a warm, cloudless morning. Lisa's light seems gentler than I ever remember it being here.

"Ademola would make a good guard," I muse out loud.

"Yes, he would," she agrees.

"Maybe he can recruit some new guards from among the newly freed peoples, to replace the ones that were lost in the battle. They can live in one of the houses up here, to protect you."

"That's a good idea," she agrees again.

"I have another one for you." I pause, gazing out over the hill. The city of Skíringssal stretches out below, giving way to the placid fjord. The same as it's always been and, at the same time, irrevocably different.

"Yes?"

I sigh. "I think you should hold a funeral for Alvtir *and* Balli. Together."

She draws back in surprise. "You want me to give him an honorable burial? Why?"

"To show the people that you are not your father. You honor the dead with an even hand." I wrap my arm around her shoulder. "Besides, if there's anything we've learned, it's that no matter what they did in life, the dead deserve to rest."

She gives me a strange look.

"What?"

She opens her mouth, then closes it. "It's nothing. You're right, *as always.*"

After Ingmar, Hetha, and Wisna send the carpenter to the hall, they get to work building makeshift funeral rafts for Alvtir and Balli. Freydis pitches in, but they refuse to let me help. It frustrates me to be so idle, but I know I need to save my strength until I heal.

I ask some of the newly freed people to spread the word that the funeral is to take place at nightfall. It was Freydis's idea that I be the one to ask, instead of her. She said they'd be more willing to do it for me.

Night takes its time falling. In addition to the seven of us, Ademola, Nyeru, a handful of freed thralls, and maybe a dozen of the remaining *hird*men and guards show up for the ceremony. None of the cityfolk come. No one loved Balli, but no one loved Alvtir either. The soldiers have come out of respect, and the thralls have only come because, as Freydis said, I asked.

We lay flowers around Alvtir's body. By the time we're done, her raft looks like a shrine. Balli's raft remains barren, save for his corpse.

As soon as the first stars are visible in the night sky, I bring Hetha a torch. She dips an arrow into the flame, setting it alight.

"May the smoke of the fire carry your spirit to Valhalla," Freydis recites. Wisna pushes Alvtir's raft into the fjord. The receding tide carries it out. When it's far enough away, Hetha draws back the bow. The arrow soars across the water and lands on the raft. The brilliant flames dance in the darkness.

"Go with your ancestors," I murmur in Soninke. Then we do the same for Balli.

After the funeral, I decide to stay at Alvtir's for the night. Hetha and Wisna join me. The dogs come bounding out of the woods at our approach. I'm oddly glad to see them.

"I thought they were gone," I say, scratching one's ears as she leaps on me.

"So did I," Hetha says.

It feels strange being back in Alvtir's house without her. But I'm still so exhausted, despite sleeping all of yesterday away, it doesn't take long for me to fall asleep.

Alvtir holds the hand of Mawu-Lisa on her right and the hand of Odin on her left. They lead her somewhere I can't follow. I reach out to her and she turns back and meets my gaze. Something in her ice-blue eyes soothes me. I look down and realize that I'm holding An-grboda.

"It's yours now," she says.

And then she's gone.

46

YAFEU

All eyes turn to the seven of us as we enter the Great Hall. It feels like the whole of Skíringssal is crammed inside. The tables and benches have been taken away, the floor swept and scrubbed. But the memory of bloodshed lingers, like a smell with no source.

We follow behind Freydis, Ingmar supporting me by my elbow, as she parts the crowd, approaching the throne. Ademola and Nyeru nod to me as I pass.

I hope Freydis will acknowledge her debt to all the former thralls in the oath she takes today. Hearing her throw the weight of her honor behind them might help their former masters resign themselves to the change.

Before we reach the throne, Freydis falters, blanching. I follow her gaze to where Yngvild and Helge stand off to the side, guarded by two Soninke men.

My heart aches as I imagine what Freydis must be feeling. Yngvild's hair is bedraggled, her dress covered in dirt. But she holds her head as high as ever as she stares her daughter down, a hand resting protectively on her enormous belly. Nothing can lower that woman's chin. If I didn't hate her so much, I might respect her for it.

Freydis continues to the dais. Angrboda lies in its sheath on the throne; it felt fitting that she should swear the oath on Alvtir's sword instead of her father's. But when she reaches the throne, she doesn't pick it up. Instead she turns to face the crowd. The six of us follow suit, positioning ourselves a few steps behind her.

It feels like a dream to stand at the front of this hall—the same hall where I first met Freydis, where she saved my life at the *Dísablót,* where I saved her life at her wedding to Hakon, where I was freed from slavery and became one of Alvtir's shield maidens—and look out over a sea of mixed faces. Eyes bloodshot with grief, eyes pinning us with unspoken accusations, eyes bright and glossy with new hope. All of them waiting to see what happens next.

Freydis draws herself up to her full height before addressing the crowd.

"King Balli's reign over Agder has ended," she calls out. I'm impressed by the firm, steady timbre of her voice. "It is a shame that so many lost their lives along with him. They were good men, though the one they died for was not. Now the battle is over, and we must look to the future. We need a leader who will unite us and restore honor to this kingdom. I know I am next in line for the throne by blood. But I relinquish my birthright and nominate another queen."

She turns to me.

"Yafeu."

The hall erupts into chaos.

I stare at Freydis, too stunned to speak. Shouts swirl together, echoing around the lofty hall. Some of approval, some of outrage.

My head starts to spin. The hall tilts on its axis.

Freydis holds up her hands until the commotion dies down. "Yafeu is the queen you deserve," she continues, meeting my incredulous gaze with a look of unwavering conviction. "She is

Úlfheðinn—but more than that, she is a leader unmatched in valor and honor. She slew King Balli with my aunt's sword, a sword forged from the iron of the gods. The Allfather put that sword in her hand. He chose her to lead us, as he chose her to fight for him in battle. I will serve as her adviser—if she will have me."

A familiar cackle bursts from the back of the hall. I catch a pair of mismatched eyes through the crowd: the skald.

All hail the dark queen . . .

"Approach, Queen Yafeu," Freydis says, drawing my attention back to her. Dimly, I feel Ingmar release his hold on my elbow, letting me stand on my own. I glance at him, but he looks just as surprised as I feel. So do the others.

What has Freydis just done?

My heart hammers in my chest, my throat. I walk toward her with as much dignity as I can muster, masking my limp and clasping my hands together to keep them from shaking. Her one mossy-green eye glistens with an emotion I can't read. She picks up Angrboda and drops to one knee before me, raising the hilt to my quivering hands.

I peer down at Alvtir's sword, then back up at the crowd. A hushed expectancy has fallen over them. My stomach convulses. My face burns from the inside out.

I can't be queen.

The doubt begins to choke me, its grip tighter than the grip of that thief in Koumbi Saleh.

But my arm moves of its own accord. Before I know it, I'm holding the sword above my head.

It's as if one of the gods lifted my arm for me. But which god? *Whose* god?

"AAOOOH!" I hear Ingmar shout behind me.

"AAOOOH! AAOOOH! AAOOOH!" First the shield maidens, then Dag, then half the hall join in.

"AAOOOH! AAOOOH! AAOOOH!"

I feel the thunderous roar in my bones. My heart threatens to burst from my chest, but no longer from fear. Something pure and potent swells within me. It's unlike anything I've ever felt before.

"AAOOOH! AAOOOH! AAOOOH!"

I was a thrall. I was a shield maiden. I was a "black elf." I was *Úlfheðinn*. I was an outcast. I was *jugu*.

Now I am a queen.

"AAOOOH! AAOOOH! AAOOOH!"

But the more I gaze at the ecstatic faces of the men and women who fought with us—at Ademola and Nyeru, at Bronaugh, at so many others—the more I understand: This isn't about me. It's about them. Their *belief* in what we fought for is what has given me this power. Now I must try to be worthy of it.

I must make our vision real.

When the chant finally dies down, I begin my oath:

"I swear to serve every one of you—even those who fought against us. I swear never to demand your loyalty, but to *earn* it, in everything I do as your queen. Above all else, I swear to uphold your freedom. Together, we will build a new Skíringssal. Without thralls, without masters. We will live as one people." I fall silent; that is all I can think of to say.

Ademola thumps his chest approvingly, and the rest of our people follow suit. The karls—the farmers and fishermen and craftspeople and their families—shift uneasily on their feet.

Freydis steps in: "Bring my mother forward. And Helge."

The guards grab Yngvild and Helge and walk them over to us.

"You heard the queen," Freydis says crisply, loud enough for all to hear. "Both of you will labor alongside everyone else to fortify Skíringssal. We will need every free hand to clear the land, build new houses, and gather enough food to last us the winter. No one will be spared from toil. I know you all have questions, but for now, go back to wherever you call home. Tomorrow, after Sól descends, we will feast in Yafeu's honor!" Scattered cheers erupt again at that.

As the crowd begins to file out, I pull Freydis aside. Ingmar, Dag, and the shield maidens hover around us, uncertain. There's a longer conversation she and I sorely need to have, but that will have to wait until we're alone. For now, I focus on my most immediate concern. "A feast?" I ask quietly. "Why? You said we need to save food for winter."

"Because it will help them accept you as queen," Freydis says firmly. "Much will change, Yafeu, but you will have to abide some of our customs if you're going to bring the people together."

"Generosity is the first step to loyalty," Ingmar adds. "And with former master and thrall feasting side by side, it may help them to accept the new way of things."

The karls are muttering to one another, careful to avoid brushing shoulders with their former thralls on their way out. "I can see your point."

Ingmar reaches out and grabs my hand. I squeeze it tightly.

I'm still gripping his hand as Bronaugh pushes the wrong way through the crowd and approaches me.

My heart drops. As soon as I see her expression, I know.

47

YAFEU

The lump in my throat thickens as I push open the door to the barn.

Airé's body is next to the firepit. Bronaugh has closed her eyes, to make it look like she's asleep. Even if I couldn't feel the stark absence of her *nyama,* the pallor in her skin all but confirms it.

Tears well behind my eyes. I feel Ingmar's hand on my shoulder and I shrug it off angrily. I grab a shovel and head back outside.

The late-afternoon weather is jarringly pleasant. It makes me even angrier. I jam the tip of the shovel into the earth. Again. And again. A viscous warmth seeps through the bandage on my leg. The wound stung miserably the whole way to Broskrap's farm, but I ignored it and set a brisk pace, ignoring Ingmar's protests as well.

"Yafeu." Bronaugh lays her hand on the butt of the shovel. "*Stop.*"

"Let me do this for her!" I growl, elbowing her aside. I hear a muted *thump* as she hits the ground.

Ingmar's arms lock around me from behind, constraining me.

Rage nearly consumes me as I fight against his embrace. "NO!" I scream as he pries the shovel from my fingers. I writhe in his grasp like a wild animal. He grunts but holds firm.

"It's okay," he says into my ear. The unbearable tenderness in his voice cuts through the rage, touching something raw.

"You don't understand!"

He sinks to his knees, taking me with him. "It's okay," he repeats.

I sag in his arms, too exhausted to keep fighting. Too exhausted even to sob. The tears spill out without fanfare, dripping down into the pathetic hole I've dug. Slowly, Ingmar releases his hold.

"She never forgave me," I say weakly. "I wanted to save her, but all I did was cause her pain."

"You *did* save her." Bronaugh gets up, dusts herself off, and crouches in front of us, placing a palm on my wet cheek. "She just couldn't see it. She was sick for a long time."

I meet Bronaugh's soft brown eyes. "Do you think she's with the gods now? Even though she didn't believe in them?"

She looks at the ground. "I don't know."

Bronaugh sits with me while Ingmar finishes digging the hole. By the time I get up, Lisa has dipped behind the hills, streaking the sky with purple and pink. It doesn't seem fair that the sunset should be so beautiful.

"I want to be with Airé," I say, my voice hoarse.

Bronaugh nods. Ingmar helps me back to the barn. Bronaugh lights the fire and I curl in my old spot beside it. Ingmar lays down beside me and wraps his arm around me again. This time, he's not so much holding me in place as holding me together. As I drift into unconsciousness, I hear the scratch of Bronaugh moving Airé's body outside.

The next night, we feast. We sacrifice a bull to Odin and Mawu-Lisa from the king's personal stock, which is now mine. Freydis and Ingmar were right: Karl and thrall eat side by side, albeit begrudgingly. Fritjof plays the lute and sings songs to my glory, which makes me highly uncomfortable. Luckily the overflowing ale dulls all sense of embarrassment for the night. Rulers are expected to drink a lot, Hetha tells me repeatedly. I indulge her as much as I can without losing my wits.

As exhausted as I am when the feast finally ends, I can't bring myself to go to Freydis's room for the night. It feels like I'd be going back in time, like I might fall asleep in my old bed and wake up to find that I'm still her thrall, and all this was just a dream.

So, yet again, I force my tired feet to carry me to the only house in Skíringssal that ever came close to feeling like home.

FREYDIS

The sizzle of the fire in the hearth lulls me into a half sleep. My mind drifts idly from thought to thought, my gaze bleary on the unadorned oak walls. There's something oddly comforting about this room. The simplicity of it, the smallness. Or maybe it's just that it isn't mine.

I'm still so sore and weary from the battle; I'm glad that I managed to slip away from the feast early, and grateful to my *dísir* for helping me find my way to my aunt's house in the dark. I couldn't go back to my old room again—not after the nightmares I had last night.

Of course, the door flies open at the thought. I surge upright, then relax at Yafeu's startled expression.

"What are you doing in my bed?" she asks. "What are you doing here *at all*?"

"I-I guess I assumed you'd want my old room to yourself."

Her brow furrows. "Why would you think that?"

Not knowing how to respond, I say nothing and get out of her bed. She sighs heavily as she plops down on it and kicks off her boots.

I hesitate. "Is something wrong?"

Her eyes lock onto mine. "Why did you do it, Freydis?"

"Do what?"

She scoffs. I bite my lip but resist the urge to look away. I may not be as brave as she is, but I am not without courage of my own. "I didn't think to rally the thralls to our cause. *You* did. They pledged themselves to *you,* not me, because *you* promised them their freedom. The same is true of Ingmar and Dag and the shield maidens. They didn't fight for me, they fought for *you.* Now they all look to you for guidance. Even *I* look to you! I meant what I said in the hall, Yafeu. The people need you, whether you like it or not."

Yafeu looks away but says nothing. I let out a heavy sigh. "Besides," I add. "My father sent someone else to fight his battles, and look where that got him. If I were queen, I'd just be repeating his mistake with you. You would be my Alvtir, when you should be much more, as she should have been."

"Did you do it for the people, or for *yourself*?"

Her question is a bright light, illuminating a dark place inside me. I struggle not to recoil. "Both things can be true," I say quietly.

Yafeu rolls away. "Good night, Freydis."

I hesitate for a moment, then slip into the only other bed. My aunt's bed.

Yafeu is angry with me, and I can't say I blame her. But tomorrow will be a new day. A better day.

Or so I hope.

YAFEU

I am woken late in the morning by Nyeru. "It's time for your coronation ceremony," he says, shaking the grogginess out of me.

I wince and grab my pounding head. "How did you know where to find me?"

"The gods led me to you," he says. I cut him a look. "And I asked your friends," he adds with a boyish grin.

"I'm already queen," I grumble. "We don't need another ceremony."

"Not to our brothers and sisters, you're not."

He signals to two brown-skinned women, who stand shyly behind him, then leaves me with them.

Even alone, the women are strangely bashful in my presence. I
do my best to put them at ease, asking them questions about themselves while they comb and braid my hair. I learn that their names
are Kansoleh and Gundo. They were both clothmakers in Wagadu.
They tell me of the trials they endured on the long journey here,
and the hardships they suffered on the farm to which they were
sold. They tell me again and again how grateful they are to me for
their freedom. I keep insisting that they freed themselves. By the
time they've tamed my hair into three thick braids intertwining
down my neck, I can tell they feel more comfortable with me, and I
with them.

I reach for one of Alvtir's tunics, but Kansoleh clears her throat,
stopping me short. To my surprise, Gundo holds out a beautiful yellow kaftan. I recognize the fabric from one of Freydis's ornate
dresses. She must have helped the women refashion it for me.

I thank them each profusely as I throw it on, admiring the handiwork. It's deeply fulfilling to wear the clothing of my people again;
I don't even mind that it's women's clothing.

If only Mama could see me now. The thought brings a lump to my
throat and tears to my eyes.

My headache has mostly abated by the time Nyeru returns. We
let the elder set the pace as the four of us head down the trail into
the city.

We find the shield maidens, Ingmar, Dag, Bronaugh, and Freydis
already waiting with my people at the harbor. It thrills me to see
the brown faces outnumbering the ivory ones for once. Ingmar
ogles me with obvious delight, at which I roll my eyes. But I give
Freydis a tentative smile, which she returns with evident relief.

Soon Fritjof and some three dozen *Majūs* arrive. Most are craftsmen and -women from the town, or former thralls, but I recognize a few soldiers among them, to my great surprise. The reverence on everyone's faces when they look at me makes me feel increasingly awkward and ill at ease. Was this how Freydis felt when she was the princess? That would explain why she was always so jittery.

Finally, with maybe forty in attendance, Nyeru paints my face and commences a traditional prayer to the gods. I remind myself to have one of the weavers from Wagadu make the robes of a Soninke priest for Nyeru; he shouldn't have to go around in a thrall's tunic any longer.

He finishes the prayer and gestures to one of the brown-skinned women, who hands him a circlet of Aggrey beads with a wide smile. I open my mouth to protest—the beads must have been hers from home, or she took great pains to make them here, likely in secret— but one look from Nyeru silences me. It won't do any good to reject this gift now.

Nyeru places the circlet on my head. I feel humbled and over-whelmed, but I do my best to look regal as he chants yet more Soninke blessings to the modest, half-bewildered crowd.

If only my family were here. If I told them about this—about everything that happened to lead me to this moment—they'd think I was making the whole story up. Well, maybe not Mama and Papa. Mama would say that this was my destiny all along, and Papa would say I forged my own fate. I still don't know which of them is right. I *do* know my brothers would laugh in my face. I can almost hear their teasing in my head, and it makes me smile despite myself. *A queen? You? Legba will fly down from the sky and slap our bottoms before you become a queen!*

When the ceremony is finally over and the people begin to dis-perse, I start feverishly scratching an itch under the circlet. It's been bugging me since Nyeru put it on.

"You'll have to get used to dressing like royalty." Ingmar closes the distance between us.

"Never," I say, taking his hand. "Too uncomfortable."

"Do you plan on being the first queen to wear a training tunic around Skíringssal?"

He's joking, but I like the idea. I shoot him a mischievous grin. "I plan on being the first queen to do *lots* of things."

48

FREYDIS

*E*ven through the heavy mantle of night, I can see Father's silhouette towering over Yafeu. His back is to me. He doesn't know I'm here. His sword is drawn; it won't be long until he deals the killing blow.

The runes on Angrboda sing to me. I can't see them in the darkness, but I hear them in Fritjof's dulcet tone: ansuz, *the power of Odin, king of the gods, first in wisdom;* thurisaz, *the power of Thor, the great defender, he who fells giants; and* tiwaz, *the power of Tyr, the force of justice and the order that governs all beings.*

I pick Angrboda off the ground and rush toward Father. He raises his arm to strike, and I raise mine.

But this time, he turns to face me. His lichen-green eyes, so like my own, betray his shock as he realizes what I'm about to do.

I thrust Angrboda into his heart.

* * *

I wake with a start to a knock on the door. I sit up and rub my good eye with the butt of my palm. My heart is still pounding. I've had the same dream ever since the night that I . . .

The night that we won, I remind myself fiercely. I force my mind's eye to let go of Father's face. To picture instead the faces of the freed thralls on the day Yafeu became queen. I picture how the shield maidens looked at her, brimming with admiration and pride. Even Ranveig was almost happy that day.

Killing my father made that possible. Killing my father set us all free.

The knock sounds again, more insistent. "Sorry to disturb you, Pri—um, Freydis." Orm's voice filters through the door. I'm glad he survived; this guilt would be even worse if he'd fallen. And I'm glad he chose to stay and pledge himself to Yafeu. So few of the other guards did. "There's a messenger here for you."

My heart sinks. "Just a moment," I call out.

I glance at Yafeu's empty bed before dragging myself out of my own. The hard sunlight streaming down through the smoke hole tells me that the hour is late. These days, sleep never wants to relinquish me.

I dress quickly, letting the brisk movements clear the dream-fog from my head. After a few halfhearted attempts, I give up on taming my hair into a braid and decide to leave it down. After all, few men will even notice, much less leer at me. Most people prefer not to look at me at all. I thought Astrid and Solvi, at least, would revel in my ugliness, but even they avert their eyes when I pass.

I try to position my locks so that they form a curtain over the mutilated side of my face, but it's no use; the scar is glaring. Lastly, I throw on the wolf vest Yafeu made me and open the door.

Orm and Demba, one of the freed thralls, stand on either side of a tall, lean man I don't recognize. There's an imperious look in his eye as it meets mine.

Somehow, I already know who sent him.

"You're Harald's man, aren't you."

* * *

The wind is bitterly cold today, carrying the promise of an even colder winter. It makes my scar twinge. I pass some of the newly freed people wheeling a cart full of apples into the cookhouse. Ademola wipes sweat off his brow and waves politely. I return the gesture.

Much has changed since the Battle of Skíringssal—as it's now called—and the crowning of Yafeu. Ingmar was made the *stallari* of the new *hird,* though Yafeu will almost certainly lead them herself when the time comes to fight again. Ingmar oversees them for now, with Hetha, Wisna, and Dag lending their skills as captains. The four of them have been given the remaining ships. They've been recruiting men and women alike to fill out their legions, and to serve in Yafeu's personal guard, led by Ademola.

Young women are joining in droves, far outpacing our expectations. They come from all over Agder, and even from beyond our borders, renouncing their former lives and allegiances, trading their sewing needles for axes, wielding kitchen knives as daggers. All inspired by tales of the *Úlfheðinn,* the great wolf-warrior, Odin's chosen queen.

If Ranveig was upset that she wasn't made a captain like Hetha and Wisna, she does not show it. She clings fiercely to Yafeu, playing both puppy and guard dog at Yafeu's side. I can scarcely get a moment alone with Yafeu now, save for at night, when we both fall into our beds in my parents' old room. Neither one of us wants to sleep alone. Not yet.

Bronaugh and Nyeru were chosen to speak for the former thralls. With their help, we persuaded most of the farmers to accept a temporary arrangement: The farmers needed all the help they could get during the harvest, and the thralls needed food and a proper place to sleep. It's not a lasting solution, but Bronaugh checks in on them constantly, making sure they are fed well, compensated fairly, and treated with dignity.

The first matter we had to deal with was where to put the rest of them. Few of the departed guards or *hird*men had homes of their own to give away. We cleared more of the eastern forest around the *hird*'s encampment and used the gold and silver Father stole from the Saracens to pay the karls to help the freed thralls build as many new homes as they can before winter. Almost everyone in the city has been involved in one way or another. The woodworkers craft the walls and roofs and beds; the blacksmiths forge the rivets and nails. Those who have no other skill cut logs or uproot stumps. Of course, the soil can't be cultivated there, but a home on barren land is better than no home at all.

We might have built enough to accommodate everyone by now, but the *hird* itself is growing faster than we can house—or feed. It's a fine problem to have, but a problem nonetheless.

When we're not building new houses or ships, we're building up our stores of food for winter: winnowing and milling the grain, drying apples and beets, pickling squash and cabbage, butchering livestock, salting and smoking the meat.

But for all the toil, there is much levity as well. Color has begun to bloom across the once-gray city. Yafeu's people make paint out of bearded iris and turnsole and paint the sides of the newly built homes. They dye their clothes in bold, bright hues and weave them together in intricate patterns, patterns I've never seen or imagined before. Some of our weavers and jewelry-makers have even been working with theirs, creating unusual new necklaces and styles of dress. Their handiwork has proven popular with merchants from other lands, providing the city with a much-needed influx of coin and materials.

Still, skirmishes do arise between my and Yafeu's peoples, and the burden on us both to keep the peace is a heavy one. At least we have each other to lean on.

Laughter erupts to my left. I turn to see a beautiful dark-skinned woman walking by, playfully pushing away the beaming Northman beside her. They banter flirtatiously in a mix between my language and Yafeu's, and I'm reminded of how she and I communicated in those early months. Gods, that feels like ages ago. The man wraps the woman in his arms and kisses her as she melts into his embrace. They're both still grinning when they pull apart.

The purity of their joy forces a smile to my lips, even as I feel a stirring of envy. Would that woman ever have felt such joy if she had lived the rest of her life as a thrall? Would she have been able to fall in love—true love—with one of my people? Likely not.

My hand reaches reflexively to my scar, my fingers tracing the jagged edges.

When I first saw my face in the pond, I was convinced it was the curse of the Dead City. But with all the good that has happened since then, I'm not sure anymore. Perhaps it's not so much a curse as it is . . . a price. After all, the gods demand a sacrifice before they answer our prayers. We must give something of ourselves before receiving their favor. Perhaps the girl I once was is part of that sacrifice, the cost of a new dawn for Agder. How selfish would I be to think my beauty is more important than that?

At least, that's what I tell myself. In my heart of hearts, I am more lost than ever.

Before I met Yafeu, all I desired was to marry for love and to become a queen. These were desires born of circumstance, but they were all I ever knew. All I *could* know. Then Yafeu came along and turned everything on its head. I realized what I needed more than anything was the freedom to *change* my circumstance, to make my own choices.

And yet, now that I have that freedom, I find I don't know what to do with it. My old dreams are dead: Yafeu is queen, and rightly so, and no man will ever love me with this hideous scar. Where does that leave me? What will bring me joy? Or, if joy is beyond my reach, is there something else I should strive to achieve? Some sense of fulfillment outside of my duties? Despite the many spells I've cast, despite seeking out Fritjof's guidance time and time again, I still have no clear answers. The Norns have woven me an altogether different tapestry than the one I'd pictured; I cannot yet see their design.

I am grateful, at the very least, for my new role under Yafeu. I know in my heart that it won't lead me to the answers I seek, but it fills my days with purpose enough to distract me from the questions. For now.

Yafeu made me her primary counselor and ambassador and put me in charge of minding "the old Agder"—the craftsmen and merchants in the city, the farmers, and Father's jarls and their farmers in the various provinces throughout the kingdom, many of whom are Thingmen. I am helping them all adjust to the new regime.

The jarls are proving the hardest to manage. Some of them bowed willingly to Yafeu when we informed them that the taxes were to be reduced in light of the diminished harvests. But many simply couldn't accept a foreigner—or a woman—as their ruler. Yafeu promised to honor their status as jarls and continue holding the seasonal Althing, but that alone wouldn't appease them. Several of them returned with our messengers to Skíringssal. After many days of heated discussion—during which time we were forced to provide them with our best hospitality, at no small expense— they agreed to *consider* acknowledging her rule and pledging their fealty, so long as they have a speaker in Yafeu's inner council. Any day now, their speaker will arrive in Skíringssal.

Given the news from Harald, I'm glad we'll at least have today's council meeting to ourselves.

I push open the door of the Great Hall to find Yafeu bent over a table, studying the map we found in my parents' room, her brow knit in a familiar expression of worry. The indigo cloak I gave her falls over her shoulders like a blanket. Ranveig, as always, hovers nearby. Her jaw tightens when she sees me, but Yafeu looks up and smiles in greeting as I approach.

I recently convinced her to have the Great Hall redecorated. The best weavers of Skíringssal joined with the best weavers from her homeland to create tapestries of our gods rejoicing together to adorn the walls. At Yafeu's insistence, I made one myself, of Odin and Nana Buluku—the "Allmother," as some of the people have started calling her—dancing hand in hand, their arms ringed around the trunk of the world tree. I threw my whole heart into the weaving, spending every spare moment at the loom. It was a welcome distraction to narrow my focus, to feel the familiar movements in my fingers once again. I'll never forget Yafeu's reverent expression when I finally gave it to her. I glance at the wall as I pass it now, taking in my creation with more than a little pride.

Soon we're joined by Ingmar, Dag, Nyeru, Bronaugh, Hetha, and Wisna. As soon as all of us are seated at the table, I jump in before Yafeu can: "I know we have much to discuss, but first, I have urgent news I must share with you all, as it concerns our safety." I pause until Yafeu gestures for me to continue. I take a steadying breath. "A messenger arrived today from Vestfold. Harald is allied with Hakon of Trøndelag. He has taken Hakon's daughter Asé as a wife. I don't know why Harald wished to inform us of this, but for some reason of his own, he has."

Dismay ripples across the table. Everyone takes a moment to absorb the news.

"Our enemies grow in number every day," Yafeu says grimly, looking down at the map. "Hakon in the north, Harald in the east. With the two of them joining forces, we need allies of our own more than ever."

Ranveig scoffs. "We don't *need* anyone. We are the best warriors Norveg has ever seen. We should attack Harald now, when he least expects it. Raze Vestfold to the ground before he and Hakon can bolster their defenses."

Everyone looks disturbed. Yafeu shifts uncomfortably. "I don't think it's come to that yet, Ranveig," she says quietly.

"However, if it does come to that, we will be prepared," Ingmar says. "Word of the *Úlfheðinn* queen is spreading throughout Agder, and beyond. New recruits arrive at our shores every day, eager to become warriors. They pledge themselves to the prophesied queen before I can even take their names."

Yafeu fixes her dark-amber eyes on me. "'The prophesied queen'? Where would they have heard such a thing?"

I let out a nervous cough. After Yafeu became queen, I sent for Agder's most renowned skalds and had them craft the story of our victory into a song. They've since gone from house to house, spreading the song across the land. Now the story has taken on a life of its own. I've heard the people say that Yafeu brought strange and powerful gods to Norveg, and that she is blessed by those gods and ours alike. I've even heard whispers that Balli's daughter is a powerful seeress who foretold that the city of Skíringssal would fall to a fearsome warrior-queen from Africa, who would build an even greater city from Skíringssal's ruins.

I'll never admit it to Yafeu, but I like to imagine that there's a kind of truth to these whispers.

"They say you can't be killed," Wisna chimes in with a smirk. "That Odin himself possesses your body, along with the gods of your people, and they wield their will through you."

A dark look passes across Yafeu's face. "I don't want such things said about me."

"It is necessary," I reply. "People must be in awe of their leader, even revere them, for their loyalty to be indisputable. And no one is more worthy of such loyalty than you. You ripped the kingdom from the grasp of a tyrant. They need to know it."

"It serves the people to exaggerate my deeds? That's something your father would say."

Her words cut too deep, as usual. I glower at her. After a moment, Wisna's gruff voice pierces the silence: "The newcomers have a strange name for the city. They call it Yafreby."

"The freed people use the same name," Nyeru adds, turning to Yafeu. "They speak in a blend of our two tongues, as you and I once did."

I think of the couple I saw on my way here. "My people are picking it up as well. Perhaps we should formally change the name of the city to Yafreby, and teach the language to all."

"Those things can wait until after winter," Yafeu says, her tone decisive. "Let's return to more pressing matters."

The meeting wears on into the afternoon. Yafeu decides to convert the Great Hall into a shelter for the winter for whomever needs it, rather than ordering any of the karls to house either the freed people or the new soldiers, to avoid causing further friction. We're just beginning to discuss the plans for the upcoming Althing when Helge bursts into the hall, gasping for breath. Her apron is drenched in sweat.

"Helge?" I ask. "What's the matter?"

She scowls at Yafeu and musters a very unconvincing bow, then addresses me. "Your mother," she says. "You must come at once."

Mother's screams carry across the small hill. The knot in my gut tightens as we near the bath chamber.

It feels like only yesterday I was outside these same doors, clutching that whalebone and praying fiercely to Freya to spare my brother's life. The memory sends a shudder down my spine as I open the door.

Mother writhes in the middle of the room. Birth water stains her dress. A flicker of anger crosses Mother's sweaty face when she sees me. She doesn't want me here. Yet this time, she has no choice. She has no one else.

There are still no midwives in Skíringssal. I sent word to the nearest towns weeks ago, but no one came. Even knowing that my father was dead, unseated by his daughter and a former thrall, they still feared punishment if they failed to deliver a live babe. I can hardly blame them.

"He's coming," Mother pants. "He's coming now."

*   *   *

Compared with the agonizing, days-long births Mother endured before, this one almost seemed to end before it began. One moment I was rushing to Mother's side, the next I was watching in awe as a tiny baby boy emerged into Helge's steady hands.

Wisps of his blond hair are slick against his head. He's too small. Too frail.

For a moment, sorrow consumes me—but then Helge pats his little chest, and he cries. Loud, strong cries.

He's alive.

Helge quickly severs the cord and hands him to me before turning back to Mother.

I wipe him down and wrap him in a clean cloth, holding him against my chest. He quiets, and soon his impossibly small hand wraps around my finger. I am filled with a tremendous, radiant joy, the likes of which I've never felt before.

Then Mother moans and begins writhing again. Helge shoots me a dire look. "Twins," she says breathlessly.

My throat tightens as I remember Fritjof's words:

They'll come in a pair, one light and one dark, the sons of Balli of Skíringssal.

A shudder moves through me. With a gut-wrenching scream, Mother pushes one more time, revealing a full head of dark hair.

This time, Helge must pull the babe's body out of her. The boy is larger than his brother, his screams even more powerful.

Helge wipes the second babe with a cloth and swaddles him. She hands him to Mother, and I quickly do the same with the first. Mother cradles them against her bosom, one in each arm. I've never seen her look so happy, so blissful.

But when she meets my gaze, her face falls.

"I know you have no loyalty to your own blood," she says hoarsely. "But if you let *anything* happen to them, not even Hel will take you."

Her words pierce my heart. "Yafeu is not Father," I shoot back. "She would never hurt an innocent child."

"Promise me!" Mother's voice quakes heavily. "I have no reason to live, save for these babes." She lets the tears fall, and I feel my own tears betray me, brimming behind my eyes.

"Oh, Mother—" I reach out to her, but she recoils from my touch.

Even in the throes of her darkest fears, she won't accept my comfort.

In all my life, the worst thing I ever did to her was live. I *survived*, when the others did not. For this alone, she will never forgive me. Not even with two healthy boys in her arms at last.

I let my hand fall to my side. "I will do everything in my power to keep them safe," I say. "I swear it by the grace of Freya, the might of Thor, and the wisdom of Odin."

Her shoulders sag with relief, which I take as a sign of her acceptance. I make to leave, then pause, lingering at the doorway. "It's a new day, Mother. Don't ruin their hearts with hatred."

With that, I leave her behind.

49

YAFEU

In the summer I hunted barefoot. I loved the feel of the grass around my toes, the crunch of pine needles under my heels. But it's too cold for that now, so I've reluctantly donned my clunky leather boots. One mindless step would scare away the game, but we no longer have enough cover from the foliage to hunt on foot anyway.

So Ingmar and I find ourselves sitting on a low branch of a wych elm, shrouded in part by its sparse yellow leaves. Ingmar says there are many of these trees where he's from in Ireland. Its arching stems are strong yet supple, like him. The spruces and firs would provide better cover, but their branches are too tightly packed to climb and too frail to support our weight.

There are few deer this time of year anyway, and none are active in the late afternoon. We've laid a few traps for hares around the wood, and now we have nothing to do but wait. Ingmar entertains me with stories from his wild early days in Byzantium, his sea eyes wide and dancing as he acts out some brawl he got into with a group of Greek traders in a taverna.

I can tell that today we're hunting only each other.

"How can you move around so much and still keep your balance on the branch?" I ask. "Aren't you afraid you'll fall?"

"Oh, I've fallen plenty of times," he says, grinning. "Though it never stopped me from climbing back up. My mother always worried I would break my back."

"There aren't many good trees for climbing in Wagadu, so my mother didn't have to worry about that."

"She only had to worry about the lions getting you," he teases.

I smirk. "Lions are lazy. It's the hippos you have to watch out for. They're vicious on a *good* day."

"Don't forget the crocodiles," he adds.

Crocodiles. Like the one Papa stared down outside Jenne.

The memory triggers a surge of emotion. I scratch the back of my neck and look away, surveying the forest ground through the gaps in the leaves. "Not much game today."

"No," he agrees. Abruptly, he swings his leg around and shimmies down the trunk, hopping to the ground.

"Where are you going?" I call down.

"I could use a bath." He grins up at me. "Care to join?"

We float on our backs in the warm water, watching the steam rise and fade into the brisk afternoon air. My fingers have begun to prune, but I want to linger here for as long as I can. Aside from our "hunts," Tyr's grove is our only respite from our duties—though our excuses for coming here are even thinner.

Ingmar dunks under the water and comes back up, running his hands over his slick brown hair. His beard always looks redder when it's wet.

My gaze falls to his torso. I trace a finger over the many scars there, trying to memorize each and every one of them. The muscles of his stomach ripple like waves, hardening beneath my touch. "I needed this," I murmur.

His eyes are soft and hooded. "A queen deserves to take a little time for herself, now and then."

"Tell that to Ranveig," I reply, regretting it immediately as my worries, only just subdued, stir awake again. I stifle a groan.

Ingmar's own expression turns grave. "The others are starting to worry about her," he says softly. "Several months have passed since Alvtir's death, and she hasn't even begun to heal. If anything, she seems to be getting worse."

"Who are we to say how she should grieve?" My tone is harsher than I meant it to be. I really didn't want to talk about this today.

Ingmar says nothing. I find my footing and heave myself onto the bank. The cool air is a shock against my wet skin, which is bare except for my cloth wrappings. I start drying myself briskly with the spare linen we brought, trying not to look at him as I do.

But I can't help but admire the way the droplets of water slide down his taut chest, how the muscles of his arms flex as he lifts himself onto the bank far more gracefully than I. He catches me staring, and the corner of his mouth pricks up in response.

I look away to hide my smile, but he reaches out and pulls me against him. Somehow his wet skin is searing where it meets mine. A fluttering sensation spreads from my lower belly as he lowers his mouth to my throat. The touch of his lips sends lightning through my limbs. I gasp before he catches my mouth with his. I kiss him back with fervor, throwing my arms around his broad shoulders. Before I know it, I've lost all sense of time and place. There's nothing else, no one else in the world but us.

All too soon, he breaks the kiss and rests his forehead against mine. We rest like that for a long moment, catching our breath. The insects hum all around us; the birdsong leaps from tree to tree.

When he finally speaks, his voice is fainter than a whisper.

"I love you, Yafeu."

Twin bolts of excitement and anxiety race through me. My heart pounds in my throat. "I love you too," I say.

He grabs my hand and pulls me onto the grass on top of him, planting kisses all over my face, my head, the scar on my neck until I'm squealing with laughter. I meet his liquid gaze, and it pulls me in like a riptide.

"I want you," he whispers into my ear, nipping at my earlobe. A shiver runs down my spine, and not from the cold.

I trace a line down his neck with my nose, pausing to kiss his collarbone. I feel his arousal pressing against me, and with it the reality of where this is leading. Reluctantly, I roll off him. "We can't right now," I explain. "Freydis can make a tea that prevents . . . anything from happening, but the herbs she needs are not in season."

He sits up, twisting slightly to face me. "Would it be so bad to have a child?"

I stare at him, too shocked to respond.

"Presuming . . ." He hesitates, a blush rising to his cheeks as he takes my hand. "Presuming we were to marry?"

My throat constricts. He continues before I can respond. "Neither of us has a family to arrange such things for us, but that means we're free to follow our hearts. My heart chooses you."

A wave of warmth washes over me. Overcome, I cup his cheek in my palm, feeling the bristle of his beard against my fingertips.

He relaxes into my touch. "So . . . will you? Marry me?"

I draw in a deep breath, searching for the right words.

I love Ingmar. More than I ever thought possible. But marriage? I've never even considered it before. There was no chance of finding a husband back home; all the boys in my village thought of me as *jugu,* and I had little regard for them in return.

And *children*?

That possibility extinguishes the last of the embers in my blood.

With the heavy burden of Yafreby resting on my shoulders, the last thing I need right now is a child.

Even if I weren't the queen, I know in my heart that I'm not ready to start a family. Not even close.

"My heart chooses you too, Ingmar," I say finally. "But I can't have a child, and I can't marry you. Not now."

He winces, drawing back as though I've struck him. My chest clenches at the raw hurt on his face. "Because you're the queen?" he asks.

And other reasons, I think. But I don't say it aloud. "Because we still have so much hardship ahead of us. Everyone is looking to me—to *us*—to carry them through it."

"A king is expected to have a family. Why should a queen be any different?"

"We *do* have a family," I say reassuringly. "The others are our family. That's enough for me. For now."

He opens his mouth to respond when the trumpet sounds in the distance. At first, I'm relieved by the interruption. But then I remember the meaning of the short, rapid blasts:

Strangers at our shore.

My mouth goes dry. Ingmar and I share a look and jump to our feet. We throw our clothes on hastily and sprint back to the city.

We arrive at the harbor to find at least three dozen soldiers—including Ademola, the shield maidens, and many of the new recruits—armed and assembled, waiting for us. Ingmar nods his approval, prompting the new recruits to stand even straighter. At the sight of us, a wild-eyed Ranveig rushes over, ready to shield me from whatever, whoever is coming. I grimace and look to the fjord.

Wisna is standing at the edge of the shingle, shielding her eyes with her hand. "That's no merchant's skiff," she says ominously.

"It's an Iberian ship," Ademola says, stepping forward. "I recognize the design."

"An Iberian ship?" I squint at the fast-approaching vessel. I can just make out its details: a long hull with a towering aftcastle and three triangular sails, each emblazoned with the same swirling symbol.

Fear blossoms in my chest. I don't know the Iberians, but I don't like the thought of any unexpected visitors. Not when Yafreby is still so vulnerable. It's not myself I'm afraid for—with Ingmar on my right and Ranveig on my left, I pity anyone who comes for my blood today—but the new recruits. They're eager to prove themselves, but they're nowhere near as ready as they think they are.

Then again, no one is ever truly ready for their first battle.

One of them brings Ingmar his ax. He tosses it from hand to hand, keeping his eyes trained on the ship. "Positions!" he shouts. I watch as the recruits arrange themselves into neat rows and assume battle stances, brandishing their weapons. It eases my worry somewhat. They may be untested, but at least they've been learning from the best. I cock an eyebrow at Ingmar, who answers with a wink.

I turn to face them fully. Men and women alike, standing shoulder to shoulder. My soldiers. My warriors. At the fire in their eyes, the *Úlfheðinn* rears its head inside me. I let it suffuse my *nyama* as I address them. "Be on your guard," I order. "But don't attack until I give the word. No matter what happens, know that you've made me proud today."

I turn back to the fjord at that, not wanting to see the effect my words have on them. Not wanting to see their eyes blazing even brighter, burning with a reverence I haven't earned, knowing that someday, if not today, such reverence might lead them to their deaths.

I unsheathe my two daggers and twirl them around my wrist. Friend or foe, whoever steps off that ship will have to reckon with me first.

"I wonder what a Saracen ship is doing this far from home, this late in the year," says Freydis, coming to stand next to Ingmar.

I grunt in frustration. "Do you enjoy making me worry about you?"

She shakes her head. "Something tells me they're not here to pick a fight."

I consider her words as the ship draws nearer. It's full of men—men of many different colors. Some have light-brown complexions, somewhere between mine and the *Majūs'*; some are even darker than I am. Those who aren't rowing raise their hands in the air—hands without weapons. A gesture of peace.

The tension in my shoulders eases. Still, for caution's sake, I keep my daggers out, knowing the others will follow my lead.

Rather than attempting to dock, the men drop anchor and leap over the side of the ship, splashing into the frigid water. They're dressed head to toe in unwieldy layers of cloth, covered in green capes that drag behind them, slowing their movements. They don't look prepared for a battle at all.

I lower my daggers but don't sheathe them, gesturing to the others to lower their own weapons. Only Ranveig doesn't comply, her slender legs still bent in a fighting stance, both hands gripping the hilt of her sword. Before I can say anything, a deep male voice rings out, shouting something in a language I don't recognize. But the voice itself . . . something about it is familiar.

Its owner reaches the shoreline and glances around, as though searching for someone. He's tall and slim, his skin is the rich color of powdered acajou bark. Ranveig moves to step between us, but I motion for her to stay put. The man clocks the interaction and, realizing I must be important, stops where he is and nods politely at me in greeting, his hands still raised by his head.

But I'm no longer focused on his hands. The dimples on his cheeks have stirred an old memory. A face I once knew better than any other.

Could it really be?

"Papa?" My voice is barely a whisper.

But then a second man catches up to him—a man with the same

dark skin and easy smile. Two brothers, clearly, from their similar bearing.

My heart sinks. I shouldn't have let my foolish hope overwhelm my senses like that. I'm no longer that naïve little girl who conjured the image of her papa in the desert, desperate to believe that he'd always be there to save her. I've saved myself too many times since then.

I take a moment to study the brothers. Both have gauzy silk cloths wrapped around their heads and long tunics with elaborate detailing. They wear the same capes their shipmates wear, except theirs are a deep-scarlet color. And though they have the bodies of men, their faces are young. They look my age at the oldest—maybe even younger. Whoever they are, they're no ordinary traders.

"Please, put away your weapons," the first man says in the *Majūs'* tongue, his accent stilted.

"We are here in peace," adds the second one. "We are friends of your leader, Alvtir."

The second man's voice is familiar too. But I can't place it.

Satisfied that they pose no danger, I sheathe my daggers and signal to my warriors to stand down. "If you were friends of Alvtir's, then you are friends of ours," I call out, motioning for the brothers to approach.

I can feel Ranveig bristling as they do. They keep their chins low out of respect, but the closer they come, the more clearly I can see their faces.

Faces that unlock a door in my heart.

The ice in my veins gives way to a bursting warmth.

They pause, uncertain. Then their eyes go wide as they recognize me in return. I race forward before Ranveig can stop me. My hands are trembling as I reach out to touch each of their cheeks.

"Kamo?" I whisper in amazement. "Goleh?"

My brothers. My brothers are alive. My brothers are *here*.

As if in response, Lisa comes out of the clouds that very moment, bathing the shore in light.

Kamo touches my hand with his own, the expression on his face mirroring my own wonder.

"Henda?" he croaks.

I never thought I'd hear it again.

My name. My true name.

ABOUT THE AUTHORS

WILLOW SMITH is a singer, songwriter and activist.

willowsmith.com
Facebook.com/OfficialWillow
X: @OfficialWillow
Instagram: @willowsmith

JESS HENDEL is a writer based in Los Angeles. She received her BA in sociology from Amherst College and her MFA in writing for screen and television from the University of Southern California.

X: @JessHendel
Instagram: @jesshendelwrites

ABOUT THE TYPE

This book was set in Chronicle, a typeface created in 2002 by Hoefler&Co. It derives from the Scotch Roman typeface family originated by Alexander Wilson and William Miller. Historically, the Scotch Roman style worked harmoniously with book printing, yet faced limitations when paired with fast-paced printers, such as those used for newspapers. Chronicle was developed as a typeface that would translate well into different styles of media usage.